For upcoming books and news visit:
http://www.journeyofrise.co.cc/

To Elizabeth,
who provides love, inspiration, and happiness every moment.

Journey of Rise

Map of the Sectors

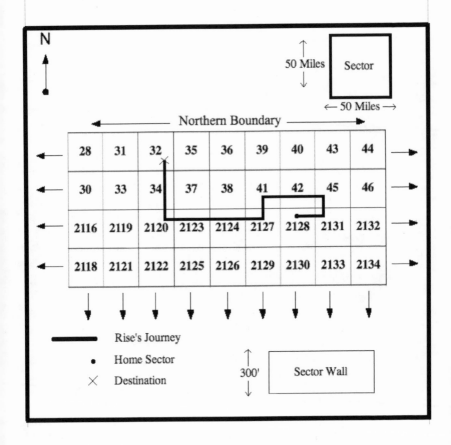

4

Part One: Sector 2128
Chapter One:

The small child's hand gripped the large hand like a chain link. Young as he was, the child still understood that this tall stranger saved his life. Together they traversed the community of tents and scrap metal shacks. It was well into the middle of the night, and the fires outside each dwelling were no more than whispers of smoke. There was very little light except for one residence, a metal shack with the faintest shimmers of a few candles inside. That petty light might as well have been the sun itself to the weary travelers.

A few hours earlier the poor child had been locked in a cage when Rise found him. A sleeping gang member had been the only guard. Rise had done well in sneaking the key away and opening the cage, all the while keeping the child silent. He even made his way out of the Writh Gang's lair undetected. His folly occurred when they were hiding behind a pile of debris just outside the lair. A Writh patrol caught him off guard and he was forced to hide quickly. But the watchful eyes of the last in the procession saw the child's foot sticking out of the rubble. The Writh waited until the rest had gone into the lair before he went to examine what he saw, probably thinking it was an abandoned shoe, a treasure not to be shared with the rest of the group. It was dark, yet the magic of the Writh Gang is in their vision. The glowing green eyes of the guard spotted the man and the child. He stepped back shocked when he discovered them. Rise had whispered, "Don't do it."

He reached for his sword and stood up. The guard grabbed the sword at his own side.

"Don't do it." Rise closed his eyes and dismissed the memory of killing the guard.

As the memory of the encounter faded, the man and child approached the candle-lit habitation. The door flap pushed aside and a woman emerged, "I hear steps." She just caught sight of the two.

She yelled into the house, "Come quick!"

The woman ran towards the oncoming travelers. The boy broke his iron grip with Rise and ran forward, "Mommy! Mommy!"

The tears of the mother fell before the two even embraced. A man emerged from the house and ran towards the hugging figures. "My son! My son has come back to me!"

Rise stood his ground, a good ten feet from the huddled

mass. He turned to walk away quietly, but the sword at his side made a clinking noise that awoke the parents from their bliss.

"Wait, don't leave." The father stood up.

Rise turned and hesitantly walked towards the man.

"I owe you everything, Rise. Ask what you will of me, I am forever in debt to you."

Rise scratched his short white hair, "What's done is done. I ask for nothing."

He was just about to leave again when the mother embraced him from behind, her head on his shoulder, "Thank you, thank you..." He saw the glimmer of a tear drop off the elbow of his leather overcoat.

"You're more than welcome." He gently pushed her away. No sooner had she retracted than the father re-approached with an outstretched hand. Rise shook it quickly. "I must go."

"Not just yet." The father reached into his wooly overcoat and pulled out a small bottle half-full with a light red liquid inside. "It's ten years old, not bad for a wine. Please take it, it's the least I can do."

Rise looked at the wine bottle as if the man held out a gemstone. "Maybe, this one thing." He took the wine and said his goodbye.

The small toddler was waving with a pudgy hand. Rise began to wave back but a sharp pain in his shoulder stopped the movement. The Writh guard did not die easily.

He walked onward through the sleeping community. From the back Rise could be mistaken for an elderly man. He had premature white hair, which often aided him in battle. They overestimated his age even though he was in prime physical condition. His life in the sector developed muscles built for survival, and his continuous protective acts toned them even further.

For ten minutes he walked, until at last he came to his dwelling place. It was relatively separate from the others, about 15 steps from the closest neighbor. More luxurious in nature than most, he was quite proud of his home. A scrap metal fence, five and a half feet tall surrounded a large tent. The whole diameter was 35 feet across. Unlike his neighbors, he possessed an unlimited supply of warm water and a guest area.

He swung open the rusty gate and to his surprise saw many candles lit inside his tent and the silhouettes of five men all taking the liberty of his comfortable chairs. He heard a familiar voice, "Ah, there he is now. Told you he'd be back soon."

Rise opened the huge tent and walked in. An old friend immediately greeted him. "Rise, you made it back! Is the child..."

"All is well, Bespin. Who are these men?"

A man with an animal skin coat that draped to his feet stood up. He must have resided in Sector 2131, the neighboring sector. It was known for having acres of cattle grounds. It was a very rare thing to hear of someone who had traveled to a different sector. Generally, it was assumed they lied. It was a life or death matter of finding a way through the giant walls, and it mostly ended in death. Sector 2131 was east of the one Rise lived in. The hunter was armed with a broad sword and many smaller knives. He stood a good head taller than Rise and extended a gigantic hand.

Rise shook it, recalling how the child's hand looked compared to his own. "What can I do for you?"

The tall man had a surprisingly gentle voice, "My name is Barton, commander of the Raven Hunters. We've traveled from Sector 2131 and need your assistance. This is my troupe..." He went off naming each one. Rise only retained the name of the first. "Perhaps you have heard of us?"

"No."

"I see... I'll get to the point. We need one more to our group, a translator, one who can speak the old tongue. Your friend has assured us of your ability. We can promise you one tenth of..."

"You want to go into the ruins?" Rise shook his head. He knew exactly where this was going. "The Writh's are the only ones still active in the old tongue. I don't plan on wasting my mother's gift to me on translating threats for a battle-hungry bounty hunter. I'm sorry, I will not go back to the ruins so readily. You better find someone else."

The large man looked down at Rise with a hateful glare like a fire just before it starts to crackle. "You turn us down too quickly, *friend*. At least listen to what we've been..."

"I've heard enough. I will not barter for you, especially now."

"You would turn down the Raven Hunters? This will make you rich..."

"Please leave. I have no interest in hunting gangs or their treasures."

The tall man was silent. His lips were moving, but anger held the words from being uttered. Finally, they spilled from his mouth into the air, "You coward! You won't risk the ruins because of the Writh Gang! You're a coward, and you've wasted too much of our time already!"

Bespin started to yell, "You call this man a coward..."

Rise lifted his good arm and signaled Bespin for silence. He was tired and just wanted to get this over with.

The expedition leader continued issuing insults and ranting until at last he gave up and motioned for his men to follow him out of the tent. He grumbled something as they walked away and slammed the gate. Soon their noise was gone, leaving Rise alone with his friend.

Bespin stood an average height with short brown hair and a young face full of compassion. He was a handsome man who never lost his childlike delight in discovery.

"I'm sorry, Rise. Thought you'd give anything for an excuse to go up against the Writh's again..." Bespin paused and smiled. "Oh, I understand. You want them to ask Trent."

Rise walked over to a pole with hooks on the top that served as his coat hanger. "Why would I want Trent to go? The man is... a waste."

"That's exactly why. He's the only other person who fluently speaks the old tongue..."

"He's not that fluent," Rise quietly said.

"Whatever, the point is there is a mean streak in you after all." Bespin laughed.

"I would never wish for anything to happen to Trent." Rise went to remove his leather trench coat that was one size too big for him. As he slipped his arm out he winced in pain. His shirt was torn and stained with a small amount of blood.

"You okay?" Bespin went to the crates by the table to prepare some tea.

"Yeah, I'll be fine. I'm not going back to the gang territory so soon though, they'll have a doubled regiment searching for me. They're probably still looking for me within the ruins.

"I've had enough of those terrible glowing eyes. As far as I can tell, their magic is somewhat weak. They can see in the dark with those eyes, but that's about it. No other powers, at least from what I've seen."

"And you want Trent to go in your place because there's a chance he might not come back."

"I don't hate the man as much as you think."

"You have nothing to fear of Trent."

"I don't fear him," Rise retorted.

"Jealous, then." Bespin had his back turned so that Rise

could not see him smiling. He was making the tea with some mint leaves that Rise had been rewarded with for some past act of protection long forgotten.

"Jealous? Why would I be jealous?"

"Because he's the only one who loves Beline as much as you do. He's your only competition."

Rise was silent. Bespin took the prepared tea leaves and walked over to a side of the tent where the ground was dug up. There was a ditch about two feet down and six feet across. A large metal pipe was almost hidden in the ground. This supply of hot water was known only to Rise, Bespin, and Beline. With the help of Bespin and his tool-savvy mind, the pipe was tapped and they could now take the hot water whenever they wished. Where it came from, where it went, who it served, they did not know and they did not care. It was preheated water; a treasure that made their lives just a small bit easier. Rise always felt that it once served the ruins, many years ago when it was a city, long before anyone could remember. The pipe was a technological marvel of a dead society. It was now reduced to supply hot water for three people.

Rise came over with a cloth and had Bespin wet it with the steaming water. The water not used fell to the dirt and descended through the mud. The rest of the tent was carpeted with a large, flat slab of scrap metal covered with old torn rugs for comfort.

He continued, "Jealous of Trent? No. Beline sees nothing in that idiot. If he were any more repulsive, we'd have to bury him like the useless corpse he is."

Bespin was still smiling. His work of annoying his friend was done. It took a lot for Rise to flat out insult someone. He mixed the tea in the two wooden bowls and turned around. Rise unsheathed his black serrated sword and began to wash off the blood stains with the cloth. Bespin's smile faded quickly. "How many?"

Rise took a solemn look like a religious man about to confess his sin. "Just one. He was alone, but he saw me and the boy hiding."

Bespin placed the tea next to Rise and slowly began sipping his. He then placed the small bag he always carried on the table.

"What's in the bag?"

He got the usual response. "Just some things I found in the ruins. Old tools I'm trying to put to new uses."

"Anything good? Anything worth risking your life in the ruins for?"

"If I ever figure out what they do, I'll let you know." Bespin patted his bag.

"One of these days you'll show me what you find in the ruins. You probably know the layout there better than the Wriths do."

"I can guarantee you of that." Bespin grinned, "I could wander through that place with my eyes closed and avoid all the Wriths along the way."

Rise carefully cleaned the sword. When he was satisfied, he placed it back in the sheath which normally latched at his side and hid beneath his big coat.

"Were the parents at least grateful?"

Rise quickly pulled out the wine from his coat pocket. "To a small extent. The father said he would do anything for me, yet I doubt that he would." Rise slowly began to drink the wine. It saddened him that out of the thousands of people who lived in Sector 2128, he only knew two that would risk their lives in return for him. Three if he counted the old man, but he was in no such position. Rise made a living out of risking his life for others, a lifestyle which earned him the name of "The Giver." Although Bespin could not fight, Rise knew without a doubt that his friend would quickly pick up a weapon and feebly try to defend him. Beline would do the same.

The Giver patted Bespin on the back as he stood up.

"What was that for? You're not so fond of the touching people stuff."

"Nothing." Rise quickly drained the wine and went rummaging through the crates for more liquor. "This stuff is amazing. I used to be able to lose the cares of this wretched world after a few sips. Now it seems to take a lake of it just to faze me."

Suddenly they heard footsteps outside. The gate to his dwelling was swung open and a moment later the figure of a woman in her mid-twenties entered. She had shoulder-length blonde hair that was thrown every which way with green eyes that were wide with grief.

"Beline..." Rise started.

"Come quickly, you two! The old man is dying!"

Chapter Two:

Beline was short with blonde hair that fell to her neck, and her mouth was full of pretty teeth, a possession few held after their twenties in the sectors. She was clean, which was one step of beauty that many neglected in these days. Her eyes were a deep green that Rise knew well. Nowhere else had he found a more brilliant green. No where else had he found someone as kind and dear and sweet as her. She was truly an emerald that had been discarded into a pile of coal. She had been with the old man all day, sitting by his bed, except for now when she ran to find Rise. He had been sick for a week and getting steadily worse. The eccentric old man was like a grandfather to the three of them, yet he was obviously crazy. He mentioned of grand adventures traveling the different sectors of the kingdom. Sure people could sneak into a different sector maybe once in their life, but the risks were not worth the benefits. The Raven Hunters were a perfect example. Perhaps they did travel a sector, but they still needed Rise's help, which he did not offer. The risks were not worth it. The Dark King's servants would find that person. His magic was beyond powerful. It was best to take your chances within your own sector. Stories people brought of other sectors, even the old man, were of places not much better, or sometimes even worse than the current one resided in. Traveling the sectors was against the law and too dangerous. Few ever attempted such a thing.

Rise forgot his fatigue and quickly followed the two out of his dwelling. It took them five minutes to find the old man's shack. It was small, only about ten feet long and five feet wide. A single cot took up most of the room. A small iron stove with a chimney pipe trailing through the roof was the only other possession inside the shack. The old man coughed violently as if someone were kicking him in the ribs.

The old man stopped coughing, yet his eyes were wandering. He was going fast. He smiled; even at his age his teeth were beautiful. He had taught the three of them how to keep them healthy, a trick many neglected in the sectors. "My beautiful children."

He sat up ever so slowly. "Beline, Bespin, and Rise. The children I never had."

"How you doing, old timer?" Bespin clasped his hand.

"Never better my boy," he wheezed. "Where's that pack of yours?"

Bespin felt his shoulder and the strap was not there. "I must have left it at Rise's place. Please excuse me." Bespin left nervously, feeling exposed without his pack.

Rise and Beline stood crowded together over the old man. He smiled at the sight of them so close.

"When are you two going to marry?"

They both lost their stern composure. Beline smiled and turned away slightly, Rise did not make eye contact except to the floor.

The old man chuckled before any of them could deny it. "You two are both stubborn enough never to admit it. Oh well, some day you will grow up." He smiled at them with soft eyes. "Beline, could you leave us alone for a while?"

"Certainly." She turned and walked out, accidentally making contact with Rise's hand with her own. His eyes darted to the touch and then quickly back to the old man.

When she left and closed the door flap the old man whispered, "I saw that look. Admit it, just once before I die. Do you love her?"

Rise took the seat and folded his arms over his knees, but said nothing.

The old man changed subjects, "I want to get this out of the way before my coughing fit returns." Already his voice was slightly weaker. "When the three of you were young, I told each of you to keep track of how many nights you saw in your life. Myself, I have kept careful record of my age. When we forget our past we forget ourselves..."

"I must admit that I haven't kept track of that for many..."

"Let me finish, boy. I know you three have lost count, but that is okay. You were the oldest of them, but not by too much. That is all I can remember. Of my own life I have seen 40,132 night falls. My father told me one day I was 1,825 night falls old. From then on I kept count."

Rise waited for more of the story, but the old man seemed to have completed his topic. "What about it?" Rise asked.

Then the old man acted as if he suddenly remembered something. "Out of the 40,132 night falls I have seen, there hasn't been a sighting of the moon since the number 9,112. That was when the black clouds first appeared. They came from the direction of what everyone assumes is the castle of that monster of a king, cursed be his name. That was also just after the sheriffs and skelguards began taking people instead of just killing them."

Rise had heard this story before, another ranting from the crazy old man.

"I think there is a connection to the Dark King's purposes and the captured people. Before that the sheriffs and skelguards just killed the criminals of the law, except on very rare occasions. Now a criminal has a good chance of merely being arrested. But there is something evil about those dark clouds."

Rise disliked this story in particular. To this day, he hated the sight of the black swirling clouds that consumed the night. Every night they came, from the direction in the northeast. He had heard stories of the moon, yet never seen it. If it did exist, and only at night, nothing could be seen through those clouds. But by morning they were gone. This pattern repeated day after day.

"Rise, listen to me. You were young, not quite a man, when your parents were arrested. Before that time you always spoke with me of how much you loved Beline. She would often remark of you as well with tender feelings, yet you both never told each other. After your parents were taken, you never spoke of loving anyone. Why do you not forsake pride or fear of rejection and ask her? It's been too long. No man can do much without a companion in these troublesome times."

Rise sighed. "Old man, why do you torment me with this? If I did marry her, but I'm not saying I will, and I lost her, I would have no reason to live."

"Would it not be like that if you lost her now?"

"Why should I marry her? What if she doesn't have the same feelings..."

"She does. When she was younger..."

Rise snapped, "People change. She might not still feel that way."

The old man chuckled again. "Settle down. You are a young fool, yet I always liked you best. Don't fear emotional attachment because you might lose it. Fear never having it. That's what keeps us apart from the sheriffs. Just because you lost your parents doesn't mean you will lose your future wife too."

"She is a good friend. I see no reason to..."

"I will stop dodging my point; a young man blinded by youth cannot see clearly. I want you to leave the sector. You, Beline, and Bespin. All of you need to leave before it's too late."

Rise shook his head, "You believe now I should leave the sector? This is crazy..."

"Please, don't call me that."

Rise fell silent. He knew he hurt the old man's feelings.

His mentor spoke softly, "I know people think I'm crazy. For years I have talked about traveling sectors. Each of these square, roofless prisons I have talked about as if they were nothing. I have revealed secrets that only a traveler would know, yet people still refuse to think I have accomplished it. Rise, I am not crazy..."

His coughing fit relapsed and Rise rubbed his shoulders to try to calm him. After a few minutes he relaxed and slowly began talking again, though slightly weaker. "I have been to over 100 different sectors. I know that each one is 50 by 50 miles. I know that it is exactly 300 feet to scale the walls. I know that each sector has giant numbers painted at each of the four walls to remind the people which prison they live in. I know that guard posts are situated 20 miles from both ends on the top of the concrete walls leaving a ten mile gap between them. I know that it is too dangerous to sneak through the wide doors at the middle of each of the walls. I know that the safest way to escape a sector... is to go over the walls. I know you have your doubts. Yes, there are many skelguards. Yes, the wall is 300 feet high, and yes, it is easy to get caught... but I know the timing. Rise, of all the things I have told you, listen most carefully to this. The Evil King has been plotting something. I know it! Every sector will be overrun with skelguards. It is at the time when they align in four rows that you must escape..." He began coughing again. Between coughs Rise could make out, "Leave soon." The coughing stopped just long enough for him to utter, "Don't you see? Already there are more skelguards than before! Leave..." He coughed himself to unconsciousness, and Rise waited by his side, listening to the erratic breathing.

He tried to think. The old man was always puzzling. Were there really more skelguards than in his younger days? Was the King planning something for Sector 2128? Did the old man really... no! Of course not! It was all just crazy ramblings from an old man. Rise bowed his head. That old man was like a father to him, and he loved him dearly. However, his lies had taken a toll on him over the years. Rise's bowed head quickly fell into the sleep he forgot he needed.

He was wakened by a ripping sound. The old man had a small knife in his boney hand and was cutting through his pillow. He seemed dizzy and weak, just barely able to rip open the pillow. He reached in and pulled out the worn clothes that were stuffed inside the sack and only stopped when he reached the bottom. He pulled something out, yet Rise could not see it with his closed fist.

"Goodbye, Rise." The coughing fit began violently. The old man was rocking the cot almost to its edges. He dropped the knife to the floor and collapsed on his cot. It stopped as suddenly as it had started, and the old man was dead.

14

Bespin and Beline heard the sounds from outside and came running in. They knew the old man would probably want private time with Rise as there had always been a bond between them. The sounds of the old man dying were too much for them to keep their post. "What happened? Is he..."

Rise nodded his head.

Bespin squeezed around Rise and put his hand over the old man's face. He pulled down and closed the eyes shut. "Goodbye, old man."

Beline sniffled and began to sob slightly. Bespin had a single tear drip down his cheek. Rise remained motionless, just staring at the floor.

Rise wanted to console Beline, he wanted nothing more than to hug her until both of their lives were worry free. Yet, he did not move. Bespin and Beline were now embracing. Rise felt no jealousy, just a little angered with himself, angered with life, and angered with the old man for dying and leaving them without a father. He had lost two fathers in his life now.

"You two may go tell the others in the living space. I will attend to readying the body."

They both stopped their tears and released from their grip on each other. They stepped out to tell everyone.

It was almost morning, but the dark clouds still swirled leaving the land looking dark and gray.

The pressures of the world were getting to him. "I need a drink." He almost checked his coat for a small bottle of liquor but realized he left it at his dwelling.

Rise turned his attention to what was in the old man's fist. He slowly opened it and pulled out a piece of paper. He placed it in his pocket. Rise had no desire to read it at that moment. He needed a drink.

Chapter Three:

The old man's body was put to fire early in the morning. A burned body could not be turned into a skelguard. Rise had gone home to find his jacket to fight off the cold; despite the quickly dropping temperature he would not miss the old man's funeral. A large crowd of about 500 people gathered. Most knew the old man, some came only for the spectacle and warmth of a crowd and fire. His shack had been scavenged by close friends until it was bare, even

15

the metal from the stove and chimney pipe had been stripped, all to be used by the lost souls of the sector.

He now sat inside a disheveled bar. It was the only half-respectable building within the living space. His company was mostly the older men of the sector. It seemed that only the elderly had enough spoils to still trade for alcohol. The bartender smiled at Rise, displaying a set of horrific teeth. "This one is free. Since you knew the deceased. Who knows, it might even be strong enough to turn your hair back to its rightful color."

Rise took the glass and drank it quickly. He closed his eyes to feel the liquid reach down through his body with its chilled fingers. It was the only way to forget the troubles.

"I would like another, if it's not too much trouble."

"It is. First one is free. The second will cost you."

Rise felt his pockets for something to barter but found nothing except a small piece of paper.

The door to the small, dingy bar opened and a familiar voice said, "Rise! You weren't at the scavenging. You know the old man would have wanted you to have something of his."

Bespin was followed by Beline. They took two worn-down seats from the side of the bar and placed them next to Rise.

Beline rested her arm on Rise's shoulder. He never looked up, but kept his eyes on a few scratches on the table. Bespin took his shoulder pack and unzipped it. He reached in and pulled out a few things and handed them to the barkeep to pay for three more drinks; a few gems it looked like.

Rise only lifted his eyes when another glass was placed in front of him. Beline and Bespin each received two because they knew the old man as well. Rise downed the next glass, forgetting about the piece of paper in his pocket.

The three sat there silently, each with separate thoughts, but all about the same topic. It was Bespin who broke the silence. "My first memory of the old man was him cleaning up a scraped knee. I was playing in the ruins and fell off a cement block. My parents were out scavenging so when I made it back to the living space, my face covered in tears, the old man cleaned me up and even gave me a newly stitched pair of pants that would cover up my injury. He didn't even tell my parents I was in the ruins."

Bespin pushed one of his glasses in front of Rise. Rise pulled it up to his lips and drank it.

"My first memory of him was wiping my teeth with a wet rag." She smiled slightly and Rise felt the entire room could have been blinded by her beauty. "He showed me lots of other things too. When my father was taken..." She paused to wipe at her wet eyes. "When he was taken, the gang did not have to respect the marriage rights. Three Wriths came into our house. They tried to steal her and me, but mother fought... until... the leader lost patience." She took a deep breath. "The old man appeared out of nowhere, holding a magic stick. He pointed it at the leader but missed on purpose. A warning shot. I remember the yellow flower vase exploding. I remember the click and then a large hole in the ground below the leader's feet. They ran. That wonderful old man was just in time to save my life. He even tried to bring mother back..." She made no sound of lament, but the tears fell quickly from her eyes. She pushed one of her glasses in front of Rise. She never really liked the stuff anyway, and just one was needed for the ritual remembrance.

He looked over at Beline who was still crying. He did not touch the glass for sake of the remembrance. She removed her arm from Rise and buried her face in both of them. Rise wanted nothing more than to take her in his arms, to hold her, to make sure the problems of life never harmed her again. He wanted to make her happy.

Bespin placed his arm around her. "Come now, Beline. Let's make this an honorable remembrance." He was fighting back tears as well.

She took a few seconds to compose herself. They each grabbed their glass, all three of them. Beline spoke first. "To the old man."

"To the old man."

Rise finished, "To the old man."

They each drank the glass. Bespin and Beline both coughed afterwards. Rise stared past them, at nothing. He was a man in need of sleep, yet his mind was working hard. He thought of the old man. It was he who had shown him how to use the sword. The old man had effectively saved his life many times over. Every time Rise drew that weapon he remembered the teachings of the old man. In spirit, the old man was with him every battle, every beating, and now he was gone!

Rise tightened his grip on the weak glass. It burst within his fist. Rise flinched and the pieces that did not sink their teeth into his palm fell to the table. He looked startled as his mind awoke from his thoughts.

"Rise!" Beline grabbed his hand and looked at it

carefully. He loved the way her hands felt. They were not smooth, but they were not deep callused like his were. She was picking out shards of glass from his palm, and he could not take his eyes from her face.

He did not notice Bespin smiling. Bespin knew just as well as the old man that the two completed each other, like the link of two hands helping each other up.

"There, we just need something to cover your hand with."

With his spare hand he checked his pockets for something to wrap it with. He felt the piece of paper from the old man.

The bartender placed a spare rag he kept under the counter on the table. "Use that before he bleeds on the table. And you better pay me back for that glass."

No sooner had she bandaged him than he sat up, the paper hidden in his fist. "Thank you. Both of you. I must go. I'll see you later tonight."

"Don't forget," Beline said, "you're helping me move into the living space tomorrow."

He nodded distractedly and walked out of the bar. He unfolded the paper and began to read it.

Chapter Four:

Rise held the paper in his hands. There was a drawing etched with charcoal. It showed a rectangle comprised of smaller rectangles. A group of the smaller rectangles were etched harder than the rest, making an uneven square of them stand out.

"Rise!"

His concentration was broken in a mist of annoyance. Rise thought to himself, *Anyone but him.*

"Hello, Rise!"

Rise turned to face the on-comer, who stood a good deal taller and much wider. He had darker skin from many naps in the noonday heat. His round body was edged with a few muscles on his shoulders and his face was round with no straight edges.

"Hello, Trent."

"Hello. Hey, what do you have in your hands?"

"Nothing." Rise closed his fist over the paper.

"Oh, let an old friend see..."

"What do you want?" Rise placed the paper in his jacket pocket.

"I just got hired by a troupe of bounty hunters, they look professional, came all the way from Sector..."

"Trent, listen to me closely. I'm in a hurry..."

Trent smiled, "I promise I won't take long. Anyway, these bounty hunters want me to go to the ruins with them. They want me to translate the old tongue so they can talk to the gang. I was just wondering what Beline's favorite color was?"

"Why don't you ask her yourself?"

"I want it to be a surprise. The bounty hunters are negotiating a trade for treasures. Please don't tell her, but I'm going to bring her back a huge gem, whichever color she loves most."

Rise stayed silent just long enough to run the scenario through his head. Trent was stupid enough to barter for treasures from the gang. They would not take kindly to it. He, and the bounty hunters would be killed or captured for this. And of course, Beline's favorite color was green. Always had been.

"Trent, I don't have to warn you of the dangers. Don't be stupid."

"It's great to have friends who care."

"I'm not..." He let it go. Trent was not listening anyway.

"Don't worry. These bounty hunters are good. They promised me full protection. I'm not much for a fight."

Rise shook his head. "The ruins are huge. These bounty hunters know nothing of this gang. They probably only heard stories of the treasures they have. I won't lie, the few times I snuck into their lair I have seen a few priceless treasures. Yet, each time I barely escaped and only by shedding needless blood. I will say this only once. *Do not go.*"

Rise turned and left Trent staring at the back of his head. "And her favorite color is green." Rise whispered that to himself.

When Rise found the old man's shack he felt a slight queasiness in his stomach. It was empty. Nothing remained except the shell of the hut, and the floorboards. It would be three days before the ritual of mourning was over and the rest could be stripped clean.

Rise looked at the drawing. It did not make sense to him. "What are you trying to tell me old man?" He lowered the paper, and it was not until that moment that he realized the floorboard formations. They fit exactly with the markings on the

19

paper.

Rise found the boards on the floor that matched the diagram from the paper. He felt along them with his rough hands. A group of them were bound as one; a hidden opening. He removed his sword and jammed it into the edge. His long black jacket was collecting dust from the floor, but he was too occupied to care. His sword was a black metal, with a six inch serrated tip. He pried it upwards and the etched boards came up in one piece. There was a long hole dug into the dirt with two objects wrapped in cloth.

He picked up the one on the left. It was heavy and clanked when he set it on the ground.

The sound of people walking close by startled him. Two people were laughing, but they were still a good 20 feet away. Rise pulled his overcoat open to block the view anyone might see of the objects he was looking at. In his kneeling position they would assume he was still mourning. The voices passed.

Rise unwrapped the first object. It turned out to be two. One was the magic stick the old man had used to scare away the gang members from Beline's house many years ago. The old man had scorned him every time he used that word. He never knew why the old man hated the word magic. The magic stick was intact, the shoulder rest and the two long metal barrels seemed almost polished. The second was similar to the magic stick, yet fatter and shorter. It had a single barrel, but a thin metal cable was wound up inside a housing at the base of the metal. A point like a short spear was half submerged in the barrel. From the base to the tip it was just over a foot. A long cylinder rested on its side with glass at both ends. Rise looked through it and to his amazement found it to be a small telescope with an X drawn on one end. He had always wanted a telescope. Perhaps this was a more powerful magic stick.

He removed the last object from the hole and unwrapped it. It was a book, written by the old man himself. The pages were thick, and the binding was done by a small rope. The words were etched in something similar to charcoal, but smaller and more pointed. The front was written in the old tongue. The title when translated read, "Journey of Trek." In the old tongue it was spelled Terk. The same principal applied to Rise's name. In the old tongue it was Ries, yet the pronunciation was the same as well as the meaning. Move up, ascend, soar, and increase. Rise never felt worthy of his name.

Rise smiled. "So old man, your name was Trek."

Rise quickly rewrapped the items within the cloth and

concealed them under his coat. He headed out for his dwelling. He had much reading to do.

Chapter Five:

Rise leaned back in his chair. It was already nightfall, and it had taken him that long to read the book from cover to cover. The first three pages were actually cleaner than the others. It seemed the old man had placed those in front although they were written last. When translated it read:

The many journey and treks I have accomplished have led to four major discoveries.

The first: There is no paradise sector. The myth of the perfect sector is false, which was my reason for leaving in the first place.

The second: The Dark King and his followers are in every sector. When his gruesome skelguards appear in monstrous numbers, LEAVE.
Occasionally, a sector will receive this bizarre attention from the King and be destroyed.

The third: There is no escape from the sectors. Sure, a man can travel them easily enough if he knows the trick, and I have even found the northern boundary. It is far too heavily guarded on the top of the wall, and beyond is a valley no man can travel. Unfortunately, I have not discovered a west, east, or even southern boundary. Just more sectors.

The fourth: We have a past. We must remember that life was not always this bad. Everyone in every sector has a past that must not be forgotten. I have taken all the stories I have heard and compiled them into what sounds the most reasonably true.

The history on the next few pages described another royal family known as the Tetriach. In the family were three siblings. Two princes and one princess. The king and queen were dead and the children fought to keep their dying empire alive. That was when the great migration was accomplished. The war was postponed for the change, but quickly returned. The empire was losing again, yet a gift

21

from the skies allowed them to take control. That was when the Evil King was manifested, cursed be his name. He was the only survivor of the children. With power from the heavens, he crippled every nation and made them all slaves to him. The sectors were built to imprison the populace. With his magic (Rise was taken aback, but the old man really did use the word magic) he created the skelguards, the walking dead, mindless warriors, to serve him. He appointed trusted men to be his sheriffs. These fools were bred to serve the Dark King. The sheriffs were still mostly human, however they mindlessly obeyed anything the King ordered. The sheriffs would keep the skelguards in line. Each sector has just one sheriff to control an army of skelguards. The last piece of that section stated, "We all know these terrors in our lives. I write them because the only reason we don't know our past is because someone did not write down what was obvious in their lives. Maybe some future generation can use these words. Maybe the future will be a better time, without evils like the King and his sheriffs."

Rise feared the sheriffs almost as much as he feared the clouds. The skelguards, despite their ghastly appearance, were not as dangerous. At least they waited for orders before they acted... most of the time. The sheriff was unpredictable. He could do anything from shooting a person in the thigh and letting them to bleed to death, or having the skelguards use that poor soul as target practice for their magic staffs. The worst thing Rise had ever seen was a mother beaten to death by the skelguards at the order of a sheriff. When she was dead there was a high pitched cry. She had been concealing a baby within her arms. "Bring it to me." The exact words of the sheriff still brought nausea to his stomach. They gave the sheriff the baby. He dropped it to the ground and drew his magic stick. Rise had turned away just in time to miss the atrocity, but the loud bang echoed forever within his skull. It pounded from wall to wall in his head like someone beating a carpet clean inside his brain.

No common man had ever seen the Dark King, yet it was under this rule that these terrible acts happened. If someone did their best to avoid the sheriff and the skelguards, all would go well. There were also the few laws to consider. If one obeyed the rules of the King you might live: Do not speak objectionably about the King. Do not attack a servant of the King. No loud noises. No complex machinery or inventions. Absolutely no trespassing into different sectors. As if the massive walls and guarded doorways were not enough of a deterrent, an actual law was made about it. Those laws were the sum of existence for the people. In the sectors a person lived or died by these laws. Of course everyone broke the laws in some small way. Rise always wondered what would be considered a complex machinery violation. On his left wrist he braced a light source. By pressing a button the glass bulb would light up so he could see in dark places. It of course required a power source, a cylinder with a small bump on one end. These were very rare, but a man deep within the living space had a machine that could put the magic back in them. Because of the threat it could be considered an invention, Rise kept it hid under his coat sleeve. It was one of his most useful tools in his dealings.

The rest of the book was about the old man's journeys and even a map of the different sectors. Just a small piece of the overall picture, but it was a map, something Rise thought could never be done of the sectors. Even a north boundary was found. Each sector was a 50 mile square surrounded by 300 foot concrete walls. Each wall had two guard towers and was constantly patrolled by the evil skelguards. When Rise saw that the maze of sectors ended somewhere in the north, he was disappointed by a small inscription. "No escape through north way. Protective barriers." There was no way to escape the sectors.

A few sectors were etched black. Rise could take a hint about avoiding those ones.

Rise found a part about how to use the short magic stick with the telescope mounted to it. The book continued:

The grapnel is a tool you must protect. NEVER allow the King or his servants to see this invention. This is the secret in traversing the sectors. Make sure the leather strap is hung over your shoulder and under the opposite arm. Use the scope to aim the grapnel. Pull tightly against your shoulder, set the X in the scope no more than a foot from the top of the wall. Pull and hold the trigger and brace for the release. The spike will embed itself where you aimed the X. Let go of the trigger to recoil the cable and hang on tightly. Use your feet to keep from ramming into the wall as you ascend. The leather strap around your torso is your only safety precaution. DO NOT LET GO WHILE ASCENDING.

Rise laughed at that part and kept reading:

The grapnel will leave just a few inches of cable when you reach the top. Pull yourself over. Once on top, you have two options for releasing the pike from the concrete. There is a red button on top of the grapnel that will retract the small claws and pull the rest of the cable back into the casing. There is a secondary release attached to the pike itself. Just turn the base of the pike next to where the cable attaches. Either way will pull the spear tip back into the barrel.

You will see that each sector wall is only ten or fifteen feet wide. Walk to the other side and fire directly between your feet. Push the green button under the handle, then descend the other side of the wall. The green button allows the cable to unwind slowly enough without dropping you. Once you reach the bottom, hit the red retract button.

The timing is the most important part. As soon as the two skelguards walk by each other in the middle of their patrol get your aim ready. Wait a few seconds and then pull the trigger. If you attempt this at any other moment, the skelguards will see you. This is the only moment when both of their backs will be towards you. Once again, this is only when *two* skelguards pass each other. Groups of three or four will not work.

Rise was glad he had something physical to remember the old man by, but his doubts of its truth spoke louder than the whispered memories. It was a remembrance of the old man, nothing more. There was no possibility that the old man had done all this. He did not travel the sectors, he did not ascend the walls or even make a map of them. It was all written ramblings of an old man.

He still smiled thinking of himself trying to do that. His whole world, the ruins, the living space, Beline's house, all of it resided in his sector. There was no reason to leave. He would never, ever, not even if his life depended on it, try something so foolish as escape to another sector. It was impossible.

Chapter Six:

When Rise awoke the next morning he quickly bathed and readied himself. It was important to help Beline move quickly into the living space, the somewhat safe area where most of the decent people in the sector resided. The majority of those in the sector lived in the central living space, far from the walls and relatively safe from skelguards. Her house was separated from the main source of residential shacks found in the living space. It was because of this location that her mother was the victim of a gang attack years ago. Her house was passed on for generations to her family and it meant more to her than any amount of bartering. It was located within six miles of the ruins; too close for comfort. The Wriths inhabited the west of the ruins, leaving the east relatively safe, but they had been known to wander to other areas.

People often scavenged in the eastern area of the ruins. Huge concrete buildings still stood, but none more than a few stories high. The rest was a maze of broken glass and rebar-infested concrete, with the majority of the buildings at waist level. A once great city stood here, but was now crippled. Many speculated the living space did not begin to compare itself to what the ruins used to be. The amount of debris in the ruins indicated the buildings were once giant figures in a thriving world. A few shacks and huts were nothing compared to the buildings that once scraped against the sky itself.

The Writh gang had been a part of this sector as long as people could remember. Those who felt the cravings to steal and hurt others found the proper company and lived as hated men in the ruins. Together, with their other gang members, the Wriths thrived on their bestial urges.

Beline's father died slowly of a fever sickness, leaving the two women to fend for themselves. When the Writh's learned that a woman was available they instantly began plotting. All the Writh women were either born within their community, or stolen. None ever joined willingly. Because Beline's house was so close she was an easy target.

When the old man showed his magic superior to their own, the gang left. He cursed them, warning them if they ever returned to the house he would destroy them. But now he was dead. His magic was useless. It was agreed many years ago that when the old man died it would be best to move Beline before news spread into the gang territory. Rise pondered over the magic that once belonged to the old man. He not only had the grapnel, but he also had the very same magic stick the old man used. Perhaps he could be Beline's new protector. He quickly dismissed it. It was not worth the risk. It was safer if she could be moved into the living space of the sector, closer to him. If she moved into the old man's shack, it would not be destroyed by scavengers. The only problem was that Trent lived close by, a short walk away.

Rise began walking to leave the living space. It took half an hour or so to cross the entire thing, maybe a little longer, depending on the passing of the people. The only thing to slow him down was being careful not to trip over a tent peg; the community lived close, one reason that they were fairly strong as a whole.

It was assumed every sector contained a living space. It was the residential area where all the "decent" people of the sector eventually moved. It was usually away from the gangs and popular stalking grounds of the skelguards. It was the only space available where people might try to live. In this sector it was situated in a small valley where hills rose around it just slightly. On the north side of one of these hills was Beline's house. Beyond that was the ruins. After the ruins were the very walls of the sector itself. The ground around the walls was cleared of any debris and hills. This small area was where most of the skelguards would patrol. They guarded from the top of the sector wall and the bottom. A large metal door was found right in the middle of every wall to allow only servants of the King to pass. All these doors were watched closely. Usually, the only time they opened was to allow the ration vehicles to pass and distribute the food.

Rise stopped dead in his tracks. "What's that doing here?"

His comment was heard by a man close by. "It's been walking through the living space since day break. Wretched thing! It's a sad day when they don't respect the boundaries of our homes."

Not more than 40 feet away stood a skelguard. Its hideous appearance only added to the fear it instilled to the very marrow of the people. The power of the King knew no bounds. Not even death stopped his servants from carrying out their duty. The skeleton was probably once someone from this very sector, but taken years ago by the sheriff. The skelguard was clothed in typical sheriff uniform with brown pants, overcoat, and black boots. A drawing of an iron fist was stitched to its chest, a symbol of the King. Strands of coarse hair hung from the back of the skull down to its shoulders. The dark red splotches where the eyes should have been glowed deep within the sockets. The almost grin of the skull was no friendly embodiment. In its boney hands, a spear with a fat head was held. A quick turn of the bones in the wrist would erupt a fireball from the staff with deadly accuracy. With a few turns, the temperature from the fireball was hot enough to melt steel. Anyone trying to escape would get their legs melted together. These monsters stood seven feet tall, and everyone knew to keep from any form of eye contact with them.

Rise remembered seeing a poor soul many years ago

trying like a futile madman to destroy just one skelguard, yet the Dark Lord's power was too much. The man had stolen a magic stick, a big one. It was a large metal cylinder that rested on his shoulder. He aimed and shot the creature in the back from sixty paces. A loud whistling noise followed by a deafening boom were etched memories in Rise's head. The skelguard was knocked to the ground, but nothing more. It stood up. The man threw down the large magic stick and fired from a small crossbow on his arm. The arrow hit an invisible casting just centimeters from the skelguard. The spot that was struck glowed light red for a brief second as the bolt bounced off. The magic surrounding the skelguard was too powerful.

The Evil King could not be stopped. His minions were indestructible. The same light-red force could be seen around the sheriff from time to time. Whenever something came too close to contacting the sheriff it would glow on that spot. They were perfectly surrounded by the magic, like an invisible armor. The man that had tried to destroy the skelguard so many years ago, had tried pulling another weapon from a strap on his back, but the sheriff had commanded the skelguard not to fire. The man pulled a dagger and ran for the sheriff. The sheriff pulled out his magic stick, his hands and shoulder glowing red from the contact of the metal, and shot the man from three feet. The sheriff wielded a sword at his side, but he chose to use the unavoidable magic. There was no honor. There was no fighting back.

Rise watched the skelguard walk around, never turning its neck, yet always aware. Everyone around it was silent, and no one dared to approach it closer than 30 feet. Every time it passed a dwelling those inside fell silent.

"Since when do they come this close to the residents?" Rise shook his head.

"This is the first time I've seen them like this when they're not hunting someone."

Rise walked away, leaving the stranger to stare at the skelguard. Rise kept his distance from the skelguard. Wriths, rogue bounty hunters, they were nothing compared to the magic of the King. True, the Writh Gang did have a strange magic that made their eyes glow green in the dark, but they were still just as mortal. Night vision was not as lethal as the walking dead. Rise had killed plenty of Wriths, but no person had ever killed a sheriff or a skelguard.

Rise saw three more skelguards, all wandering in the living space. "Why don't you stay near the walls, where you belong?" he muttered. He started to wish he brought the old man's magic stick, just for comfort. Maybe the old man was right about there being more skelguards. No! It couldn't be. It couldn't. Things could not get worse.

He made it almost to the end of the living space, no more skelguards in sight. A lone figure in a dark cowl stood a few feet from a shack on the edge of the living space. Just watching. He did not move. He stood very straight. Too straight. Writh members were taught to stand and sit straight. Rigid.

"One way to be sure."

Rise did not have the magic stick, nor the grapnel device, but as always, he carried his sword hidden under his trench coat. Walking silently he crept a foot behind the man and uttered a greeting in the old tongue.

The man answered back in the same language. The Writh member immediately recognized his mistake and quickly jumped forward, pulling out a sword. He shook his head in disgust. Wriths knew never to reveal their gang affiliation by using the old tongue in the living space. The cowl was tossed off his head, revealing a man with a very square face and huge neck muscles. He was shorter than Rise but built like a fist. The Writh member cursed at Rise in the old tongue. Rise warned him, "If we fight, the skelguards are going to kill us."

The first blow came fast, just as Rise suspected. He stepped back and drew his sword like a striking serpent, easily evading the strike. In the old tongue he muttered, "So be it."

The square faced man handled a thin sword, the ones that would bend easily, but it was sharp with dual edges and allowed him to move it quickly. Rise tilted and lowered his sword to block the rapid jabs. The Writh stepped forward and swung widely, aiming for the side of Rise's throat. Rise ducked. He regained his posture and continued to block the strikes. The Writh again swung for his throat. Each time the Writh swung that direction his right foot stepped forward and to his left for better balance. Each time. Now Rise just had to wait. He continued to block, not making one offensive counter strike.

A small crowd was gathering, about twenty people, but it quickly multiplied. In the front of the group was the family whose boy he saved. The small child was still holding onto his mother's hand. The father was there too with his wooly coat. Rise glanced at the sword scabbard at the dad's side, however the father merely continued to watch with vague interest. It was the same for the others he had helped. He quickly counted eight people who called themselves his friend from past favors, and that was just at a glance.

Rise continued to move and block as the grunting of the Writh became heavier. He was becoming angry. Each swing was quicker than the last and Rise almost started to worry about keeping up.

"Rise!" Bespin pushed forward through the crowd. He was reaching into his shoulder pouch for something.

Someone grabbed Bespin and forced him to the ground. It was the man in the wooly coat. As he pinned Bespin to the dirt he yelled, "Keep it a fair fight!"

Finally! The right foot forward and slightly to the left. Rise ducked and swung upward as he took a long step inward. There was a slicing sound as his sword cut away some flesh from the Writh's hand, and then a clank as the tip hit the Writh's sword. The enemy sword fell to the ground and the gang member doubled over, grabbing his crippled hand. Rise kicked the sword away.

He heard vague shouts from the crowd, "Finish the Writh!" "Kill 'em!"

Rise holstered his sword to the disappointment of the crowd, and violently pulled the Writh to his feet. The square faced man could now only wield a burning hate in his eyes. Rise had both hands around the dirty shirt collar. In the old tongue Rise told him, "If I catch you spying for recruits again, I will finish the job. Go back under your rock!" Rise fiercely shoved him backward. The Writh ran, cradling his hand like a wounded animal. The Writh yelled over his shoulder in the old tongue, "I'll come back for you!"

Rise shook his head. That young fool. The Writh's had hunted him before, but somehow he always pulled through.

Bespin ran over. "I tried to help! That idiot in the..."

Rise continued walking with Bespin following. "It's all right, Bespin. Thanks for the thought." He smiled and patted Bespin on the shoulder. "What were you reaching for, inside the pack?"

"You going to Beline's?" He quickly changed the topic.

"Yeah."

"Good. Good luck with the moving. The old man's shack is still in good shape."

Rise scratched his head. "You're not helping?"

"Nah, I figured you and Beline could use some alone time."

Rise did not respond.

"And," Bespin continued, "I plan on doing some spying on that group of bounty hunters. They took Trent with them this morning, and I was going to see how *negotiations* were proceeding. Maybe make away with a little treasure."

"Don't get killed."

"Don't you worry about me. I've been practically living in the ruins since I was a boy."

Rise nodded and Bespin headed off in a slightly different direction. He was heading towards the left of the ruins, where the Wriths resided.

Chapter Seven:

Rise saw Beline's house, one of the few old constructions that was still intact. The ruins probably contained many of these types of dwellings, but they were now swept under a carpet of rubble. Rise smelled something that seemed to reach within him and bring warmth to his whole body. It was baked bread.

It had been a while since he ate bread, a rare treat.

Beline came out the door holding a loaf of bread in an earthen pan.

Rise smiled and took it as she offered it to him. "This is wonderful, it wins me over the rations." He leaned in close and smelled the bread. "Thank you."

"Don't think of it as a gift," she smiled, "I have to keep my beast of burden full of energy."

"Do you want to go inside and have one last meal in the house?"

Her face gloomed. "I think we should do this quickly. I saw some Writh spies go into the living space. I think they came to confirm the rumors of the old man's death. Did you see any on your way here?"

"Just one. But you're right... let's get this done."

"Thank you, I've loaded most of my things into the cart. I don't want to leave the bigger stuff behind, but the old man's shack is so small." She looked towards the ruins nervously.

"You can take it. We can put it in my home with the rest of your things. At least until you find a bigger place. I have enough room."

She kept staring into the ruins, "No, no, please, let's just move it now."

"All right."

She showed him in, and they quickly found the last of

her smaller belongings that would just barely fit in the old man's shack and stacked it in the cart outside. The bread was tempting him for a break in their work, but Beline would not allow it. She was nervous.

"Where's Bespin?"

"He went to watch the bartering."

She was quickly looking through her house for any special belongings she might have left. "What bartering?"

"A bounty hunting clan came asking me to help them translate the old tongue. I said no and so they hired Trent."

She gasped slightly, "Trent? Why would he do something like that?"

"He's an idiot."

"No he's not. He's a very nice man."

Rise changed the subject, "Bespin went to spy on them and I guess if things went well he'd try to earn some profits."

Beline was not seriously worried about Bespin. "He knows the ruins well, not even a skelguard or the sheriff could find him there. He'll be fine."

She put her hands on her hips and sighed, "Well, that's everything I need."

Her dwelling was bare to begin with, but now it was even more spacious. The house was completely made of wood and some carpenters from long ago had taken their time in crafting it. The shacks and tents of the living space were no comparison to the craftsmanship of the ancients. Beline stood in her empty home and took a deep breath. She turned to Rise and said, "Maybe one day I'll be back here. If the right circumstances happen."

Rise nodded, "I can start hauling the cart as soon as you're ready."

They walked outside and Rise put on the shoulder harness and began to pull on the cart. The wooden wheels moved slowly, but eventually momentum was built and Rise began to pull it easier. It took too much energy to try to talk while pulling, so Rise did his favor in silence. Beline was not talking either, she was disturbed by something. She continually looked over her shoulder in the direction of the ruins. Not until they had gone some way down the hill and the ruins were hidden behind the slope did she exhale and begin talking.

"Thank you, Rise."

He nodded his head.

"Oh! What was I thinking? I'm sorry, I must have been

distracted, let me help you."

Rise broke his silence to utter, "No, I have it..."

But she was already squeezing into the shoulder harness next to him. Her strength was not outstanding, but her physical presence so close gave him more energy.

"Thank you so much Rise, this has been a difficult day. I never actually thought I'd have to leave my home. But this is no time to look back; at least I'll be closer to those I care about."

Rise nodded.

"Do you remember when we were children and the old man gave us speaking lessons?" Beline asked.

"Yes."

The old man taught them the art of speech, how to make it prettier and more effective. It turned them into effective barterers. Grammar was the first lesson he instilled in the threefold friends. The old man taught them things that even a sheriff would not have learned. He had taught them art, carpentry, cooking, and fighting. Rise was the only one of the three to pick up on the latter lesson.

The living space came into view; just a short way to go. Another hour of pulling the cart and they would arrive.

They talked for some time about the old man. Rise had deep feelings for him, yet he kept his sentences short. It disturbed him that Beline was doing most of the talking. She deserved someone who was as passionate about things as she was. She could become excited about the simplest pleasure in life and could practically write a book about it. Her and Bespin both. Rise wondered if the difference between them was his ability to fight. He was the only one of them to really focus on combat. Perhaps that had dampened his zeal for the simple pleasures that his two friends maintained. He stopped talking all together and just listened to her.

Beline was still going, "I wish I had paid more attention during his art lessons. I loved the things he used to draw for us. I still have many of them at the house. Maybe someday we can go back and get them... what's wrong?"

"Nothing."

"You haven't said anything for a while. I miss your, "Yeah, and yes, and I remember that."" She imitated a man's deep voice while she tried to mimic him.

He smiled a little. "I don't speak that well."

"You talk just fine. You have better speaking skills than you let on. Anyone who can take a year's worth of lessons of the old tongue from the old man and remember it the rest of his life has a gift."

"My mother taught it to me. The old man just helped me to memorize it." He looked at her from the corner of his eye, enjoying her company. For a brief moment he considered telling her he loved her. He quickly dismissed it and looked straight ahead.

"Something's wrong. Just tell me." She was getting short of breath from the work.

"Nothing is wrong."

"All right, if you don't want to tell me, that's fine. But I wish you would, we've known each other our whole lives practically. As long as I can remember you've always been there. You've always been there for me." She stopped at that suddenly, as if she didn't mean to say it and quickly moved on, "Uh, how much longer do you think this will take?"

"If you're tired don't worry about it, take a break. I'll be just fine."

"No," she leaned in just slightly more towards Rise. "This is fine."

They walked and Beline spoke, "I've been working on a new poem. I need some paper though, to write it down."

"Let's hear it."

"Okay, it's about children. I don't have a title for it yet:

Simple eyes and simple minds,
make the real treasures more sublime.
Playing with sticks or skipping stones
our sector's children can weather any storm.
Mothers and Fathers all of us are,
We protect the young ones from the monsters afar.
With eyes of birds we peer down on our treasures,
Protecting them with all our endeavors.
Should we lose a child to the mystery of lifeless,
The only thing we know is: gone is something priceless.
The children are gemstones to the poor, water for the thirsty, and a support for the weak,
All beautiful creatures that shine bright
no matter how bleak.
To have the cares of a child once again, to run and play and forget adult cares,
Because once you grow up, you have nothing but terrible loathsome scares."

Rise liked it. He kept repeating some parts in his head, but he did not say anything out loud.

They pulled the cart for another hour and finally stopped at the old man's bare shack.

"You didn't like it."

"What?"

"The poem."

"No I thought it was beautiful. Sounds like you really like children."

"Just the children of others," she laughed.

They continued to move her things into the shack.

She packed it literally full of her belongings and Rise brought a stored cot from his place to her new home since her old bed did not fit.

"Listen," he said, scratching the back of his head, "now that you live this close, if that place ever gets too cramped you can come on over anytime..."

"I most certainly will! You're the only person with hot water ready all day."

They were both sweaty from the work, yet Rise found her just as beautiful. "Beline..."

"Yes?"

He stood quietly for a short time, "Would you like to get a drink?"

She put her arm through his and they began walking to the shack of a tavern.

He enjoyed her company, and as far as he could tell, she enjoyed his. They were close friends, but he did not know if that was all they were. It was confusing to him. If she did return the feelings, and if they did get married, and something happened to her, he would have no reason to live. He did not want that risk of losing someone so close. But the old man's words returned to him, "Would it not be like that if you lost her now?"

Chapter Eight:

The two sat at the bar, Rise with his alcohol, and Beline with water and crushed mint leaves. They traded half the loaf of bread for their drinks. Rise was close to finishing his third.

"You're doing that quiet thing again." She smiled at him.

"I've just been thinking."

"There's a change."

He chuckled slightly.

"Thank you again for helping with the move. I doubt anyone else in the living space would have had the courage to help someone who lived so close to the ruins."

"They're brave enough when they need something to barter with."

She took a small sip of her water. "Rations are coming today. Good thing too, I'm almost out."

"No one has seen the sheriff for a while. Think he'll be there at the ration distribution?"

"I hope not. He looks almost as scary as the skelguards."

Rise said, "I'd rather take my chances with a skel. At least they have to follow orders. That sheriff has too much freedom. Morceff doesn't deserve that power."

"Don't talk such things. The King's magic heavily protects Morceff. And don't you dare try to prove otherwise. I don't know what I'd do if you died. I couldn't bear to lose the old man and you."

Rise stayed silent. Those words hung in the air in front of him and refused to leave. He wanted to tell her. He had to tell her. He thought it out in his head, the exact movements he would use. The precise way his lips would say, "I love you." He ran it over and over in his head. His mouth instantly turned dry and sticky, as if he swallowed a spider's web. He finally forced it open.

Before a single sound could escape his dead-bolt mouth, a distraction occurred. A crowd of people suddenly walked by the door to the tavern. Words could be heard from certain noisy individuals, "The rations are here."

Beline jumped up and grabbed onto Rise's arm and pulled him off the seat, his mouth still open. "Let's go, I don't want to be last in line."

Rise sighed. His courage sank back down to his knees and his heart seemed to follow. Maybe it was better this way. Maybe he was just not meant to tell her.

They followed the crowd. Soon, they were just two ants out of a colony. Thousands of moving bodies herding towards the call of their only reliable food source.

Finally, they made it and stood a few hundred people back from the front. Not a terrible spot.

The line formed around the main road of the sector. A huge door in the wall allowed giant vehicles to transport the disgusting food rations. Four main roads, usually avoided by commoners, ran through the sector forming a + through the middle, to allow the King's vehicles access. The doors were heavily guarded; nothing except ration vehicles went in or out. Once a month a troupe of the giant vehicles would pass by, each one going to a farther sector. Then they'd go back during the night. It was the only time the massive concrete gates were slid open, and it was the most dangerous time to stand too close to one of the walls. The skelguards were on high alert at those times, and many innocent people were torched alive.

"I know you hate these crowds, but I promise we can go somewhere peaceful after this," Beline said.

A few hundred skelguards formed a line around the people, keeping them in order. The skeleton monsters always stood poised with their lances, ready to spew magical flame on anyone that would dare cross that ever vanishing line of "unacceptable conduct."

They stood as compact as sand in a desert, being pushed by a relentless wind. Slowly they made their way to the front of the line. A large vehicle that was about 80 feet long was parked. Out of the back of the cargo area a few unhappy men pulled out the ration cases. They were clothed in fine garments, clothes that actually fit their bodies. Clothes that were tailored, not scavenged from the rubble. They never made eye contact with the residents. They worked at the palace of the King, and as such they were hated. Anyone who worked directly for the King was considered an abomination. Their clothes were already covered with the saliva of the people. Rise saw the person in front of him spit into the man's face while taking his ration pack.

Beline took her ration pack and said, "Thank you." Rise snatched his and they quickly walked out of the crowd.

Beline said, "These ration bags are getting lighter each time." She shook the pack and heard the contents slosh around.

"I don't believe so." They made their way around the huge line of people, staying a good 30 steps from the guarding row of skelguards. Rise was looking around to see if he could spot the sheriff. That wretch was nowhere in sight, which relieved him greatly.

"Are there more skelguards this time?"

Rise shook his head, "You're sounding like the old man."

"Is that a bad thing?"

Rise stayed silent at this. The death of his mentor was still stinging him.

Beline wrapped her arm around Rise's torso and the only way for him to walk comfortably was to put his arm around her shoulders. Again his mind seemed to stab his body, trying to get him to tell her.

"You know, Beline, you're my best friend." Rise stopped there, it felt awkward to him, as if he just spoke a language he didn't know he possessed.

Beline looked up at him questionably. "I didn't think you would get drunk after just a few glasses."

He laughed. "You always know just what to say." Once again he stopped his sentence short of what he wanted it to convey. His heart was kicking him in the chest and he felt sure that with her head so close to him she could hear it too. He took a long deep breath, one that felt like it could have filled six lungs. In his mind he said it once and clear, "I love you." He opened his mouth.

Beline jerked to the side suddenly and squeezed Rise tighter. "There he is!"

Rise's jaw snapped shut. Sheriff Morceff was watching the huge ration line make its progress. Three skelguards surrounded him, each with their lances at their sides. His magic stick was at his side, and a sheathed sword on the other. He was an ugly man, a face that seemed to have been stomped on and nailed to his body. His black hair was long in the back, tied in a pony tail. He was five and a half feet tall and stood with his nose higher than any man deserved to have it.

"Let's move away from him," Rise said quietly.

The sheriff's gaze was on a group of children. His hideous grin seemed to stretch from his cheeks to his ears, like a fruit sliced across the middle. He said something quietly and pointed at one of the small boys.

The three skelguards immediately walked forward at the signal from the sheriff. The child saw the three skeletons approaching him, their awkward walk, the glowing red eyes, the sadistic grin; all part of a ritual that was seen too frequently. They were going to arrest the boy.

Rise stopped walking. He was 30 feet behind the sheriff.

Beline gasped as the three dead guards surrounded the boy, towering over him. Someone, who must have been the father, stepped forward. Rise could not hear what was said, but he knew the deadly routine. Everyone knew it. Even the father knew it.

The sheriff rasped, "Bring the boy and the father to me!"

The father quickly leaned down and told his boy something. The boy ran into the crowd before the skelguard's hand could reach him. Morceff strode forward. Each step he took caused a light-red color to shine at the bottom of his feet as the magic barrier surrounding him hit the dirt.

Rise stood motionless as the sheriff dragged the father out away from the crowd, screaming at him, "You wretch! You filthy peasant!" The area around the man's collar was light-red from the magic barrier around the sheriff's hands. The barrier only became visible when something made contact. The skelguards just watched as mindless drones.

Morceff slapped the man in the side of the head with his magic stick.

By this time, the line stopped moving and the crowd of people morbidly stared.

Rise realized his fists were clenched and his knuckles were as white as a skelguard. Rise had two fears in his life. First, those hideous clouds that came out during the night. The second was the sheriff. He was completely unpredictable and commanded a legion of dead warriors. The dangerous Morceff would kill any man, woman, or child if he felt it was for the benefit of the Dark King. From what he heard, every sheriff in every sector was like this. Some even worse.

The man curled himself up and took the beating as dust stirred up around him. Morceff was still screaming curses when he finally decided to stop, but this was only to pull the man back to his feet so he could throw him to the dirt again.

Everyone knew this event as if it were already written out. Whenever the sheriff would try to take a child the parents would try to hide them. If the child was sent into a crowd someone would find pity and hide the child. Then the parent was beaten to death in replacement of the lost child.

Beline seemed to shake more with each blow the father received. The father of the child quickly pulled loose. Beline and Rise had seen this act before also.

The father pulled a knife and lunged at the sheriff. Morceff stood perfectly still and watched in amusement as the knife blade bounced off his torso with a red glow. The magic barrier. Impenetrable.

As quick as a thrown stone, Morceff put his magic stick up to his shoulder and pulled the trigger. Rise blinked his vision away from the sight. A loud bang clapped Rise's ears together.

When he opened his eyes Beline had her face buried in his chest and the father of the boy lay a good five feet away from where he had been standing.

"Take the wretch's body!" Morceff blew the smoke from the tip of the weapon with a smile.

His three personal skelguards stiffly walked over and carelessly picked up the body.

Beline was shaking. Rise patted her back. "Let's go. It's over."

Chapter Nine:

They walked towards Rise's dwelling, arm in arm. It was not the feeling Rise wanted. It was a hollow pit in his stomach that was gnawed out by grief. Both of their arms locked together served to sustain them both. Rise wanted to be the steady hand, but he found himself picked up just as much by her as she was by him. No matter how many times they witnessed atrocities like that it still hurt. Rise knew that this would affect Beline for a long time to come. This only carved more of a hole in his gut. He knew the routine. He knew that within a few hours he would have moved on. Completely. Not Beline. She was sincerely sorry. She deserved someone who cared as much about the problems in the world as she did.

He shook his head ever so slightly, a movement that only Beline felt through their physical connection. He was powerless to help. He saved many people of all ages from gangs, thieves, and fools. Some were battles almost epic, some were not. Yet, he could not save anyone from the clutches of the King's men. They were impervious and he feared them. No man could strike fear in him. No man, except for a sheriff. No man except Morceff. At that moment he was not The Giver. He tried to take his leave.

"Don't go. Please." Beline tightened her grip on him.

Rise could feel her looking at him. He could not raise his head. There were too many thoughts pulling it toward the earth.

She was silent again. They passed six tent dwellings before she spoke. "You have no reason to keep your head that low. You could not have saved him. No one could. Morceff is too powerful. You'd have been an idiot to try. And I could not have watched you die. I couldn't."

Rise stayed silent. They were near his house.

"It's okay to fear a man..."

"I do not fear him." Rise looked at her gently.

"Well," she said, "I do. And so does everyone else. Only fools don't."

They had reached the home. Beline sat herself down in a wide chair and let Rise dish out the rations. They had a good meal. A good, quiet meal. A good, quiet, two hour-meal.

Beline was surprised that it was Rise who broke the silence. "You're right."

"About what?"

"I do fear him." The words had to be ripped from his throat. Rise could not believe what he just said.

Beline was a little off balance by that, but not for long. "I wasn't expecting that. The Giver, admitting his fears? Why me?"

Rise was hoping with all his heart that he understood that last question correctly. He might be able to explain it the way he wanted to. He had to be sure before he continued.

"What do you mean?" He cleared his throat, a nervousness that Beline did not even comprehend, though she suspected.

"Why would you tell me that? I've never seen you, ever, admit to being afraid of someone. Why... tell me that?"

"I..." He looked around for something to drink, but quickly remembered he already finished his storage of alcohol. "I don't know. Maybe because... I trust you." *Coward! Tell her!* He felt his heart tugging him like a leash. *Take the chance.* He heard the old man's voice, urging him to just tell her.

"No." Her words broke Rise's spirit for a quick moment. He almost feared she was hearing him argue with himself.

"No," she continued, "That's not the reason. You trust Bespin as well, but you never tell him such things."

"Because..." Rise saw Beline's posture straighten slightly at that word. Her eyes seemed almost hopeful. "Because... it must be the alcohol."

Her posture slouched, her eyes dulled. "Oh."

That was all she said.

Rise quickly stood up and took the dishes they used to be washed by his supply of water.

Beline stood up and said, "I think you have one other fear, Rise The Giver. You're afraid to tell me something. When you

40

can do that..." She left. Suddenly and quietly she left.

Rise stared wide-eyed at the tent flap shaking. She left. She was mad at him.

Rise threw the glass dish to the ground. It only bounced on the soft carpet. He smashed it through with his boot. He could have told her. He could have. He should have. He heard the old man in his mind again, telling him all about how he missed the best opportunity to tell her. Just the thought of her being mad at him, or even worse, *let down by him*, sickened him to the very bottom of his stomach. Of all the horrible events of that day, one image lingered in his mind. That look she gave after he blamed the alcohol for his words. Her face was completely crushed by those words. He inflicted such pain on her. For a brief second, he considered himself a monster worse than Morceff. Why didn't he just tell her the truth?

"Beline." He said out loud, "The reason I told you was because I do trust you. I trust you more than myself. I trust you completely with my whole life essence. I trust you to be my friend, my companion, my one perfect love. I trust you so much, that I offer you the one thing that is hardest for me to give away, my heart. Please let me be able to trust you... to... to... love me."

Then he understood it. There was no doubt in his mind. She loved him too. It was the only explanation for her actions. He would tell her. His back straightened like an arrow at the exact instant released from a bow. Just before he left his dwelling to tell her, something caught his eye. It glimmered under a worn desk. He bent down and picked it up. It was a full bottle of alcohol he had forgotten about. An old brandy that twinkled with the help of a nearby lantern.

He slouched slightly. He began to think about the situation again. What if he were wrong? What if she did not return his love? Maybe she was really mad at him. Maybe that thoughtless word would drive her into Trent's arms, the farthest possible place away from him.

He took a drink from the bottle.

Chapter Ten:

Rise awoke suddenly as the pain in his head stabbed him down to his spine. His vision was blurry, but only until his eyes could focus on the dry bottle of brandy he held in his hand. *Just one drink, to calm my nerves*. His head felt like it was full of water from

41

that stupid mistake.

He sat up slowly, rubbing his forehead. He propped himself up against a seat and rolled the bottle across the carpeted floor in disgust. He had no idea how long he had been out.

Rise looked outside and saw that the sun was descending. "Couldn't have been more than eight hours." He sighed to himself. "Now, or never."

He turned his attention to the direction of Beline's new home. Like a steel grafted arrow, he knew his course.

It was strange to him that Beline's new home was the old man's home. Just strange that life goes on anew. The old die, the young take their place of suffering.

The Giver was uncertain whether it was the effects of the alcohol still in his blood, or that he finally won over his fear. His real fear. The fear that was greater than the evil clouds. The fear greater than the sheriff. He would tell her.

A fire was already warming the small shack. Beline's chimney spewed smoke upwards into the sky. Just before Rise brought himself to knock and enter, he caught site of the evil clouds. They were coming from the north with tremendous speed. Just before nightfall they would envelop the whole sky, swirling like a dark warning, dissuading anyone from looking to the sky for hope.

He shivered and knocked on the door.

"Come in."

He walked in. Beline was tending the fire in the stove heater with a metal poker. She did not look up. She did not need to. She recognized the footsteps. Beline spoke slowly. "Earlier I came back to apologize for what I said." Rise felt relieved until her next words, "But I found you drunk on the ground. I figured you'd be happier with the bottle, so I left."

"I'm sorry..."

"Goodness! I can still smell it on you!" Her voice did not change, it was not a yell. It was worse. It was a straightforward voice that told Rise there was no mistaking it: he had let her down.

He tried to fight the pain in his body, the gut twisting pain of disappointing her, but he had no idea what would conquer it. Then he knew it. He had his opening.

"I let you down. Somehow, whatever I did failed you. The worst part of having people that care for you, is not living up to what they expect of you."

She looked up at him. Her beautiful green eyes were still angry.

"If it means I never have to drink again..."

"It's not that! I thought you were going to say something to me. For the first time in our years of friendship, I thought you were actually going to *say* something. Something from you, not the person you pretend to be."

It only gave him confidence. It was time. She did care about him. "I trust you. When I told you that much, I meant it... and more. You are always there when I need someone. You are the only person I fear failing. Something I just now realized."

Her eyes softened. They were ten times more brilliant. It was time.

There was a voice outside, a distant yell, "Beline!"

Rise looked around confused. Beline did the same. It came again. "Beline! Help me!"

She rushed by Rise and looked out the door. "Trent?" She stepped outside.

Rise came outside as well.

Beline looked out across the living space, "Is that Trent? What's wrong with his legs?"

The chubby figure was limping and holding his arm. "Beli..." He collapsed between two tent dwellings a hundred feet away. People stopped to stare, but offered no help.

Beline ran forward and Rise quickly followed. By the time they reached him a crowd had gathered, but no one checked to see if he was alive.

Beline bent down and rolled Trent's thick body over. Blood was stained all over his shirt. His arm was dislocated at the elbow, and the end of a broken arrow was submerged in his right thigh.

Beline gasped. "Help me get him into the shack!" She maneuvered to try to pick him up under one arm, but Rise gently, ever so gently, pushed her aside and with great effort managed to pick him up.

Trent moaned but was quickly losing consciousness.

Rise had just enough strength to plop the body onto the cot in Beline's new home. The crowd followed them to the front door but after a few minutes they tired of watching Rise and Beline treat familiar injuries and relocated back to their business.

Trent was grasping something in his hand so hard his knuckles were white. A small golden chain squeezed out between his fingers. Rise went to remove it and startled Trent so badly he sat up quickly in the bed and jerked his hand away. "No!" He was confused. "Where?" He looked around like a frightened child.

He saw Rise and immediately calmed down. When he saw Beline he smiled. "I have something for you." He tried to sound normal, however the pain was manipulating his voice. His eyes, burdened with suffering, were nearly closed.

"Trent, listen to me. What happened?" Rise kept a stern voice.

Trent's head was wobbling back and forth. He was in sheer agony. "My elbow... it hurts so bad."

Rise knew this type of bend in an arm. It was easily fixed. He positioned his hands on both sides of the dislocated joint, and not too gently forced it back into the proper place. Trent screamed in pain. It quickly passed and he sighed deeply. "Thank you."

Rise despised the politeness for some reason. He should have left the elbow the way it was. He would rather have dealt with Trent's pain-contorted face than that stupid grin.

"Beline, I have something for you." He said it this time with a blissful stare.

He shakily held out his hand. He dropped a thin gold chain necklace with a square cut emerald into her palm.

Rise blurted, "Where did you..." He knew the answer. "What happened at the meeting?"

Beline looked at Rise and then back at Trent.

"Don't you like it?" Trent asked.

"Silence that, and answer my question. What happened to you and that idiotic bounty hunter group?"

Trent now turned his attention to the piece of arrow in his leg. "They shot me. And they sliced at me. I... I... don't remember. I'm so tired. Do you like the present?" He smiled with glazed over eyes at Beline.

"Yes, Trent. It's beautiful." Her bottom lip quivered as she examined his injury.

"Hardly compared to you." Trent smiled as he slowly laid down. He was losing consciousness again.

Beline gave an effort to smile at the compliment, but her eyes stayed concerned with Trent's condition. "Poor Trent. I can't believe this. He's been stabbed so many times. The blood..."

Something deep in Rise's mind started yelling at him. Rise looked at the emerald Beline held. A stolen treasure from the gang. The blood. They must have attacked the bounty hunters. The blood. Despite his warning Trent went along, his childish love for

Beline blinding him. The blood. He was willing to die to give her one stupid treasure. Then he understood.

The blood. With a wound that great there would surely be enough to track.

He quickly peeked outside the small shack. He saw two men, just as he feared, each covered in red cloaks. Writh Assassins. Like wolves following a scent, they had tracked him down. The people avoided such monsters like a corpse. They passed through great crowds of people with plenty of space. They looked up for just a second and saw where the trail of blood led. To the shack. And there was Rise staring at them.

Rise reached for his sword but already the gang members were running for the shack.

His hand contacted his leg. His sword was not there. He remembered taking it off in his drunken haze.

He turned around and saw the hot poker in the stove. "Stay inside and give me the emerald." He held out his hand, the bandage was still on it from Beline's mending.

She looked confused. She glanced at Rise and at Trent's unconscious body. "He'll probably die, all because he brought this to me."

"Beline, please! Trust me... as I trust you." Their eyes locked. She gave him the necklace. As she did he reached behind her and grabbed the fire poker.

"Stay inside."

He walked back out. The assassins were close, only 30 steps away. Rise hid the poker behind his back, hoping they would not notice any small amount of smoke emerging from behind him. He threw the necklace at their running feet. They did not stop. It was bad. They did not care about the treasure anymore, they wanted Trent.

The assassins stopped a few feet from Rise. "We want the fat man." The assailants were young, just barely men. Their countenance was strong, and so were their frames. The one on the left had dark skin while the other was pale.

"You have your gem, now leave."

The second assassin turned to the first and uttered something in the old tongue about Rise's hair. The second one looked stunned. "It is the same one! Perfect. We've been looking for you as well. No one steals from the Wriths without having a blade put in their ribs!"

They advanced towards Rise.

The assassins threw open their cloaks and the one with dark skin revealed a wooden crossbow. The pasty one drew a sword.

Rise quickly swung the poker from behind his back and forced the crossbow to the ground. An arrow was released before it dropped and flew by his ear. It embedded itself into the doorway of the shack. The dark skinned Writh struggled to recover his weapon while the other one charged with the sword.

Rise sidestepped and heard the sound of his leather coat being torn. The one with the sword crashed into the wall of the shack. Rise spun outwards at the dark skinned one and kicked backwards with all his strength. The force snapped the knee cap sideways of the dark skinned Writh. He howled in pain and dropped his weapon for the second time. Rise was just in time to step over the disabled gang member as the one with the sword regained his balance and came running.

The Giver threw the hot poker straight at the face of the on-comer. It was not enough force to run him through, just enough to scrape his face and singe his skin. The moment it took the Writh to check his face for blood was all Rise needed to bend down and grab the crossbow. He pried the bolt from the wall of the shack and loaded it with one swift movement. He pointed it at the Assassin.

"You will not kill me, or the fat man. Help your friend up and leave. I swear that if I see either of you two again, I will kill you both!" Rise kept the crossbow aimed as the two wounded men limped off angrily together. The one with the shattered knee cap would not be back anytime soon. They hobbled off towards the ruins, being eyed by passing spectators.

Beline's hand touched his shoulder. "Thank goodness!" She hugged him and breathed heavily. "They were after you too?"

"Different story."

"I'm just glad you're fine. If I lost you..." She shook her head. "It's funny, look at them walk away. They're wounded and hated, yet the people let them pass. They're too apathetic to act. They just let them leave so that they can return to haunt us later."

"The people here aren't much for a fight. It's safer if they let them be."

Beline walked forward and found the emerald on the ground. She slowly put it around her neck after wiping the dust off. On her way back to the shack she put her hand on Rise's arm. "Thank you."

Rise followed.

Trent was awake, yet he was still bleeding profusely. He

had limped all the way from the ruins. *The ruins...* that nagging voice in the back of Rise's mind was back.

"Good, Beline. You're wearing it. I hoped you would like it. I thought green was a good color, the same as your eyes."

Then Rise realized what was bothering him. "Trent, where's Bespin?"

"Beline, I love you." Trent started to cough heavily.

Rise just stared at him. Never had four words burned Rise so intensely. He just said it? Just like that?

"Wha..." Beline was taken aback. "No, no. Trent. Where's Bespin? Please tell me."

"Okay, for you." He was gasping. "When I ran to escape, I saw him spying on us from a rubble cliff. He was spotted by the Wriths, and I saw a few go after him. He ran. That's all I remember before the arrow struck my leg." Trent was gasping desperately for air.

Trent grabbed Beline's hand and held it to his bleeding chest. With the last bit of air in his lungs he said, "I love you."

Beline could only stare. Over the years in the sector she had watched people she knew die. It hurt every time. She turned to Rise and regained a slight bit of composure. "Please Rise, go save Bespin."

Rise nodded and left to retrieve his sword. As soon as Bespin was safe... then he would tell her.

Chapter Eleven:

Rise strapped his weapon to his side and grabbed a few gems he stashed for emergency bartering. He considered taking the magic stick the old man had left him, but he realized quickly his lack in understanding of how it worked would only hinder him. He was more comfortable with the sword.

The Giver walked out of his dwelling with a purpose. His friend was in danger.

He began marching through town, his eyes fixed only on the direction of the ruins. The Wriths would be in full force. He almost considered it an option that they might actually attack the people in the living space during his absence. It was strange to Rise; he never thought of himself as a protector of the living space itself. A Writh attack was out of the question. They were cowards at heart, and even these apathetic people would fight back if they were attacked.

His vision was broken by the sight of a skelguard. It was wandering the living space freely. He quickly went around it.

Someone grabbed his shoulder. He knew the touch. He turned around to find Beline equipped with the crossbow that had fallen from the Writh. She wore a thick jacket patched from other jackets of various colors. "Do you have any arrows?"

Rise smiled just at the corner of his mouth. "You don't need to come..."

She interrupted him, as he knew she would, "He's my friend too. Now, do you have any arrows?"

"I'll buy you some. And for crossbows they're called bolts." He noticed the emerald necklace she wore. "What have you done with Trent?"

She seemed to choke on the words. "His body can wait. Bespin could be in danger."

They took a slight detour and found the blacksmith pit. The ground was dug out into a hole 15 feet wide and 15 feet deep. Inside this hole the smithy set up shop. A large dark skinned man was at work making shovels. Rise climbed down the rope ladder with Beline following him.

The blacksmith looked up from his work, sweat pouring down him like a waterfall. He placed the hammers down. "The Giver! How's the dagger working for ya?"

"It broke."

"I see. Maybe you're stabbing too hard."

"I need some bolts. And a small quiver."

The blacksmith smiled, the gaps in his teeth were darker than the soot he wore. "It'll cost you..."

Rise gave him three gems. "You owe me a new dagger."

"Fine."

The blacksmith pit was dug 15 feet into the ground with an equal radius. It contained a small wooden cupboard that shelved swords sticking straight up like unkept finger nails. From underneath his wood shelf he pulled out a quiver filled with bolts, each handcrafted.

Rise snatched it. "I hope they last longer than your dagger."

He handed the quiver to Beline, and they climbed the ladder, ignoring the muttering from the blacksmith.

They continued to the edge of the living space. Four more skelguards were spotted along the way.

Chapter Twelve:

They reached the ruins in the middle of the night, stopping only to drink or eat out of Beline's meager supplies. They kept to the east side of the fallen buildings, the most likely way for Bespin to have fled. "With the Wriths after him, he could be hiding anywhere," Beline sighed.

A fog was settling onto the ruins. The remains of the ancient concrete buildings were almost covered by the mist. Above, like an evil twin, the swirling dark clouds danced.

Rise switched on the light attached to his wrist. It was weak, but better than nothing.

They walked through a well known trail. The ancient buildings were looted years ago. The biggest one seemed to have been a marketplace of some sort. It used to be a treasure trove of goods. Ancient displays of clothes and other goods had been stripped bare before any of them were born. Bespin would not be there. Nor would he take the main trail. He knew the rubble alleys too well for that.

Beline was quiet, but it issued from strength, not cowardice. Rise could not believe how well she was handling it. So many scares in one day, yet when their friend was in danger, she could rise to become the force motivating him to continue. He knew she was steel-willed, but this impressed him.

"This way." Rise began climbing up old concrete blocks that had caved-in probably centuries ago. He helped Beline avoid the crevasses that sank down hundreds of feet into the sewers of the ancient world.

"He could be anywhere." Beline sighed again. She was getting nervous for Bespin. She shivered from the cold as she clutched her coat.

"We have to try. He'd do the same for either of us."

Beline quickly pulled Rise down behind some rubble. "Look!" she whispered sharply into his ear. Below, on the main trail he saw the green eyes. There were six sets of them. The magical night vision of the Wriths was a powerful force. Every night they wore specialized eye glasses tainted with some glowing spell. Prey usually did not escape their sight.

"This way." Rise crouched along the edge onto the other side of the huge pile of rubble. It seemed to have once been a building. They crept their way to a new trail. They quickly crossed it and climbed back up to the top of another rubble heap.

Rise and Beline began to realize how hopeless the search was. The ruins were elaborate in the daylight, and even more confusing in the fog. Still the two did not stop. Nothing could make them stop.

The pair found the tallest building in the ruins that was still standing. Rise and Beline quickly ran through the door. The fog was already billowing through broken slits from old windows. They climbed a long flight of creaky stairs and emerged on the rooftop.

They were a good 60 feet above the ground. "Wow." Beline had never seen such a high view. Most buildings in the sector would never span upward more than 20 feet. The fog's evil fingers were running along the contours of the ruins. There were numerous glowing green specks all over the debris slowly moving about. "There's so many Wriths," Beline whispered.

The fog made the distance difficult to see, but at least from this height he could keep on eye on the gang members that were in the immediate area.

"Have you been to this spot before?" she asked him.

"Yes."

"Oh."

He looked at her. She was comically menacing with the crossbow being held in her feminine hands. "Was that not the answer you wanted?"

"No... I was just hoping you wouldn't go back to your one-word answers."

"Let's find Bespin," Rise stated, hoping to change the subject.

He walked towards the stairs. "I know the formation they're using. They sweep between three points they have picked out, usually the tallest buildings, in groups of four. It hasn't worked on me, and it won't work on Bespin. He's safe."

Beline knew Rise endured many confrontations with the Wriths and usually avoided the subject. "How many times have you... been here?"

"Enough."

They quickly ran down the flight of stairs and out of the building.

"What do we do if we come across any?"

Rise knew what she was really asking. "Don't worry. You won't need to use it." He nodded towards the crossbow. "I'll

50

take care of you."

"I know you will. Because if I get turned into a skelguard guess who I'll be hunting first."

Rise laughed quietly.

They made their way quietly through the ruins for a couple of hours. They avoided six groups of Wriths. So far they avoided all potential conflicts. Rise knew that she could never kill anyone. She hated death of all sorts. As far as he knew, no power in the sector would force her to take a life.

They traveled for two more hours without any sign of Bespin. A sound broke their concentration.

Loud marching footsteps came echoing through the walls of rubble. A group was close.

Rise looked around and noticed they were pinned inside a huge semicircle of rubble with jagged glass spikes. The walls were too steep to climb. "No!" he hissed, looking around desperately.

Around a corner came the first set of green eyes in the fog. They quickly noticed him and more green eyes appeared. Rise heard Beline gasp. It was that gasp that gave him motive, he would never let anything happen to her.

He glanced behind him and saw hope. A small slit of hope. Rise grabbed Beline by the arm and quickly led her through a small passage that was dug through the rubble. He pushed her through it as fast as he could run. They heard the footsteps coming after him. Rise glanced behind him and saw that a few climbed the sides somehow and were trying to flank him on top of the rubble canal. Their magic green eyes were following him, staring at him, trying to find his vulnerabilities.

Rise turned just in time to slice his already wounded shoulder on a shard of glass sticking out of the canal. He ran harder. The Wriths were closing in.

It was then he noticed he was in a part of the ruins he never encountered. He was at the mercy of the rubble. They came to a clearing of knee-high scrap metal piles.

He glanced behind him and saw the gang closing the distance to ten yards. The ones that tried to flank him were now making their way down the sides of the rubble, like vengeful ghosts in the fog.

The Giver turned and pulled Beline behind him. He drew his sword. A couple of them were speaking in the old tongue, "It's the white haired man."

Rise saw quickly that he was being surrounded. More

51

green eyes were appearing from the rubble. They were completely encompassed by Wriths.

He heard the bow strings tighten from somewhere in the dark. Rise realized he was going to die, and worse yet, Beline would die. There was a strange peace that settled upon him. They were together.

Rise closed his eyes and grasped Beline's hand. "I..."

"Rise! Beline!" Bespin's voice was like a knife cutting through the fog.

It reached the small enclosure and echoed. The Wriths looked in every direction. Then they saw him. Bespin was running along the top of the closest pile of concrete. His skinny body was moving as fast as he could manipulate it. With striking speed, he pushed one of the Wriths from the top of the wall before the gang member could locate the source of his echo. Bespin jumped and landed just after the Writh. He landed 15 feet below, now on the same level as his two friends, and rolled to distribute the pain in his legs. The Writh did not land so gracefully.

That's when the bow strings launched. Dozens of arrows came flying through the air, all directed at the new threat. Rise heard Beline scream as they saw the deadly streaks fly through the air towards their friend.

There were red glows as the arrows bounced off his body like swatted flies.

One Writh had stepped forward and swung his sword straight at Bespin's torso. Bespin was knocked to one side, but the blade bounced off with a red glow. He backhanded the Writh across the face and continued running.

"Rise, CATCH!" Bespin threw a small square object from his hand at his friends.

Rise caught it and quickly saw the large red button. He pushed it just before the first arrow struck him.

Chapter Thirteen:

Rise braced himself for death. For a split second he focused on only one thing: He never told Beline that he...

The arrows bounced off Rise and Beline like wadded paper. The device Bespin had thrown them encircled Rise with a magic barrier. He looked to his hand holding Beline's and the glow it created. As long as their hands were locked, it appeared she gained the same protection.

More arrows. More dull thuds. Rise smiled. He coughed out a nervous, disbelieving laugh.

Bespin pulled on his arm, a red glow illuminated from the point of contact, "Come on! Hurry!" Rise almost wanted to stay with his new found power. Teach the 50 Wriths that surrounded him a final lesson.

The three friends ran. The Wriths just stood and watched them, their green night eyes more glaring than glowing. They made no move. They knew their power was useless against a red magic barrier.

One or two Wriths followed at a safe distance, probably just scouts. Bespin soon had them so interlocked into different caverns of the ruins and canals that even Rise could not remember which way he was going. "Have we been here before?"

"Nope. Quickly, we almost lost 'em. Wow, do I have something to show you two."

"Yes you do," Beline nodded at the device Rise held. "Where did you get that?"

Bespin answered between breaths, "I found an ancient room... I just have to show it to you. I can't even describe it. It's... amazing. It's the answer for everything.*Everything*."

Soon, they were completely lost in the fog and crumbled buildings. Bespin led them to a large mass of shredded metal and concrete. Bespin pulled a large metal plate to the side and revealed a very dark, very small tunnel. "Crawl through." He waved them on. As soon as Rise broke hands with Beline the shield dissipated from around her.

Rise realized the light on his wrist was still on, so he led the way. Bespin closed the hatch behind them as he followed.

When they were running Rise placed the contraption in his pocket, yet he was still glowing whenever he touched something. To his surprise, he realized he was not actually touching anything. His hands and knees were less than a finger thickness from the ground as he crawled. He could only feel the smooth surface of the magic barrier between his hands and the ground. "How did you do that?"

"It's magic. It's ancient magic and you'll see soon enough. No more questions, the tunnel will echo our voices."

They crawled until their knees ached. They finally reached a hatch. Rise went to turn it but Bespin whispered to him, "No! It's a fake. It'll lead you right back to the top. Pull the small handle to the side of the hatch."

Rise felt along the side and soon found a small hidden lever. He pulled it, and a square section of the wall slid open, revealing a room with enough space to stand, leading to a polished stone stairwell.

"What is this place?" Beline asked.

"I have no idea," Bespin said. "But you two are gonna love it."

"We must be deep under the ruins by now," Beline marveled.

They were led down the stairs until they came to a door. Their steps sounded out of place on the level stonework. Bespin opened it and the light almost blinded them. It was a large white room illuminated from what seemed like all angles. It was a candle-less light and it was one of the most amazing things Rise ever witnessed. It was an ancient building... completely intact. A building from before people dwelt in tents and shacks. A building *constructed*, not just scrounged together.

"I found this place when I was hiding from the Wriths. I spent the whole day exploring it. Actually, I suspected there was a big find in this area for quite some time. I just never discovered that lever until recently."

The room seemed to be lit by magic. Many consoles with colorful lights were arrayed along the walls. In the middle was a round table with a magical picture floating above it. It showed a map of the ruins... yet they could see people moving on it. It was as if they were watching the ruins from a giant's perspective.

"This is amazing," Beline said as she tried to touch the floating picture. Her hand went straight through it, blurring the edges.

Bespin hit a button and the image disappeared. "More about that later. Look at this." He dumped the contents of his shoulder pack onto the table. Many different devices, all magical in nature no doubt, were sprawled across it. "I found this a couple months ago." He showed them a device like the one he threw to them, except more weathered and beaten. "Which reminds me, I need that one back. Make sure to turn it off."

Rise hit the button on his device and watched the barrier dissipate from around his body. "I should have asked you more about your adventures in the ruins."

Bespin smiled and pushed the button on his own device. A protective barrier around Bespin dissipated. "It creates a magical barrier. The same one Morceff uses, I'm sure of it."

"Is this how the King uses magic?" Beline asked. "Does the King still use this place?" She looked around nervously.

"I don't think so." Bespin said, "You can trust me on that. Anyway, I found that first magic button a couple months ago. I found the tunnel but not the latch. It wasn't until today that I accidentally found it while I was hiding from those Wriths... Trent was hit pretty badly, Beline. Those bounty hunters were slaughtered." He reached out and touched her shoulder.

"I know about Trent," she spoke just above a whisper. "I'm just glad you're safe."

"I found the switch and spent the rest of the day exploring this place. I found more of those buttons laid in a display, I found some magical weapons too. This whole place... whoever made it, knew the magic arts well. I want to show you the hall."

There was only one passage that lead into a straight hallway with many metallic doors. Rise walked forward and bumped into a magic barrier that was blocking the hall. It flashed red as he doubled back.

"Now, you're gonna love this." Bespin picked up one object from the table he dumped from his pouch. It was similar to the magic stick the old man had left, but it looked shinier and was small enough to be held by one hand. It was also different in that it consisted of only one barrel instead of two. Bespin pulled the trigger and a distortion shot across the room into the magic barrier. There was a sizzling sound, like wet wood burning and the whole barrier flashed red for a brief moment. "Now try it."

Rise walked through it. He stayed silent. The implications nearly made his heart stop.

Beline stared at the object in Bespin's hand.

"This magical weapon is what we've been waiting for! This is the key," Bespin said.

Rise stared at the twenty doors, all lined up through the hallway, and then turned to face Bespin.

"The key to what?" Beline asked.

"The key to what? The key to rebellion, Beline. The key to fighting back!"

"Don't talk such with me," she stammered. "Everyone who fights back dies. It's that simple Bespin. If you fight back, you die!"

"But look at this! This thing will destroy a magic barrier for a good five minutes... which, by the way, I'd step away from there if I were you, Rise."

Rise glanced at the overhang of the passage where the invisible barrier had first been. He quickly stepped away, in fear that it would crush him if it came back.

"Rebellion?" Beline sighed. "Talk like this is enough to get us all arrested. Rise..." She looked at him pleadingly for support.

"Bespin, this is amazing. I've never seen such a place. But rebellion can wait. What else is in here?" Rise was actually showing intrigue in this place. Deep down, he felt if this place were real, maybe the old man was not so crazy after all. Maybe his wondrous stories had some truth in them.

Bespin seemed a little disappointed that his rebellion idea was dismissed, but quickly moved on as he shuffled all barrier buttons and strange small magic sticks back into his pouch. "This was how I found you guys." He began to press buttons on the table.

Beline was amazed at just the finger work alone he was doing. All the different colored buttons looked like a puzzle to her, especially since the only labels on them were in the old tongue. "How long did it take you to learn this?"

"A couple hours." He did not look up from his frenzy of button pressing.

The picture of the ruins eventually came up. "Rise, you might be able to help. The instructions are in the old tongue. What do you make of it?"

Rise walked over and began skimming the buttons. "Well... here is the alphabet, a button for each letter... I've never seen most of these words before. Zoom+, Zoom-... ESC... PowerSrg... EMP... I don't know for sure."

Rise now took his attention to the floating map. "It looks like it shows a quarter mile around where the tunnel started." The map was comprised of only light greens and dark greens. Every few seconds a disruption of a line came circling through, refreshing the green map. Human figures were walking in formation... Wriths.

"That's how I found you guys," Bespin repeated. "I've been playing around with this thing so long my eyes hurt. It's probably more useful than I could ever imagine."

"It's too small, how did you know it was us?"

Bespin began pulling on a black stick that was above the alphabet board on the table. A small square began moving on the map. He then pressed the Zoom+ button and the square in the map enlarged. Rise could now make out the individual features of the Wriths as they passed. "Amazing."

"Your white hair stands out like a campfire. You were pretty easy to spot. I almost didn't think it was Beline when I saw the crossbow."

She laughed lightly and began to distribute some food and water from her supplies, which they all ate readily. She then found a chair in the corner and sat down. She watched from the small distance, trying to group her thoughts. This was one of the few times she witnessed Rise so... childlike, so intrigued. He was almost happy. It was an exploration for him. It was like before... before his parents... Maybe he was happy. She smiled. Guilt instantly swooped in for yelling at him for drinking.

There was a quick loud sizzling sound. They all turned except Bespin. "Just the magic barrier coming back for the hall." He and Rise continued working at the buttons. .

After an hour, they learned to use the magical map well.

Rise cleared his throat; there was a massive amount of dust in the room. "It looks like the map has a limit of a mile. We can't look beyond the ruins. Can this table do anything else?"

"Yes, but I want to show you some stuff before we go on. Beline, please stay there."

"I want to see it also." She stood up.

"It's all right Bespin, she can see whatever it is."

"Whatever you wish." Bespin hit a few buttons on the table again and the magic barrier blocking the hallway sizzled away. "Come on."

"How did you do that from there?"

"I didn't figure that out until after I got frustrated and shot the barrier. Somehow, that table controls all the barriers in this place. Makes it easier, since I think that barrier destroyer stick has only a little power left. It used to have more green dots on the barrel. I think it represents the magic left."

They walked through the hallway and stopped at a door somewhere in the middle. "I can unlock this door from the table, but I can't get the other ones to open." He pressed a panel on the side, and the door slid clunkily open, dust falling from the cracks. An overhead light came on. Inside was a room with a large round table. Thirty five chairs were placed around it. It was a room of death. Skeletons half-eroded were sprawled everywhere. They wore strange green uniforms. The ones closest to the door were still in a sitting position. Others were sprawled across the floor, some leaning over the table. The smell was unbearable.

Beline staggered backwards, and Rise wanted to join

her.

Bespin quickly closed the door. "That's why I don't think anyone has used this place for a very long time."

They walked back to the table. Bespin hit a few buttons and the barrier blocking the hallway came back. "I'm sure I'll figure out how to open the rest of the doors. In the meantime, I think you guys need some sleep."

Rise was going to object, but then he saw Beline's face. She was tired. She was so strong, and she had gone as far as she could. He knew that if he stayed, she'd stay.

Rise put his arm around Beline's shoulder. She was surprised, but made no objection. "We have some work to do at the living space."

She nodded. "Poor Trent." Her eyes were watering.

"One more thing." Bespin poured out his contents and again gave Rise and Beline a magic barrier button. "Just in case, you know... look at the back. There should be three green dots. The first one of these I found had just one. When it disappeared, the magic grew weaker until it stopped. So I believe there's a limit. Use them only when you need to. And these."

Bespin handed Rise a small wire coil. "It fits around your ear, and I speak into this magic box here." Bespin showed them a hand-held box with a single button. "The ear part, and this part both have those green dots. I think they have full magic. I can talk to you, but you can't talk to me."

"I don't understand."

Bespin spoke into his section of the device.

Rise jumped as he heard Bespin's voice directly in his ear. "Amazing. I can hear you... a little creepy to have you in my head, but this might be useful."

They all smiled a little.

"I'm going to stay here and try to see what else this table can do. You guys get some sleep."

Rise grinned to no one in particular. Rise had known Bespin for so many years, ever since they were children, and still his friend impressed him. His intelligence deserved a better canvas to paint on than the wicked world they lived in. For so long Rise viewed himself as the protector of his group, yet today he saw Bespin's true talents shine. His passion for the ruins, the secrets he kept in his bag, and his innovation for new devices had all come together this day to save them all.

They began walking away when Bespin asked, "Did

Trent..."

Beline shook a little and choked down a sob. "He's dead. He died... for me." She felt the necklace at her throat.

"Come on." Rise pulled her gently back the way they came.

They made their way out of the tunnel and emerged back into the ruins.

As they began to walk away, a voice in Rise's head said, "Hey! Put the metal covering back. I don't need just *anyone* finding this place. If you remember, I've got some bad neighbors." Rise was startled by Bespin's voice.

He shook his head. "This will take some getting used to." He replaced the metal plate.

"While you've got me in your head, I think you should just kiss her. I'll even turn off the magic map and let you do it in private... oh, no time for that. You got some Wriths coming."

They walked through the ruins, Bespin's kind voice directing them safely away from the Writh patrols. From his watch point, Bespin was looking after them.

Chapter Fourteen:

They made it back to the living space by morning with no further incidents. Rise and Beline told Trent's family of what happened. After that, Rise went to his home and rested for half of the day while the funeral progressed. He took a quick bath and washed his teeth with a rag. Even his shoulder found time to be bandaged. He found an old bottle of fermented oil he received from helping someone. There was enough left to make a pleasing smell hint around his body.

Rise even checked his appearance in a small shattered mirror Bespin had given him. He wanted to look perfect. It was time he told her. It had to be now.

The doubts persisted. That emerald necklace she wore, a reminder of Trent. So much death in just a few days. He glanced around for a bottle of alcohol, but found none.

"Here goes." Rise walked out of his dwelling. He was surprised to see her meet him halfway there.

"I was coming to visit," she said.

"Me too."

Rise noticed she made a strap and attached it to the

crossbow. She carried it slung over her shoulder. He did not like it.

"Why the weapon?"

"The same reason you carry one. It makes me feel safe."

Rise held her hand. He hated the idea of her carrying a weapon. He would protect her. "I don't carry a weapon for how safe I feel. I carry it to protect people worth protecting. Like you."

She tilted her head to one side. "Have you been drinking again?"

"No..." He jerked his head to one side and grabbed at his ear. He felt the device Bespin had given him.

"Is that Bespin?" she asked.

"Rise!" The little voice came sharply. "Something's happening! I know you can't speak to me, but I hope you're listening. I found a way to view the entire sector from the map. I've been trying to find you two, but I can't. You guys need to come back here *now*. The gang is doing something. It looks like an army... There! I found you guys. If you can hear me, wave your arms."

It was strange to Rise that Bespin could be watching them. He waved his arms slightly. Beline lifted one eyebrow at his actions. "Must be Bespin. Hopefully."

Bespin continued, "Please, come back here. The skelguards too... they're everywhere. They've lined up in four huge rows on the east wall of the sector."

Rise felt his heart stop.

"What's going on?" Beline asked.

The memory of the old man came running back to him. *It is at the time when they align in four rows that you must escape...*

Rise grabbed Beline's hand and pulled her back towards his dwelling. "Come on! We have to make it back to the ruins, something's happening. But first I have to get some things."

They ran to his home, hands still locked. Rise quickly found where he stashed the book and two magic sticks the old man left. "Just maybe... maybe, old man."

He took his coat off and slung the grapnel over his shoulder just as the old man instructed him. The leather strap held it securely to his body. He placed the book in an inside pocket in his jacket. Beline grabbed some dried meat and an old water skin. Rise put his coat back on to conceal the grapnel, and carried the other magic stick in his hand.

Rise and Beline ran hard. They followed Bespin's helpful voice that led them the entire way. According to him, they dodged six skelguards and even some Writh spies in the community.

Hours later, they were in the ruins and Bespin quickly led them through the maze of long abandoned buildings and back into the hidden place.

The journey took five hours with Beline at his hand. Rise noticed letters on the walls that he did not see the first time through. "EMP Station 4." Whatever that was.

Bespin clasped both of their shoulders, "Thank fortune you were wearing that ear piece. Look at this."

Bespin pointed towards the floating map. "All of these, are skelguards. They're hunting the Wriths."

"Those all can't be skelguards. There's got to be thousands of them..."

Bespin moved the map lower and made a portion bigger. "Look at that. They're lining up on the east side of the sector. It looks like they're going to hunt out everyone. They've already started with some of the Wriths in the ruins. Probably the group that would give them the most trouble."

Bespin moved the map back to the living space. The sight made Beline feel weak in the eyes. They wanted to shield her from the atrocity. They watched the skelguards at random blast some with fire, while others were dragged by their hair to be arrested. Many large metal vehicles were driving around the sector as well, following the skelguards. They were arresting people by the dozens!

"What is this?!" Rise snapped. "They're killing so many!"

Beline was having problems breathing. Rise quickly helped her to the chair.

"Rise," Bespin motioned him back to the map. "It's Morceff." He pointed.

Morceff, with his magic stick, was barking out orders to a few hundred skelguards at his command. He was taking over the living space. Rise saw the familiar faces of the sector being dragged away to the vehicles to be arrested. Others were being consumed by the magical fire of the skelguards. Even Morceff was pointing his magic stick and killing a few.

"No! NO! That MONSTER!" Rise slammed his fists onto the table, disrupting the map for a brief moment. "That ROYAL MONSTER!"

Rise was pulling at his hair in frustration.

Bespin was just staring at the map, watching the deadly dots move like poisonous ants.

Rise removed the magic barrier button Bespin had given

him. He looked at it nervously, and then held his gaze at the image of the sheriff.

"Bespin, give me that device that destroyed the invisible wall."

Bespin glanced at Rise, and then to Beline questioningly.

"Don't you think about it, Rise!" Beline stood up, her eyes watering at just the thought.

Rise held out his hand and Bespin quickly pulled it out from his pouch. "Are you doing... what I think?"

"Just a little rebellion." Rise turned the magic breaker in his hand without taking his eyes off the sheriff. The enlarged picture showed Morceff striking at random people in the scared mob. The people were running everywhere, like a horrified frenzy of flies with hundreds of deadly spiders feeding off them.

"Rise! You can't! Please, we're safe in here. Maybe it'll be okay," Beline pleaded.

"NO!" He realized it was the first time he had snapped at her. "Too long have I watched him murder. We've sat by too long as he did whatever he wished while we suffered! TOO LONG! This must end."

Beline ran over to him. "Then I'm coming." She patted the crossbow awkwardly.

Bespin stood by her side. "I'm coming too."

The site almost melted Rise's iron-will to tears. His two friends were willing to die to help him. His only two friends were willing to die for him. "No. I have a plan. I need you here. Bespin, you'll have to direct my steps. Beline..." He looked at her eyes. They were frightened, they were dilated, and they were green. They were so beautiful.

The corner of his eye saw Morceff's ugly face on the map. He was beating a young woman that was trying to flee from a skelguard. "Beline... please stay... in case they find the entrance, you're the only one with a weapon." That would keep her safe.

Rise removed the grapnel and placed both it and the magic gun from the old man by the hallway barrier. He would need every spare pound off his body for the run.

The Giver turned and ran out. Beline realized she missed the opportunity to hug him.

Bespin began giving directions as he tracked Rise on the floating map.

"Please, come back to me." Beline sat down on a chair

and took a deep breath.

Chapter Fifteen:

It did not even occur to Rise until he was out of the ruins that he was going to die. It didn't matter. He ran harder. He was going to die, because for too long Morceff killed innocent people. For too long he had gloated of his power, and for too long he had made Rise feel like a coward. Rise would have fought six Wriths to protect an animal, yet he would not even fight Morceff to save a child. Too long. He ran harder.

The only comfort he maintained was the magic barrier and the strange magic breaker. It was no use. He doubted the same magic that made that invisible wall was as powerful as what protected the sheriff. The King was all powerful. His minions were the walking dead themselves... he could not defeat a sheriff. Yet, he was going to die trying. Too much death. The Giver would finally give all that he had to give. His life.

Bespin directed him and Rise made it to the living space without incident. The crowd was screaming, trying to run, but they were boxed in by thousands of skelguards. The small community was now completely corralled.

He saw Morceff. He was yawning and sitting upon the dead body of a man in a fur coat. He idly barked orders to his skelguards. "For the King!" He would point and Rise watched in horror as a crowd went up in flames.

"MORCEFF!" Rise yelled.

Morceff looked around curiously and unafraid.

Rise set his glare upon the sheriff and marched forward. He placed the button that would create the barrier in his pocket in front of a hard flat object. It was the book of the old man he had forgotten to leave with Bespin.

Rise acknowledged his plan in his head. As soon as Morceff drew his sword he would draw his, and then he would press the button hidden in the coat pocket. The magic barrier would be drawn around himself, and he could battle Morceff in a fair fight.

Rise walked by six skelguards. He had never looked at one so close and the sight unnerved him. He kept his eyes averted the best he could. He fixed his gaze on Morceff. "Morceff. Today, you die." Rise's voice was steady, controlled. Nervous.

Morceff laughed and pulled a magic stick from his side.

Rise could only curse at his stupidity as Morceff pulled the trigger. There was that horrible, deafening sound. There was a horrible pain in his chest. He felt his feet leave the ground. He landed on his back with a thud that knocked the air out of his lungs. He coughed roughly.

"Rise!" Bespin's voice rang in his ear and he heard Beline scream. Instinctively he loosed the ear piece so that it was still wrapped around his ear, but facing the opposite way. He did not want to hear them scream as they saw his death from the impersonal floating map. However...

He was alive. He felt inside his pocket. The magic barrier creator was destroyed... and the book... the book had many small holes in it, but they never made it through all the pages.

A shadow fell over his body. Morceff was staring at him, the morning light shining right over his shoulder. The magic stick hung limply at his side. His face was contorted smugly.

Rise almost snarled as he sat up. The smug look on Morceff's face turned to shock. The Giver kicked his foot outward and knocked the magic stick from Morceff's hand. Before he could reach for his sword, Rise was on top of him. He felt the hard invisible wall as he clawed at Morceff's face and torso. Red light seemed to emit everywhere he tried to reach the sheriff. The magic barrier.

The skelguards immediately approached, lances drawn and ready to fire.

Morceff landed his two fists into Rise's shoulders, forcing him away. With his legs now free, the sheriff booted Rise in the chin with a glow of red at the impact. Rise felt his face go numb and the blood seemed to ram the top of his head and then back to his mouth. He fell off the sheriff.

"DON'T FIRE!" Morceff yelled. "THIS ONE'S MINE!"

The skelguards retreated back to their business. They knew their master was safe. They silently obeyed, never uttering a word.

They both drew their swords. Rise tried to reach for the barrier breaker, but he quickly found he needed both hands on his sword to fend off the wicked strength of the sheriff.

Morceff was sloppy. Rise barely calmed his nerves before he realized it. Around him the skelguards were going about their business, arresting some, killing others. However, he remained unharmed because this sheriff wanted him as a trophy. Murderer.

Rise swung his sword to the left, knocking an opening for Morceff's torso. He took the plunge, but his sword bounced off with a red tint. No good. He was able to slice once at Morceff's face. Same thing, no effect.

His heart was beating fast, combining with his nervousness and adrenaline, making his attacks shaky and uncontrolled.

Morceff was back on his attack. His wide swings would have made Rise almost laugh if it were a normal opponent. This was a servant of the Dark King, invincible.

They continued fighting. Rise dodged tent pegs that seemed to be deadly spiderwebs for him. He ducked as Morceff sliced and blocked when he lunged.

Morceff was sweating, not used to the physical exertion of really fighting. His lips were curled and he was spitting in rage. "DIE! DIE! DIE!" He screamed.

Rise ducked as the blade ripped a hole in a nearby tent. Sparks flew as he jumped back to dodge the sword as it ricocheted off a scrap metal shack. Everywhere Rise heard screaming. Panic had sunk its jaws into the people.

In the distance, he saw an army of Writh warriors running towards the living space. They were fleeing from a large scale group of skelguards that were chasing them from the ruins. He hoped they did not find Beline and Bespin. Whatever was happening, the King was making a full invasion of the prison Sector 2128.

Every time Rise went to reach for the weapon, Morceff would double up his swing and knock the sword almost loose from Rise's grip. He needed both hands.

Morceff was sloppy, out of shape, and yet invincible. Rise felt like dying and giving up every time he made contact with the barrier around the evil man. That quickly passed as he heard the screams of children and women in the distance.

He found they were fighting over the blacksmith pit. He glanced down and saw the body of the blacksmith face down, his figure still charred from the flame of a skelguard.

They fought along the top of the pit for what seemed like an eternity of sweat and rage. Rise had been cut twice now, and bore large scratches on his chest. Morceff was unwounded.

Rise called himself stupid for overlooking the magic stick. In hindsight, it was just like Morceff to fire on him. He should have known to activate the button sooner. He was originally worried of it running out of power in the middle of the fight, but now he was more worried of his own energy running low. He was starting to get winded.

He saw a child being dragged by his feet towards a gray vehicle that was piloted by a skelguard. A cage was set up in the back for the "fortunate" ones to be arrested.

Then The Giver saw it. The small hands of the boy he rescued from the Wriths days earlier... those small innocent hands, were clutching at the charred dress of his mother. Tears were streaming down his face as he was trying to pull his mother to her feet. He was trying to run away with her from all the death. Her body did not stir.

Morceff yelled, "Give it up you peasant! I'm gonna kill each and every one of you!"

Through clenched teeth about ready to snap from their gums Rise yelled, "NO! MURDERER!" Rise swung with all his might, knocking the sword out of Morceff's hands. Morceff stumbled backwards and was waving his arms trying not to fall into the blacksmith pit.

Rise pulled the magical weapon Bespin had given him and fired. There was a red flash, and the sheriff fell backwards and vanished into the pit.

There was a crash and then a horrible, high pitched scream.

Rise looked down into the pit. Lying with his back broken and three swords from the display rack sticking through his torso, the sheriff did not stir.

Rise dropped to his knees in shock. He did not believe it. It could not be real. The weapon broke the barrier. No one could kill a sheriff. The magic of the King was unbreakable. He killed a sheriff. He killed a sheriff! He shook his head. "No, I was supposed to die..." The Giver was supposed to give up his life for his friends, trying to protect them. Now what was he?

He looked at the silver weapon in his hand. This device destroyed the magic barrier of the King's servant.

"The Giver just killed Morceff." A voice in the distance.

"I don't believe it. Morceff... is dead?" More voices.

Rise realized that people saw it. Despite all the chaos and death, a few stole a moment to witness the impossible. They saw the death of a sheriff. One of the King's most protected warriors now lay dead, sprawled across a sword display cabinet. And The Giver was the reason.

He didn't want to hear them. He didn't want to believe

them. He put his ear piece back in. It could not be happening. He felt as if the magic of the King would strike him dead instantly, but it never came.

"Rise! I can't believe it... you just... Morceff! Rise... it worked. Run! Run now! Skelguards, they're coming for you!"

Rise saw two skelguards approaching behind him, lances drawn. He was selected to die. He fired on both of them with his new weapon. There was a sizzling sound as the barriers broke, and the skelguards dropped limply to the ground in a contorted pile of bones. Without their barriers, they seemed powerless.

"Run! Straight!"

Rise obeyed. He ran. With the help of Bespin's voice in his head, he hid in many spots, and played dead in others. Rise found it strange to play dead as skelguards went by. He felt as though he should fight. He always relied on his instincts. And now, he was following Bespin's voice. He wanted nothing more now than to see his two friends' faces one last time. This was too good to be real, to a kill a sheriff and live. Rise felt he had been robbed. Robbed of the chance to give his all. To give his life for his friends. The Giver became dazed and perplexed. He mindlessly obeyed Bespin as he directed him. The mindless procession took him five hours to complete.

Rise found himself, once again, back in the ruins with his friends. Awaiting death to find him, for it would surely come.

Chapter Sixteen:

Rise was exhausted. They all sat in silence for a while, none daring to speak out of fear they would cast a hex on their good fortune. They were alive, the sheriff was dead, and that was all they needed to know.

Rise was the first to speak up, "Rebellion." He looked at the silver weapon he used to destroy the magic barrier. He turned his gaze to Bespin. "How many of these did you find?"

"Just two. But I'm sure there are more in here, I just have to get the other doors open. I found a visual instruction on how to use some of the magical weapons that I think are hidden somewhere in this building."

"Bring the map back to Morceff's body."

Beline grabbed onto Rise's arm. "Don't worry, he's dead. It really happened. That monster is dead."

"I just need to see it. I have to be sure."

Bespin brought the map back to the blacksmith pit. Without the sheriff, the skelguards just walked around without any sense of direction. As the map honed in on the blacksmith pit, an unusual sight greeted them. The villagers had taken the opportunity of the confused skelguards to pull the sheriff's body out of the pit and tie him to a recently erected stake. His body would not burn honorably. It would hang there until the birds themselves finished him off.

Rise rubbed his temples. Something in his mind was pestering him. "So the King's magic can be broken. We need to open those other doors."

Bespin began his work at the table. He had figured out how to keep the map in the background while he worked with other floating words. "EMP STATION 4. LOG/OFF. MENUS. MAP <SONAR TERRAIN ENHANCE 3D>. HELP FILES...." Bespin worked quickly through each.

Still, something in the back of his mind would not go away.

He felt the holes in his jacket, and he felt the book hidden underneath. He pulled it out. The holes were small but numerous. They did not affect the reading of the book too badly. If the book had been five pages thinner Rise's chest would have taken more than a bruise. That was it!

Rise remembered something in the book. Some small thing that was mentioned by the old man. Something he dismissed as fast as he read it, believing it was just another fabricated story.

He quickly thumbed through and found the page. It was just a couple of lines. It warned of an enemy less powerful than the King, yet more of a threat than a sheriff. An elite hunter. The Evil King apparently had a sheriff for every sector, but one elite for every hundred sectors. This human was invested with more magic powers than the sheriff, and was rumored to be able to fly and fight with such speed that he was invincible. The old man himself quickly dismissed it though. Only one sector had a story of this creature, and he only truly believed the stories that had origins in more than one.

Rise slammed the book. He knew it was too good to be true. He could not kill a sheriff and live through it. His whole mind and body knew it was only a matter of time before one of those elite guards went searching for the man who killed Morceff. He knew it was true. There was no fighting back, there was no victory. How else could something this great have happened?

Beline came over to Rise. "What's that?"

Rise placed the book under his coat. "A remembrance of the old man."

He sat down on the floor. His legs were tired. Beline did the same and wrapped her arm around him and rested her head against his shoulder. Rise realized how tired he was. Beline looked up at his face and smiled. She unlatched the green necklace Trent left her and placed it around Rise's neck. They were silent at this act, and Rise thought it better not to ask. It would only make him seem foolish to her. She had a reason, and that was more than good enough for him. Beline knew that even though Trent was badly wounded, he still managed to make it all the way from the ruins to the living space to give her that necklace. With any luck, it would allow Rise to come back to her should they ever be separated, no matter the distance. It would keep him safe. With all that had happened, she had a sinking feeling more was to come. They were soon both asleep.

Bespin glanced back at them, smiled, and returned to his work. He seriously doubted he could get those doors open.

After an hour he stopped to look at the map again. His mind needed a break. The four rows of skelguards, probably thousands in number resumed their mission and went making an east to west sweep of the sector. Something had stirred them to action. At least half the familiar faces he knew were dead, the others were arrested, soon to die or serve the King. They were not leaving anyone. It was a total invasion of the sector right above their heads. He felt safe in his underground lair. Yet... he looked at the peacefulness of his two slumbering friends. His friends, no, his family was right here with him. He missed nothing and no one on the surface. He was safe with his friends. They were all strangely at peace, like a dreary dream that was forgotten after waking up.

Rise's dreams were horrible. He kept seeing Beline die, over and over again, while he lived. He killed the sheriff, and he lived. It wasn't right. The Giver was supposed to die.

"Rise... wake up. Something's happening."

Rise stirred and looked up at Bespin. Beline was asleep, resting against him, and he gently lowered her to the floor.

Bespin pointed on the map. "Look here. The skelguard line completely stopped once it came across Morceff's dead body. They've been standing there for a while..."

"Who's that?" Rise pointed to a figure, not a skelguard, standing in front the dead body.

"Don't know. He just showed up a few minutes ago.

He's been staring at the body the whole time with that metal box to his eyes."

The figure was strange to look at. His whole body seemed covered in metal strips, an armor Rise never encountered before. One long magic stick was attached to his back. Just below the shoulders were two slanted cylinders with burn marks on the edges.

"Bespin. You've been a great friend to me. Better than those in the community ever have. You and Beline both. I think I'm going to die."

Bespin stared with eyes of glazed ice. "What?"

Rise just gazed at the metallic armored man studying the body. A skelguard dragged a man to the metal figure. The metal one seemed to perform a brutal interrogation. The beatings happened faster than anything Rise had seen. Movements that could only be achieved by a rigorous training routine. It was a literal blur. The man seemed to give the right answers, and the beatings stopped. The skelguards took him away. The metal man's head pointed up, and the two cylinders on his back ignited in a small controlled flame. To their amazement, the hunter quickly flew through the air with the control only a bird could master, and was off the map.

"What was that?!" Bespin gasped.

"That is what's going to kill me. By now he's probably figured out where I am. Beline is right. We can't fight the King. The sheriff was pure luck. The King knows one of his servants is dead. He won't respond kindly. You and Beline should leave. Hide in the ruins." Rise said it all so calmly to Bespin, while his gaze was completely on Beline's sleeping form.

Bespin put his hand on Rise's shoulder. "Even if that thing is coming here, even if you think you're going to die, you know we won't leave you. We die together, we survive together."

Rise rubbed his shoulder nervously. It still stung a little.

"Besides," Bespin let go and walked back to the map, readjusting it. "You don't really think you're going to die."

Rise looked up at him. "And why do you say that, old friend?"

"Because, if you really thought you weren't going to survive the day, you would tell Beline you loved her. But, you honestly think you still have time. So, I honestly think you're going to live through this battle."

"Please, take her and leave. Hide before that thing gets here."

"Nope." Bespin located the flying hunter. "Wow, he's on

a course straight for us. He's making good time, too. He'll be here soon. Better be prepared." Bespin walked over, ever so calmly, to his pack and dumped all the contents. "Beline!"

She quickly sat up. He handed her another barrier button, and the small metallic magic stick that broke barriers. "Something's coming for Rise. One of the King's monsters."

"What?" she asked, confused. She was rubbing the tiredness out of her eyes. "What is it?"

"Rise wants us to leave him alone..."

"No!" She stood up from the floor. "Not now. Not ever."

"Beline..." Rise started, yet he knew she would not leave. "I... thank you."

Bespin laughed. "You still think you have time. Perhaps we will live through this."

There was a deafening sound, and dust and chunks of metal and concrete went flying through the air. An explosion ripped away the exit. Dust was everywhere, a cloud of sheer loudness and pain.

They were all knocked to the ground. The dust cleared and the daylight crept into the building. There was a buzzing sound like a thousand bees.

Rise saw a dark figure in the cloud, descending through the newly formed door. It was the hunter filled with powerful magic.

Rise looked around the room. Bespin's lower body was covered in small concrete slabs. He was unconscious, and a small trickle of blood from the back of his head ran down onto the floor. Beline was to Rise's left. She was shaking slightly, face down, but there was no blood. She had been knocked harshly to the ground.

That sight angered him greatly.

There was a metallic clank. The hunter was walking towards them. Each step was a loud heavy bang of metal. The dust settled, and Rise saw a man completely covered in shanks of metal. His helmet was round with two small slits for unseen eyes. A raspy voice echoed, "The white haired man. The peasant gave a detailed description of you. You killed Morceff."

Rise coughed and stood up, the pain in his legs was excruciating. No weakness. Only anger.

"Answer me, peasant."

"I did." Rise drew his sword.

The creature laughed. "Don't even try with me. You cannot hurt me."

Before the hunter could finish his last word Rise pulled

the same magic stick that broke Morceff's barrier and fired. The disruption flew through the air and struck the hunter. It pushed the monster back one step, nothing more. The creature had no magic barrier. It needed none.

"You idiot! I'm an elite hunter, beyond your powers. Beyond Morceff. You're not the first one to discover one of the old EMP stations in the sectors. There was one other. He was the first person to kill a sheriff. Don't feel too jealous, you'll die just like him."

Rise pulled out the magic button. With speed only capable of the wind, the creature swung his foot perfectly across Rise's hand and then swooped downward and smashed the button to pieces on the ground, all without ever actually touching his hand. "Beyond you."

Rise quickly placed the useless magic breaker into his pocket and tightened his grip on the sword. He looked at Bespin's unconscious body. He saw Beline trying to get up, but she contained no strength.

The metallic man stepped forward. "I am one of the few proud ones to be serving the King directly. I am his most elite warrior. I have killed many powerful men and women for him. Now it is your turn."

The monster disappeared. Rise blinked. Impossible! Rise looked around anxiously. Something was moving towards him, a small distortion in the air like ripples in floating water. It was the figure of a man running at him. There was a sharp pain in his wrist and then his chest. The sword flew from his hands.

The hunter reappeared inches from his face, a horrible rusty smell from where his mouth should have been. "I see you." His words were ice down Rise's back.

He felt a metal hand slap him hard against his face; he knew his cheek had split open. Then cold fingers around his neck. Then the pressure. The horrible pressure of darkness floating around him. He managed to choke out the word, "Beline!"

The monster dropped him. "Who?"

It turned towards Beline, who finally stood up. She saw Rise's crumpled figure and screamed in rage. "Don't you touch him!" She ran at the monster, completely unafraid. That creature backhanded her so hard across the face that Rise feared he had killed her. She fell to the ground, smacking her back across a wall of rubble.

Rise stood up, a surge of anger acting as a spring.

Bespin was right. He was not going to die today. Nobody, NOBODY, dare do that to Beline in front of his eyes.

He screamed and threw his body into the hunter. It stumbled forward slightly. The sheer weight was impressive. Rise could barely move it. It spun a graceful kick into Rise's stomach and in the same movement jumped with the other foot and came back up into Rise's face. He tasted blood.

Rise was picked up by one hand of the monster. "The King has decreed your death, peasant."

The monster set Rise on the floor. He did not struggle. He just stared with hate-filled eyes. He would not die today. His anger would keep him alive long enough to repay that monster seven times what he did to Beline.

"I have killed 602 individuals. Each one I have looked into their eyes. Not with these hollow slits of machinery, but my real eyes. Every person I execute for the king makes me a stronger, better man. I'm also trying to understand my enemy, how anyone in their right mind could oppose our loving King. All I see is pure idiocy and ignorance. After I execute you and your two friends, I will be at 605, a new mighty warrior."

One solid hand held Rise, while the other slowly slid the metal helmet off. There was a pale man underneath with patchy hair. A weak looking man. A pitiful man with powers he did not deserve. Wires, ones similar to what Rise wore for his wristlight, came out from the metal suit and into the man's skull. He was more armor than man. Rise stared into the blue eyes of the beast, not breaking his gaze.

"Your power is mine." The hunter raised his metal arm to crush The Giver's skull.

Rise did not close his eyes, but stared right back at the monster.

The monster's pale head jerked forward quickly with a snap. His mouth shot open revealing grotesque teeth and the pointed end of a crossbow bolt. His blue eyes receded to the back of his head and the body crashed limply onto Rise with the bolt sticking straight through his mouth.

Beline stood directly behind the hunter with the empty crossbow. Her face was white and her eyes glaring. She killed for him. Beline killed someone to save his life.

He knew it. She loved him.

Beline stared down at the body of the King's servant. She was in tears but her voice and eyes were steady, "I told you not

73

to touch him."

Rise pushed with most of his strength to get the dead metal beast off his body. It clanked to the floor and Rise quickly stood up and hugged her. "Beline I..."

Bespin still lay without moving. She quickly broke the hug and ran over to Bespin, throwing the weapon to the ground in a plume of dust. "Get up, please! Get up!" She tugged at him. He stirred slightly, and she let out her breath. "He's alive."

That was when the first skelguard dropped clumsily down the hole.

Chapter Seventeen:

The world was as slow and blurred as a burning coal. The skelguards were awkwardly dropping down the hole blown open by the first explosion. Beline just killed for Rise. She loved him... he would not die.

"Grab Bespin and run for the hallway!"

Rise drew his magical weapon and fired upon the skelguards. The distortion hit the first three and they went limp on the ground before the fourth even dropped through the hole.

Beline was struggling to free Bespin from the rubble. Rise stepped over the carcass of the hunter and continued firing upon the skelguards. Rise did not give them time to react. As soon as they landed and their knees buckled, Rise fired.

He took one brief moment to consider how strange his life instantly became. A day ago he was fearful of the sheriff and his army of undead warriors. Now he was killing them as spiders under his boot. It was not right. Something bad was going to happen.

Bespin screamed in pain as he finally awoke from his stupor. His legs were broken. He used what was left of his strength to help Beline remove the rubble from him. Rise fired into the invisible wall, opening up the passage to the hallway. He turned and shot one more skelguard. They kept coming like puss from a wound. He would kill them all. He quickly pulled the grapnel under his coat, and sheathed his sword that was on the ground.

Beline was struggling, but now she was using all of her strength to help support Bespin, his legs loosely dangling. She dropped him back to the floor. It was too much for her alone. "Help us, Rise!" She screamed, tears sliding down her face. She was desperate. Time was slow for Rise.

He then realized his mistake. They could not open the doors in the hallway. "We're trapped." He was slightly pleased to hear himself speak as he always did. Direct. At least some things in his life stayed the same.

Bespin pointed to the fallen hunter. "Take those metal spheres off his belt!" He gasped it out. His face was red and contorted from the pain he was enduring.

Rise pulled them like oranges from a dead tree. He continued firing on the intruding warriors. A nice bottleneck was being formed with their bodies.

He backed up and handed the three metal pieces to Bespin. No skelguards were coming at the moment. He took the chance to lift Bespin up on his shoulders and ran for the hallway. Beline yelled, "They're coming!"

Rise quickly laid Bespin down on the floor more roughly than he wanted to. He immediately turned and fired down the hallway. Now there were three dropping in at a time. He was late on the last one and nearly gave it enough time to shoot the staff of fire.

They were halfway down the hallway. A good 40 feet lay between them and total entrapment. "We need a way out..."

Bespin spoke quickly through his pain, "The table had moving picture instructions of these things under the weapon index." Bespin pulled a small pin from the top and threw the ball down the hallway with a grunt of pain. It landed right next to the last few doors.

Bespin shielded his face with his arm and Rise and Beline instinctively followed. There was a loud bang, and a hole was ripped through the end of the corridor. Rise was amazed at how destructive this magic was. Perhaps it was this same magic that destroyed the ruins years ago. This building, though old, looked new, but after a few minutes with this magic it was resembling the surrounding wreckage.

He heard more skelguards dropping, five at a time. He continued firing, the magic collapsing the dead warriors.

Beline was dragging Bespin, who was obviously trying to disown any pain he felt. Rise grabbed one of the orbs from Bespin, pulled the pin, and threw it at the pile of skelguards. He picked up Bespin, and the three friends ran for the newly made hole on the other side of the hallway. With each thumping step, Bespin breathed heavily, his legs like two dangling iron chains.

The newly exposed room was huge. As they ran, Rise

felt the explosion behind him and heard the sound of metal collapsing and the strange hissing noise of the magical equipment breaking apart. He glanced back to see metal collapsing, making a temporary wall from the invading forces.

The room was thirty feet tall and at least fifty tent dwellings could have fit inside it. The square room was bright with white tile, and had circular doors five feet in diameter. The doors were spaced two feet apart equally around the room. Above each one Rise read the same sentence in the old tongue, "Escape Pod."

"Escape? Perfect!" He glanced into the closest round door. It was a small metal chamber with a comfortable seat and many colorful panels, like the table they used to access information. It looked as if each chamber would barely fit one person.

Beline was glancing back nervously between Bespin and the hallway. "Do we have any magic barriers left?"

Bespin painfully reached into his pack and pulled out two, handing one to Beline. Rise searched for his and remembered the hunter smashed it. "Don't worry," Bespin said, "One can protect at least two people. We'll be safe until we can figure out these doors." He coughed and Rise shuddered. It was the same cough the old man made moments before his death.

Rise pushed a green button on the wall. The door hissed open. "Well that was easy."

They all peered into the room. They heard the sound of metal and concrete falling. The skelguards were working quickly. No telling how many new enemies dropped down.

Rise crawled inside and began inspecting the panels. All the buttons were green or yellow, except one big red one in the center. In the old tongue it read, "Launch."

"Launch... launch... I don't know that word!"

Rise stepped back out of the pod. "Okay, we have to activate three of these doors." Rise pressed the green button for the next closest door. A strange obnoxious noise beeped at him, and red letters glared above the door, "Malfunc. Low-Fuel."

Rise punched the button. Another beep. "No!" The door would not open. Beline ran to the opposite wall and began pressing green buttons trying to find another pod that would open. None of the doors except the first would open.

They frantically ran the sides of the room pressing all the buttons. They met in the middle. "No! It can't be like this!" Rise grabbed Beline's hand and they ran back to Bespin, who was slumped at the first door.

"We've got to squeeze in..." Rise started.

"Watch out!" Beline cried and pushed him out of the way of a hurtling fireball. The magical flame missed both Beline and Rise, yet Rise tumbled into the open pod, a soft plume of smoke coming from his jacket. The skelguards had made it around the rubble. They were a deadly shot even from the end of the hallway. The flame sizzled the metal wall into black char.

Rise fell into the chair of the escape pod and his feet kicked upward, pressing the red button unintentionally. The door slid shut.

Rise and Beline's eyes met through the thick glass in the door. They were so green. The most beautiful eyes he had ever seen.

A creepy voice that was neither male nor female startled him, "Launch sequence commencing. Emergency escape procedure."

The room began to shake. He pressed his hand to the glass. Beline's waist was grasped around by Bespin's hands as he quickly pressed the button for the magical barrier to protect them.

That horrible hidden voice echoed, "Malfunction. Fuel source deficient. Battery power minimal."

Rise's eyes and Beline's were only focused on each other. Their hands were inches apart by the glass. "Beline!" He yelled. The chamber allowed no outside sound.

He saw her lips form, "Rise!" but no word was heard.

He felt his eyes watering. The room was shaking violently now. "I LOVE YOU!" He yelled with all his heart, all his soul. She never heard him.

A violent wave of fire engulfed Bespin and Beline as Rise was only able to watch from within the pod. The barrier Bespin created around them shone red as they were knocked to the ground unburned. The magic barrier had saved their lives. Three skelguards quickly hobbled over.

Instantly the horrible image in the window grew smaller, and Rise realized the chamber was leaving at an unthinkable speed. It was stealing him from his friends.

Rise beat the chamber as hard as he could. He felt his knuckles split, his finger nails rip, and his toes crack. "Beline! Bespin! NO! NO! NO! NOOO!"

He felt strange. His body was weightless for just a moment. He felt the chamber turn, and he looked out the window while beating it with his fists. The pod was flying through the air, leaving his friends hundreds of feet below. He was probably the first peasant to see the sectors from the view of a bird. It was shocking.

An unending grid filled with equilateral squares of a dark evil land. He saw a northern boundary of the sectors, many, many miles in the distance, yet it was a barren land of dirt and sand. As for the other three directions... they seemed to span forever of relentless sectors. Roofless prisons. The chamber turned, and he realized it was falling. He must have been a mile up in the air. His fists stop beating as the voice startled him.

"Malfunction. Thruster 1-2 low fuel. Commencing emergency landing." The light turned red inside the chamber. It tilted downward, and he saw the sector below. His sector. Burning. Many fires were everywhere, but mostly in the living space. Those horrible vehicles were taking people away. The sector was being abandoned.

His mind was flooded. Beline. Bespin. Here he was, hurtling through the sky, now falling. He then realized with his current course that he was going to land in a different sector. His heart wanted to implode. Too many impossible things were happening at once.

He had a vision of all the people he knew, disappearing. What if the King decided to wipe out all peasants? The other sector would be a wasteland as well. He did not care much. His heart was ready to collapse just with the thought of Beline and Bespin being arrested.

He began to sob. His breathing was staggered. He tried to get a look at the new sector he was uncontrollably heading for. The headless voice spoke again, "Activating crash shielding." A metal frame engulfed the window, and he was in a dark red tint with only his tears and sobs.

"Beline! No! Bespin! Anybody!" He collapsed into the plush seat and two leather straps magically came out and pulled his body tightly into the chair to prepare him for the landing.

It seemed to take an eternity, and just as he felt the horrible impact, he thought of Beline, Bespin, and the old man... who traveled the sectors.

Part Two: Sector 2131
Chapter One:

Darkness. A shadow of a shadow. He was alone.

Every muscle in his body hurt. His hands were too stiff to move because of the caked blood on his knuckles. He was lying on his side; his neck hurt. He could not see anything.

And then he remembered. He was alone.

"They're gone." He said it as simply as he could. "They're ALL GONE!" He squinted his eyes, trying to smother every tear he felt welling up inside him. He wiped his eyes quickly. "Beline. My Beline."

He shook his head. He must have a clear head. First things first. Self preservation. They had the magic barrier, they would be fine for a little while. He could still rescue them... just not right now. He was not even sure where he was exactly. Had he really flown into another sector, or was it just his dizzy mind?

He began to look around, and just the simple movement hurt his head. He saw a blinking red light. He slowly, painfully, reached out and touched it.

There was a hiss, and the whole chamber seemed to roll slightly as the door slid up, spilling stabbing rays of light into the pod. The leather straps from around his body released and he stumbled out.

Rise emerged shakily and took a good look at the pod. It was small, round, and very wrecked. There was still smoke from the crash. He landed in a junkyard of scrap metal. The pod left a small crater and drag-trail. Only by a matter of twelve feet or so had he missed the side of a half-intact building. He did not recognize this place. The walls of the sector were a few miles away.

Rise realized he needed to hide. He killed a sheriff, a hunter, and many skelguards. He could not believe what had happened. At any moment, he would wake up back in his own sector. His mind began to drift back to images of his friends. He saw the old man. No! He dismissed it. No time for that. *Have to keep on track.*

He began to pace painfully and mutter to himself, "If the King sends more after me, I have to hide until I can fight... simple. If they see that..." He shook his head at the obvious trail the escape pod left.

His mind went to Bespin. That look of pain on his face when his legs... *No! Focus!*

Rise began to walk through the scrap metal heaps. He needed to find this sector's living space. A voice in his head began to argue with him. It told him to find a place to hide for the first day, and then seek out people. Get a feel for the place.

His mind finally did it. He was drowning out the thoughts as hard as he could, but it returned. He thought of Beline. He did not dismiss it right away. He let his mind stay just long enough to get a look at those green eyes. Then he rejected the thoughts as quickly as he could. Hide first.

He could have been walking for hours, he was unsure. The huge walls of metal scraps rose to provide a chilling shade. This scrap yard was huge, probably as big as the ruins in his sector. His head hurt, and his judgment of time was all wrong. He found a small pile of scrap metal that was half-made into a shelter. There was one spot where the metal was singed together. The occupant was probably killed by a skelguard not too long ago. It would do for now.

It was dark inside the barely built shack, but the wind was blocked. There was one table, one chair, and a couple of large rags for a pillow in the corner. There was a faint smell of mildew emitting from the pillows, but nothing too terrible. There was still enough light outside for him to see without aid of his wristlight.

"Supplies." He dumped out everything he had. He was still carrying the cumbersome grappling stick that the old man left him under his coat. As always, his trusted sword was at his aid. He still carried the small magic stick that broke the invisible shielding used by the King. All but one light was gone. It was low on magic. He still had the ear piece but could not talk to Bespin. He listened for a few minutes, hoping with all his heart Bespin would talk to him. Nothing but silence. Rise decided to hide it in his pocket, fearing it would make him stand out too much in this sector. He also had the book from the old man.

He pulled the wobbly chair over and began to read it. He turned to the chapter about the different sectors and found the map.

He found Sector 2128. His home. "It seems like... I traveled east." East one sector was 2131. He followed up on the page where the old man wrote about it.

The old man complained so much of the apathy in this sector. All he did for one whole page was complain about how the people gave up hope here, only to spare one line about how much scrap metal there was for scavenging and inventing. In his log, it stated that he stayed there for two weeks before getting tired of it.

"You might have been right after all." Rise sighed, regretting that he did not believe the stories sooner. He would give anything for some "crazy" advice from the old man.

And then he felt it. The one supply he forgot about. The necklace. The emerald necklace that Beline gave him. She knew they would be separated. Somehow she knew it.

That was when The Giver collapsed and wept. He cried for many hours. The dark clouds came, the light disappeared, and the night followed.

The loneliness was unbearable. In his old sector, he knew so many "friends." He knew they were not really his friends, but he missed them now. He was alone... except for three friends, the old man, who was more of a father, Bespin, his brother, and Beline, his love. They made life worth living. All the times he gave of himself to help others, all the battles, all the scars, they were not for the people he was helping. They were for his three friends, who truly believed in hope. They believed in the good. They were passionate about life. And now they were either dead or in the clutches of the King.

"That's where this ends!" He screamed it to the heavens of his metal shack, the sound echoing in his ears like a haunting reminder of his promise.

He would track down the King himself. He would find Beline and Bespin's fate. He would find their threat, he would confront it, and he would free them. He grasped the necklace. If they were dead... the King, cursed be his name, would pay. The sparks of rebellion would burn him alive.

His sleepiness hit him unexpectedly. He quickly dropped to the floor and wondered if his zeal would survive the night. A night without alcohol, but with plenty of dreams of Beline.

Chapter Two:

He awoke to the sound of a group of tiny feet bustling into the shack. His hand reached for his sword as he lifted up his head. Rise was confused for just a moment.

Four children, all with fake skulls over their faces, were looking down at him. The eyes stared at him through their masks. They each had a stick.

Rise looked at them suspiciously.

"Mister, what are you doing in our hide?"

Rise wondered if the children actually built the shelter. He would have been impressed if they did. "Sleeping."

"Oh. Well, we're playing skelguards and peasants. Why is your hair white?"

Rise did not like the idea of children playing skelguards. He gathered his things and walked stiffly past them, his body still sore. The children went on with their business, "Woomf! I burned you!" They were pointing their sticks at each other. "No! I burned you first!"

Rise shook his head and was grateful when he was out of hearing distance of that foul play. He was finally coming to the end of the scrap heap. The whole sector seemed to be made up of little hills. He saw quite a few smaller ruined buildings, nothing like the ruins in his sector, but they reminded him of home. He realized he would trade anything to have it back the way it was. Whatever the King was doing to his sector, he was sure it would spread. It set him on edge that at any moment the rows of skelguards could appear and wipe out this sector as well.

The sky was cloudy, almost as if it were about to rain. He looked to the west, towards home. He could just barely make out the wall of this sector and the smoke billowing from his old one. If the King had been doing this when the old man was traveling the sectors, there was no telling how many sectors were destroyed and how many were left. He smiled as he finally realized he believed the old man's stories.

He walked through the last of the scrap yard and found a slew of two story buildings that had their upper portions destroyed years ago. He saw small fires inside some and the smoke was escaping through the cracked windows. He was leery about approaching, but thought that perhaps in this sector the living space was the ruins, and the gangs hid elsewhere. He never thought that ruins could be a safe place. Such a different world on the other side of the wall.

Rise's stomach growled at the thought of fires. He needed something cooked. The hole in his stomach was just another pain added to his physical and emotional trauma.

He approached the community. All the people he saw gave him no notice. He tried to talk to a few, but they ignored him. The clothing here was much the same; rags that were scavenged long ago by their parents.

It was strange. No one was talking. These people might as well have been skelguards. They seemed stuck in a routine of gathering water, cooking food, and... no weapons. Nobody held a scabbard or bow.

He heard someone talking, "Please friend, I guarantee this pelt is from a healthy goat. It'll keep you warm..." He heard the second voice, "Go away. I have nothing to barter with."

Rise saw a person in the middle of the town that stood out. He was in bright colored clothing. He recognized it from somewhere. It looked like one of the men from his old sector. It was one who claimed to travel sectors, a news gatherer as they called themselves. They were known to be expert barterers, often found with exotic goods that they claimed were from other sectors.

Rise hurried through the apathetic crowd and found the brightly colored man. The news gatherer was short, probably in his early twenties. He had a boyish face with dark curly hair.

"Excuse me," Rise said.

The man turned and took a step back. "I know you! Yeah, I do. You're the guy with the white hair."

Rise just looked at him.

"You killed Morceff."

The words surprised him. It was no longer a dream. "You were there?" he asked slowly.

The man lowered his voice. "Oh yeah, I was there. Unbelievable. How long were you planning that assassination?" The man in the colorful clothing was talking fast.

"Never mind that, how did you travel the sectors?" Rise asked.

"Friend, that is a secret us news gatherers must keep. But, since you seemed to have traveled one as well, if you tell me how you did it, and if it is the same, I'll tell you."

Rise shook his head. "I am not entirely sure how I got here."

"I know what you mean, my friend."

"Can you help me get back?"

"Ha!" The man slapped the pelt he was holding. "Are you crazy? Well, I guess if you attacked a sheriff you must be. Once that sweep of skelguards happens, a sector is dead. Gone. Nothing in or out. Personally, I just thought they were rumors from the other news gatherers. Once a sector dies, the number of skelguards increases on the walls. Anything that gets within a hand length of the wall is killed. They have eyes that do not quit, and an aim that will not wander from its victim. In the ten years I have been doing this, I've heard three rumors of a sector dying. What I have been told is the doors that allow the large food vehicles access are sealed up. Skelguards melt them together. That sector is dead, no way in." The man was fingering a gold ring on his left hand.

"So, you use the food vehicle access to get through a sector?"

The colorful man laughed at his own mistake. "You are smart, warrior. What is your name?"

"That is not important..."

"Oh I think it is. Otherwise, I shall have to call you the white haired slayer of Morceff, and my tongue is lazy..."

"It's Rise. Listen, two of my friends are trapped in there. I saw..." He shook slightly at the memory, "skelguards taking them."

"I don't understand, Rise. If you saw skelguards take them... they're either dead or arrested. You can be honest, did you run away?"

"No! Well... No!" Rise wanted to strike the man for that thought. "A strange vehicle... never mind. They are not dead! They had a magic barrier, the ones the sheriffs use."

"This story gets better and better. You're almost as good at spreading rumors as us news gatherers. But, I'm afraid if the skelguards could not kill them, it seems to me, they were arrested. The barrier could not protect them from that."

Deep in his being, Rise knew that was the answer. He wanted to avoid it, but if someone else said it as well...

Rise clasped the necklace.

The colorful man sighed, "I am sorry. Truly. Friends are a wonderful thing to have, so I hear. But trust me, you will find no friends here. This sector is the worst in hopefulness I travel to."

"What sector is this?"

"2131."

"Well, the old man's map is accurate."

"You have a map of the sectors?" The colorful man was in awe. "Peasants don't usually have one. I sell those, at least those that are in my territory. I go to ten different ones, and so do my fellow news gatherers. Canyon would not have it any other way. Well, now mine is down to nine, since your sector closed up. I barely escaped myself. I was able to hitch one last ride on a vehicle that passed through before the skelguards sealed it up. Now I will wait my travel term until the next food vehicle. Next meeting, I will have to explain it to the other news gatherers."

Rise did not care. The colorful man saw that, but he loved to talk, and to find someone in this sector that would listen was almost worth a good barter.

The black haired news gatherer asked, "Rise, what will you do?"

"I will find my friends."

The colorful man nodded in agreement. "What if you cannot?"

"Then the King will pay."

"Oh, you are a rebel at heart. I have some advice,

consider it free, just because I like you, and you are the only person who actually lets me finish my sentences in this sector. If rebellion is what you wish, travel north of this sector. The one north of this sector is 45. I have an acquaintance working there, another news gatherer, you will recognize the uniform, it looks like mine." He pointed to his red and black squared shirt, and faded yellow pants. "Although I doubt you will see him, most of the time he will be in hiding. That sector is plagued by war and strife. Sometimes I think I would rather have the excitement than this graveyard of apathy..." He saw Rise losing his attention. "Anyway, he speaks of a mysterious group of rebels, ones that..." The news gatherer lowered his voice, "want to dethrone the King, cursed be his name. Personally, I don't think it's possible, but my eyes open a little wider every day. Until 24 hours ago, I thought sheriffs were invincible. But apparently, you push a white haired man at them and they throw themselves onto a table full of swords."

Rise asked, "Do you have any food?"

"No, sorry friend, and good luck finding it here. These people will not help you. Wake up, you dead fellows!" He yelled at the somber crowd walking by, ignoring him. "You know, I cannot wait to tell other news gatherers I met the man who killed Morceff."

"I will make do. Thank you, I'll head north."

"You did not get my name, friend Rise."

"I don't want it, but thank you just the same." Rise walked by the colorful man. "One more thing." Rise yelled over his shoulder, "Do you use magic to travel the sectors?"

"Ha! Hardly." The news gatherer laughed and pointed at the ring on his finger that he had been fidgeting with.

That was all Rise wanted to know.

He walked through the crowd. He saw many women, none as beautiful as Beline. He saw many men, none as loyal as Bespin. He saw many elder ones, none as wise as his friend. And none would share food.

It was a full day of wasted wandering, and as far as he could tell, the whole sector seemed to be one big living space, except for the expanse of scrap heaps.

He found one family, a particularly fat one, eating away at roasting animal flesh. They had a small fire in front of their tent. The parents and the two children ate slowly.

"Excuse me," Rise approached them. They, just like everyone else who was walking by, ignored him at first. "Hey, you, the fat one. I'm talking to you."

The fat man raised his head. His eyes were sunken slightly at the corners. He went back to eating.

"Do you suppose," Rise continued, "that you could share just a small portion of that food with me?"

"No!" The fat man barked.

"It's not as if you haven't eaten more than your fair share. In my sector, fat people are rarely seen."

"Leave us alone, you beggar. Earn your own food."

Rise had one brief moment where he wanted to kill the fat man. The thought of that violence made him sick. Hunger was driving him mad. How could Beline love such a person with horrible thoughts like that?

"I apologize." Rise quickly walked away.

Rise wandered the whole day with nothing to eat. He lost count of the people or families that turned him down. If just one person of each of these families spared one bite he could have been full by now. As for the meat, he could not tell where they were getting it from, but he smelled the flesh cooking constantly.

He needed a drink of alcohol. If only drinks were as common as the roasting pits.

He saw a man with an animal skin coat walking through the community. He carried a dead beast on his shoulders. The animal had horns sticking out of its head, long horns that looked gnarled, like old man fingers. The man carried a bow and long knife at his side.

Rise ran through the crowd and caught up to the man. "Hunter, where did you find that meal?"

"Leave me alone."

"Just tell me where you go to hunt."

The man sighed, never once breaking eye contact with his feet. "Life is hard enough without beggars, please, leave me be." The man did not sound angry or offended. He sounded... depressed. Just like everyone else in this sector.

"Why can you not spare me three seconds to help make life easier for another man?"

The man shook his head. "It doesn't matter. We hunt, we eat, we die. The only difference is when we are killed or arrested by the King. Skelguards know no pity."

Just the thought of the animal roasting was enough for Rise's mouth to start watering. He turned his attention to the direction the man came from. It was a large grassy slope that looked as if it curved into a dense valley. Only a few scattered tents broke the monotony.

Rise began jogging, the weight of all his collections becoming burdensome. He was tired and needed shelter and food.

He followed the trail to the grass away from the community. The hill did indeed flow into a valley with a forest hidden in the center. It made the small grouping of trees in his sector look like a pitiful herb. He never really thought that trees could grow so dense.

A drop of water slid down his nose. The rain was descending. It would not last for long, the night was almost here and the dark clouds would push the healthy wet ones away and replace them with their dry, cool breeze. Rise wandered into the forest and quickly found that many stables were built. Small wood huts that spiraled at the top were placed close to each stable. The spiral allowed smoke from their furnaces to escape. Rise saw some animals; he assumed they were pigs from the descriptions of others in his sector. There were some goats, which were also in his old sector; good for milk.

He stared at the fat pigs. Some roasted pig flesh would hit the spot.

"Hey, beggar! Leave my cattle alone, or I..."

Rise was surprised to hear an actually angry voice. Finally, someone who was not apathetic.

A man emerged from the hut with a gnarled club. "Hey, wait a second. You have white hair."

Rise said, "I was wondering if I could trade you something for a meal?"

"Please, come on in. Any man with enough magic to kill a sheriff is welcome for a meal in my house. Come along. I'll slaughter a nice fat one."

The hut was about 20 by 20 feet. A small shed was built onto the outside with a chopping block that was covered with blood. The man told Rise to make himself at home and walked into the rain. A few minutes of squealing, followed by a wet thunk eventually turned into dinner. Rise could not take his eyes off a bottle on a worn-down shelf. It looked like an alcoholic drink.

The man was strong, not huge, but with lean muscles. He used the same muscles for his chores of herding and harvesting, and it showed in his subtle yet precise movements. His hair was black and he stood probably a good head and a half taller than Rise. The man prepared the pig by cleaning and bleeding it. As he did so he said, "Feel free to have some wine. I have plenty more bottles

87

being readied for the next few months. Wine grapes are probably the only food we actually cultivate here. I am one of the few that truly understands the magic of making wine. I think you'll be impressed."

The man handed Rise a wooden cup with a bloody hand and Rise eagerly poured some wine into it.

"Drink as much as you can."

An hour later the pig smelled great and to the man's great surprise, two of his bottles were gone, and Rise was still coherent. "You must drink a lot."

Rise said nothing.

"The pig is ready, I'll dish us up."

Rise ate and drank quickly, forgetting that it was getting dark outside.

"Why?"

The man was startled that Rise actually asked something. "What?"

"Why did you do this for me? No one else in this sector..."

"I know the feeling. They are all very depressed. I've heard from many news gatherers that this sector is one of the saddest things they have seen. The news gatherer that came by earlier to barter for hide, told me of a white haired man who defied the Evil King. Believe me, I know life is horrible. Skelguards, the sheriff, all death at any corner. But, man is good about adapting. I wonder if things were ever better? A time with no Dark King, cursed be his name. The people here have lost hope. They say, "Life is bad, we might as well die." I say, "Life is bad, why make it worse by losing hope?" Oh well. Life is life after all."

Rise wanted another bottle, but knew it would be rude.

"Oh, look at me. I have talked your ears to death, and we still haven't exchanged names."

"I should be going."

"Not so fast, my stranger friend. It's night. I don't know about your sector, but here skelguards hunt very often at night. Stay here, I have an extra blanket somewhere."

Rise started, "I can't take your hospit..."

"Be quiet. I will not have a man as powerful as you exposed to the skelguards. Perhaps someday there will be a use for you. A man who can kill a sheriff is a powerful ally."

The man gave Rise a blanket, and a spot was found on a sheep skin carpet by the bed for him. The tall man took his own bed, which was hardly big enough for him.

Rise closed his eyes. He finally had time to think, and it only saddened him. He wanted to keep moving and avoid the haunting thoughts. He saw his friends and his love. They were constantly in his mind. They seemed to be painted to the back of his eye lids, but the only portrait he saw was their uncertain death.

A voice came from the dark, "What is your story?"

"I have no story." Rise wanted to sleep, yet he was grateful for the conversation that distracted his mind from the truth of his situation.

"Do not give me that stranger, after all I have done for you, the least you can do is tell me about that green necklace you kept fondling through dinner."

Rise bit his lower lip, and even in the dark he was sure the man would notice his weakness. It was in this darkness that Rise eventually told him everything.

He hoped he could get out before the tall talker awoke in the morning. He had to figure out his next course.

Chapter Three:

Rise was startled by someone moving around him. It was the tall man.

"How late in the day is it?" Rise asked groggily, rubbing his closed eyes. He did not like the idea of someone standing over him while he slept.

"Oh, about four hours since the dark clouds vanished. Here, warrior, I have something for you. It will keep you dry on your quest."

The man handed Rise a pig skin hat with long brims that drooped down loosely in the back. Rise had seen similar ones, but never found an excuse to use one. He hated hats, but he knew this might be an advantage. The water would easily drip off backwards and avoid even touching him. It would also be good for on-the-spot shade during the hot days. It might make a good barter to someone else.

"What quest?"

"Oh come now, I may not be smart, but I am a great judge of personality. You, for a fact, will not stop until you find your friends. Even if they are dead, you will not stop until you either die or kill the King who is responsible." The tall man was helping Rise to his feet. "That hat is not only meant to keep the rain from your head. If word spreads that a white haired man killed a sheriff, you'll be executed before you even realize you've been spotted. A man such as you; motive, power, and brains, should not die so easily."

The tall man handed Rise the book, his sword, and grappling machine. "You even have the equipment for one worthy of a quest. Your answer is not in this sector. Apathy does not deserve a man of your motive. I know that somewhere out there, or so say the news gatherers, that there is a rebellion. I don't believe in it myself, call it my only form of hopelessness, but if it is out there, you are a powerful man who will do great things. If the King, cursed be his flesh rotting name, is dethroned and the walls of the sectors that separate the human family are destroyed..." He took a deep breath, "That would be a glorious day and I can say that I did my part by sending the white haired savior with my good will. Now, stranger, be gone and find your answers. Beline and Bespin are waiting for you, I know it in my heart."

Rise was pushed out and the door was closed.

Rise just stood there for a second, holding his possessions. He still was not quite awake yet. He quietly readied his possessions and decided to get moving.

Maybe the old man traveling the sectors was not such a funny thought. Maybe it was time The Giver tried it. Rise remembered the news gatherer speaking of his friend to the north, the one who would know of a rebellion.

Rise turned north and could just barely make out the top of the 300 foot wall. It would be a long walk, but the tall man filled him with food and purpose. With the thought of Beline's smile, Bespin's helping hand, and the old man's watchful eyes, he set out on his "quest."

As he passed people, he could have sworn he caught some looking at his hair. He previously did not recall anyone in this sector giving him such attention, so he put on the pig hat. He felt ridiculous, but safe.

Even the people in his old sector, although they would not fight for him, would give him food if he pleaded with them. This sector was too far lost for his time, and he wanted to leave before he saw a sheriff or a skelguard.

The wall grew closer and he could eventually make out the huge yellow lettering that spelled out Sector 2131. Each of the four walls, in the exact center, would have the sector number printed on them. It was a reminder of what prison they were to die in.

Skelguards patrolled atop the giant walls. One could see

them marching at the very edge. They were not unknown for shooting people at random who came too close to the walls. Rise saw another scrap metal heap thirty yards from the concrete wall. He would hide in there until nightfall. First, he needed to review the book of the old man.

He pushed a few metal plates aside and sat in a small hole he made, the only light came through one bare space he left open for reading. He took out the book and reviewed the instructions for the grappling machine. After he examined the machine itself, it seemed logical that the old man's directions were correct. "Hardly magic after all."

He laid it to the side and reviewed the map. According to the square grid, the sector north of 2131 was 45, the one that the news gatherer spoke of. The information the old man left for that sector described similar things to what the colorfully dressed man said. It was war stricken with gang riots and pure poverty.

It was amazing to Rise that just across that wall was a completely different world. It was made up of similar people, the same oppressive hand, and yet completely different circumstances.

His sword was tested, tried, and true. His skills were fair enough. His love for his friends was a fire that would never give out.

He would wait until the ever approaching nightfall.

His careful eyes were watching through the small hole and he began to understand the patrol pattern of the skelguards atop the wall. He was even beginning to predict them, and he would find their weakness.

Chapter Four:

Rise shifted his weight to accommodate the six-hour cramp in his leg. He felt something in his coat pocket. He reached in and found that the tall man left him some roasted meat rolled up in a package. He gladly ate half of it, and continued his watch. The old man was correct. If there were a time to use the grapnel, it would be just as the two single skelguards patrolling the middle of the wall passed each other. Rise could just barely make them out. So far, it appeared as if his hiding spot was a secret to them. If they came in pairs, it was no good because they walked in unison. In groups of three it was no good because they would stand there too long. But just about every hour, two singular skelguards passed each other on the top. After they passed, there was a good four minutes of peace.

Four minutes, to scale up the 300 foot wall, and down the other side.

The book warned him as soon as he retracted the grapnel, to run, just in case he was slow and the guards were returning. This was it, he could really do it. He and the old man, almost together again. Even in death he was still teaching him things.

Rise realized his legs would be too stiff to make the run, so he again rearranged himself, his legs sticking straight out.

Half of him wanted to try to get back into his sector, just to explore the wall, see whether there was an unprecedented amount of skelguards patrolling it, but he now believed the old man's warning. Everything else was happening the way he said it would. His sector was dead. It would only waste time checking it out.

His eyes continued on the skelguards patrolling the north wall. They never failed to keep formation or timing. No wonder the old man was able to explore so many sectors. It was the first time Rise viewed them as having a weakness in their patrol. Even when he was using the magic breaker to cripple them, he never viewed them as weak, probably because he did not believe what he was seeing. The whole experience was a blur, a painful blur that ended with Beline's face growing smaller and smaller. He blinked and dismissed it. He needed to focus. He needed to regain his nerve.

The formations repeated themselves, and, as the time before, it was only safe after the single patrol passed. It was a couple of hours after nightfall. Another hour or two and he would try it. He had to be sure the formation would not change. Then he would be one step closer to his friends.

Rise suddenly realized he needed a plan. The tall man was right. He would not stop until this matter was finished. There was no giving up. He needed his friends. He cringed at that thought. The Giver was motivated by selfish reasons. The fact that they needed him was a secondary thought. It saddened him. He placed the book back into the large pocket in his coat.

A plan. He needed a plan. His friends needed him. This man who knew of a rebellion could point him to another sector. He must spend as little time in each sector as he could. Time was the key.

Time. He needed time. And here he was wasting it. Planning was wasting time.

He pulled the grapnel to him. Next possible formation, he was going. He long since memorized the buttons on it, read the instructions over and over. He knew how to do it, but a lot could be said of practice.

He pulled himself out of the rubble and walked forward to the wall. He stopped 20 feet away, at the last rubble pile between him and the open space to the wall. He was looking practically straight up at it. It would be hard for a shot. He pulled away some of the metal scraps and hid under the last pile. Through a small hole he could just barely make out the tips of the lances of the skelguards as they marched. It was the closest he could get to the wall for a decent shot.

However, if he moved closer, perhaps the skelguards would not have a shot at him either. He did not want to risk it. Their magic was unpredictable.

Time was escaping him, but still he waited. A sickening feeling came over him that as soon as he would try to use the grapnel, their pattern would change. Again it stayed the same. An hour drifted by, the dark swirling clouds daunting him. This was the moment.

Rise placed the pig hat under his coat, not wanting to lose it on the ascent... the very high ascent.

He shook his head violently; no fear would overtake him. He felt the necklace against his skin. The emerald necklace. Beline's eyes were a prettier green.

Rise pointed the grapnel upward and peered through the scope. He lined up the X a few inches from the ledge. The loud bang almost knocked him to the ground, but he took the brunt with his shoulder. He watched the thin cable strike like a gargantuan snake, and the pike buried itself into the concrete. The line went taut.

Rise held a firm grip and hit the recoil button. His arms were nearly ripped out of their sockets as the machine sprang to life. He was traveling at a speed that rivaled the escape pod. He had that same sick feeling as when he saw Beline and Bespin's figures shrink in the distance.

He held on tighter and used his feet to keep his body from scraping the wall as he flew by the huge yellow lettering that read Sector 2131. Before he knew it, he reached the top. It was a true shot, only a foot from the top of the wall. The world shrank beneath him, leaving him breathless. He reached up quickly and found it very difficult to pull himself over the wall. The old man must have been young when he did his travels.

He did not expect the top of the wall to feel like concrete. He was expecting something... different. It felt so ordinary. So... peasant-like.

Rise made it to the top and quickly released the grapnel

by twisting the end. It automatically finished recoiling.

It was amazing. The wall had a few guard posts far in the distance. He could just barely see the backs of the skelguards on either side of him as they wandered away. He was undetected.

It was as if the sounds of the separated sectors joined atop the wall. He heard the wind blowing from Sector 2131 with the silent apathy, and from Sector 45 he heard many screams and sounds of magic sticks exploding. He heard swords clashing, brawling, and yelling. It was horrible. That was his destination.

He ran 15 feet to the other side of the wall and fired the grapnel between his feet. There was a small hole in the wall almost exactly where he was going to shoot. It was probably one of the old man's descents. Rise took a deep breath before his nerve jarring leap. He was amazed as he jumped the wall looking at the entire sector. No one but him and the old man ever saw such a view. He was sure of it. It was a sector of ruined, ancient, concrete buildings, broken glass, and rubble. It was as if the ruins were the entire landscape here. Many places for fighting and war. In the middle he saw the tallest building his eyes had ever seen. It stood probably 200 feet up; a large tower made of wood and concrete hodgepodge.

Gravity caught up to him and his senses as he was slowly descending into the new sector. He saw the flashing lights between distant buildings of magic stick fire. He landed on the ground a few seconds later. He hit the recoil button and the machine pulled the cable back so fast he feared the pike at the end would stab him.

There was a black smoke cloud coming towards him, as if a great amount of earth was recently torn apart. It was probably due to one of the small pockets of war.

He needed to find some shelter first of all. And water. He forgot how pleasant his home was with the running water.

Rise had landed between two small buildings, each with their roofs ripped off long ago. The concrete remains of them were scattered around his feet. The buildings had many windows, but no glass remained in them.

The evil clouds mocked him from above as Rise took his first step into Sector 45.

Part Three: Sector 45
Chapter One:

    Rise was surprised to see a group of people huddled in one of the abandoned buildings. The door was open just enough for him to make out the mass of people. It was a group of 20 children, none older than ten. Little girls and boys, all with dirty faces, and wrapped in shredded blankets. The only clean looking part of them were their eyes. Their pure innocent eyes were staring at him.

    Rise slowly stepped forward and pushed the creaky, dilapidated door. It loosely swung on rotting hinges. Something did not feel right. The air changed quickly. The eyes of the children looked above Rise. He quickly stepped backwards and avoided an axe swinging downward. Rise grabbed the handle just below the head with both hands and swung hard, pulling a man from his small perch just above the door.

    The axe was ripped from the man's hands and he landed with a thud like a pan being dropped on a wooden floor. The fall knocked the wind out of him, but he stood up quickly, and through ragged breaths hissed, "You stay away from them! Murderer!"

    Rise put his hands up and dropped the axe, "I had no intention of harming the children."

    The man examined Rise in the dim light, his eyes darting quickly over practiced areas. "You are not a Crow." The man was as dirty as the children. A patchy red beard outlined his square jaw. He was short, and held himself straight with a hidden strength. His forearm displayed a skin drawing of shards of glass.

    "I was merely looking for shelter. I shall go elsewhere."

    "Wait, you are not a Shard either? Neut?"

    "I'm not from this sector."

    The man eyed him curiously. "You are not a news gatherer either. And you came here... willingly? Must be your first time here, and I guarantee it will be your last."

    The ground shook, the air thundered, and the sound of debris hitting walls could be heard not more than 100 meters away. More explosions. More screams.

    The children's eyes did not leave Rise. They sat motionless, like curious birds atop a clothing line. They did not move. They reminded him of something that he could not discern at the moment, and it left him feeling at edge.

    "I'm looking for the news gatherer of this sector," Rise said, directing his attention back to the man with the patchy red beard.

"I have not seen him lately, but if he's even in this sector this time of the year, he would be in the compound."

Rise was curious as to what he meant by "this time of the year." He asked, "Where is the compound?"

"Due north, right in the middle of the sector. You'll not miss it. It's a large tower."

Rise turned to leave.

"No! You can't go now. The great war is upon us. Wait one night, it should be over before tomorrow. The Shards and the Crows are trying to kill each other."

Rise nodded toward the skin drawing. "You're a Shard?"

"No! Never say such a thing! I would much rather be a Neut and be safe with my family, but no one under the middle age of years is accepted. They would kill me before I got close to the compound. An elderly man like you... you are young." The man just now took the time to look at Rise's face. Until now, his attention was probably used to looking for gang identification, and of course white hair. White hair meant easy prey or non-threatening.

Rise wanted to leave, but information was often worth the trial of listening. Time was again slowly running through his fingers.

"What's this big war?"

"The great war is during the time of year just before it starts to chill again. All the gangs turn on each other, in hopes of trying to wipe each other out." The man paused, thinking. "For now I am part of the Shards, just because they can protect me until I am old enough to join the Neutrals. As soon as I look old enough, I will scratch this horrid skin marking from my arm with my own fingernails. For now I am the guardian of the children. Since you are new to the sector, you probably don't understand half of what I said." The man was in no way talking strident, but he obviously felt highly of his knowledge. "Each year, the great war occurs. I don't think they mean for it to happen like that, but it falls the same time every year. It gives them just enough time to train the next batch of warriors."

Rise looked over at the huddled children. "And those are your newest batches?"

The man heard the anger in Rise's voice. "No! They are a good three years from being fighting age. Do you think I would join a gang of monsters? No! The Crows, they use children of all ages!"

There was another large explosion and many screams.

Rise saw the children not even flinch at the noise. "They're very brave. Why are they not being protected by more than just you?"

"They were. It used to be 30 of us guardians. We were taking them by a secret way to the training grounds. All of our young are raised in the homestead and then brought out to the training grounds. Those who make it to be of age eventually recruit themselves to be a Neut."

"Where are the other 29 guardians?"

"They were taken by a party of Horbs. It was pure chance they happened to be on the same trail that day. There were arrows everywhere, but we stood and fought! What you see is what survived. The plan was to make our way along the wall of the sector until we arrived at the hidden training grounds."

Rise was curious. This man did not once speak of the sheriff or the skelguards. "What's the name of the sheriff here?"

"Ah, the demon of the Spring! His name is Ekheart. Him and his skelguards are not the threat this time of year. They hunt during all the other parts of the year. This, however, is the time of the gangs. I hardly see them around this time. The destruction is what they want anyway. They have their wish. This war is one of the most vicious I've seen."

Rise felt he knew enough. "I'll leave you to your task, guardian. I need to make my way to the compound."

"Stranger, do not go. I... I could use some help to get these kids to the... the training grounds. I noticed the sword at your side. You are a warrior. Please help us."

The Giver wanted to do nothing less, but, time was once again slapping him in the face. Beline and Bespin were out there somewhere.

"I must go, farewell guardian."

"Stranger! I want you to see something." The man pulled Rise by the back of his coat. He was desperate. "Korbe. Come here for a moment."

A small boy with tousled brown hair walked over. He was no more than ten years. His round face housed two almond eyes and a round nose. His small plump hands carried a crossbow awkwardly. It was the same innocence Beline held when she carried her weapon. He was silent, and walked with a straight back. "Stranger, this is Korbe. Tell him how old you are, Korbe."

"Nine years next week, sir."

97

Rise clenched his jaw.

"Korbe, what was your tally today?"

The boy's young voice was as steady as a man's while as pitched as a child's, "I killed four Horbs today, sir, two with bow, and two by strangling."

Rise noticed the small rope that hung at his side.

"When we were overtaken, not only the guardians fought. This young boy and a few brave others took up the weapons of the dead Horbs and fought with us. They would have been killed if they did not. The Horbs and Crows are especially horrible monsters. They will not hesitate to kill the children of the other gangs.

"Thank you, Korbe, go sit back down." The small boy carried his weapon back to where they huddled.

Rise felt the anger growing. Small children killing. The cowards in this sector used their own children! With a low, controlled voice Rise said, "You make me sick. How dare you recruit children!" Rise was reaching for his sword but saw the eyes of the group of kids. Those white helpless eyes were stuck on him. Whether he liked it or not, this man was the only hope for the children.

"Stranger, this sector must not make any sense to you, but it's the way things are. The sooner I get them to the training grounds, the sooner they can learn to really fight. Then they can protect themselves, they live longer, they're able to be a Neut, and then they live in peace as a Neutral and raise a family within the compound. Their whole lives depend on this journey! Please help us!" The man clasped Rise's two shoulders with steady hands.

Rise did not make his decision on the speech of the horrible man. He made it on how Beline would have decided; by the twenty pairs of helpless almond eyes and round noses.

Chapter Two:

The man that disgusted Rise pulled out a badly drawn map. Before Rise could look at it, he quickly sketched something off with a charcoal marker. "So much for the first plan." His eyes glanced around. "Here is where we are, and here is our destination, and this line is our path." It was a crude map of the entire sector and Rise took a brief moment to memorize the layout of the compound before turning his attention to the trail they must take.

Another explosion shook the earth. "What is that?" Rise

asked.

"Fighting, of course."

"How do they have so many magic weapons?"

The man thought about it for a while. "I'm not entirely sure. I know our ancestors in this sector found a huge supply of it, a few men skilled in the magic arts learned how to build them and replenish them. Today, we rely on what we have in stock. I suspect the reason we never run out is because of the sheriff, a true feeder of flames. He must get a sadistic thrill of death. He probably supplies it."

Rise pointed to the map. "Every 30 feet we will find shelter, and then in groups of three sneak the children into it. Proceed again until we make it all the way."

The children seemed to be looking at their guardian questionably. He saw this and said, "Remember, *quietness*." They seemed confused, but agreed by silently nodding their heads.

He turned his attention to Rise. "That will take too long. We must reach there before sunrise." He paused. "Because we will have no cover at day."

Rise thought about it. "All right. Every 100 feet. That should give us enough time."

The man smiled. "Move out!"

The children stood up straight like stakes. "March!" The children began moving towards the door. "You will obey master... uh, what was your name?"

He hesitated. "Rise."

"You will obey master Rise with the same devotion you give me."

Rise said, "You stay here with the children while I head for our first safe point."

Rise followed a trail between buildings and caught glimpses of a few scattered fights of the war. None were close enough to affect their journey, yet they were near enough for uneasiness. The fighters were really dependent on magic sticks. He had never seen so many warriors use them. People could kill from 100 steps away and not think twice of the life they took. Both sides used the honor-less weapons. There was no valor in this war.

Rise found a building that was ripped apart from the inside out, its framework sticking out like broken ribs. He waved to the group, and the children followed with the man last in line. Even if Rise did not agree with what they were doing, at least the man cared for them. He was quite protective of them and kept a vigilant eye for enemies.

They all huddled together, and Rise peeked around the corner to make sure of the safety.

A lone skelguard was patrolling the area. He was walking between two long buildings that they needed to pass. Rise pulled out the magic breaker and shot the skelguard without thinking. The gun made a funny noise as the creature dropped clumsily to the ground. Rise checked the back and saw that there were no longer any colored dots. He remembered what Bespin had said about its magic running low. The magic was gone and he discarded it.

"We're safe for now. Move."

The man smiled, "I knew our stranger would be of assistance. Impressive."

That was all the man said about his encounter of the skelguard. Most would have thought Rise was above human to possess such power, but this man was focused on something else in life, not fear of the skelguards. He struck Rise as strange and only added to how much he disliked him.

The whole night proceeded this way, and Rise's only comfort was that the man carried a water canteen, which Rise liberally drank from. The water was foul, but it was wet. His nerves were shot from the lack of alcohol in his system, and his hands were getting shaky, but the water did help a little.

Throughout the night Rise kept noticing a small girl with dirty blonde hair. She possessed emerald green eyes. Rise could not help seeing Beline's face in the small child's complexion. Rise forced himself to look away. He could not believe how much the small girl looked like a young Beline.

Two hours were left in the night by the time they made it to the last segment.

They turned east and were now a few hundred feet from the giant sector wall. The explosions were more distant now and only a few scattered commands from rogue leaders could be heard in the distance. They came to a ridge of concrete and grass.

The man said to Rise, "Just below that ridge is the building. I will take over from here, we do not need any... miscommunication."

"Very well."

"I will come to get you when it's safe. But, I must take the children."

Rise was hesitant for some reason to let them go. For a moment he feared he did not wish to release them because of his

100

sense of power as a leader. But it was something else. He just now took the time to look into the man's eyes. They were dark and vacant.

"March!" The man yelled and turned his face away. The children marched to a small wall of concrete slabs that overlooked a square building 200 feet down an embankment of rubble with posted guards. Rise could not make the guards out clearly, but he saw they all held magic sticks. At least the children would be well protected.

The man pulled out a cylinder and raised himself just enough to look over the wall down to the building. Then he held the cylinder to his eye. Rise remembered the telescope attached to his own grapnel.

The man smiled and placed the telescope in his pocket.

Rise grew uneasy.

The man whispered some command in a language that Rise did not know. The children pulled on a side of their clothing and blankets wrapped around from their sides. A hood from each plopped down, and they quickly placed them on. Rise saw that the cloaks blended in with the concrete masses. Even from a close distance, Rise was having trouble making them out.

"Now!" the man hissed. The children threw themselves over the wall, and the man did so as well. They vanished down the dirt hill.

"What?" Rise asked himself.

Rise pulled out his grapnel with the shoulder strapped still wrapped around him. He peered over the wall and looked through it at the guards of the training grounds. They were oblivious to the children coming. Rise did not think it wise to sneak up on their own people. A miscommunication like that could prove fatal...

Rise noticed a skin drawing on one of the guard's forearm. It was a marking of a black bird. A crow.

Rise looked down the hill with the scope and found that the children had made it halfway. They were hiding behind concrete slabs, blending in. They were preparing their weapons. It was then Rise remembered how they looked in the building, all sitting there with watchful eyes. They had reminded him of buzzards perched in a tree.

They were not on their way to the training grounds. They *were* the warriors.

Chapter Three:

Rise felt sickness wrap around him like a moldy blanket. The children, those innocent children, made the first shots. Three adult guards fell before the others realized the ambush. They did not hesitate to fire back. The small Korbe boy took an arrow to the arm. The force snapped his body back like a loose sail in a storm.

Rise fell to his knees behind the small concrete wall and vomited all the food he ate hours before. His stomach was scraped clean of any nourishment, and his mind squeezed dry of any tranquility. Only anger and absolute disgust were left.

He pulled himself back up to the short wall and peered down into the horrible valley. A quick estimate calculated 50 bodies, only a few were children. The remaining kids were placed all around the complex, two at each entrance, while the red bearded demon began throwing metal spheres through the glass windows. A cloud began to slowly emanate from the building. A yellow sand-cloud filled with glass shards erupted from the spheres in the buildings. The few men left in the complex began running out of the doors, coughing and holding their chests. The children killed them all as they exited.

Rise turned around and stared into the maze of ancient buildings that lay before him, putting his back to the atrocious, inhuman act. That behavior was what the sheriff would have wanted. Rise slowly slid his back down against the wall, his ears blurring the sounds of yelling behind him. He was ready to faint and did not notice his collapsed leg was in the middle of his pile of vomit. He sat there until his body seemed to lose itself. He forgot time and he could have been sitting there days for all he knew. He could see Beline's face, smiling. He saw Bespin's face, smiling. He saw the old man's face. It quickly disappeared and was replaced by a square jaw with a red patchy beard. There was no telling how long Rise was sitting there before the man appeared.

"Thank you my friend! We destroyed those dogs! I bet you wish you could fight as well as these children." He motioned his arm to the group of kids that survived. They surrounded Rise while he was in his trance-like state. They were all smiling. Not pretty childish smiles, but dangerous, inhuman grins. Some were bleeding. Korbe had an arrow shaft sticking out of him, and he cradled a broken arm. The nervousness of their eyes from before the battle was replaced by murderous, pleasure-seeking eyes. They enjoyed what they had just committed.

Rise hazily stood up. The loathing he felt was intense enough to melt any action he dare to take. He was so mad that he could not move. That monster was ready to sacrifice children for his own gain. Rise's mind went numb from searching for a word to describe such evil. There were no words for Rise to describe his anger in the old tongue, or the new.

"Oh, my friend. You have something on your pants. Allow me..." The man pulled a rag with red stains on it from under his shirt. He quickly wiped off the vomit from Rise's leg and threw the rag away.

"Thank you," Rise said numbly.

And then Rise hit him. Hard. A viper strike could not have matched the speed and ferocity. Rise felt his index and middle finger crack as they were sprained against the square jaw of the red bearded man. He felt the skin he struck expand against the teeth of the monster. As he followed in with his shoulder, he felt a few teeth of the beast snap and separate from its gums.

The children watched in horror as their master fell to the traitor. They did not let his body land before they drew their weapons. He heard bow strings bend, daggers slide from their sheaths, and the heavy breathing of blood thirsty little monsters. They held their stances. They would make no move without their guardian leader. Rise did not care. He almost preferred death at this point than the memories he just incurred.

He reached down and pulled the dazed man to his feet by the torn collar of his shirt. He held the red bearded monster's face three inches from his own. He stared into the beast's eyes and then spat in his face. "You make me sick." Rise spit the words out. He pushed the monster of man away from him.

Rise stared at the small heathens and felt disgust at what these children had become. He bit his lip but quickly released it. With a controlled pace Rise spoke to the little demons that glared at him with blood-hungry eyes. "The sector I come from is a beautiful place. Or at least it was. It was no better than most others, but it had one thing that you should all be envious of. We protected our children. Even if our wives never gave birth, we were all fathers. We were the eyes of birds as we watched our children of the sector. True, we often did not watch our fellow adults, but the children were priceless." As Rise spoke, he saw the bow strings return to their original tautness, the daggers lowered, and the eyes less murderous. They were not monsters anymore. "The children were gemstones to the poor, water for the thirsty, and a support for the weak, you beautiful creatures shine no matter how bleak. You beautiful creatures..." He caught himself looking at the blonde child. A tiny Beline. "You will never know what it's like to be a child. To run, to play, to forget the cares of the adults. Yes life is bad, but we all had childhood to look back and remember fondly. Except you. To have the cares of a child once again, to run and play and forget adult cares, because once you grow up, you have nothing but scares." He remembered those words from somewhere. It was the poem Beline wrote. "Should we lose you to the mystery of lifeless, the only thing we know is: gone is something priceless.

"This monster has robbed you of life's greatest gift to you. Innocence. I'm sorry my children."

The children were no longer demons. They were dirty children with a heavy burden. They were abandoned children with tears in their eyes. For the first time in their short lives, they heard the voice of someone who cared for them. They all dropped their weapons. They looked almost ready to cry as they stood dejected and abandoned. It was probably the first time in a long while they had time to feel remorse. They looked at each other, and then stared at Rise.

"No child should have to kill. No adult should cower enough to make his children fight." He pointed to the bearded man who lay on the ground. "That monster has stolen life's greatest gift from you. Please, remember this day, and do not repeat it."

He heard one of the children say, "Was that man daddy?"

Rise made himself disappear between the shadows of the buildings and never looked back. He heard the harsh voice of the red bearded man yelling at the children. He could not make out what was said. Then there was a scream followed by only wind. The red bearded monster was destroyed by what he created. Those were not children, those were small hardened warriors. They would return to their homes and go back to fighting. The lust had been placed in them at an all-too-young age.

As he walked through the sector, he did not notice which way was east or north. He did not care how close or far away the explosions and riots were.

He thought back to his speech he had made. "See Beline, I have more than one word answers."

104

Chapter Four:

His head hung low. He wore his adventurous spirit below his feet. Rise wandered aimlessly through the war scarred land. He found a torn building resembling a broken spine sticking out of the ground and decided to make it his temporary home. The building had been blown apart many years ago, no telling how long. Its supportive girders now looked like broken bones sticking through a concrete chest. Even the buildings in this sector looked like death. Rise found an especially dark corner and collapsed into it.

He made it to his new sanctuary without coming across any real battles. A couple of thieves tried to knife him on his way, but they ran when they saw the sword. Even in the middle of a sector-wide battle, the rodents still tried to rob and pillage.

Despite all the tragedy, a small, ever weakening part of him wanted to live.

Rise was almost invisible in the shadows, his black coat blended perfectly with the darkness. He was completely helpless. He knew no friends. No food. Barely a shelter. And he could not keep dodging battles forever.

The Giver sat for hours, listening only to his stomach growl and his dehydrated lungs heave. His body shook, but not from the cold. He needed alcohol. The hole in his stomach needed more than food.

He saw Beline's face shrink in size hundreds of times, as if the nightmare of the escape pod were painted onto the very air in front of him.

The sounds of two men struggling hand to hand snuck up on Rise. He turned to see two men fighting just outside his shelter. He was annoyed at the inconvenience. A large man wearing only tattered pants was fighting a very small man in a tan robe and cloak. At first, he felt sorry for the little man. His opponent dwarfed him by double his size in every direction. The large man seemed to have a cobweb of enormous veins that linked his entire body from the outside; a man bred for heavy lifting and killing. It was impressive, but Rise found himself fascinated by the small man's technique. It was entirely defensive. It was beyond defense. He never needed to block one blow, he never needed to brace for anything. He simply would not be hit.

Each gigantic forceful punch from the large one seemed to pick up the dust from the ground as he swung. The smaller one twisted, jumped, lunged, and turned perfectly each time. Neither was armed, and the battle turned so that the large man's back was facing Rise. He lunged at the small man. He turned just perfectly to avoid being snatched up and ripped apart by the giant.

From his angle Rise saw the brute slowly move his hand behind his lower back. Tucked away in the back pocket, Rise made out the shape of a knife.

The brute lunged with a speed that would defy a blink, but with the same result. The little man twirled in a whirlwind of tan robe, and the big man seemed to float through him. He missed and fell to the ground. He pushed himself back to his feet and began to corner the small one into the building. Rise watched the battle with indifference. His vision was glazed with depression. Despite his admiration for the small one, he did not care who won. It was another needless battle in this sector.

The large man swung his knife many times, and some blows seemed to pass straight through the small man like air. The brute began screaming and spitting as sweat poured off his huge body.

Despite how close they were to him, they did not spy Rise in his dark corner. He saw them get closer, inches away from him, and still he did not move from his kneeling position.

Just when it seemed the large man lost all his energy, he managed the impossible. He somehow managed to grab the small man by the neck. He raised the man four feet off the ground. His arms were such that the short man would not have been able to reach across and hit the brute even if he were trying. He never made an offensive strike. As the brute raised his knife with the other hand to finish off the menace, he took a step back. He tripped over Rise and as he fell back the small man flipped out of his grasp.

The thug blinked his eyes angrily at the strange bump in the shadow. Rise saw the exact instance he was noticed, and three veins in the man's head seemed close to exploding. Rise knew the big man would stab him. He knew this was the end. That was the moment he knew he lost all hope. He would not avoid it. It was time to embrace death. He closed his eyes and stood up, spreading his arms outward, waiting for the sweet cool blade to pierce his chest.

"You're slumped, old man." The voice was deep and soothing. It was the voice of the person who would bring him to Beline.

He smiled.

Chapter Five:

Rise waited for the sweet cool metal to pass through his heart. It never came. He opened his eyes in time to see the short man kick the knife from the giant's hand and as soon as his foot landed the other came up and across the side of the big man's head. The small man could not have weighed more than 120 pounds, but it was as if the giant was struck by a concrete slab. The dust from the small one's foot exploded into a cloud as he struck down the giant.

The giant fell and landed limp as empty clothes but heavy like a boulder. It was the single most impressive fighting technique Rise ever witnessed.

The short man quickly turned to keep his back from being exposed to Rise, a habit that was formed by years of living in the sector. The man's eyes were strange, they seemed more square than others he had seen, almost as if they had been slit with a knife around the corners. The short man had black hair and a mustache that he grew only on the sides of his lips. They dangled like strings below his chin. The hair was just beginning to whiten on a few patches and he was clearly a decade older than Rise.

He just stared at Rise, his square eyes almost looking through him.

Rise slowly bent down and picked up the knife. The short man raised an eyebrow, waiting for what the next action would bring. Rise extended the knife handle first. "Kill me."

The man tilted his head slightly to the side. "Why would you ask such a thing?" The man's voice was deep with an accent Rise could not place.

Rise once again saw Beline's face, this time she was smiling. He saw Bespin's face, this time he was smiling. He saw the old man's face, this time he was smiling. "My life is over."

"I doubt that. You... are younger than your hair portrayed you. Very strange." The man snatched the knife from Rise's hand and threw it into the shadows. "Besides, the war will be over tomorrow. Things will look different, I promise you that. A good night sleep is all you need.

"I am Chuce, a healer." He pulled out a flask of water. "Here, drink as much as you like."

Despite his thirst Rise found .himself wishing it was alcohol. As soon as the first wetness touched his tongue, he knew the flask would be drained. His thirst was quenched, but his body still shook from his withdrawals. He handed it back to Chuce and wiped his lips with his sleeve. He heard the stubble on his face begin to scratch the leather.

"Already the explosions have started to ease. It will be morning in a few hours." Chuce placed a hand on Rise's shoulder. Rise reluctantly began to follow him. "Come with me. I doubt I'll find another alive this close to the end of the war."

They walked out of the gutted building and into the rubble filled streets. There were still bursts of screaming and explosions, but it seemed to be slowing down. "They're using the last of the magic they received from the sheriff. It will all be well shortly."

They walked through an open square that had recently been home to a battle. He saw the remains of both Shards and Crows. Bodies were mangled and even in the twilight the blood was appallingly visible. At least 200 died in this battle. Rise found it hard to cross while Chuce did not hesitate. "Surely this is not the first battle scar you have seen?"

"No... but it's the first war scar I've seen."

"Ah, you must have hid all your life."

"I'm not from this sector."

Chuce nodded. "You are somewhat conversational for a person who claims his life is over."

"You're probably the first person to say I'm conversational."

Chuce chuckled. As they passed a building Rise saw an enormous monument. It seemed made of wood and concrete. A huge tower stood in front of him. Never before had Rise seen such a tall standing building. It was just a little shorter than the walls of the sector itself. He recognized the tower from his descent. Chuce was leading him to it.

"That is the compound. It's the only safe place during wartime."

The ground shook as a battle erupted nearby. Several people ran from behind a building as it collapsed in the distance. Rise heard screaming from behind him. Not a scream of pain, but of a lust for blood. He turned and saw a wild man with many scratches and bruises running at him. He seemed to have emerged from the rubble itself, as if the evil in the sector spawned him out of metal and dust.

Chuce said, "It's amazing. They don't care who they kill. The spilled blood has made them go mad."

Rise saw more people like the mad man. They wore no

gang tattoos, yet they were just as crazy. Fortunately, a few met in battle and distracted the one that spotted Rise and Chuce.

Within seconds the very place they were standing was home to another battle. Fifty people seemed to have crawled from the spaces between fractured concrete and the rubble floor. They scurried like rodents from cracks and holes. A riot was breaking out, and they were caught in the middle.

"I know you say you have no reason to live, but please, give it one day. Survive this night and perhaps we can help each other."

Rise was still depressed, but trusted this man. He braced himself by pulling out his sword. A few people tried to engage him as they made their way slowly through the riot. Rocks were being thrown along with shards of glass. A few crude weapons were swung rather close to Rise. He deflected them, and pushed the attackers back into the mob where they were engulfed. His fingers were extremely sore but he fought on.

Chuce, however, seemed to move like a shadow through the crowd. Nothing would touch him. He would sidestep or bend his neck at just the right moments to avoid being blindsided or accidentally struck by a blood-thirster.

There was an explosion somewhere off to the right. A magic sphere was thrown into the midst of the crowd and the bodies spilled to the ground limply.

Finally, they made it through the thick of the fight. They slowly began to climb the side of a collapsed building that fell at an angle to create a ramp. It led up the natural hill landscape the ancient city was built on. They watched their step as they dodged broken windows below their feet. They reached the top, and Rise saw they were a few minutes journey to the compound. It had many windows for very tight security.

Rise turned around and saw the very place they had been standing was completely engulfed in war. It was no mere riot. Hundreds now flocked to this new place looking to satisfy their blood craving.

Within a few seconds Rise saw 300 people die, and still the flood of fools continued.

Chuce shook his head. "After the gangs kill themselves off, many of the common people begin to fight each other. War does strange things to people. Don't worry. You'll be safe at the compound. I have no idea what this must look like from a stranger's perspective."

"Am I old enough to enter the compound?"

Chuce laughed. "Old enough? What are you talking about?"

"Don't you have to be a certain age to enter it?"

"What fool told you that?"

Rise gritted his teeth. "A red monster."

"I do not know of any red monsters. Just fools and followers. We welcome any that come, no matter how old they are. Mothers often bring children to live here while they return to their husbands in the gangs. Some people would rather fight and live in hate. The choice is theirs to make."

They walked on towards the compound. A few scattered gang members were still wandering the area. The black smoke of war seemed everywhere, blinding the gangs from finding their remaining victims. Rise and Chuce encountered no further disturbances all the way to the massive base of the compound.

There was a giant gate made of wood and concrete at the base. It was a sliver compared to the large base of the compound. The tower seemed to sprawl upward with just as much impressiveness.

At the sides of the gate stood two miniature towers, 30 feet in the air. Two men sat in each one. Each tower was equipped with the biggest set of magic sticks Rise ever saw. The barrel of each could fit him inside, and the length was no less than eight feet. Chuce caught him staring at them as they made their way to the front.

"I swear to you we are peaceful. But, even the peaceful need assurance. They will not kill you."

"Death would only relieve my pain," Rise muttered.

"At least you're remaining positive."

A loud booming voice echoed from the tower as a black guard spoke to them, "Identify!"

"Chuce and... a guest," Chuce echoed back.

The loud voice yelled, "Kill them!"

There was a pause. Then laughter. The man from the tower yelled, "It's no fun when you bring back ones that aren't afraid to die, Chuce. I thought your job was to find the motivated ones?"

Chuce laughed, "Be silent and open the door."

The man complied, and the gate was lowered on two huge chain mechanisms.

"Enter! If you dare!" The black man in the tower ended the sentence with a mock laugh.

"You know," Chuce yelled, "that's the reason we don't

have more company."

"Shut your mouth, little one. And don't think I forgot you owe me a drink!"

Rise quietly asked him, "Is he speaking of an alcoholic drink?"

Chuce laughed and showed Rise the interior to the compound. A massive wood stairway spiraled upwards to the top. Many floors could be seen extending from the stairs. "Fifty floors, many of which are below the ground level, and 3,000 inhabitants. Well..." He looked at Rise. "Now we have 3,001. The food is not bad, if you like roots that is. Underneath, I will have you know, is the sector's largest root farm. It is my honor to give you a complete tour of the compound." He ended the speech with a smile.

Rise still maintained a grave expression.

"Don't worry, before long I will have you convinced that your life is not over."

"You have one day." Rise stated it very plainly with no anger or distrust in his voice.

"Well, we better get started then. I think you need a drink."

Chapter Six:

It seemed difficult for Rise to imagine this huge building as the sector's living space. People were constantly moving back and forth between small tented shacks built along the walls. These cubicles maintained a bartering system more complex than any Rise had seen. At one moment a commodity would be near priceless, the next it would be as worthless as dirt. The whole bottom floor seemed to be a huge space built only for bartering. People would trade items from one stand and then rush to the next.

"This is our buying and selling floor." Chuce pulled at his mustache as he spoke. "This whole place is based on an image we found incased in glass. The founder thought it was some sort of enlightenment from the past. Let me show you."

Chuce led him across the crowded floor of hurried people. Rise quickly noticed that the clothing in this building was different... it looked... unused. People were wearing these fine garments and selling them. New clothing was hard to come by. The only time he ever obtained a piece of clothing never before used was when his mother made him a tiny jacket. Materials were just too hard to come by. Everyone in this place wore garments that would have made a sheriff envious.

They found a large concrete stand right by the enormous stairwell. The stairwell spiraled upward with cross beams making walkways to the other floors. It reminded Rise of looking upward at a gnarled tree. The concrete slab was intact, and the picture was well maintained. It stood ten feet square and seemed to have been painted. The artist must have had unlimited colors to work with. The painting showed a large crowd with many pouches that they carried by a strap slung over their shoulders; shiny pouches made from a material he did not recognize. It reminded him of a building found in the ruins, at least what it should have looked like before it became a memory. The people were going to different stands. Some were buying clothes, others had food. Rise turned and realized the people were behaving just like the giant image. He was seeing the same thing, only not as glamorous. The people here were trying to live a thriving life like the picture. It still could not compare. Well structured selling booths, like the ones in the picture, were long gone.

"Below us are the working chambers. When a child is born, it's decided where he will work. Some working chambers prepare roots that we grow underground. Others make clothing. Hundreds of different items are constructed down there. Then, they are brought up here to be traded. Amazing what an ancient painting can inspire."

Rise was curious that through all this time Chuce never asked for his name. He was pleased, but simultaneously confused.

Chuce, noticing the pause added, "See, already I would bet your impression of this sector is improving."

Rise shrugged. "It will take more than clothes and roots to change my impression. The death outside those gates is too great."

"Perhaps you would like a new jacket? That one looks tattered... a new pouch, one that fits on your back? You seem to be carrying a lot of tools. Perhaps there is nothing here that can interest you." Chuce chuckled, "Perhaps your life is over."

"Do you have alcohol?"

"Ah! Of course. You need a drink after your journey. And food. And rest! Of course! The basic necessities!"

Rise looked backwards to the huge doors. In this building he could not hear the screams. He could not see the bloodshed. These people were hiding. He shivered.

Chuce led him through the crowd to a stand with a wide array of colored bottles, each containing an alcoholic beverage.

The man in charge looked up with expectant eyes as Chuce drew close. "Chuce! You found one!" The man was cleaning a glass drinking container and pointed with his rag at Rise.

"Yes, I found one lost soul. He comes in pretty handy when he hides in the shadows."

"How so?"

"Never mind. A story for later. Our guest needs a drink."

The man poured Rise a drink out of a complicated glass vase. Rise drank the whole glass.

Chuce seemed a little surprised. "Wow, we have an expert."

The man looked at Chuce. Chuce nodded and the man gave him another.

This time Rise drank it slower, allowing him time to see his eyes in the reflection of the liquid. It was not his eyes looking back. It was Beline's.

He drank it slowly.

The liquid soothed him. Even though he needed more to feel a real effect, his nerves seemed to settle just from the thought of the contents flowing through his blood.

"Come, enough with the drink. You need food. I'm sure you have seen some horrible things in this sector. But forget those. You are safe here."

Rise silently obeyed, wishing the alcohol had more of an effect. It did however settle his nerves and headache, and dulled the pain of his fingers. Maybe the pain was more in his head.

Chuce led him back to the stairwell and they began their ascent. Hundreds of people walked by just within a few minutes of climbing. The stairs were made of wood planks, and the stairwell itself was 50 feet wide. It seemed to go on forever. Rise did not know that man could make such things in this current time. As they passed each floor, he noticed a red painted number was etched on the side of a plank. The ground level was marked 21 and Rise remembered Chuce saying that many floors were below the ground. They made their way up a few floors.

The 24th floor was surrounded by a fence. It was filled with children. The floor contained young ones that were still being carried by their mothers, and others just about to enter adolescence.

"This is our nursery. Our children are watched by many gracious eyes."

Rise saw some adults in blue clothing supplying food

and entertainment. Many rooms were created along the walls. Some of the children were sleeping. A whole floor filled with the future. The enormous building contained something truly important after all. At least amid the materialism, they still knew what really mattered.

Rise shook his head as he remembered the children he first encountered. They were war battered, murderous, hideous demons. Just four walls away were children that had the life they deserved.

"Friend, you have a solemn look. Does the end of your life have something to do with children?"

Rise sighed. "You have monsters in this sector capable of misleading beautiful young children and mutilating them into beasts."

"I am aware of that. The first time I saw a gang use children to fight I cried for days. But, our children are safe here."

"What about sheriffs? Skelguards? These walls can't keep them safe from the King's magic." Rise spoke those words with a little bit of trouble. So far he survived the powers of the Dark King, yet he still knew he was going to die for it. He did not want to bring the curse to this place.

"The skeleton warriors and the sheriff stay away from this place. It's part of the agreement." Chuce went silent.

They continued up the stairs.

"What agreement?"

Chuce seemed embarrassed. "The sheriff says that he will leave this place intact and harm no one... if once a year we release 300 grown men and women into his custody. He arrests them, and the rest are free to live here. Part of my job as a healer is to find people to replace the ones we lose by finding those in the sectors who wish for peace."

Rise stopped walking. "You made a deal with the worst monster of them all."

"No! Friend, no! If you only knew. Everyone who stays here puts his name on a wood plank. Every year, 300 are selected out of 3,000. The 300 are probably taken to the palace."

"You're deceiving yourself! The King is probably tying them up with stones and drowning them!" Rise was starting to get angry.

"No, that can't be. The sheriff supplies us with... materials and seeds for our gardens. He encourages us to become good at our trades. It's my belief that they are slaves in the palace. The King surely needs people to make things for him."

Rise was almost satisfied with that answer. "What happens if a person chooses not to stay, and not have their name on a plank?"

Chuce looked at him suspiciously. "That has never happened. But, you are a strange one. You are very shrewd. Too shrewd. Normally by now I have the new ones into a nice bed resting. They wake up and that's when I tell them they must get a job here and work. A day after that I tell them about the plank, but by then they are too absorbed in this wonderful life. They forget all about leaving. You are the first person who has asked for our secrets before even making it to his resting room."

Rise trusted this man. He felt no deception in his voice. "Why are you telling me the truth? You could have made up lies and tried to get me addicted to this life."

"A healer never lies. A healer only... heals. As you meet the rest of us, you will learn our code."

"Chuce, what if I decide not to stay?"

He laughed as they passed floor 35. "Why would you not stay?"

"I told you, my life is over. Nothing this place can give me is worth my time here."

"Tell me your name. You have avoided that long enough."

"Rise."

"Very remarkable name. It has a connotation of becoming better than what you think you can become. A truly hard name to live up to. Tell me, Rise, what is so far beyond you that you can't rise any further?"

After a long pause, very quietly, almost in a sob, he blurted, "Beline."

"My friend, Rise. You're not the first one here to lose a love. Give it a few days. We cannot replace her, but we can give you a life. Stay here, work, eat, live."

"Live. Eat. Work. And gamble your life to the King, cursed be his name. I can't stay. I must find a way to end my life. If the sheriff won't take it..."

Chuce looked confused, but interrupted anyway, "You said I had one day. Get some sleep and tomorrow you can end your life."

Chapter Seven:

Rise was led to the 41st floor and showed an empty room. Inside was a bed and a wash pan. The wooden floor creaked while he walked over to the window. It was amazing to look out. He had never been on a structure so high, other than the wall of the sector itself.

He could see more of the sector than he wished. Every now and again, a few lights would spark somewhere in the allies of destruction. A few fights would still break out, but it was obviously slowing down; too many corpses to fight.

Rise shook his head. Meaningless destruction. The sort of disease Beline would give every part of her body and soul to defend against. And that sweet creature was now in the clutches of the King. He had to distract his mind. He promised Chuce one day.

Slowly, he took off his jacket. He placed all the things he carried on the bed. He was still carrying the grapnel and book. He still had the horrible pig hat and his trusted sword. He found the ear piece and listened to it. With all his heart he hoped to hear Bespin's voice; nothing but silence. He put it back on the bed. It had been a long journey. He could not even remember if that was all he carried. And then he felt the necklace around his neck. The green one. Beline's. He delicately placed it on the bed.

His nose espied a familiar smell. It was a sweet smell. He turned to a small table; the only other object in the barren room. It had a surprisingly clean silver bowl with a lid. Removing the lid he found freshly baked bread and a canister of wine. He ate the bread ravenously and took the canister within two large gulps. Not even enough wine to lull him to sleep.

All the rooms on the floor were along the walls of the tower, surrounding the stairwell. The floor stretched out from the four walls until the catwalks to the stairwell met them like fingers. It was no wonder the nursery was roped off. He wondered how many fools in the past had fallen off.

The door was a mere sheep skin blanket nailed against the two upper corners of the door frame. The bottom did not quite reach, and Rise depressingly entertained himself by watching the shadows of people walking by. He heard fragments of many vain conversations. Many laughs. The sounds of death and the cold weather from the window made an odd amalgamation with the laughter. These people were delusional. The sector they loved was under attack, and yet they entertained themselves with their riches.

He remembered his sector. He missed the relative peace before it was destroyed by the sheriff.

Rise now turned his back to the door and walked to the window. His sullen face was a mocking reflection. Somewhere, in the shadows, in the darkest depths of the broken buildings, the King's will was after him. He killed a sheriff, and he should have died for it. He survived that elite monster. He should have died from that. He escaped a gang attack, and killed many skelguards. The King's will for him was death. He was certain he would die. It was just a matter of when the will of the King would finally reach him and slowly place its destined fingers around his neck.

It was the King after all, who enslaved the world. It was that wretched monster that wielded more than magic, the same who erected the sectors and imprisoned humanity. It was that immortal beast that few had ever seen, and he maintained a dark purpose for the world. Rise defied that all powerful monster. In some small way, Rise felt he was the first to defy the King like this. And for that he would die.

Beline was as good as dead. The magic barrier would surely have worn off by now. Bespin, bless his heart, was soon to be a lifeless corpse next to her.

Rise fell onto the bed amid his only possessions, and for the first time in days, fell asleep on a full stomach but an empty heart.

He awoke to a knock on the wall. He rose lazily and noticed the sun shining through the window. Chuce pushed aside the sheepskin and walked in.

"What a wonderful morning. The dark clouds are gone quite early."

Rise grumpily sat up. He knew he had dreamed of Beline, but his memory of it was gone.

The Giver stared at the healer. "Your day is almost up, Chuce."

"Rise, my friend, you are too eager to die. Your life is precious, and I will show you just how precious. This is the morning of rebirth. Come and see for yourself. The children have already spread the flowers of the new year."

Rise grabbed his coat and possessions. He would not leave them out of his sight. He felt safer with them against his body, especially the necklace.

117

The tower was empty. The crowd was gone. They made it to the bottom of the stairwell and exited the tower through the large gate. The gate guardians were still on their post.

"Chuce!" The black man yelled. "About time you woke up!"

Chuce dismissed him with a friendly wave.

Rise saw a mob of people surrounding the tower. It was the residents, all 3,000 of them. For the first time Rise saw many people wearing the same robes as Chuce. "Those are the other healers. You may accompany me. They won't mind."

The crowd was cheering the healers as they walked through. A good 200 healers were encircling the tower. They began their walk.

Rise noticed people in black cloaks following the healers. They each pulled wagons bearing an imprint of a flower on the sides. In the wagons were piled pieces of wood.

Rise saw many dead bodies in the ruins. Many bloody battles were fought for nothing. Yet, the blood was hidden. The bodies and the blood were covered with white flower petals. "This is the work of the children. Early in the morning, just as the sun comes out, we send them to flower the dead. We healers look for survivors, and the peace makers collect their bodies, and burn them. We start afresh while the gangs wait for their next batch of warriors to grow. It is a sad cycle, but this is the joyous time of rebirth. The war is over.

"We will make our way towards the wall for six miles. Don't worry about the sheriff or the skelguards. They will not interfere with this sector until tomorrow."

Rise felt cold and placed the floppy pig hat on his head. It helped some.

His friend smirked at the headpiece, but said nothing.

Rise followed Chuce as they walked the bloody ruins. Once a wagon came across a body, the wood was used to start a small fire and burn the corpse.

Rise saw someone up against a slab of concrete. He was injured, and just barely alive. It was the first time Rise did not feel like The Giver when he saw someone's pain. There was an emptiness for the person and his agony.

"Over there!" Chuce said, finally noticing the man.

Rise was shocked that he carried no desire to help. His depression seemed to overwhelm his sense of humanity.

Chuce ran to the man and took out a water container

from his robe. He made him drink.

Rise began to examine the injuries and forced himself to help.

He was no older than a young man.

Chuce examined him and looked up to Rise. "This is the work one of the magic rounds. If you ever see one of them rolling at you, get away as fast as possible. In my opinion, it's the worst way to die. Your body is ripped apart in giant sections, and you die watching what used to be your limbs smoke from the heat. He's lucky a hole isn't where his chest is."

The young man struggled to breathe and never opened his eyes. He gasped through parched lips, "I heard children giggling."

The healer pointed to the flower petals on his body. The children apparently thought the man was dead.

Chuce whispered to Rise, "This is strange. It's been a long time since I have seen a survivor of the war myself. I've heard of others finding them, but this is a rare event. You should be happy."

"Yes. I suppose I should be."

Chuce applied some herbs to the burns and forced the man to open his eyes. They were brown.

"The war is over. Make your way home." The man stumbled as he tried to stand up.

Chuce turned and did not look back. Rise followed, but looked back at the poor man.

"Rise, don't think it heartless. He's beyond more help. He will die before the night. It's best we look for more survivors."

"Why look if you don't help them?"

Chuce stopped and looked indignantly at Rise. "I did help him. We helped him. We gave him more life than he would have had without us."

The rest of the morning continued the same. They finally made it back to the tower half an hour before nightfall.

"Why didn't we enter all the buildings?" Rise asked.

"Because those were gang territories. They need no help. We look for the mostly innocent people. The gangs will not bother anyone for at least a week. Their leaders are dead and once again no one came out with an advantage. It's strange though... we didn't find as many bodies as normal. Almost as if the gangs are realizing this is a waste."

Rise found it disturbing to his soul that it could have been a bloodier war.

Chuce led Rise inside the tower where everyone was back to work. The crowd was bustling and trading goods. The root farmers were back in their underground caverns. Chuce decided to take Rise back to floor 24. The nursery.

Chuce opened the small gate and led Rise through the playing children. He introduced Rise to a few men in blue coats. Rise could not remember their names.

"Well Rise, I have nothing left to show you. Please stay in the nursery before you decide to end your life. Maybe the hope of work, survivors, and peacetime will not bring back your spirit, but perhaps the future will. I'll return when the time is up."

Chuce left and Rise picked his way gently through the mob of kids. He made it to the protective railing and leaned over it, looking downward beyond the staircase. He let out a long sigh, wishing he could just end his life. He felt if he could end his life he would be closer to Beline. He did not know it, but he felt it.

The rope he was leaning on shook slightly. He turned his head and saw an eight-year old girl playing with the rope railing. She discovered a hole in it that just might be big enough for her to wiggle through and play on the forbidden part of the catwalk. He looked around for a blue coat but found none close enough.

He walked over to the curious girl and gently pulled her back.

"No, darling. It's a long drop."

She looked up at him. She carried a tattered cloth with burns on it.

"My name is Emily," she smiled. "Where is your blue coat?"

"I don't have one, Emily." Rise bent down and found the problem with the railing. A rope had come loose from its knot, and he quickly tied it back to safety.

"That is a pretty necklace," she said, squeezing her tiny blanket.

"Thank you. But it's not mine."

"Why are you sad?"

Rise was taken aback. This small precious child had more insight in her than many wise men. Unfortunately, that meant she had probably been through a lot for her short life.

"I like your hat."

Rise bent his head low and smiled. He forgot it was still on his head.

Emily saw Rise's pause and decided to ask him a

simpler question. "Can I wear your hat?"

Rise placed the hat on her head.

"Why is your hair white?"

Rise smiled, just a little. "Because it makes me look old and wise."

"Oh. You must be really old if you have white hair."

"I'm getting there. Why were you hanging so close to the edge of the ropes, Emily?"

"I wanted to fly. I saw a bird outside my window do it one time. I don't see many birds. Why were you so close to the edge?" As she swung her arms outward like wings he noticed a slight burn on her forearm. It looked a few years old.

Rise sat down on the floor and picked up Emily and placed her on his lap. "Because I was very sad."

"Oh," she said. She looked down at her cloth. "You can have this if you want. It makes me feel better. It used to be my mommy's before I came here."

Rise recognized the burn marks from a skelguard's staff.

"No, darling... you keep it. I'm happier now."

"Okay, but you can have your hat back."

She placed it gently on his head.

Rise saw all of Beline's kindness in that little girl. He saw her pure love, her untouched kindness, and her unwavering sweetness.

"Emily, you remind me of a friend. The friend this necklace belongs to. She was a very sweet woman."

"Where is she?"

Rise bit his lower lip and then pushed it out. "She was... taken away from me."

"Oh, like mommy."

"Yes. Like mommy."

Emily was quiet and tugged at her cloth for a while. Then she spoke in the sweetest voice Rise could comprehend, "Well, if you are sad your friend is gone, you can be my friend. And then you will be happy again."

"Emily... thank you. You are a beautiful girl. Now, why don't you go play with your friends?"

"Okay." She got up and ran to her little friends. They were dancing in a circle singing a song they only knew the small words to.

"Beline, you would have loved to see this place. This could have been our home." He clenched his eyes shut. He no longer wanted to die, yet he no longer wanted to live without Beline. He wanted her with him. They could help raise the children in the nursery. What better life could he have than helping the future grow up?

Then Rise saw it. A uniform he recognized. It was the colorful uniform of a news gatherer. Rise ran and jumped the railing onto the catwalks after the man.

Chapter Eight:

The youthful face had prodded the coals inside Rise back into a burning flame within him. If he were truly to contemplate the end of his life tonight, he might as well learn as much as he can beforehand. Too many people spoke of rebellion. It was no coincidence. Thoughts of his own murder were put back in their place by desperation for Beline's life. He still had hope buried deep in his soul, and his heart was pounding to the new rhythm.

He ran to the stairs after the man in the colorful uniform. "You there! News gatherer! I know your friend from Sector 2131!"

The man stopped briefly, looked at Rise, and continued his ascent up the immense stairs. "Talk faster stranger. I have urgent news to bring to the meeting."

Rise trailed slightly and noticed the man's pants were ripped at the knees. He saw the enormous calves the man possessed; he traveled the stairs repeatedly. He found it hard to keep up.

The news gatherer was a bald man, short and gallant. He carried a folded cloth that appeared to contain documents.

"Do you speak of rebellion against the Dark Lord?" Rise huffed. They climbed two levels rather quickly.

"Not in the open such as this."

"Where then?"

"None of your concern."

Rise grew impatient. He suddenly felt Beline's presence hanging by a thin grip. "You will answer me, news gatherer."

"I will not, you arrogant scat! Leave me be! I have to make it to the meeting."

At level 49 the stair apexed into a four by four foot slab of concrete stairs. They reached the top of the tower. The news gatherer pulled out a key and opened a hidden compartment. A round lever was just barely visible. The news gatherer pulled it, and a trapdoor sprang open and a rope ladder dropped down.

"Peasants are not allowed beyond this point!"

The news gatherer slammed the chamber for the hidden latch and climbed up the ladder. The trapdoor closed quickly after the ladder was pulled up. Rise felt the cold air pass over him from the door.

Rise ran down one floor to level 48, his legs aching from the climb. He ran across the catwalk and pushed his way through crowds of people. Rise rushed into a room that was built along the wall of the tower and found a room like his, except with a young couple enjoying a meal.

"Excuse me," he panted.

He removed the grapnel and busted the window through with the end of it. The couple stood up afraid and offended. Rise leaned outward and fired the wall-climber. The tip ripped into the tower wall a few inches from the ledge and Rise jumped out. The lady gasped as his body disappeared out the window.

It was a long drop, and the cold wind took him by surprise, like a plunge in an overly cold lake. He swung wildly and felt sick as he looked downward onto the entire sector. The tower went straight down for what seemed like miles to Rise. Shaking his head, he refocused on the roof. The young couple peeked their heads outside and watched Rise.

He ascended slowly to the top. Rise propped his feet and put his hands over the top ledge. He pulled his body up and soon found himself peering upon the large roof of the tower. His fingers found a sizable slit that ran along the entire top ledge of the roof. It was the news gatherer's meeting. Despite the wind and chill, they remained on the roof.

The wind was scraping against the building so they did not hear him climb over. Most of the crowd kept their backs to him anyway, as they were all encircled around a point in the middle. The crowd was 300 strong and very intent.

Rise pulled his grapnel up and back under his jacket. He made sure his trusty pig hat was nice and tight on his head, and began walking towards the crowd. They remained silent, no one spoke.

Then he heard a muffled voice carried in pieces in every direction the wind would take it. It sounded like an order. Out of the slit in the ledge, a rumbling noise was heard. Rise halted. A thin metal sheet was being pushed upward by some hidden gears. The canopy rose along the entire parameter of the roof. The extra shielding created a quiet atmosphere and protected them from the wind.

A discernible voice then echoed off the metal walls with surprising clarity, "The meeting will now begin!"

Before the voice finished several others began to yell, "What about the siege?!" Others yelled, "Tell us about the sheriff!"

The podium master was still unseen to Rise, but his tone of voice seemed to denote he expected them to interrupt him. "I have reviewed most of your testimonials. A few are late arrivals, but if a late one wishes to speak of something very important, let us hear it now."

There was a pause. "Very well," the voice continued. "There are three matters that are of high concern in our area of the sectors. First off, the attacks the King has been making on specific sectors. Second, the rumors of a murdered sheriff. Lastly, the attack of this sector and the siege of this very tower."

Rise felt his moment in the brief silence and yelled to the unseen voice encircled by the crowd, "What of the rebellion?!"

A few heads turned curiously and saw him. They began to murmur and point. Soon Rise had the attention of 600 eyes. There were murmurs of, "A peasant? Here? Commoner?"

A very old man made his way through the crowd. He wore a very long white beard which contrasted his dark skin and stood erect with a cane. His left hand held a gold ring for every finger. He wore the same uniform as the others, but it was not quite as tight. He slowly parted the crowd with his powers of respect.

"How did you get up here, peasan... stranger?" It was the same deep voice he heard echoing, yet quieter now, more personal.

"No matter. Tell me of the rebellion against the King! I must know how to reach it!"

The man narrowed his eyes. "We news gatherers hardly fight, but we do kill spies. An animal like you suits to be the King's pet. Sneaking around, spying..."

Rise took great offense at being called the King's pet. That Dark Lord had Beline imprisoned somewhere or perhaps even murdered her. Her sweet voice could already have been silenced from this world, and this old man dare say Rise was a slave-animal for that monster?

Rise pulled the hat from his head and slapped the old man across the face with it. The entire group flinched. The man did not look angry. He held his arms up and signaled them to be calm.

He stared in amazement at Rise.

Rise looked around confused as the anger slowly dissipated from his body.

Many in the crowd seemed bewildered by their leader's refusal to let them exact punishment. And then they saw it too.

Rise pieced the last of it together. They were staring at his hair. The second issue they had to discuss, the murdered sheriff. They were referring to Morceff.

Chapter Nine:

Even the old man was speechless. The failing light outside cast strange shadows over his face as the swirling clouds began to come from the north.

Someone came pushing through the crowd, "Excuse me, let me through please. My white haired friend! So good to see you still alive!"

Rise saw the first news gatherer he met on his journey. The young news gatherer with black hair pushed his way to the front. His face was gristlier with stubble, evidence that he had been in a hurry to make it to the meeting. "This is the one I sent the report to you about! This man killed Morceff!"

The man wanted to continue speaking to the 300 others, but Rise interrupted and spoke directly to the older news gatherer, "How do I find the rebellion? My friends were arrested, and they need my help."

As if the crowd were thinking the same thing, all except his friendly news gatherer scoffed at him. He realized how strange he must have sounded, but he wanted to skip beyond the more tedious explanations. His friends could still be alive.

The old one spoke, "Of course your friends were arrested. Name one person, in all the years of this wicked world, that has not lost a few friends to the King? Eh? Name one, PEASANT!"

"You use that word like you're the King himself, old man!" Rise narrowed his eyes and clenched his fist.

"The rebellion is a lost cause! Every man or child capable of thought knows that!"

Ever since Rise first heard of the rebellion, he never took the time to think it could be a waste. It hurt his enthusiasm for it.

"You're standing in the way of my friends, and it's

125

unwise of you to do so." His teeth were clenched tight enough to snap.

"Your friends are dead! Anyone arrested is either dead or serves the King and is as good as dead! Give it up stranger and leave us! We have more important things to discuss than your hopeless causes!"

It took all of Rise's inner strength not to strike the man. It would only make things worse.

The old man was an expert debater and saw the pause in Rise's speech. "You need to leave now before you make a fool of yourself. You will not find your friends. They are dead. Move on with your life, like everyone else in this forsaken land."

Rise felt depression slithering up like a suffocating snake. The old man talked as if he knew Rise's friends were dead for a fact. He seemed to know far more than Rise could ever hope to.

The man was satisfied with the longer pause and spoke, "You should leave now."

His friendly news gatherer spoke up, "No! Master, this man can fight. If the rumored attack is true, we need everyone we can find to defend the tower."

"Don't give this peasant more knowledge than he needs! Silence!"

Rise hated being called a peasant by another man who lived in a sector. Only the King and other royalty like the sheriffs used that disdainful word.

"Master, please." The friendly news gatherer bowed. "Please."

The gesture seemed to relax the leader some. "You're right."

He looked to Rise and said, "What is your name?"

Rise did not feel like revealing it to him, yet he knew if he were to get anywhere it would be through this arrogant man. "Rise."

"Well, Rise, you are free to stay and listen in on our meeting. You may learn something."

The old man made his way back to the middle of the roof and began his speech.

"My followers, the day Canyon has feared is approaching. He has received word that some 20 different sectors, although hundreds of miles apart from each other, are being destroyed. No sources have been able to get inside due to the heavy restraint of security. We have no idea what the King is planning.

Canyon remembers the days when the sectors were first built. He said that the day the sectors fell would either be the day of our liberation or our doom. Seeing as how the King is behind it, we can be assured of doom. Slowly, this horrible havoc is coming. Our sources don't know of any pattern. It seems that the King is randomly destroying sectors and placing them in heavy guard. Don't be fooled by this, nothing the King does is random. We must find out why this is happening. Over the past 100 years, Canyon believes that 42 have been taken.

"True, there are still thousands of sectors to destroy before man's doom, but we don't know when the very sectors we live in will be attacked. For now, my faithful ones, go forth and find more information. Canyon will soon have a plan, but we need more information. You have pleased your master and Canyon as well. A messenger has informed me that he has dispatched some trainee gatherers to deliver you extra food rations in whichever sectors you will return to.

"You, news gatherer of Sector 2128, your sector is lost. Please keep to your normal route excluding 2128. If all goes fortunately, you will not have other sectors fall anytime soon."

Rise was surprised to hear the name of his own sector mentioned. He watched the kindly gatherer bow at the speaker's commands, even though the old man could not see him through the crowd. His echoing voice was like a light to this people, and Rise felt that he could speak over a cliff and watch all 300 of them fall after the voice.

"I know this can be frightening, but have faith in Canyon."

The crowd repeated "Faith Canyon."

"Now, I have received word that this man Rise, has indeed killed a sheriff. Don't put your faith in him, remember Canyon's knowledge is far greater. Whatever magic this man has used, I have no doubt he cannot repeat it. That's why he's hiding in this sector. If he were a real sheriff hunter, he would not be in hiding."

Rise strangely felt no offense over this. He knew he would die. The man spoke only the truth. Perhaps he too was falling for the hypnotic voice.

"I was informed long ago by our leader, that only one other sheriff has ever been killed. I know our stranger has done a fine deed, but it will not happen again in so short a time." Rise felt the man was trying to rig the conversation for something of more

127

importance. He was deliberately making sure they would not think too highly of him.

"Next on the agenda, an urgent cry must go forth. Directly after this meeting my children, do not return to your route of sectors. Remain here and search out the ruins more thoroughly for survivors. Don't spend more than half a day and bring back any that can fight. All our reports indicate that the sheriff of this sector plans to destroy this tower by tomorrow's night. We have 24 hours. Our sources say fewer than ever have died in the war. The sheriff planned this. He has recruited the strongest ones to siege us. He wants this tower destroyed and the sector back into ruins. Apparently, the tower agreement will soon be void."

The crowd gasped.

"Your captains have been issued with the challenge of taking every fighting person and getting them ready for battle..."

"We can't defeat a sheriff!" A distant voice in the crowd cried out.

There was a pause and then all eyes shifted to Rise. The friendly news gatherer slapped Rise on the back. "My friend is our hope. I know he can defeat another sheriff." He whispered into Rise's ear, "I hope you still have that magic stick."

Rise did not wish to correct him at this point. It might work out to his benefit.

The old man looked shocked at his lack of control in the situation. His voice was slowly being ignored. He was not used to it.

Rise walked forward into the crowd. The old man watched in agony as Rise possessed the same power to part the people. With few words spoken, Rise earned their respect. Rise walked straight up to the podium master.

"You can't fight an army led by a sheriff." He looked straight into the eyes of their master. Not more than two inches separated them. "It won't matter how many people you bring to help. By tomorrow night, this tower will fall."

The man maintained a strange grin on his face, but he was frowning. He knew what Rise was doing. But it was too late. The crowd was in Rise's hands.

"Let the stranger fight with us!" "We have no chance! At least this man has killed one sheriff!" More cheers rose from the crowd.

The man whispered to Rise, "This tower has been my home for many years. It has been the strongest and safest meeting place for my news bringers. It will not fall. And since my children view you as a trustworthy source of hope, you will stay and fight with us."

"No." Rise spoke it loud enough for the people closest to hear. They in turn repeated it in shock. Within a few seconds, the crowd was aware that Rise was declining the offer to fight with them. This could prove bad for the old man's image.

"What do you want?" he hissed.

"Tell me about the rebellion, and I will stay and fight."

The podium master of the news gatherers smiled; he was angry. He did not pause before his answer. He already knew he must give Rise the information. "Two messengers of the rebellion are coming here sometime in the dusk tomorrow to exchange information with me. Meet them at the outside of the gate, get your information, and then help defend this tower! It will be a man and a woman. Tell them you are looking for The Control."

"Fair enough." Rise shook the old man's hand and applause broke out in the crowd. They received a champion warrior to defend their tower. They could not stay and fight for they were not warriors, but they carried the conversation skills to persuade others to fight for their meeting place. It reminded Rise of a bird he once observed in his own sector. It would wait for a smaller fowl to build a nest and then evict it. None of the work and all the benefits; these news gatherers would use the people in this sector to fight for their tower. The tower provided shelter and hope for them and the people of this sector. Even some of the gangs respected it. Rise felt no doubt in his heart they could convince people to fight for it.

The old man pulled Rise close to him and whispered, "But I warn you, they will not help you. You may join them, but they will not help you. All you will have is a lifetime of unfulfilled expectations. Your friends are probably long dead."

Rise wanted to crush his hand but he quickly released it. He walked towards the trapdoor. He had all the information he needed.

Chapter Ten:

Rise found his quarters and fell onto the bed. He forced himself to stay there. If he stayed to fight, he would need his strength.

His dreams were restless, and he kept seeing plans failing in his head. If he were accepted into the rebellion by the

129

messengers, he would still have to stay in the tower and fight. He gave his word. If that was the case, then he would surely die.

He also realized that if they won the battle, and he was not accepted into the rebellion, there was always the threat of arrest. A last chance to see Beline. A desperate chance he would not fail to take if needed.

He also dreamed of the nursery, all the young faces of the future. This appeared to be the safest place for them. He could not let the tower fall. Without the defense of the tower, this sector would eat these people in one satiable bite. They needed him to win this fight. Win? There was no winning this fight.

Then he saw his death. The sheriff without a face, the sheriff of this sector, running him through with the same sword that killed Morceff. It was a hero's death. He did not fear it. He expected it. And yet, at the same time, he knew he would not die if Beline were still alive.

There were hurried voices and steps outside. It woke him from his dreams. The sun was blocked now by clouds, not the evil swirling ones, but the fluffy ones of mid-day.

Rise walked outside of his room and found hysteria. Men wearing full plates of armor and weapons could be seen mingled in with those in plain clothes. Some gathered their riches in blankets and were trying to flee. "News spreads quickly," Rise muttered. The crowd was pouring out of the doors like a boiling pot of water. They knew it was time to run. They might have been the cowards, but they were the smart ones.

He caught sight of a woman in a blue uniform and followed her.

"Excuse me, what's going to happen to the children?"

She had long brown hair and pointed cheek bones. Her eyes were nervous. "We're taking them below, to the root caves." She stared at a few white hairs that had snuck out from under his pig hat. "Are you the warrior? The sheriff killer?"

Rise glanced away. "Thank you for the information."

"You're welcome." As she turned to head for the stairs she said, "My children are depending on you, warrior."

The words dug into his ears. He could not provide the victory they wanted.

The men and women who did not pack their belongings to flee, began to arm themselves. Many held magic sticks, none like the one Rise used to destroy the sheriff. Many also carried swords. Some were armed with clubs and some with bows. Any object that could be used to beat someone to death with.

Rise saw a female news gatherer leaning against a rope safeguard. She was simply observing the crowd. Rise asked, "How many did your people find to fight?"

"None," she said. "The gangs are advancing through the ruins as we speak. A few skelguards and Ekheart are leading them. They should have us surrounded by dusk."

The woman was amazingly calm. Her red hair shined white from the sun peeking through a window.

"So..." Rise looked around at the scattering crowd, "This is it? How many are actually staying?"

"So far, only about 300 have left. Same as what would have been drawn by the sheriff anyway."

"And you news gatherers do not intend to stay?"

"No." She was rather cold about it. "We're not warriors. Besides, these people would die for their tower even if we weren't here. They need it more than we do. We can always find a new place to meet, but this is their living space. Their home."

"How do you plan on escaping if we're being surrounded?"

She smiled. "We news gatherers have our secrets."

Rise spied the podium master walking down the immense stairs, his noble cane more or less leading the way. The old man deliberately made his way to Rise.

"Ah, Rise. I was just coming to get you. Chuce said you were sleeping." It was the same smug look.

"The ones of the rebellion... have they come?"

"No you haven't missed them." He nodded to some parchments tucked under his other arm. "They would not leave without the intelligence."

"You lead the way."

Rise followed the man down the stairs which his legs were still not used to. Despite all his running about and adventures, these stairs tested unique muscles.

He followed him down to the lobby, where he saw a mass of men with heavy armor plates, wide swords, and shields. They were fortifying the lobby. Rise saw men with arrows and bows heading up the stairs, as well as those who carried magic sticks and the exploding spheres. They would take the high ground. Rise maintained a strange sense of peace. It was all happening too fast for him to be swept up in the anxiety of the moment.

Rise stared at the huge painting as they walked by. He

wondered if the ones in the picture ever had to defend their selling and buying place. The picture looked more peaceful. No warriors, just peasants purchasing.

They made it to the enormous gates. When the guard saw the podium master he quickly opened the huge doors.

Rise saw the large magic machines guarding the gates; their deadly barrels looking to the horizon for prey. Any army without magic would surely fall to the giant weapons.

"Those turrets will protect us from them getting through the gates."

Rise pondered over the new word turret, and turned his attention to the ruins. He saw a few people fleeing into the debris. He knew the approaching mob would kill them before they fled too far into the sector.

"What of the sheriff and the skelguards?" Rise asked.

"We have other things to worry about. The man appointed in charge of defense is not as strong now that the hour is nearing. He's afraid. I fear our walls will crumble before the sheriff even arrives."

They walked a little way outside of the tower. The black silhouettes of destroyed buildings and rubble encircled the landscape, preceded by the dark outline of the sector walls. The tower stood as a tree thriving in parched grounds. Rise had no doubt as to what the sheriff wanted to do with the tree.

"Let him have the tower."

The podium master stared with cornered eyebrows. "Never. You vowed to protect it, Sheriff Slayer, and protect it you will. As much as I despise the hopelessness of the rebellion, I value their information. Just as you view this siege as pointless, you are still banded to it."

Rise only nodded.

They waited. They waited for hours. They wasted much time just watching those who would flee run for their lives, while others were getting armed for the battle. Some came outside just for some fresh air before heading back into their soon-to-be tomb. The number of people leaving became smaller and smaller. The dark swirling clouds were coming back. It was almost dusk.

"How will your news gatherers escape from this?"

"Canyon has his ways of protecting his people."

"And what of you? Will you stay and fight?"

There was no hesitation in the man's voice. "If needed. But, I'm still sending my news gatherers to safety."

Rise needed a way free from this promise. Dying here would do nothing. At least The Giver would have his chance to give his all protecting the children. He shook that notion off as well. The quiet panic of the atmosphere betrayed his hope of any surviving.

"What if it was not needed?"

The podium master looked at him strangely. "What do you mean?"

"What if none of us had to stay and fight? A worthless cause. If we stay and fight, we will die. If we stay and fight, the children will die. If we escape with them..."

"You coward!" The man hissed. "You call yourself a Sheriff Slayer, but you fear one now? You timorous fool!"

"I don't care if I die! I only care about the children you claim to protect..."

"You gave your word and you will die by it!"

Rise was silent. His honor would kill him before it helped him.

Two shadows unexpectedly appeared from the flat silhouette of the ruins. They walked hurriedly; both dressed in drab clothes. Their clothes would never draw attention in a crowd of peasants. One was a man and the other had a woman's form. Each wore a gray tattered overcoat. The male wore a blue scarf while the female wore a red one. The man was tall and skinny, like a high tree branch sprouted legs. His head was free from any restraint of hair. The woman had black hair down to her shoulders. She kept her chin up, and swayed her arms just slightly straight with an athletic walk that was not just for show. Despite her height, her forceful appearance probably kept her alive many times.

They saw the podium master and hurried their steps. The tall man was immense, at least a foot over Rise, and the woman a foot under. She glanced at Rise and then turned her undivided attention to the podium master. The tall man stood silently with his arms crossed, never leaving Rise's eyes.

The woman's voice was pleasant, despite being just a little lower than most. "I don't have to tell you about the army walking your way?"

"Not in the least. Here is the information." The podium master moved along quickly.

The woman frowned. "Come on now. Tell me if the rumor is true."

"There are a lot of rumors..."

"Give it up. Did someone actually kill a sheriff?"

The podium master grazed a look at Rise, but realized his mistake too late.

The woman turned to Rise, her black hair blowing across her face from a wind that just picked up. She looked at him, and then with a hand faster than a snake bite, took Rise's hat from his head. "Well, I actually get to meet the white haired man. I guess that means it's true." She sloppily replaced the hat.

"What about the elite guard? If he hasn't found you yet..."

"He's dead." Rise quickly interrupted her.

The woman showed obvious surprise, and even the tall man lifted an eyebrow. "You killed an elite guard?" His voice was deep and boomed in the wind.

Rise remembered the elite's head snapping back as the crossbow bolt penetrated.

"No... a friend did." Rise's tone left no room for argument of whether he wished to discuss it further, but the woman kept pushing.

"Wow, not even Lars survived an elite... never mind, where's your friend, I would like to meet him also..."

"She's gone," Rise blurted, "I need to join you. I have to join the rebellion. It's the only way to save my friends!"

"You can't back out of your promise!" The podium master snapped at Rise.

"What promise?" The woman asked.

"He swore to defend this tower!" The podium master pointed his hand full of rings at Rise.

The woman took a step closer. "Give it up, Canyon follower! Your tower is gone. You have a few hours before that army is upon you! I have not one doubt you can kill the gangs in the army... but the sheriff and the skelguards? Come on! Flee while you have a chance."

"Never! The people here will not give up their living space!"

The woman looked ready to hit him.

The large man put a massive hand on her shoulder. "Barbara. We must leave," he said with a deep voice.

"Not without promising me I can join!" Rise clenched his fists at his sides.

The woman looked confused for a moment, almost flustered.

The large man shook his head. "Barbara, he can't follow

us on our mission. We're already a day behind on the Clarions."

"What do we do, Tad? If he's killed a sheriff and survived, he could be an asset."

"Or a spy, or a dead man, or he could lead a whole army of skelguards right to us."

Rise broke in, "If you don't let me join, I will get myself arrested and find my friends without your help!"

The two were completely oblivious to Rise and the podium master as they continued their conversation. "What do we do?"

"We have him meet us at the recruiting area. If he doesn't make it, no loss. If he survives, maybe he could be an asset. Then we just have to determine if he's a spy, which can be done easily enough. We don't have the time now." He was looking around, not nervously, but expectant.

She nodded. "What's your name?" She turned to Rise.

"Rise."

"Well Rise, don't get yourself arrested between now and Sector 32, and you might just make it into the rebellion. Meet us at Joe's bar, not at night. We will catch up with you eventually."

"Where's the bar?"

"You'll find it. Remember, *not at night*."

The woman and the podium master exchanged envelopes which they quickly hid in their shirts. "Listen, podium guy, I know you don't respect our group, but I think you know deep down that this is your only hope. Canyon is wise, I'll give you that, but he can't see the future. No matter how much information he collects of the present and past, he just can't see the future. If you truly believe this man killed a sheriff and he is not a spy, don't make him die for your stupid promise. It's a lost cause."

"Do not speak like that, Barb, please. We both know of lost causes. You can trust me in my judgment. I have not failed you before." The podium master showed no design of stubbornness in his voice. A voice that rang of truth replaced the arrogant tone.

The woman was frustrated yet let the topic of Rise pass. "Alright, you have my trust. For now.

"But this is your last chance. We can help you get the children out. Just cave-in the west wall of the root cavern. Our geologist says it will hold without the west wall. Lead them through the tunnels of the ancient city. It will take you a few miles from the east wall of the sector."

"How do you know this? Only those in the tower..."

135

"Canyon is not the only one with sources."

The master said nothing.

"Let's get out of here before that army gets here." The woman pulled at the arm of her tall friend.

"That's it?" Rise asked. "You just leave me with that?"

"That's all you get, sorry sweetheart."

The woman and the man walked away. Rise felt compelled to run after them, but he knew he could not change their opinion.

"What do you think of the rebellion now, Sheriff Slayer?" The podium master had his arms folded and a grin across his face.

"We have a tower to defend."

Chapter Eleven:

Rise looked along the insides of the defended tower and could not help but wonder if he were responsible for this. Was the sheriff after him for killing his contemporary? Or was it just complete and utter chance that brought him here to die? Justice would find him, one way or another.

On the lobby floor 300 men crowded, all with swords or clubs and heavy metal armor. There was a general for the lobby group, as there was for the archers and magic stick carriers. The latter two held their stations at either the roof of the tower or the windows along the sides. The giant gate was locked, and the turret commanders were left alone to die outside the door. Despite the massive weapons they controlled, it was only a matter of time before they would die defending the tower, but still their laughing voices outside could be heard.

Rise was passively content with wandering the lobby between the bodies of guards. He felt like a warrior ant of a different color, wandering through a colony he did not know, yet was expected to protect. The podium master had long since retired to some unknown location. Chuce was nowhere to be seen, just the nervous quiet of all the strangers in armor, awaiting battle at their stations.

Rise wondered where they were hiding the children. He wanted to help protect them. If he were to die, he would rather be protecting the future than a building.

Any moment they would receive word that the army had encircled them. Any moment the explosions from the turrets would sound. Any moment the gates would be broken, and hordes of gangs would flood the lobby. The roof and the window posts would try to kill as many as they could before they entered, but it would only be a matter of time. Rise had no doubt the sheriff would send the gangs in, and most would probably die. Then the sheriff and his skelguards would enter, invincible and heartless, and probably kill everyone inside, including the children. And including The Giver.

"Rise."

He turned and saw that Chuce silently came up behind him. He was wearing his normal robes as well as golden metal gloves over his hands with sheared metal. The same was true of his knees, elbows, and shoe fronts.

"Rise... I must do something I have never done before."

"What's that?"

He smiled, pulling at his weed-like mustache. "Attack first. Do not mistake me, my training was great, but only in defense. I have never hit anyone first."

"You'll do fine. Just get really mad first. What about the other healers?"

"I'm the only one."

"What?" Rise frowned.

"The rest have fled. They didn't have the same trust in their training, apparently. The same with the news gatherers. Only a few of them are left wandering the building, and soon they will pull their vanishing magic, and leave us completely."

"These people do not want to defend their home. They all want to run. Chuce, I think they should."

"I like how you said 'they' should. Why not yourself? You're really set on dying, aren't you?"

Rise laughed and realized that many turned their attention to the only two voices in the lobby. Even the general was silent.

A voice rang as an echo from the top of the tower, "THEY'RE HERE! ARM YOURSELVES!"

"Chuce, I have to see my enemies before this battle."

"Shall we?" Chuce motioned both hands to the stairs.

They ran hard. Even Chuce's calves were burning as they ran to the top. Rise wanted his body loose and ready to fight.

They reached the roof and pushed their way through some archers. He heard many whispers, "We'll die. Look at all them!" One was laughing hysterically.

Rise saw the mob surrounding the tower. It was probably 2,000 strong, though it might have been more. Most were probably hiding in the shadows of the night. The scattered lights from candles in the tower and fires on the ground gave only half the picture. What they could see clearly was only the beginning. The shadows seemed to breathe with hidden enemies. The mob was yelling curses and vile warnings. When the sound reached the ears of those atop the tower, it became muffled by the wind and sounded inhuman. It was the howl of another monster that Rise would face.

Rise could not make out any skelguards, but he could see many lit torches and blood thirsty beasts, although for now they kept their distance. A few kept savagely big dogs under their control by chains. They stayed hidden in the rubble, a protective forest from the large turrets. Even the ones on the sides of the tower without turrets were staying hidden. They kept a safe hundred feet from the walls of the tower.

Rise noticed a man on the roof. He had two long bows on his back, a sword at his side, and a large basin of arrows at his feet. He wore a helmet with a large cloth that hung down his back like colorful hair. He was shaking wildly, as if the top of the tower were moving below his feet.

His eyes were open wide, and his breathing was ragged. "WE WILL ALL DIE!" To Rise's shock, the man pushed by a few surprised archers and threw himself off the side of the tower.

There was a hollow pit in Rise's stomach as the body disappeared over the ledge. Just that quickly, and the man was gone forever.

"I fear for our commander," Chuce said.

"Why? Was he friends with that man?" Rise asked, staring at the spot the crowd had gathered to at the ledge.

"No, that was him."

The archers lost their focus and they began to show the effects of genuine terror. Many were putting their bows down and began to ponder how painful a death of that sort would be.

"Regain your positions! That man was not worthy to lead you! Lead yourselves this night and do not tremble! You're defending your home, your families, your children, and your lives. Fight well and let your aims be true. Should this be your last stand make it a slap the King will never forget! You are all heroes this night! Your children will live because of your valiance this dark night!" Rise could not believe how powerful his voice was atop the tower. Even the wind died down just long enough for his words to

138

carry themselves to the hearts of the men.

Chuce held a pleasantly surprised smile on his face.

A man saluted Rise. Two more followed. Then six. Then ten. The entire assembly of those on the roof swore their allegiance to their new commander, the Sheriff Slayer.

Chuce laughed and dragged Rise back down the stairs. "I thought you said they should run."

"They're dead already, they just haven't hit the floor. Let them destroy a few monsters before the end."

"Be as negative as you wish, but I think you found your reason for living. Told you I would give you one."

They began their descent on the stairs. From the floors they walked by, a few archers came running and yelling. They were apparently upset at seeing their commander fall past the window.

Chuce told the bereaved archer, "Tell your general and everyone you see that Rise, the Sheriff Slayer, is our commander."

Rise began to feel awkward that he even said anything to begin with. He went from a sworn militant, to a commanding officer, all within a few hours.

He quickly filled the new shoes given to him. Chuce and Rise made sure each of the generals were ready. They finally made their way back down to the lobby and spoke to the final general.

"The first problem will be the back wall. No turrets defend it. They'll break through there first and you must hold them at bay. The turrets will kill many on the other end, so your concern, until they do break through the turret side, is to defend the back."

The general saluted him. "Yes, Sheriff Slayer."

There was a deafening rumble outside. It grew more and more loudly until finally reaching a violent crescendo that shook the floor. The entire tower creaked and moaned from the shock. Three more successive rumbles followed.

"Keep your courage!" Rise did not like addressing a large crowd. "You will show these cowering monsters how men fight! Send them back to the rubble were they crawled from!"

A small door above the gate opened, and a dark skinned man yelled, "The sheriff just collapsed several buildings! We have no clear shot until they charge!"

The generals relayed the message to their troops.

Rise shook his head. "So much for the turrets helping defend before the attack."

Chuce said, "Rise, they will attack soon. You must

defend the children. Should we fall, I will rely on the Sheriff Slayer to protect our little ones. They're hiding in the root caves. Let no one enter the lower levels."

Rise nodded.

He ran to the stairway leading to the lower levels. He quickly ran down the uneven steps and found the small militia force guarding the entry to the hallway of the lower levels. It was a small door, just barely big enough for one person, however it was guarded by 30 strong men.

Rise was surprised to see the podium master. He carried a long magic stick instead of a cane.

He was surprised to see Rise.

"You're still here?"

Rise stood next to him. "As much here as you are. What good it will do is still left for fate to decide."

"You carry many items under that coat. You'll fight better if you leave them."

"No."

"I don't want the person fighting next to me to be bogged down..."

"Then don't stand next to me."

The podium master was silent.

More explosions from outside.

"One last time, I ask you to forget this stubborn death. At least do as that woman said and let the children escape..." Rise said to the podium master.

"Of course we're doing everything we can to help the children, you fool! We're trying to break away the cave wall as we speak. If we can defend this position long enough, the children will have a chance. Our best miners are excavating as we speak."

As soon as the podium master finished the sentence a small explosion rocked the base of the tower. The battle had begun.

Chapter Twelve:

The sound of smaller rapid explosions was faintly heard over the shaking of the building.

"The turrets are firing," the podium master said. "You should be with the army. They respect your presence for whatever reason. It'll strengthen them."

Rise wanted to stay and help protect the children. The

podium master saw this. "No you don't. If the front line falls, then by all means, come back and help us. Or are you a coward?"

Rise turned and left, frustrated with the old fool.

He made his way back up the stairs and sure enough just his presence seemed to make the men stand taller, but it just made him uncomfortable. The building was crumbling and creaking in some parts, and the back wall was beginning to display long cracks in the cement and mortar. The men in the lobby could only stand and wait. The battle cries of the archers on the floors above leaked down the massive stairwell, as well as the cries of pain as some were hit.

"I hate this sector," Rise mumbled to himself.

The back wall was nearly broken through; a large crack began to form. Rise pulled out his black sword slowly. He felt the blood pump through his veins at a quickened pace, his heart beat expeditious but controlled. Steady.

The back wall broke open, just a tiny bit at first. The murderous look of gang members came into view. They were slamming large hammers into the flesh of the building, carving a wound into it. Rise wished for a few archers, but knew they were above doing their part. The hole was larger now and a less than intelligent marauder tried to crawl through. The armored guard in front made quick work of him.

Rise was five rows of men back, but he squeezed his way through towards the front. The hole was made big enough for a man to walk through, but any who tried were also slain. The floor began to spill over with blood.

There was an explosion behind Rise.

He turned to see a large chunk blown inward from the outside. The remnants of one of the gigantic turrets sprawled across the floor into more pieces than his eyes could track, knocking an array of soldiers to the ground.

The next turret exploded into the compound just as the first one. The wall was losing its defense. In an instant, their two biggest weapons lay dead on the ground. Soon, the tower gate would be broken through. Rise saw cracks forming on the other side of the tower. They were coming at all angles.

Just as Rise was expecting the back wall to give way, the large gates splintered. This took the platoon in charge of defending the front by surprise. They expected a slow process like the other wall. Now they were throat-high into battle. Swords clashed and magic sticks fired. Rise yelled, "Keep your positions! Hold them!"

141

He was sure no one could hear him at this point. It was just as good. He was glad to pass his mantle of commander back to where it came from.

He ran to help the platoon under the most pressure.

A mob of gang members inundated the lobby. They did not make it more than thirty feet in. The guards were strong and would not break their position.

Rise saw a guard being ganged up on by three. It was amazing how well he held his ground, but he knew it was only a matter of time. Rise sliced the side of the third one's arm. This angered him and he turned to attack Rise. As he swung horizontally, Rise ducked and shouldered him into his two friends. One was run through by his companion. The other two were quickly taken care of by the guard.

"Thanks, Sheriff Slayer!" He was breathing hard and continued his defense against any intruder he saw.

Rise saw a skinny man who bore the flags of many gangs on different parts of his body. The sheriff had united the gangs. The man wore them like bandanas on his arms, legs, thighs, and head. He screamed wildly and swung two boards with nails driven through them. He clobbered a few guards before he was overtaken. Rise saw a few more of these berserkers and realized that one of these blood-crazed goons would take out three guards before they were beaten down. Rise devoted his attention to these.

He saw the body of a guard underneath a dead gang member. He grabbed the sword in the guard's hand and lobbed it through the air. It rotated twice and then stuck hilt-deep into the back of a berserker who almost blind-sided a guard.

Rise felt the heart-sinking sensation of an arrow fly by his face. The subtle sound of wind combined with a crisp noise that brought death. It just barely missed, but he heard the agony as a guard was hit meters away. He spotted the enemy archer. Three very large men were protecting him. The three giants surrounded him and used their broad swords to ward off any guard that approached.

Rise saw an abandoned round metal shield on the ground. He picked it up and saw the archer and his protectors just within the gates.

He was beginning to tune the sound of battle cries and death out of his head. Rise could not afford to be distracted. He pulled the shield into his chest with his arm around the edges and flung it outward. The large disc spun through the air and caught the closest protector in the side of the head. He fell to the ground stunned.

Rise saw an intruder running at him from the corner of his eye. The intruder held a short dagger.

Rise turned to face the new attacker and saw it was a woman. Rise's mind seemed to stop. She came ever closer, obviously heading straight for him. He did not know what to do. The woman ran at him screaming, her matted hair hung down to her lower back. She raised her bloody dagger above her head. Rise realized what had to happen. He killed her.

He made it quick and gently lowered her body to the ground. He grabbed the dagger out of her hand.

Turning towards the other two archer protectors, he saw four guards taken out by these women warriors because they refused to attack.

"Show them no mercy!" Rise shouted to the men, feeling it a vain effort amid all the noise. To his great sadness, they heard him and complied.

Rise threw the dagger at another of the protectors, but the handle hit this one in the face. It angered the giant, and he ran towards Rise, yet a guard slammed his sword into the man's shin as he passed. The giant collapsed and Rise finished him as he lay there in pain.

The archer saw the threat and pulled an arrow out.

"Attack the archer!" Rise yelled.

Five guards that heard him ran for the small man. One was hit in the neck with an arrow, two more were taken out by the remaining giant before he was overpowered. The last two ran the archer through and Rise heard the scream of a woman.

These barbarians used a large portion of woman warriors. It sickened Rise.

A horrified notion came over him that they would use children, as he had seen the others do. To his relief, he saw none trying to enter the broken gate. He would sooner die than slay a child.

Rise caught an intruder across the face with his blade. The man dropped motionless. He made his way through the battle and grabbed the bow and quiver the woman archer was still clinging to. He fired three shots before he began to miss. He slung it over his shoulder and pulled his sword out.

A new noise that seemed out of place caught his ear. He turned to see a large wolf growling. A thick heavy chain dangled from its collar with a severed hand at the end. Two arrows hung loosely from the sides of the animal.

It lunged at Rise, pulling the big chain like it was a ribbon. Rise spun to the side and brought his sword straight down into the face of the beast. It did not stop the momentum, and he was knocked off his feet as the chain painfully smacked his knee. The body of the wolf began to spasm and Rise quickly pushed it off. He grunted in pain as he stood up.

There were more new sounds behind him. Battle sounds of swords replaced the yelling and hammering of the wall. The back wall was breached. Rise turned and saw this new flood of death. He noticed the other wall was beginning to crack. Soon the lobby would be overrun.

Rise began his run to the other side of the lobby. A club swung by his head and he ducked under it, ignoring the attacker. He rested the bow over his shoulder and decided to keep his sword ready.

Then he saw a man that never failed to impress him. Chuce was battling with his golden gauntlets.

That small man was fighting four at once. Just as Rise was ready to fire a shot to help, each of the four men lay on the ground wounded or dead.

A man ran at Chuce with two swords. He swung the first one high and Chuce ducked. The second one came low, just after the first. Chuce jumped and extended his legs straight out into the knees of the attacker. There was a crack, and the man fell as Chuce rolled over and delivered a spiked blow with his elbow to the back of the man's head. Another came running towards him from behind while he was still on the ground. This man held a chain. Chuce pulled his feet over his head and rolled to a standing position. As soon as he had traction, he spun a kick into the side of the man's head. A second kick, from the other foot, landed into the enemy's face before he finished falling. Every move was an art form.

A club struck Rise on his shoulder; it was an awkward swing and only left a bruise. Rise swung his sword and slashed the man's hand. The enemy dropped his club and then lunged at Rise, biting him on his neck. Rise hit the ground on his back and kicked upward, knocking the man off him. Rise rolled and stabbed forward, finishing him quickly.

He saw one of his men being overtaken by twin assailants. Each was shorter than Rise and displayed red hair that was glued upward in spikes with black leather armor strapped to their bodies. They each held two axes and made a great team. The

144

brothers ran for Rise.

Rise swung horizontally as hard as he could, making contact with the wood handle on the first assailant, cutting the blade off and knocking the first one off balance. The second one swung while the first regained his footing. Rise ducked but felt it scrape along his back. The next swing Rise pulled his sword upward and deflected, and then kicked the second man in the stomach with his boot. The first dove at Rise but his swing was cut short by an arrow that struck him in the back. Rise ran him through and quickly spun the sword back just in time to stop the axes of the second man from making more than a flesh wound across his chest. He kicked the man in the same spot, harder this time, and then swung the sword and ended it.

His breathing grew heavy.

Rise ducked as he heard the whistling sound of a spear, and picked up one of the axes that the brothers dropped. Rise saw an enemy archer and flung the axe. He was never good at hurling objects like that, yet by pure chance, it stuck into the archer's bowing arm.

A sharp thin pain sliced its way across the back of his thigh. He dropped to one knee out of surprise and jabbed his sword back without looking. It made its way through the stomach of another berserker. The beast swung wildly as his life slipped away, cutting Rise three more times in the back. Rise had the horrible feeling of slowly being overcome with pain.

He reached to the back of his thigh and felt a small foreign object. The nail from the berserker's club found a new home in his leg. He felt the shallow six-inch trail it left, leaving his finger tips coated with his blood. He wrapped his fingers around the nail and pulled it out, grunting in pain.

The third wall was breached and more ran into the lobby. The lines were breaking. The middle was still free from any battle and the stairwell was untouched. He knew it was only a matter of time. A quick look at the bodies showed Rise that just as many of each party were killed. His group could not afford an equal amount of loses.

He glanced back and saw a small pile around Chuce. He was sweating profusely. His energy was being sapped by this evil.

The fourth wall was cracking.

Rise wondered if the children made it through the tunnels yet. Curse his promise.

He quickly put his sword down to use the bow. He shot

the last of his arrows into a mob of intruders and did not watch long enough to know if his aim was true. Rise left the bow on the bloodied ground and grabbed his sword.

A portion of the fourth wall was blown open and the last of the defensive positions was gone. The whole perimeter of the lobby was now a war, but thankfully the stairwell was untouched. As hard as they were trying, the defenders still had not allowed them to enter all the way to the massive stairs.

Chuce quickly immobilized the two that were fighting him and Rise ran over to help.

"I bet you're ready to sign that plank now, make your stay here permanent." Chuce said as he slapped a sword away from his face with his metal gloves. "As you can see, we have the best activities here."

Rise deflected a club from hitting his head and then kicked the intruder square in the shin with the heel of his boot. He slapped the man in the face with the broad side of the sword and elbowed him in the stomach. After sending him to the ground with a head butt to his face, he turned to see Chuce once again engaged in a three-on-one fight. Rise turned his own attention to fighting a small quick man who wielded a light axe.

The intruders gained another foot towards the center, and the flood was still pouring through the cracks. It was endless, as if the sides had been blocking an ocean of evil. Now it was vented into the compound.

Rise was growing tired, and the weight of his possessions was not helping him, but he would not let them go. Each cut and bruise he obtained seemed to scream through this flesh. The axe came too close to Rise's head and he realized he would not be overly concerned if he lost the pig hat. While the man pulled back Rise sliced the end off the axe and cut the man across the torso, not a deep cut, but one that stung. Then, using both hands, he swung the handle of the sword into the man's temple, knocking him to the floor. At the same instant Chuce sent his opponents to the reddening ground.

Four unsuspecting guards were taken out from the side by another archer with a viper-quick draw. Chuce saw the archer and made a desperate dash between fighting bodies. Rise turned to face another woman warrior. The thought disgusted him. Fortunately, she was intercepted by a guard and Rise turned to help another guard who was fighting despite his wounded arm.

Chuce fought the three archer protectors with the same

grace, yet slightly slower. His energy was giving out. He broke the kneecap of the first one, spun with the other foot and jammed it straight into the man's throat. He saw the archer pull an arrow for him and yanked on the third man while falling backwards. The third protector took the arrow and Chuce quickly took care of the archer.

More arrows and an occasional spear would be thrown into the crowd. Rise felt it strange that he still had not seen a single skelguard. He did notice however, that some of his archers were taking position on the stairs of the lobby. They fired at the giant holes in the wall to keep the evil at bay.

A fist struck Rise across his face as he felt the blood start to leak out of one nostril. The fist belonged to a giant black man who held a short sword in the other. The sword was closely following his fist and Rise spun just enough to keep his chest from being cut open, yet sacrificed his side. Rise rammed his sword into the giant's armpit and out his shoulder. It screamed in deafening pain, which attracted more archers to take aim on the giant.

Rise wiped the blood from his face and checked his side. Not too deep, just a little more than a scratch. The giant finally fell with eight arrows sticking out of his back and legs.

He spotted a man in a tight all black body suit. His limbs were long and skinny, and he made quick deer-like movements. He carried one of the explosive magic balls in his hands. He did not stay to fight in the battle but ran straight towards the middle. The man made it through the thickest part of the battle, and then made a surprisingly high leap over the last of the barrier of guards. He was running for the entrance to the lower chambers.

Chuce was now fighting five men at once. Two held him by his arms and he was using his feet in an almost magical way to fend off the other three, yet it looked as if he were going to lose.

Rise saw the man with the black body suit making his way to the entrance of the root cave. He shouted and ran after him. If the enemy threw the magic weapon down the stairs, the children would not have the protection they needed. Their defenders would be blown apart like chaff caught in wind. The man stopped at the stairwell and threw the bomb down. Rise was a few feet behind as the sphere was dropped. He yelled and rammed into the dark one at his fastest pace. They both went tumbling down the stairs. Neither had time to attack the other until Rise landed with a thud twenty steps below. They were at the entrance to the caves where the podium master and the last of the children defenders stood. The dark one landed a few feet away, but was in worse condition due to his smaller frame. Rise had dropped his sword on his fall and it spun across the floor.

Rise looked up and saw the eyes of the podium master and the rest of the men gaze at the magical ball that was rolling towards them, the look of death in their eyes. Without them the children would be helpless.

"NO!" Rise yelled and pulled himself to his feet ignoring all pain and blood he felt on his body, and jumped to cover the sphere, hoping his body would muffle it just enough to save the children protectors. He felt the peace of The Giver come over him as he knew he would die to give the children a fighting chance.

He closed his eyes and embraced his death yet again.

As he was wondering what the pain of using his torso as a human shield would be, he realized a sufficient amount of time elapsed. The magic ball did not work. It was a failure.

He unclenched his eyes and looked up at the men he attempted to save. They all heaved a sigh of relief, except the podium master who looked more disturbed than ever. The others turned their attention to the man in the black suit who shakily stood up. One of the men released a crossbow shot to the dark man's chest. He collapsed without a further fight. Rise went to pull himself up and was surprised not only by the pain in his body, but by the hand of the podium master helping him up.

The podium master led him away from the small group with his head hung low. Two of his protectors followed them. Rise picked up the sword, the podium master purposefully avoiding his eyes. "I feel I have misjudged you, Sheriff Slayer. Until now, I thought you were a spy."

Rise's knuckles were still white from grasping his sword during the battle. He inspected his hands carefully. "You did?"

"Yes, I had to be sure before I would allow you to leave. If you deserted your task I left orders with the generals to have you killed. As much as I hate The Control, for now we need each other for information. They're decent people, and I will not send them a spy. A spy of the King would not have cared if the children died."

Three distinct, loud knocks echoed from the enclosed side of the root cave door.

"There it is." The podium master said, "It's the signal that the women and children are safely through. If we would have had them flee into the sector, the sheriff would have tracked them down and murdered them. At least now they have a chance. Master Sheriff Slayer, I release you of your promise. This world would be a much better place with more people like you. Your selfless action has won your freedom and life."

"Sound a retreat, you fool!" Rise hissed. "This battle is lost!"

"Though I despise the rebellion, perhaps Barbara was right. Maybe they are the only hope for this world. It's time I make my escape, and you should do the same."

Rise said it again, "Sound a retreat!"

The podium master gave a strange smile. "Canyon does possess knowledge beyond you, and he has a way for me to escape. You, on the other hand, need my help." The podium master gave Rise one of his rings. He removed it from his pinky. Rise eyed it suspiciously.

"The tower will fall," the podium master said.

The men who were standing with the podium master looked shocked. They looked shattered and desperate for some glue of command.

The podium master continued, "I was a fool for thinking we could win. Even now I hear the battle worsening." He removed three more rings and flung them at his followers. "Save yourselves! Run while there's time!" The men did not bother to pick them up. They wanted to murder this man who pulled them down to this engagement of death. They edged forward slowly. Some were purposefully loading their bows. Whether they were hesitant or savoring the moment, Rise could not tell.

The podium master did not care. He turned back to Rise, "Sound a retreat, whatever good that will do. If you are truly an important man, one that will shape the future of this world, you will survive this. Today was the first day I doubted Canyon's ability to solve our problems, but in your one selfless action I saw all the wonderful love, courage, and hope that preserving this race requires. Perhaps you will play a bigger part in the overall picture." His minions were a few feet away. "I bet you're curious as to how news gatherers are never caught? Farewell, Sheriff Slayer." The podium master turned a square portion of the ring, and his body disappeared almost instantly. The magic stick he held fell to the ground, and Rise heard quickened steps just barely above the sound of the battle.

Rise remembered the magic the elite guard possessed of invisibility and it filled him with rage. How could they use that evil and tie it to rings? It was a royal magic and shouldn't belong to an earthly item. He swung his sword into the air where the podium master had been standing. He hit nothing. "You coward!" Rise yelled into the air.

The group of 30 men stopped in their place. They turned and made an urgent dash for the rings on the floor. Rise decided to make his exit before they came looking for his. He painfully limped up the stairs.

He was staggered at how much ground was lost within a few minutes. The remaining guards, probably 200 strong, were reduced to a concentrated circle towards the middle, a few feet from the stairwell. A few archers came down the stairs and were firing from the railings into the lobby and more were joining them. Rise quickly found Chuce still in battle. His face was bloody and it looked like his nose was broken. The bodies were piling up.

He ran and tackled one of the two men attacking Chuce. The man fell on his own sword and did not get back up. Chuce's legs seemed like two short snakes, sneaking in every direction as he battled. His leg seemed to go straight up with as much force as a hammer into the man's chin. He pulled back, flipped, and drove another foot into his chin, knocking the man unconscious.

Rise saw an arrow float by his face. He hated that feeling. Before he could turn his head, he heard Chuce cry out in pain as the arrow stuck in his chest. Rise turned and saw Chuce's body take the impact like a twisted rag. He fell backwards and made no effort to cushion his fall. His back cracked against the floor and his head was resting against the stairs.

"CHUCE!"

At that instant, a shrill whistling sonance sailed through the room and exploded into the large painting. The sound was so loud Rise needed to cover his ears. It rocked the foundations and destroyed the tapestry into small flames of canvas. It was now burning trash scattered in the midst of an ever intensifying battle.

The army lost 50 more men, and the circle was now enclosed around the giant steps. Rise pushed his way through smaller battles and fell next to Chuce. He was just staring at the arrow in his chest.

"It missed your heart," Rise said.

"Well that's good news," Chuce muttered it through curling lips. "But I think it got something else important."

Rise stood erect next to Chuce, his sword poised, ready to defend this wonderful man's body as long as he held breath.

Chuce tugged Rise's pant leg. "Friend, listen to me."

Rise looked down at Chuce's bleeding face and was happy to see that his eyes were pain free. "Friend, go find your reason to live." His eyes rolled back to his head and his breathing stopped.

"No!" Rise yelled it through clenched teeth.

Rise closed his eyes and let his inner consciousness make his decision. He reached down to put the ring on Chuce's dead finger, and twisted it. He watched Chuce disappear, and yet he still felt his hand. "At least your body will have peace in death. Farewell, my friend." Nothing would harm his friend further. He was now hidden from the evil that swarmed around him.

Rise stood and let the air fill his lungs. A faint, sad smile crawled across his face, "May you trip many enemies." He could almost hear Chuce laugh. He composed himself to defend his friend's body, but the words came through his mind, "Go find your reason to live." Rise saw Beline. She was almost as real in his mind as if she were standing right in front of him. His reason to live.

He would not die today.

The vision blurred out of existence and Rise saw what he feared. The red eyes, the awkward walk, the deadly spear. The first of the skelguards clunkily walked through the crack. No hope of escape that way.

Rise ran up the stairs. He sounded the retreat, hoping they could push their way out back through the cracks and at least a few could survive. He did not look back as he alerted the escape to the archers. Too many floors, too many faces he knew would die. He felt guilty that he could not save them all. The only thought keeping him from dying with them was Beline's smiling face. That image left no second thought in his mind. He lingered too long at this distraction.

Rise heard the screams as the invading force began to climb the stairs. They would kill everyone floor by floor.

He climbed all the stairs; his calves felt as if they would splinter. The long run to the last floor was nearly all the strength Rise had left. He climbed up through the hatch and found the archers still atop the roof firing into a blob of enemies they could only discern as one monster. "RETREAT!"

Only a few of the archers stopped and looked at him. They returned to shooting into the mob below.

An archer turned to Rise and said, "You should have left sooner." The archer glared with sharp brown eyes and very little teeth.

"If you retreat now you can push through the bottom and escape into the sector! Go now!"

"Sheriff Slayer, if you really killed a sheriff, you're the only real hope for this sector. You must escape. I would gladly die for you."

"You don't even know me, stranger! How can you..."

"Either way, death will come. If not now, then maybe later, by a gang attack, or a sheriff decides to use my back for a target! Eh? Either way, I will die for something I believe in. You have something special if you killed a sheriff..."

"It was luck! How can you people not see that? Run for your lives!"

The man shook his head in disgust and went back to firing the last of his arrows into the mob. "Go die in your best way," the archer said curtly.

Rise felt a little hurt but the face of his love remained in his sight. She was waiting for him to rescue her. He needed to escape.

A man burst up from the stairs screaming. "They're climbing the stairs! They're coming!"

He walked to the edge of the building, the strong wind nearly taking his hat off his head.

He felt Beline guiding his eyes, but he could not focus on what. He could not discern what she was trying to tell him.

Then he saw it.

Rise pulled the grapnel from under his coat and felt the difference in weight. "Never tried anything this dangerous before." He chuckled quietly to himself as he suddenly remembered at least a dozen other things that qualified as more dangerous.

He jumped up to the ledge and nearly fell as a gust of strong wind got caught in his leather coat. It flapped viciously and he turned his body so it would not whip around quite so violently. He fired between his feet and the grapnel stabbed through the concrete.

The mob was still engorging the building. To be clear of the army he would have to swing outward from the tower at least 100 feet. The closest structure he could hit with the grapnel was a tall rubble heap topped with the remains of a building. It had shattered barbs sticking out of the remains, but it was the only place far enough to escape, yet close enough for his plan. If he fired directly down to the adjacent building from the top of the tower, the force of his swing would splatter his body against the side of the rubble hill it stood on. He needed to fire his grapnel upward at the building. That way his swing would take him outward and up, displacing some of the force. To do that he would have to go down first. Very down.

He breathed in air and held it. His grip on the grapnel tightened, and he loosed about three yards of line from the barrel. He wrapped the leather shoulder strap tightly around his forearm. "Hope I don't go through a window." And he jumped.

There was a moment when time stopped and his heart flew to the bottom of his throat. He held no weight. The lowered arc of the cable seemed to slowly drift like a snake, and then tighten. The sound of the cable being strung taut echoed in his ears. Rise kicked off the side of the tower and swung as hard as he could and hit the release button.

He felt ready to vomit. He was hundreds of feet above the surface, and he just retracted his safety line. His body was completely free in the air. The momentum carried him away from the wall. He felt dread creep in around him and panic was closely following.

The mobs below were like flies streaming into a carcass. They were little blurs with occasional blips of torch light. He was tilting backwards and falling. He had no balance, no weight, and no control. He was falling too fast. He fired below him and to his left into the building, just missing a window in his panic. It locked and gave him thirty feet of cable. He fell past the point of contact and the cable went taut. His arms almost ripped from their resting place in his shoulders as his body jerked into another swing. He scraped across the side of the building and banged his sore knee into an overhang, scaring an archer.

Slow it down, he told himself. *Don't give yourself too much slack on the line.*

He hit the release button at the lowest part of his swing, forcing his fingers to take the action of retracting the cable again. He kicked against the wall so he turned the other direction. He panicked and fired into the face of the tower again, too far away, and too much of an angle. He braced himself for the pain he knew was coming. It made contact lower, and he began another fall.

The flies were bigger now, and the sound of their bloodlust was a deafening roar. Over a hundred feet lay between him and the ground, but not his destination. He needed to avoid the mob.

He saw the invading army fighting in the windows he was adjacent to. They had climbed quickly.

Rise hit the release button at the lowest point of his new swing, and as soon as it retracted he fired again. He saw the stunned faces of the archers that flooded the windows. They stopped firing their arrows to watch him fall. He began to fear that he might impale one by mistake.

He was too far to one side of the tower now so he turned his body, released, and fired diagonally towards the other side, yet his shot came no where near the middle of the tower. He was still too far to the left to make it to the lower building he spied as his escape. He began working his swinging and falling routine to the right of the tower. On his third try he knew he missed the mark.

The grapnel was heading for a window. Thankfully, the archer bent down to retrieve an arrow he dropped, and the cable went over his head and into the floor, just barely missing his backside. Knowing the archer was safe Rise now had to face the possibility the grapnel may get stuck in its new temporary home. It dug through wood and perhaps would get stuck on some other building material.

He hit the release button and nothing happened. He continued his swing until the line went taut on the window sill and he slammed into the side of the building between two windows, the force nearly taking the grapnel away from his hands. The leather strap dug deep into his skin. The shock bounced him back outwardly and he slowly spun in position until he hit the wall again.

Rise's arms were tired. He would have to hit the retract lever and climb back into the tower death trap.

He saw a gang member fighting in one of the rooms with two archers. He spotted Rise trying to make his escape, but was forced to deal with the archers first.

A burning sensation passed by his ear and bounced off the concrete wall. An arrow from the mob made its way to his height. Not more than a 150 feet was between him and the ground. There was a pause and then he saw the volley of arrows. They were arching towards him. Not all were good shots, but some would come close. The arrows were coming.

Rise would never know the name of the archer who pried the grapnel free from its trap, but he felt thankful for the weightless feeling.

The arrows bounced off of the building above him, some shattering, others just falling. He retracted it fully and began his free fall. He was too close to turn back now.

He saw the adjacent rubble heap of a building. He aimed and fired. If this missed, he would splatter into the mob; his only comfort was knowing he would take out a few barbarians with him. He felt the sweat pouring out of him like a strainer. The aim was true and locked in place into the side of the adjacent building.

He instantly hit the retract button and hoped it was

enough to keep him from hitting the ground.

The point of contact in the building was about 100 feet high. The grapnel seemed to retract slowly. The mob was close now, he could make out distinguishing facial marks. Arrows, spears, and rocks flew by him. He felt his feet smash into the faces of a few rioters. He felt one of his toes break, but the grapnel was now pulling him up again. He came within six feet of the ground. His arc was good. His swing between the buildings was almost over. The cable retraction picked up speed and he raced through the air quickly with his jacket flapping behind him like bat wings.

The wall of the building his grapnel stuck into was close. He was safe from the mob now, although he could feel the arrows' presence behind him.

The building sat like a spike rising above a pile of rubble, almost like a fortress of scrap metal.

He turned sideways and absorbed the blow of the collision with the wall in his left shoulder. He felt the concrete crumble slightly from his impact. His shoulder felt like half-frozen water, and his body went numb. All he had to do was hang on for just a little while longer as the grapnel ascended. He was losing focus. The wall was blurring. He felt his body scraping against the side of the building as his grapnel did all the work. Just a little further until there was a large enough crack he could slip safely through into the building.

His feet went into the crack, and he pulled himself safely inside his new building, high above the mob. Painfully, he unwrapped the leather shoulder strap from the grapnel and knew a bruise was circling around his arm from it. He retracted the grapnel and collapsed into the dark on his knees, knowing that the mob could send some of their own after him.

He had to keep moving. He just fell from a tower, swung to an adjacent building over a mob filled of the King's hate, and survived. His luck would not hold out after that stunt. The evil would find him.

Then he fell flat on his chest and knew darkness was coming for him.

Chapter Thirteen:

Rise forced himself awake. He felt caked blood across his lip. His head felt swollen, and his hands were sore. His toe was in pain, it felt almost shattered. He stiffly stood up and heard his back crack down his spine. "Ugh."

With a hand on his back and one against the wall, he peeked over the edge. The mob was still attacking the tower. They were fighting the archers at the 30th floor so he could not have been unconscious for more than a few minutes. They had ignored him after he swung by.

He wanted to move quickly, but his body refused. He turned on his wristlight and looked around. The crack in the wall narrowed to no more than a sliver after a few feet, yet it looked weak, no more than a wall of pebbles.

It took a few seconds for him to focus on the wall blocking him from the inside of the building. It seemed to spin in front of him. He leaned back and kicked it. Most of it collapsed in dirt and rocks. He kicked it again, and it all came crumbling down. He walked through and found himself in a large strange room. He was on a balcony that stretched across the wooden room. Below him were many flat benches, 50 feet in length, lined up in rows. A podium with a mark that looked like a square letter T was at the head of the benches. Despite all the dust and cobwebs, it appeared grandiose and polished. A large glass window was boarded up from the outside. The glass was stained many different colors and stretched straight to the ceiling of wood rafters and giant bells.

Spiderwebs abounded as much as the dust and it surprised Rise that no one had entered this sanctuary before. It was practically unspoiled. Below him many trading goods lay nestled in their original positions. A trove of incredible treasures was spread on the lower level. Tables with utensils for eating were set here and there along the ground floor.

Rise moved the light upward and then realized why the sanctuary lay undisturbed. It was spelled out in red paint on the rafters. It was written over and over again. The one curse that everyone in the sectors feared. It was even on the walls, parts of the floor, and benches. The King's name was written over and over again. He shuddered. No wonder this place lay unspoiled.

Rise looked down and saw a pile of rotting wood on the floor. He turned his attention to the ceiling and saw the hole that was to blame. The one gap in the entire building to let any moisture in. That was his exit point.

He was feeling slightly better now and removed the grapnel. He fired upward, and the point of contact was a few inches to the left of the hole. The force from the shot hurt his shoulder. He slowly retracted his body upward, grunting in pain. He rose by support beams and bells and was able to get his footing on a broken board that stuck out from the wall. He pulled himself up and released the grapnel from the wood. He took one last look downward. One hundred feet below him lay a completely untouched treasure trove of goods he could trade. Shiny stones, clean metal, and strange objects that could set him for life. He felt drawn to it, yet he shook his head and dismissed it.

He kicked a wood plank downward just for the justice of seeing it fall so far. He felt that he should have died from the stunt he just pulled of free-falling off the tower. He felt cheated, that he could be the one to survive all these strange situations. Something had to fall today.

The wood plank bounced off beams and made a clank sound off a large bell. It hit with a thud amid the wooden benches. No sooner had it landed than a large flame engulfed it from three different angles, each from the entrance of the building. He quickly turned off his light.

The skelguards glanced up just as Rise pulled his body into a shadow. The flame on the floor caused their evil shadows to bounce around him. The haunting red eyes stared for a few moments before they returned to their hidden posts guarding the treasure. One of the King's many traps. Their hollow, red glowing eyes were visible from all the way up where Rise stood in the shadows.

The fire was spreading as the skelguards marched off. Rise breathed deeply. He felt strangely at peace. That was the catch. He had passed. The treasure was the lure that would have killed him. He felt better knowing that he beat death by surpassing temptation rather than simply being lucky.

He pulled himself up and onto the roof of the building with great pain and effort. He walked to the side and quickly launched his grapnel again to an adjacent, smaller building. He swung and used his feet this time to brace his impact on the wall. It still hurt and jarred his body, but not as badly, yet he felt most of his strength sapped. He lowered himself and felt the lovely shattered ground beneath his feet. His entire body was still shaking.

Rise began hobbling in a westward direction. He held no plan, except to reach Sector 32 and find the rebellion. The immense pains were a secondary concern. Each cursed sector he visited seemed to add a new definition to suffering. The map the old man left in the book pointed to that sector in a west position from where he was now. It was a long walk to the wall, but the sector seemed almost empty. He heard sounds of life but saw none among the wrecked buildings and rubble.

Rise soon limped himself to the foot of the great wall just before daybreak, barely making it in time. He put the hat in his pocket and waited out the routine of the guards to pass. He eyed his target through the scope. He fired with his ever increasing accuracy. Taking the leather strap, he wrapped it on the opposite arm to avoid deepening the wound from the last time. He groaned at the thought of the pain that would be inflicted by another ascent and descent. He climbed to the top with shoulders that wanted to split.

He pulled himself over and was ready to throw himself over the other side, just to escape the horrible memories of this sector. Despite the terrible thoughts, he turned around to get one last look at the tower.

As he turned, a large emission of light came from the base of the tower. It blinded him momentarily, and then there was an ear crackling noise. The entire bottom of the tower burst apart, and Rise stared in horror as the great monument fell before his eyes. There was nothing he could do. The massacre was over.

Rise turned and began his descent into Sector 42.

Part Four: Sector 42
Chapter One:

As soon as his feet hit the dirt he painfully drew his sword. He even managed to force himself to put the pig hat on. It seemed heavier with the burden of sore muscles. He was breathing heavily, and his sweat drenched through his body and clothing. He was beginning to stink from a lack of bathing. His home seemed so far away. He feared his old luxuries, the hot water pipe, the warm shelter, the soft rugs, would be gone forever. Despite knowing his appearance was no worse than a normal peasant, he still felt dirty. He was used to better and he felt ashamed for it.

The new sector seemed to slope towards the middle. No building stood higher than a single story before they looked ripped apart from the top. He saw many scrap metal piles and no people foraging. It was almost morning, and he knew sleep was a necessity after that horrible blood spill.

Putting the sword away was hard, he felt like he needed it after the battle. He walked stiffly over to a pile and pulled back a large metal plate as tall as he was. It bent and wobbled easily making a strange noise as he did so. He collapsed and pulled it over him to provide some additional warmth. Exhaustion robbed him of any lingering dreams of Beline, yet the trauma burned horrible pictures into his head.

Rise woke up quickly and practically jumped to his feet, hitting his head on the metal. It startled a drunk man who took off running. Rise was in a cold sweat from reliving the battle of the tower over and over in his dreams.

It was morning now, and a fog rested across the sector. There was a coat of dew covering the landscape and Rise felt his teeth chattering.

He was horrified at what he saw on his clothing. Red splotches were everywhere from his boots to his coat, and he felt skin stiffness on his face. He didn't care if it were his own caked blood or not. Too much killing. If Beline had seen him kill all those people...

Rise fell to his knees in the soggy ground, and weakly stabbed his sword into the dirt. It tilted from the wetness.

"I swear Beline, I will not take another life."

He stood up slowly and removed the sword from the mud. He cleaned it on his pants, covering the biggest blood stain with the mud.

Scanning the horizon, he could not see more than a few hundred yards before the mist devoured the images. Many broken buildings were spaced out like gapped teeth in a rotted mouth. Smoke was coming from a few buildings and he instinctively made his way towards them.

He could not believe how quiet it was here. The whole sector seemed to be made of black and gray. The gray fog was everywhere, making the rubble-clad buildings hard to see. He felt robbed of color in this sector. He heard no wind. He heard no people.

He knocked on one of the buildings, but no further sound emitted from it. He continued to knock on different ones, hoping to find someone who would answer the door. After ten minutes he was about to give up hope. He could not even be sure people lived in these houses. They were awfully close to the sector walls.

Rise saw one of the many identical buildings with smoke arising from it and walked towards it. All the buildings were small, square, and dark. None had windows of any sort. An actual wood door blocked his entrance.

He knocked on it. It was a thick door.

The footsteps almost startled him; they seemed more out of place than the knock.

There was a loud clank as a lock was undone. The door opened slowly, and Rise saw a young woman in a gray robe and hood looking at him. Her eyes were half-closed and her face was dirty. The robe was tattered and stained.

She spoke with a soft, scratchy voice, "Hello?"

"Hello. Um... I don't know exactly what to say, but I'm new to this sector, and could use a hot fire..."

As she spoke she avoided making eye contact, "You poor creature." She reached out and felt his dew drenched jacket. "Come in and warm yourself."

"Thank you, I truly appreciate it."

"Think nothing of it."

Her voice never changed pitch and her head was hung low. She did not seem happy to help him, nor upset about his presence. If anything, she almost seemed sad.

She closed the door and pulled down a huge, complex lock. It took many turns of screws and bolts to make it function. It seemed too complicated for its purpose.

The house was made from an ancient building that had been torn apart long ago. The roof was covered by patches of wood and metal. A cylinder pipe escaped the ceiling to let the smoke out from the small iron stove it was attached to. The house was a square, no bigger than a 12 by 12 room. A large bed made of cloth was on the ground, more of a nest than anything. A large ripped carpet lay in many sections across the wood floor; the only bare spot was a trapdoor. The rest of the house was made up of broken-down old furniture. Broken glass surrounded some of the furniture. Battered chairs and two tables took up the remaining space.

"My name is Taiya." The woman spoke in her same manner.

"Rise."

He kept his hands close to the stove, warming them.

"Your clothes are wet, and you need a bath." She was not being snide about it. Her sad voice was too indifferent to have a strong opinion.

She removed her robe with the hood and was wearing a thick garment stitched from other dresses of different colors. It was the first color he had seen in this sector.

Rise almost collapsed when he gazed at her. She had blonde hair and green eyes. He could not tell with her hood on, but

160

now with it off, she looked exactly like Beline.

Chapter Two:

He concealed the hand he used to steady himself on a nearby piece of furniture and stuttered, "Beline?"

She looked at him with one eyebrow raised. "No... Taiya."

Rise adjusted to her face and began to see subtle differences between the two. Taiya's face held pointed cheekbones and a rounder chin. Altogether, she looked thin and weak. She also had a lack of emotion that stole away any potential beauty. She was attractive, yet detractive at the same time. There were also large bruises on her arms.

He was able to take a breath. "Oh, my mistake. You look... it's not important."

She handed him her robe and said, "The bath is under the house. I just put coals under it a few hours ago. It should still be warm. Under that hatch. I'll dry your clothes on the stove."

Rise pulled open the trapdoor and climbed down a very old rope ladder. A small bath tub with glowing embers underneath it filled most of the room. He had to duck down and almost crawl to reach it. He removed his items and clothes and put on the robe. It smelled of a sweet perfume he had not noticed before. It smelled like the yellow flowers Beline used to decorate her house with.

He placed his sword, grapnel, book, ear piece, and necklace by the tub.

Rise went to the ladder and opened the door to hold up his clothes to Taiya. She took them silently and went to dry them. Rise lowered the door and then crawled back to the bath. He removed the robe and lifted himself into the tub. His shoulders hurt the worst, yet his whole body was a brick that he needed to lift to the warm water. Scratches and cuts were etched all over his body.

Leaning his head back and letting his body soak in the warmth was the most relief he had felt for a long time. It seemed like a long time to him, he couldn't even be sure how long his journey had been progressing. Everything was starting to fade in his memory, like a shape over a hill that was just too blurry to decipher. The last bath he remembered was a short one, just to quickly clean himself to get ready to see Beline. He wished he had savored it more.

"Finally, a sector with some hospitality."

Rise was surprised to find a clump of soap next to the bath. He broke off a small piece, not wanting to waste any of Taiya's graciousness.

He cleaned himself and lathered his face and clumsily tried to use his sword to shave. It was dull from the battle, and he would have to sharpen it later. For now he would simply rest with the small ebb of soothing water surrounding his body. His toe was feeling better, maybe it was not broken after all. His fingers were even slowly beginning to heal.

He reached down and picked up the ear piece. He listened for Bespin's voice but heard nothing.

Drifting slowly into a deep, soothing sleep, he felt his muscles flatten and begin to heal.

He was not sure how long he was asleep, but he was being pulled out of it slightly. He heard voices and creaking footsteps in the wood floor paneling.

"Get out!" A woman's voice said, "I don't want to partake anymore!"

Rise jolted upward like a nail being driven into a ceiling. The sudden movement shocked his recovering body. He slowly pulled his body out of the tub and grabbed the robe. He silently put it on. The water from his body dripped off and slowly rolled against the coals, making a soft hissing noise.

The voice continued, "No one just *stops*. You'll suffer the drain just as everyone else and come crawling back. Except the price goes up each time. Are you stupid?"

"No." Taiya's voice was a firm whisper.

"I don't think you realize what happens next."

Rise grabbed his sword and quickly went to the rope ladder under the trapdoor.

The footsteps moved around above him and one stopped a few feet from the trapdoor.

"Hey, Vigg, look at that. On the stove."

"Whose clothes are... Oh, I see. Taiya has another courier. 'Fraid we can have none of that. Competition is bad for business." The footsteps of this voice moved quickly over to where Taiya was standing. "Where is he?"

Silence. Rise could hear his heartbeat quicken.

There was a slap, and Rise heard Taiya fall to the ground and gasp.

"Rip this place apart, he's here somewhere."

The footsteps above Rise moved directly over him on

the trapdoor. "Hey... I found a..."

Holding the sheathed sword in his right hand, Rise grabbed onto the sides of the rope and pulled his feet above his head and kicked the trapdoor upward with both his bare legs. The door opened, and the intruder fell backwards. Rise quickly scrambled up the rope ladder, leaving the scabbard behind.

He glanced at the fallen man and then to Vigg.

The fallen man was a small wretch with dark splotches on his skin and sunken eyes. He looked sickly pale with frizzled red and brown hair. He clenched a mouth only half-full of teeth. Despite his foul appearance, he wore fine garments. A vested blue shirt tucked into a pair of black pants that fit nicely with a belt. A belt that held a small magic stick, which he was reaching for.

Vigg was larger, as tall as Rise, but skinnier. He had the same sick skin with a patchy head of black disgusting hair. He also wore nice garments similar to the fallen wretch. A quick glance at Vigg showed all he held was a sword, which he was also reaching for.

Rise chose the greater threat and quickly collapsed his knee onto the fallen one's chest and pulled the magic stick from its holster. Just feeling the honor-less death striker in his hand was enough to make him sick and remember his vow to Beline never to kill again. He pointed the weapon at Vigg and stepped away from the one on the ground.

"Get up, Lauren. He won't know how to use that." Vigg said, "Nice hair, old man."

Rise said nothing.

Lauren stood up and wiped off his pants from the dust on the floor. He looked at the robe Rise wore over his body. "Looks like he's more than just a courier." A nasty smile spread across his face like a flesh eating disease.

Rise drove the end of the weapon into the disgusting smile and heard a few dirty teeth break. Lauren bent down and clasped his mouth with his hands as Rise kneed him in the stomach, sending him to the ground a second time.

Rise glared at Vigg as he held the magic stick in one hand, and his sword in the other. Vigg held his sword out and slowly tromped across the room with his large boots, confident Rise wouldn't know how to use the magic weapon.

"Get him Vigg! Cut him up good!" Lauren spit some red onto the floor and quickly crawled away when Rise glared at him for his comment.

Vigg carried only a thin sword, not one to match the strength of the broad sword Rise held, but it would be quicker. Rise would not underestimate him.

Vigg swung first and Rise remembered his oath. The first block deflected the blade from the side of his head. He heard Taiya scream in terror. The second attempt was to slice his torso. The attacker was slow and uncoordinated. Rise kicked him in the stomach. Vigg doubled back in pain and then ran at Rise, pulling the blade over his left shoulder to begin his swing. Rise deflected that blow too, but Vigg's body did not stop. He plowed into Rise and stomped down on the bruised toe with the heel of his boot. Rise grimaced in pain and anger. He head butted Vigg in the chest and used his shoulder to push him back.

Rise pointed the magic stick and pulled the trigger. A chunk of the floor paneling between Vigg's feet exploded upward.

"Whoa! There, that be enough!" Vigg said, stepping backward.

Lauren threw his body onto Rise, forcing him to put his weight on his bad foot. Rise clenched his eyes in pain and fell to the side against the stove. He hit a bolt on the way down and gave his back a large burning gash through the robe. He pulled away quickly and pointed the honor-less weapon straight at Lauren's face. He backed up towards Vigg with his hands up.

"Last warning." Rise held his head low but his eyes stayed on the two men. "If you come back," Rise bluffed, "I'll kill you."

"We are gone, it's not worth it, getting slumped for one lousy deal. Come on, Lauren. She'll come back anyway."

Before they left, Lauren turned and said, "What are you trying to prove? No one stays off. No one! You'll be begging us next time." The two walked out into the gray world and slammed the door behind them.

Rise limped over to a chair and supported his weight on it. He knew his back was bleeding from the stove and did not wish to stain the furniture. His shoulder was sore, his back was cut, his legs were tired, and his toe was broken. He did not want to admit it. He could not admit it. But he knew it. He was in no shape to continue his journey.

"Thank goodness. You... brave man." Taiya came over and forced him down onto the chair. "Why... risk your life for me?" The woman was actually smiling. Her eyes even committed to a few tears. She was much prettier with emotion in her face, even a sad one.

"You helped me first. You invited a wounded stranger into your home. Anyone that selfless deserves to be protected."

She blushed.

"I don't deserve your praise." She quickly added, "I think your toe is broken."

Rise looked down and nodded.

"And you probably hurt your back..." She tilted him forward and gasped when she saw the cut. "Stay still."

She went over to her half-collapsed cupboard and pulled out a ripped towel. She dabbed a corner in a pot of hot water she was boiling on the stove.

Taiya's movements were quick but shaky. Rise had the impression that something was wrong with her. Nothing offensive... just not quite right. He felt that impression when he first saw her, and now it was more apparent with her "emotional" display.

She came over and pulled at the rip in the robe on his back and began to wipe the cut.

"I'm sorry about your robe," he said.

"Oh quiet. It's a good thing that stove was hot. The heat must have sealed off the bleeding. It's not deep."

She pulled the top of the robe open and Rise quickly made sure to pull the bottom half tight around him. With his upper body exposed he felt strange and uncomfortable. "Let me put my clothes on, please."

"It's a hard place to bandage, we'll just have to make sure to keep it clean." She stepped away after wiping the cut and Rise hastily pulled the robe back on fully. He limped down the rope ladder and put on his clothes. He felt slow and awkward; the stiffness was still in his body. He bundled his possessions in his worn leather coat. He put the borrowed robe under his arm and placed the emerald necklace on his neck as he hobbled back up to Taiya.

She was poking at the fire in the stove. She turned her head and smiled at him. "Let me see that toe."

She placed all the things Rise carried on the floor next to the chair and put his foot up on a shaky crate. "It looks broken and not in position. Give me a second to get something." She erratically moved back to the cupboard and began to make a small splint.

"You seem eager to help people. Thank you for taking me in."

"I have a lot to make up for. I'm starting my life fresh. I will never partake again, and someday I will be able to move back into the community with my family..." She trailed off and then got slightly louder, "I have not seen them in so long."

"Partake?"

She came over to his foot and bent down. "You really aren't from this sector, are you?" She looked at his toe. "This will hurt." With dexterous fingers, she popped the toe back in place and expeditiously put the splint on tight. Rise made no sound or movement, yet he felt the pressure in his foot go down substantially.

"Why do you feel you need to start your life fresh?" Rise asked her as she went back to the stove for the hot water pot.

She came back and put the hot water next to his foot and gently lowered his toes into it. The water was a little warm for his foot, but just right for the splinted toe.

"Tomorrow will be the first ration day in years that I will go to."

"Being self-sufficient without those horrible foodstuffs from the King is an accomplishment," Rise said, genuinely admiring her.

She said nothing. Rise was strangely concerned by her silence. He talked to so few people that he wished to keep a conversation going with. She was one of them.

He noticed that the lock on the door was broken through. "Vigg and his friend made short work of that lock. For something that complicated, I thought it'd last longer against an assault."

"It's not to keep people from coming in."

Rise looked into her face. She was pretty. She was also thin and weak. And there was something wrong with her. Nothing offensive, but something was wrong. Her last sentence echoed in his head.

Chapter Three:

"I have been banished here," Taiya said, "along with all the others in the mist. The rest of the sector really is beautiful."

"Banished?" Rise asked. "Why?"

"Because..." She tilted her head down and looked ready to cry. Rise walked over and placed an arm around her.

She continued, "Because I partake."

"I don't understand, Taiya."

She pushed away from him. "You should go, have

166

nothing to do with me. I'm not worth time to waste on."

Rise did not move. He chose his words carefully and said, "The places I've been, the things that I've seen, prove to me that you are worth helping. You invited me into your warm home. You've bandaged me. Believe me when I tell you, you're the nicest person I've met on my journey."

She smiled as a drop ran down from her eye. "You are a nice man, Rise. Maybe confession to you will help me start my new life. I was begging for something, or someone. Some sort of help. And you knocked on my door."

They sat down together, and she took his hand. She looked so much like Beline that she could have asked anything of him and he would do it seven times over. "I start my new life free from partaking of the mull." She stopped and took a deep breath just at the mention of the word. "I know it's futile, but I have to try..."

"Mull?"

"Oh," she glanced around. "I forgot, you're not from here. The sheriff here, Traxe Paz, is a vile monster. He pays couriers to deliver the mull to the people. The courier pair who has the most rounds receives the best profit, or is spared for another day."

"What's the mull?"

"It's a bag of blue powder. If you eat half, you do not have to eat or drink for a week. Yet... it makes you... not you. When I partook I would throw myself into the wall over and over again."

Rise drew his attention to the bruises on her arms.

"Sometimes I would not remember, sometimes I would. I had one month where the only moments I remember were taking the next bag of mull. And that's why I say tomorrow is the first ration day in a long time for me."

"Why would this sheriff do that?"

Taiya shook her head. "Because he is a sick man."

"If everyone... partakes, why does the King still have a ration day?"

She sighed. "Not everyone partakes. Back when I lived with my family in the village," she paused for a moment at the word and tried to think of something. "That's strange, it gets harder to remember. Anyway, the sheriff first introduced the mull years ago, when I was small. In their craze, those who partook did great harm to those who did not. None who partook meant to harm anyone, but they could not stop taking it when offered. They began to crave it. In their blindness from the mull they would attack viciously, scratching and biting anyone who did not partake. They were banished to the area of the sector where the mist flows from the ground.

"The village oversights built these small houses and furnished them. We found out those in the mull craze can't complete any sort of methodical task. That's why the lock on the door appears so complicated. It's meant to keep us in, keep us from doing harm to others. I swore to my parents I would never take such a vile thing."

"It's strange the sheriff would only do that to a few. If the King did not have to send rations, I doubt he would. The mull could replace the rations, feed his people for weeks, and bring this world to a new low depth of terror."

She nodded and agreed. "One day when I was in my teens, I was away from the village. When I saw him, it was too late to hide. The sheriff and his troupe of skelguards surrounded me. He threw me a bag and said, 'Eat it.' I made no move to do so. 'Very well. Guards, do not let her move from this area. Kill anyone who tries to rescue her. After she eats the mull, you may release her.' He walked away, and I have not seen him since.

"Those horrible red eyes, staring at me for days, not letting me move more than a few feet, and not moving themselves. My brother came looking for me. I told him not to do anything and just leave, and let our parents know I was okay. He told me to just eat the mull, but I couldn't. I made a promise." She stopped and shook her head while her eyes pinched out tears. "They killed him when he tried to rescue me. They burned him... the smell... he... died." She was crying hard and took her hand from Rise's to cover her face as she sobbed.

Rise pulled her close to him and she rested on his shoulder. He watched the tears fall. His body still hurt, yet he would not let her grieve without a sore shoulder to cry on.

After a long time of crying, she sat herself up and wiped her eyes with her hands. Rise kept a hand on her back.

"If you don't wish to go on with your story, you don't have to."

"No, you risked your life to help me. I can tell you my story." She cleared her sob from her throat and continued, "I was tired, no food or water for two days and my brother was stolen from me. I ate some of the mull. It felt like sand in my mouth, but tasted like meat. The last I remember of that is the skelguards walking away. They were satisfied their master had inflicted the mull on me. I think that was when my first craze began. I woke up in the same spot. The ground was scratched up around me and I had dirt under my nails. I saw my dead brother and ran home and cried with my parents for hours.

"They saw the effects of the mull already in me. I was angry, thin, and pale. They tried to hide it, but the oversight of the village eventually noticed it too, especially when I was starting to have severe cravings. So I was banished here."

Rise was silent for a short time and then asked, "What about everyone else in these small buildings?"

"They're all mullers, just like me, just as worthless as me. But Rise, I will do something no one else has done."

"What's that?"

"I'll conquer it. I will never partake again."

Rise smiled. She had a will like the roots of a tall tree. "Taiya, I will help you beat this."

Chapter Four:

"I am grateful for your concern, Rise, but nobody beats it. I guess I'm only going to try."

Rise said, "You mentioned you were banished here, and no one has ever beaten the addiction. That's because you're all alone here and have no support. Believe me, I've seen many impossible things accomplished. You will beat this."

She smiled and gave him a hug. "It's good to have a friend again."

He awkwardly put his arms around her and quickly let go.

"There's something you need to know, Rise. The cravings have strange effects. I could do anything from shake violently to screaming in pain..."

"Like the lifton." Rise broke in, not really meaning to interrupt. It felt strange to him to actually want to continue a conversation with someone.

"What's lifton?"

"It's a poison from my sector. The gangs would use it sometimes on their arrows or darts. They saved it for the people they especially hated. A very painful sickness. I still have the scar."

"Which sector are you from?" She got up and poured some water from a jar into a cup as Rise talked.

"It doesn't matter now. It's gone. That vile King destroyed it... and everyone in it."

She handed him the cup. "That's horrible. I've never

heard of the King doing something like that. What of your friends and family? Did any of them escape like you?"

Rise bit his lip. "I... don't know." He took a quick sip of water, feeling awkward, suddenly remembering Beline. He felt like he was cheating her by talking to Taiya.

"That's horrible. I hope with all my heart they're okay." She looked around in silence because Rise suddenly was withdrawn.

"What, um... of the lifton? How did you survive?"

"With the help of three friends. I was a young man when it happened." She smiled as he continued his talking, relieved from the silence. "I and three others chased off a marauding band from the living space, but we fell into an ambush. We were all hit with a dart or two while retreating. The other two died.

"I had three friends back then. The most beautiful, caring, gracious woman, Beline." He stared at nothing and then slowly closed his eyes for a moment. "She nursed me while Bespin, the best navigator I have ever known, went in search of what my alternate father, the old man, told him was the only cure. A strange, purple leaf that only grew in dark, wet spaces. Bespin found it and brought it back. Somehow he found it. I owe that man my life.

"I went through the most excruciating pain as the poison left my body. I screamed, I shook, and I spit foaming rivers from my mouth. But I survived. Only I survived. Because of my friends."

There was another silence. Rise decided to break it this time. "If I can survive that with the help of my friends, you can beat this addiction."

"Yes," she said, "I think you're right."

"If it's anything like the lifton, the first day will be the hardest. If you can, and you will, make it past that, it will probably be easier." Rise knew he would have to keep her mind off it.

"You'll see the effects by night, Rise. That's when the others in the huts will take the mull. It's a bread of poison."

"We have another five hours before then."

She sighed. "That's probably when the craving will be the strongest. You really don't have to do this... if anything, I will be embarrassed by my symptoms."

Rise silenced her by putting up his hand. "Don't. The few good people in this world need all the help they can get."

"Well, let's start by getting some fresh water. I'm nearly out. There's a well at the outskirts of the abandonment."

Rise nodded. Taiya rummaged through the shelves and found a large dented bucket with a reinforced handle of wood and metal. He took it from her and followed her out the door, shutting it behind him.

His movements were stiff, his muscles still reminding him of his previous ordeals. He would need to rest for at least a few days before starting on his journey again. He felt as if the King would find him if he slowed down and seek his execution for his crimes. For now, he was helping Taiya, and that was all his mind would allow him to dwell on. They walked through the misty flat land of dark buildings and death-quiet peace. He knew people were around because of the smoke from the buildings, but he saw no one leave the huts and barely heard any sounds.

They walked through the mist mostly in silence. Then Taiya spoke, "What of your life, Rise? I have told you my grand story, what about yours?"

"There's nothing to talk about..."

"Don't lie. Someone who traveled sectors must have as many stories as a news gatherer."

"None worth telling."

She punched him in the arm, and even though it was in a more playful manner, Rise felt her dearth of strength, probably from the years lacking real food. The mull was an evil thing the King was using in this sector, for whatever foul purpose. "Tell me," she said.

He said nothing. It was the first time he felt quiet around her.

"What sector did you come from?"

He felt more comfortable with that question. "2128." He continued walking stiffly, trying to hide his pain.

"Is that north of here?"

He thought for a moment of how the grid system of the sectors worked. "South. It's closer than I realized." He stopped walking and looked into the distance facing south. He only saw fog and shadowy buildings. "Just over that wall. My sector. Dead."

"What happened?"

Rise continued walking and followed Taiya through the rocky terrain.

"The King took it."

"What happened to your friends?"

Rise felt uncomfortable again. She could tell by the way he stared at his feet.

"Just tell me." She was still probing for the answers to her earlier questions.

171

He let air fill his lungs and decided to speak. "A dear old friend, a delightful, crazy old man... maybe he wasn't so crazy. I guess my journey began when his ended. He died and left me the machine under my coat, and the book in my pocket. I didn't believe it could work, but it did. It allows me to travel the sectors, and the book was my map and guide. But, like everybody else, I thought of it as nothing but crazy ramblings from an old man. I was such a fool.

"My friend, Bespin found a hidden... I don't wish to use the word magical but I can't think of any other... found a magical place with a floating map. He discovered a strange weapon. The two of us and Beline..."

She interrupted at the mention of Beline's name, "Who is Beline, this is the second time you've mentioned her?"

"She..." he stopped. He felt ready to explode with his confession to her. "She was my love." He paused after this, and to his surprise, Taiya said nothing for a while.

"Oh," was all she eventually said.

"I never told her," Rise said. "I was about to, so many times I was about to, but I didn't. And now... you look just like her." He trailed off.

Taiya said, "What happened, after you found the magical place."

"The sheriff attacked. I watched it on the floating map as it happened. I saw him murder the most innocent of people. I wanted to destroy him. I took the strange weapon we found, I don't know why, I felt perhaps it was the last chance I had. Deep down, I wanted to die a hero's death. Not just for Beline, but for me."

"Did you actually attack the sheriff?"

Rise nodded.

"How did you escape?"

Rise pointed to a wood pump handle, sticking out of the ground. "Is that the water fountain?"

"Yes."

He slowly placed the bucket down and began pumping dirty water into it. It disgusted him. He longed for his clean water at his home. In his sector. With Beline. This place was foreign and felt wrong.

While filling it, Rise noticed the gradual slope downward of the land. A bright array of colors and sounds was echoing up. The fog blurred the colors, like squinting at a sunset. A village full of flowers and colorful plants, home to what looked to be hundreds, was nestled in the gradual inverted hump. The buildings were all made of a colorful red wood, and they all seemed to have gardens of some sort. He could see tiny specks of people tending to their areas. It was one of the most beautiful things he had ever seen. He instantly wanted a house like that for Beline. Quite a contrast from the abandonment area of mist and gray. It was a true flower village.

Taiya said, "My village. Someday, I'll return there with my family, when I free myself from the mull."

"I know you will. Come, the water is done."

She saw him shake a little with his efforts to pick it up. She reached out and helped him.

They stood close and walked a little awkwardly. It reminded him of helping Beline move her cart. He glanced quickly at Taiya. Beline was stronger.

It was harder work now; they had a gradual incline.

Taiya asked what Rise did not want to answer out loud. "You didn't answer me. How did you escape the sheriff?"

He gritted his teeth for a moment before answering through a stiff jaw, "I killed him."

She laughed. "No really, how did you?"

"The weapon stole away his magic and pushed him to his death. Like a coward I ran back to my friends, foolishly leading it to them."

"Leading what?" She stared hard at him now, looking for any sign of untruthfulness.

Rise's body shook slightly as he remembered the strokes the elite guard left on him. "An elite monster, a man half-evil and half-metal. He was stronger than the sheriff, but served the King just as eagerly, but more complacently. He needed no magic protection. He followed some trail I left, and found me and my friends. The weapon did not work on him.

"He beat me. I was ready to die, but my love killed him with an arrow. That sweet, innocent, beautiful woman killed for me. And still I could not tell her I loved her.

"The skelguards came pouring in like spiders. They found us and we retreated deep into the building. We tried to escape through a smaller pod-like thing, but the door shut with only me inside. Before I could save them, before I could even tell her I loved her, the room moved. The pod room shot me into the sky, and I landed in the sector east of mine. That quick, I lost everything I cared for."

He paused. Rise could not recall a time when he talked

so much.

"How did you get here?"

"I moved north, using the old man's machine. I Saw monsters of worse evil than I had previously mentioned. Child murderers. Blood thirsty marauders.

"I also met a friend there, a strange man with slit eyes that made anything seem funny. He was also stolen from me. That sector was a horrible place, one I will never return to.

"A false sense of security in a tower that should never have been built! I have more nightmares than I can ever dream about from that wretched place."

They walked in silence the rest of the way. Finally, the familiar silhouette of Taiya's prison came into view.

"Rise, you tell a strange story. I know liars. You're not one. I have to get something straight though. You killed a sheriff. Survived a monster I have never heard of, one supposedly more powerful than a sheriff. You have traveled the sectors without getting caught, and without the magic of a news gatherer." She laughed. "I don't want to be standing near you when your bad luck finally catches up to you."

Rise smiled, and almost started to laugh, but he noticed the soft indentations of new footprints leading up to her house.

Chapter Five:

They were 20 feet from the house and Rise slowly put the water bucket down. The door was closed, but he was sure those footprints were new. He drew his sword and walked over to the door. He listened and heard nothing. He kicked the door open. Nothing. He jumped inside and turned in case of a surprise attack from behind the door. Nothing. He went over to the trapdoor and opened it. It was dark. He shinned his wristlight and looked inside. Nothing but the tub and shadows. He closed the hatch.

Rise walked around, looked up at the ceiling rafters. Nothing.

Then he saw it. "Taiya."

She walked in and looked around the house. Rise pointed with his sword towards the table. A small brown sack was resting on it.

"Mull."

Rise shook his head. "I can't believe they'd try

something like this. Taiya?"

She was shaking. Taiya bit her lip and slowly started to walk to the sack. "The night comes."

"Don't, Taiya."

"It comes in the night. It's so strong in the night."

"TAIYA! NO!"

"The night comes. Maybe... just a little..."

"No!" Rise pulled her backwards and she snapped at him.

"Don't touch me! Just let me have it!" She scratched his face with her nails, and he swung her away from him. She ran at the bag, but Rise was quicker.

He left his sword on the floor fearing an accident, and ran to grab the bag. He pulled it just before she lunged at it, slamming her body into the table, sending it across the room with surprising strength. She fell and landed on her knees. She quickly got up, "Give it to me you peasant!"

Rise opened up the stove fireplace and threw the bag into it. A blue puff of smoke and hiss incinerated the mull in an instant.

"NO! HOW COULD YOU!?" She ran for the stove.

Rise grabbed her and wrapped his arms around her elbows and held her tight. She was stronger than she looked and began thrashing with her feet. She bent her head to bite him, but he pulled her down.

"Taiya! Stop! TAIYA!"

She stopped struggling and began to cry. Rise slowly set her upright and sat with her on the floor. He was out of breath from holding her and his weak body trembled.

She sobbed for a while and fell against Rise. She put her arms around him and cried some more. "Sorry. I'm so sorry, Rise. Rise. I can't do this. It's too hard."

Rise began to rock her. "Taiya. Don't you see? You just beat the worst craving. You're more than halfway there. Don't give out yet. You'll soon be at that day when you'll see your family again. And you'll be the first to beat this sickness. I'm here with you."

She slowly stopped crying and began to nod. "Maybe," she said between gasps of air, "I can do it. Please don't leave me."

"I won't leave you, Taiya."

175

Chapter Six:

Rise was impressed by the progress Taiya made through the next three days. He was in the middle of a limp jog through the abandonment to regain his strength. This was the first day his muscles were not hurting him. Vigg and his friend returned while he was gone and did nothing more than throw a package of mull at the door. Taiya was burning it when Rise made it back.

She told him, "They'll keep trying. If the sheriff finds out a courier lost someone, they'll be punished."

They saw Vigg off and on throughout the days, delivering mull to the other huts. All he did was cast them glares.

Not only her commitment impressed him. Her physical appearance was beginning to brighten. She was not as skinny and sickly. She was eating rations again, and Rise managed to trap a large bird for food. After three days she was already looking healthier.

Rise did not want to admit it to himself, but hardly a thought of Beline crossed his mind in those three days. It was the first time thoughts of finding a new home came to him. A new place to call home. He was also hesitant to regain his journey simply because she reminded him so much of Beline. She was kind, funny, and for the first time in his life, he was actually talking to someone.

Taiya had gone for rations two days ago while Rise hid in her shelter. She waited until night when everyone was gone to claim some of the gleaning pile that was always left behind. She feared the reaction of the community if they saw her before she was completely free of the mull. Rise and Taiya were eating some of the rations on the third night.

"Rise, thank you for fixing the table, it was always a little shaky."

"Think nothing of it." Rise was relaxing. He was actually relaxing.

It was quiet outside, just as it always was before it happened. Every night before bed, the mullers would again take some of the sickness. Yet, there were always the clicks as they turned the complicated locks.

The clicks were beginning.

"Strange, they start almost at the same time every night. Would this have been the time when you would partake?"

"Yes," Taiya said. "It always seemed strongest when the swirling clouds would come. It just seemed... right. The night

176

cravings were always the worst."

"The village I'll bet, thinks of you as a threat. Well not you, but them... the ones that partake. I don't believe they wish to harm anyone. Why else would they lock themselves inside?"

"That's true. It's not that we wanted to. It was just... we had to. But now that you've come, Rise, I can't go back to the mull. You've given me so much."

The sounds came quickly. Crashing, screaming, banging. The lonely ones in the huts were thrashing. Beating themselves, scratching themselves, and screaming into the night. The mull was doing its job.

"You know the first night it was horrible. The sounds I mean. The second night, still strange. Tonight, I'm getting used to it. Perhaps we should help them as well?" Rise asked.

"Rise..." Taiya said it so softly Rise did not hear her.

"That screaming reminds me of when the old man put some of the green pubescent leaves in Bespin's bread. He could not leave the privy for half the day." Rise was actually laughing. He was actually joking.

"Rise..."

"The old man joked afterwards that the place would have to be burnt down."

"I think I love you."

Rise grew silent. Instantly thoughts of Beline filled his head. His good mood was shattered by her words. The sounds of the night were beginning to startle him. The noises were amplified, and the walls seemed to close in. She was looking at him. She wanted an answer. She looked just like her.

"Taiya..."

"You are such a wonderful man. Caring, brave, strong. You helped me beat the addiction. I no longer partake... because of you. You are a man too good for this wicked world, and fate has pulled you here to me, where you can be healed. I love you."

Rise felt the moisture in his throat evaporate. He would rather have been in one of the huts with a screaming muller. "Taiya... as long as... I can't..."

"It's that woman you keep talking about... isn't it?" She did not sound sad, or angry.

"As long as there's hope that she's alive, I cannot promise my love to anyone else."

That last sentence caused her head to droop. "Please, don't answer so quickly. Tomorrow we'll go to the village and show them I no longer partake or have the cravings. Please, give me until then. At least have the decency not to crush my love until I have my family back."

Rise felt ashamed. "The last thing I would ever want to do is break your heart."

"I know."

They sat together, listening to the horrific sounds of the night. Rise was even beginning to make out where and who each of the screams were. He had given them names.

They fell asleep, Taiya with her arm wrapped around his, and Rise with his hand very tightly clutching the green emerald necklace.

Chapter Seven:

He dreamed of something strange. Happiness. The feeling whenever he had been close to Beline was the center of his dream, and yet she was not there. He did not even realize who was missing from the feeling. In her place was Taiya.

Rise awoke from his nightmare, not remembering it. He started and Taiya shook awake.

"What was that?"

"I don't know." Rise looked around and wondered what the imprint marks on his fingers were from. He forgot clutching the necklace in the night.

Taiya's face lit up like a child who had just remembered something. "The village! Today! Oh, I can't wait, Rise! Today!" She slid out from his caring arm and ran to get ready. She wanted a bath and to comb her hair and to clean her teeth. She could hardly control her excitement.

"Taiya, the water won't be warm. We forgot to fill the coals last night."

"Who cares? I get to see my mother and father!" She grabbed a moth-eaten towel from a cupboard and ran to the trapdoor.

Rise smiled.

He walked over to the door and threw it open. He stepped out and took a deep breath. "What a gorgeous day," he said to the fog. The mullers were quiet, in their "sleeping" state of the addiction. "No flower village, but it seems prettier today."

Two red dots in the fog's distance slowly materialized. Rise cocked his head to the side. The shape of a skelguard slowly began to loom. It was not walking directly to the hut he was in, yet the flashbacks of his previous stunts rushed through his head, all of them leading to the one ending: his death.

Rise closed the door. "Not now! Not now!" He hissed under his breath.

He saw his pig hat close to the stove. His white hair suddenly felt like a bright orange target on his head. He rushed to cover it. "Just let me get her to her family. That's all." He pulled it snugly on his head.

He opened the door slowly and peered out. The King's presence was gone from the area. Breathing heavily, he grabbed the bucket for water and slowly stepped outside, fingering the hilt of his sword for comfort.

Rise walked the distance to the fountain and peered at the flower village. It was a marvelous sight. A valley below the fog. A treasure in a rotting chest. The people in the village were in their morning rituals, preparing food, watering their gardens, or chasing down their children for a bath. He turned and saw the contrast to the abandoned land. Dark. Foggy. Ugly.

He filled the water and began his walk back. His shoulders did not hurt, his fingers were feeling almost normal, and his toe was better. He could probably run on it by now, but he did not try to. The jogging helped to regain his strength.

Rise felt alive, a fresh breath of air in his lungs. He probably started more conversations these past few days than he had his whole life.

When he made it back to the hut, he saw more footprints in the wet earth. There were boots that walked off into the distance of the fog. The silence began to trigger his adrenaline. He rushed inside and saw Taiya half-naked, trying to decide between the only two dresses she owned. He turned away embarrassed, and she laughed at him.

With his back turned he placed the water down and said, "I saw footprints, I wasn't sure..."

"Probably just a skelguard patrolling. You can turn around now."

Rise did and saw her in a beautiful purple gown with short sleeves. Her hair was still wet, and her movements were invigorating. She twirled in her dress and said, "I have not worn this since I left home."

"You look gorgeous."

"And your hat looks ridiculous."

She held out her arm and said, "Come." She giggled. Rise could not believe the transformation. Her bruises were almost gone, her sunken eyes seemed revived, and she was smiling hard enough to pull her cheeks off. She was beautiful.

He took a sip of the water in the bucket and then wiped his hands on his pants. He took her arm and walked out the door with her.

They walked quickly. Rise held his steady fast pace and Taiya bounced a little. The edges of her dress were becoming dirty from the wet ground, but she did not notice or care.

They made it to the hill overlooking the village and she pulled on his arm, "Run with me!"

Rise smiled and said, "My foot can't take it yet. Go ahead, I'll follow." He laughed and playfully pushed her. She ran.

Rise walked quickly downhill and followed her as best he could.

By now a few people of the village had spotted the two and stopped their work to stare. "I'm back!" She yelled, "I broke the addiction! I'm back!"

The villagers did not know exactly what was happening. They looked at each other confused.

The village outskirts consisted of all houses while the inside was nothing but flower gardens that circled a stone well with a wooden cover and draw bucket. The wood looked old and almost rotten. A well that had not been used for some time and looked merely decorative. Rise loved everything about the village. He smelled the smoke from the meat being cooked in various homes. He saw mothers outside their homes sewing. He saw Taiya running to a white hut. She pounded on it, "Mother, Father! I'm home!"

Rise fell quite a ways behind, but he could sill make out the surprised look of the two parents and young children that answered the door. The older ones were smiling and laughing between tears. They were hugging and embracing and spinning around. Muffled questions were being asked.

She nodded them all away and then pointed to Rise. He felt awkward from the attention and had half a mind to stop walking, yet he could not stop smiling at the sight. He could start to make out their conversations, "Taiya! My girl! My girl!" The father was even crying, "How is this possible? What about the mull? You look... healthy. Everyone! My daughter is well again! Stranger! Come inside, please, we'll prepare you the finest feast you have ever seen!"

Rise listened as Taiya excitedly told them all that

happened. The mother listened over her shoulder as she prepared the food. She was a dainty creature, barely five feet tall with short blonde hair and a sharp nose. The father was a wide man with bushy hair on his head and face. It had tints of red through the brown. The two small children's ages could not have added up to ten. A small brother and sister, they seemed completely fond of each other but they did not know their older sister. They both had their mother's nose, but their father's hair.

The hut was beautiful. The father must have been a carpenter. The inside reminded him of Beline's house. Carved pillars, chairs, and posts were everywhere. The man loved to carve flowers and plants. The whole place overflowed with beauty. No wonder Taiya was excited to come back. Perhaps happiness was closer than everyone believed.

The Father spoke, "Rise, you are positively the most kind hearted man I have ever met. Who would have thought someone could come back from the mull grounds? Ha! Glorious day! My love, finish with the food, already!" It was not a domineering voice, it was a quiet, soothing one.

"You have a beautiful village here. I've never seen so many flowers," Rise said.

"It used to have a river, but it has long since dried up. I was very little when my father built that well, but it too dried up. We have to travel a few miles to the east for any clean water, but we manage to keep the flowers, and our families watered."

The food was spread out before them and Rise could not believe at all the variety. Meat, vegetables, breads... his stomach growled obnoxiously.

Hurried footsteps could be heard outside. The noise distracted the man from the festivities, and he went to the window to look outside. He pushed aside the clean curtains and mumbled, "The sheriff is here again! Curse him!"

The mother was adding some seasoning to the meat and vegetables. "He's been here every two days for a week now. He's ruthless, searching for a white haired man."

Rise felt his heart begin to stir and he quickly lost his appetite.

Taiya looked at Rise nervously and quickly hid her surprise. "Uh, why... why would he do that? I mean... why does he look for this man?"

"He never said," the father answered. "But there have been rumors spread by some news gatherers that this man killed a sheriff. Bah! He has three skels with him, and that infernal magic stick."

Rise walked over to the window and peered out, hoping his hat covered every inch of hair. His mind was racing with scenarios, each leading to his death.

The sheriff of this sector was a short, handsome man with a rounded face that was marked with a sneer. He pulled the magic stick upward and fired into the air. The loud noise echoed to the extent of the small village. "Peasants!" His raspy deep voice called, "Come out of your homes, now!"

He spoke a few muffled orders to the skelguards who went tromping through the flower beds to the exact middle of the village. One skelguard was holding Vigg by a broken arm.

Rise stood next to Taiya and whispered into her ear, "Promise me, no matter what happens, you'll live a happy life with your family, free from the mull."

She looked at him with hurt eyes.

Rise whispered, "If you love me," he choked a little in shame, "promise me."

"I... I promise." She placed a nervous hand on his shoulder.

He did not wish to use her love, but it was for her own good.

The family began to walk outside, "Come Taiya, Rise. The sooner this is over the sooner we can eat."

Rise began to walk forward to the door but Taiya grabbed onto his arm and pulled him back. She had tears in her eyes. "No." She shook her head. "No. Don't go," she pleaded.

The father looked puzzled, "Taiya, what's wrong?"

"I must go." Rise told her. "I've put you all in danger. Better he not find out which house I come from." He pulled his arm away but Taiya grabbed at the other.

"No!" She bit her lip, and two tears fell down her face. "Please! Please! No!"

"Taiya! What's wrong?" The father insisted.

The sounds of doors opening and closing all through the village could be heard. All except the one he was in. Too late to sneak out unnoticed.

Taiya said, "Let's go outside, let Rise hide! The sheriff might... uh... not like a new face to the village. Please daddy, let us hide him!"

The father frowned in confusion. "What is this? Let's

just go out and... wait." The father turned his head to the side and walked over to Rise. With a quick movement he snatched the hat from Rise's head and stood back aghast. "You... you're the one! You're responsible for the sheriff being here!" The father turned angry, his face a deep red. He threw the hat to the ground and smashed it with his foot.

The sheriff's voice seemed directed to their house, "You peasants in the white house! GET OUT!"

The father grabbed Rise by the arm and pulled him towards the door. Taiya held onto the other half of Rise and pulled the other way. "No father! NO!" She was crying in scattered breaths. "I beg you father! PLEASE NO!" The strong man pulled Rise out of the door and threw him to the ground outside the porch.

"Here is the man you seek! TAKE HIM AND GO!"

Rise stood up and surveyed the landscape.

The sheriff stood in the center of the village, deliberately crushing flowers with his boots. He stood next to the well and seemed surprised that someone actually found the man he was looking for.

"Skelguards! Bring him to me!"

The three began walking, their staffs poised. Rise made no resistance and began to walk forward to meet the sheriff. Despite the fact he was walking towards them, the skelguard's dead hands grabbed onto him and picked him up off his feet. It was the grip of death. Their cold immense strength was a force to deal with.

The tall skeletons placed him two feet from the sheriff, yet never loosed their grip of nasty boney fingers.

The sheriff rested the upper half of the magic stick on his shoulder and began to walk around Rise. He circled him a few times and said, "You're the one? Not a giant. Just one lucky man."

He turned to Vigg who was being held by a skelguard. "Let him go. You'll live for today."

The skeleton released Vigg and he ran awkwardly away.

"I didn't think he was telling the truth. I honestly thought he was just trying to spare himself after losing a mull drop."

"Maybe you should have investigated before you broke his arm," Rise replied coldly.

The sheriff spotted a loose rock on the well. He picked up the small pebble and flicked it onto Rise. "No magic protector. How did a whelp like you manage to... I have my doubts. It must have been luck."

He put his free hand around Rise's throat and began to

squeeze, the barrier glowing red, "Do you know what the King offered to any sheriff who caught you? Not worth telling a peasant like you. You wouldn't understand the gifts of the King. To put it in simple enough words for you, it's a lot. I'm gonna kill you nice and slow, hopefully add a little bonus to my prize."

Taiya's voice could be heard screaming, "No! You horrible monster! Let him go!"

The sheriff released Rise's throat and gave a look of contempt to the house Taiya stood in front of. He yelled, "YOU DEFY ME, WOMAN?! Skelguards! Burn down their house!"

Rise felt their iron grip release and they turned to walk to the house.

"No!" The father and mother screamed, grabbed their children, and ran.

Taiya was being pulled by her father but she never took her eyes away from Rise.

Rise felt relief. He was resigned to death and felt comforted by it. It was his time.

Something scratched him below his neck. The green necklace. Beline.

The sheriff turned and punched Rise in the face. Rise saw the red glow as the magic barrier smacked into his face. He toppled backwards, almost falling into the well.

"No elite will steal my prize!" The sheriff swung again and hit him. *Now or never*, Rise told himself, remembering the necklace. Beline.

The sheriff swung again, his body off balance from holding the magic stick. Rise ducked. The sheriff's arm went over his head. Rise stood up and threw his weight backwards, grabbing onto the sheriff's body. All he could grab was the smooth surface of the invisible shield around the sheriff. It felt like an invisible metal. He pulled up and threw the sheriff over his back into the well.

The sheriff did not have time to scream for help from his skelguards. The well was not deep, only 20 or so feet. The sheriff landed in an awkward position. Rise pulled his sword and cut the rope holding the bucket and ran while the skelguards were occupied with burning down the house with their magic staffs.

The crowd gasped as they saw what happened. They watched as Rise quickly disappeared behind the cluster of houses and continued running awkwardly on his sore toe. He made it to the end of the village before the sheriff finally barked orders for help from his guards.

Rise tasted blood on his lip and spit it on the ground he quickly raced over. He stayed away from the hill leading to the forsaken lands and tried to stay downhill, hopefully being able to find the water the father had spoken of.

"Please, Taiya, just keep running with your family."

Chapter Eight:

Rise ran until he saw a small grove of trees fed by a rippling creek. The creek started from a hole in a mound. There must have been a tunnel that fed the creek below the sector walls. Rise hid in the forest for quite some time, until darkness settled. He found some edible vegetation and rested until the night. Under the cover only night could provide, he departed for the flower village. It was a long journey, and the night was probably a third over when he reached it.

He snaked to the outskirts of the houses. All the fires had been put out, and everyone was stone asleep. Rise quietly made his way through the conglomeration of houses in the dark and finally made it to the middle. It looked different in the dark. He could tell the house that was Taiya's. The remains were still smoking.

Sighing to himself he began to feel regret. He put too many people in danger. He fell to his knees.

"Don't worry, Sheriff Slayer."

Rise was startled by a voice behind him and stood up, ready to draw his sword.

A shadow was sitting against the well. He was covered by a thick blanket. It sounded like a young man, "You have courage. Many don't believe you killed a sheriff. I do. I saw what happened today. You brought that woman back from being a muller. Something that is almost as impossible to do as killing a sheriff.

"I was hoping you'd return to the village, to look for the girl. I wanted to meet you. What's your name?"

"Rise. Where is..."

"By the time the skelguards pulled him out he was furious. I think his arm was broken. Even with that magic shield... I think it just keeps things from harming him from the outside. At least that's what it looks like to me. He could still fall to his death and be smashed from the shock, even with the barrier. Kinda like shaking yolk in an eggshell. I never thought that a sheriff could be injured."

"Where's Taiya?" Rise interrupted the young man's

strange ramblings.

"I'm not sure. Her family is staying in the blue hut with some friends. The sheriff left in such a hurry to track you down that he didn't even question anyone. Taiya disappeared, probably looking for you. Before she left, I went to congratulate her on her return, but she just kept mumbling something about the night coming..."

"NO!" Rise hissed. "No!"

"It was nice to meet you, Rise. Sheriff Slayer."

He took off running and the young man yelled, "The news gatherer told me to tell you to be more careful." The shadow pulled the blanket tighter to fall back asleep.

Rise did not know what the young man meant by that, but he never looked back. He clambered over the hill and ran deep into the muller territory. He heard the screams and crashes of the afflicted in their prisons.

Finally, out of breath and energy, he arrived at Taiya's prison. Something was inside.

Rise forced the door open and stepped into a blue mess of mull. The bag had been split open on the floor. It crunched like sand under his boots. It was dark, and the only light came from the stove. Something was in the shadow near the corner. Something was curled in a ball and rocking back and forth, groaning in pain. The small light from the stove flickered in every corner except the one Taiya was in.

He bit his lip. He knew what he would find. Rise slowly walked over to the figure, the floorboards creaking under his steps, and reached his hand into the shadow to touch her.

A hand struck out and scratched his face from the darkness. Taiya emerged, her eyes were sunken, the bruises were back, and she looked thin and pale. She looked more like a monster hunched in a corner than a troubled young woman. Her eyes were glaring hideous thoughts, and she leaped onto Rise trying to bite his face. Rise pushed her away with disgust to the floor.

"You said you loved me! You promised! TAIYA YOU PROMISED!"

The creature that was once Taiya stopped her assault, and seemed startled by the loud noise. Her hand quickly scraped some mull from the floor and she licked it cautiously, never taking her eyes off Rise. They were not eyes that recognized him, they were eyes making sure that her mull would not be stolen. She crawled back into her corner like a lizard under a rock, and slurped her food from her hand. She did not hear a word Rise said.

Rise turned and walked out of the hut, slamming the door behind him.

He walked westward, ready to leave this sector behind him. There was nothing for him here.

He walked for hours and hid during the day. When night came again he continued his trek.

With Beline he was too quiet. With Taiya, he felt he talked too much. Both extremes hurt him in the end. Perhaps he would never learn, but he felt no need to speak with another person ever again.

How could he have believed she loved him? It was foolish! He felt shame and sadness looming like the west wall in front of him. Beline was willing to kill for him; something she abhorred. Taiya would not even give up the mull for him. Foolish! He needed to find Beline. Nothing else mattered anymore. The rebellion in Sector 32 was the most obvious choice of action. If that failed, he could always get himself arrested. He needed to find her.

Rise approached the west wall and instinctively waited for the opportune time. He climbed the wall with ease. He was getting faster at it. It only took him a few minutes before his feet touched down in Sector 41.

Part Five: Sector 41:
Chapter One:

Before his descent Rise noticed an incredibly lush sector that lay beneath him. It may just be the thing to take his mind away from his troubles. Instead of being greeted by shards of broken glass and half-decayed buildings, he found a field full of luxurious green grass that stood four or five feet tall, without any sign of recent visitors. The field stretched for a half-mile with a few scattered trees, some bearing fruit, to a forest that seemed to stretch all the way down the sector.

He noticed quickly that the ground was soggy and mud was already encasing his boots.

He moved forward through the grass heading west. The sun was starting to come up, and the swirling clouds slowly began to accept their banishment. Rise found a leafy fruit tree and climbed into a nook of the branches. Droplets were falling from the shaking leaves. He felt protected under his umbrella of leaves. At peace. The tree was all the company he needed for the moment.

Rise reached out and grabbed one of the red fruits. It was crunchy and moist. He devoured several before feeling full, and then stuffed his pockets with some. These fruits were not in his original sector.

He pulled the old man's book from his large pocket and opened it to the map of the sectors. He used the reference in the front to find the sector he was looking for. As he thought, west was the correct way to go. Heading west from 41 he could cross 38, 37, 34, and then north to 32. To the bar, to the rebellion, to Beline. Simple. Sector 32 was apparently along the northern most border of the sectors. To the north of 32, sectors did not exist. Open land. The old man discovered the north border. The old man never found a south, east, or west end of them. No telling how many there could be. He realized he was not that far from his home sector. Sector 2128 and 41 met at the corner. The northwest corner of 2128, and the southeast corner of 41 were joined. It tempted him to scale the wall again and sneak to a position to take a look, yet he knew the skelguard pattern would be heavier the closer he got to the corners.

A strange humming noise could barely be heard. Rise peeked through the leaves of the tree and saw an object flying through the fleeting clouds. It looked... human, but had a silver shine. It was an elite guard. The vulture was soaring a hundred or so feet above the sector walls.

Rise pulled himself back under his tree umbrella, hiding beneath the leaves. He remembered that the first somehow followed his path, but this one simply flew by and did not notice Rise. It began to descend deep into the forest, miles away. He was still bewildered at exactly how their magic worked.

He realized he was gripping his sword. He began to rethink his plan. A direct route may lead the elite right to him. He looked at the map. If he went south, to 2127, west to 2124, 2123, 2120, and then north to 34, then 32, perhaps it would throw the monster off his trail. He knew he would lose about four days or so, and the thought of making Beline wait longer for her rescue was stabbing his chest. His luck would not allow him to survive another attack from an elite. He needed to change the pattern of his journey. The direct route would only bring death. He could not help her if he died.

Placing the book back, Rise leaned into the tree with his arms behind his head. His pig hat was gone, trampled to death by Taiya's father. He felt completely naked and exposed without it. He wondered if news of his killing a sheriff had spread to here. He would have to find a news gatherer one of these days and have a polite word with him about keeping their mouths shut. Those "rumors" would get him killed.

Exhaustion was placing its sinister fingers around his head. He knew he needed to keep on the move. The elite would hamper his retreat. No hasty escapes this time. The last sector taught him the importance of keeping away from people. No more idle encounters that would betray him.

He needed sleep. His thoughts were running together like water and dirt to create a muddled vision in front of him.

Rise was not sure how long he had dozed off, but it could not have been for more than an hour. The sun did not move much, but the swirling clouds were gone and replaced by healthy rain clouds.

Climbing down from the tree into the soggy grass he began his walk through the mud feeling somewhat refreshed. He began heading to the forest, curious of what this sector was like. He also needed to find a water satchel of some sort while he was still in a sector that looked wet. Too often he was feeling parched.

He made it to the border trees of the forest. They were tall, not quite as impressive as the walls, but they were the tallest trees he ever encountered. This journey was bringing him new wonders he did not have time to enjoy, and new dangers he barely had time to react to. Rise saw a group of strange plants as tall as he was. The leaves were broad, a foot or so long and bent downward in the middle, retaining large puddles of rain water. He took his sword and cut off a leaf. He noticed it was looking a little dull in some spots from his previous battles.

He quickly swallowed four leaves worth of water, and let it trickle down to his stomach. Peering into the forest he saw no signs of life. He took his first step in and immediately felt the dry dirt under the forest canopy. He kept telling himself, *not too far*. He did not wish to meet up with that elite bounty hunter. He felt less exposed in the forest, and wanted just a peek at the town. It was intriguing that a whole sector could consist of only trees. The living space had to be somewhere in the woods.

No discernible paths, yet not too much undergrowth. It was fairly easy to travel.

Rise came upon the first sign of life, wood steps nailed into a tree. Some of the nails in the steps were bent and then hammered in, evidence of child-craft.

The tree split into two sections at the top, and in the

189

nook was a flat board. Rise climbed the clumsy ladder and sat on his perch thirty feet in the air. The green leaves were draping around him, and he felt discreet and protected on the small board. He drew his sword and pulled the whetstone from its holster on the underside of his scabbard. He placed the stone, which was looking a little worn too, in an open knot in the tree that still had some water left in it. Watching the birds and wind move the trees for ten minutes, he waited until he thought the stone was sufficiently soaked. Rise set the sword blade at a 20° angle to the stone and began moving the stone along the serrated blade towards himself in an arc. As he came to the end of the stone he released pressure, exactly as the old man taught him years ago. After both sides were done, he grabbed a leaf and was pleased with the refinement as the sword perfectly sliced it apart. He replaced his tools and was about to get down when he heard someone running. There was some laughter along with the hastened steps. A group of boys. Rise could just barely make them out, they were running east and not very close. He caught glimpses of them between the foliage, the one in lead was wearing a blue cloak. It looked as if he were being chased by the other boys. He was too far away to tell.

Rise climbed down the tree and began walking. He walked for half the day. He could now hear the sounds of the village. The ground sloped upward, and he slowly made his way to the top. It flattened out, and he hid behind the bushes for a quick survey. The hamlet surrounded a lake probably a quarter mile in diameter. The village went all the way around it, made mostly of small log huts. There were also many tree structures with rope ladders hanging from them. A town above a town. He saw a few fishers wading in the water. The family groups were busy making preparations such as arrows, bows, and fire.

Something startled him. An unwanted shape. He made out the figure of a lone skelguard standing motionless in the middle of the village. No one walked within a hundred feet of it. It was as still as a tree; waiting for something.

Small bushes that formed a hedge surrounded the town, and Rise used the cover liberally as he prowled around to the west. He saw a couple men pointing and whispering across the lake, completely unaware of his presence. He could make out the brown sheriff uniform and the metal suit of the elite guard. His heart began to pound. He had wandered too far. The two hunters were just across the small lake. They were having a conversation and the elite smashed his fist into his other hand. The sheriff looked like he nodded, but it was hard to see from his distance.

The metal man nodded his head, and there was a burst of light as the leaves around him blew away. He heard the humming noise as he floated into the air and then disappeared into the sky flying westward. He sighed with relief.

The sheriff's voice echoed over the lake, "FORM UP!"

The skelguard obeyed, and Rise saw a few that were hidden come out of the forest on the other side of the lake. The sheriff pointed to a man fishing a safe distance away. The skelguards began walking over to him. The sheriff turned his back and walked westward into the woods.

They stiffly waded out into the water and approached the man, the invisible shielding turning the water around them red. He turned and stared at them, not moving. Rise nodded to himself as he had seen this many times. This man was obviously one of those people that felt they would never get arrested. Rise felt slightly more protected in his cover of brush a quarter mile away from the excitement. He felt sorry for the man, yet was disgusted with himself for his relief. The monsters grabbed the man by the arms and dragged him away. His screams echoed to Rise and he closed his eyes. He heard the man kick his feet in the water.

He forced his eyes open and watched as the man was quickly dragged through the bushes and vanished.

Once the skeletons and their prisoner disappeared into the woods, he continued his loop. He kept low and well hidden in the brush.

He made a mental count as he began his circle. The community was 500 strong and not one of them cast a second glance when the man was arrested.

He snaked roughly 100 feet and saw an old woman bundled in blankets next to a hallowed-out dirt mound with a board over it, forming more of a den than a shelter. She had long gray hair and was blindfolded. She sat with her legs crossed and back straight. A short tree stood 30 feet from her on her left side, and a group of mean looking children had climbed it and were staring at her.

Rise crept closer. If she was really blind, it might be the chance he was looking for.

As he got closer he saw one of the boys take a small rock from his pocket and throw it at the woman. It missed by a few feet. The next one took a turn and got closer. The third was wide again.

Rise grit his teeth. What sort of children did not respect

the old?

The fourth was a dirty little girl and she threw a decent stone. To Rise's surprise, the woman bent her head just in time, and the rock flew over her neck.

An adult walked over to the tree and began yelling at the kids.

"Finally," Rise muttered to himself.

"Throw up higher! She hears it better when it comes straight at her!"

Rise clenched his fists. The blind woman just sat with her legs crossed, never saying a thing.

The adult continued to yell at the kids, "Get down from there! You can throw at her later, we have work to do! Gargier just got taken, and we gotta claim some of his stuff before his sons get back from hunting."

The children climbed down obediently and followed the man who was ugly enough to be their father. He noticed most of the villagers wore yellow or blue cloaks with animal hide pants. All the men wore beards, and all the women kept their hair short. Just an ugly community all around. He found it hard to believe that such an ugly group of people lived in such a beautiful place. The sectors never failed to surprise him.

Rise made it within three body lengths of the woman. Her right ear seemed to twitch slightly as his foot came down on a small twig. He slowly lowered himself and sat. He was intrigued by the old lady and wanted to talk to her. But, if she were not blind, and merely in some sort of meditation, he did not want to be discovered. Time would reveal.

He was perfectly hidden in a cluster of tightly packed bushes and as long as he did not move he kept silent.

A few people would occasionally walk past the old one. Some spit on her, others swore at her, calling her a waste of breath. Each time she heard footsteps approaching she would say in the sweetest voice, "Could you please fill my water jar up and bring me a piece of food?"

Six people walked by, and none did anything. The seventh gave Rise the information he had been waiting for.

"Don't speak to me, you blind waste."

Rise was angered and wanted to beat the man's smug face into the dirt. He received the notion that they were not just mean to the blind woman. They were mean to everyone. It was a community that thrived on hate and greed.

Rise did not dare move forward, not in daylight, although he felt pity for the woman. He grabbed a fruit from his pocket and after making sure no one was looking, tossed it towards the lady. It rolled perfectly beside her through the leaves, and her boney hand shot out instantly, without moving her head, to grab it. She picked it up and dusted it off. "An apple?" She laughed.

She took a few bites with the few teeth she had and took her time chewing it. After some difficulty she managed to eat three bites. Rise wished he could have offered a more gum-friendly gift.

Without turning her head she said, "I didn't think I recognized your footsteps when you approached. No one here has boots anymore."

Rise darted his eyes, looking for who she was talking to.

"Yes I know you're there. Why are you hiding?"

Rise said nothing.

"No matter," the lady said, licking at the apple. "You are a silent, kind man. No one else gets angry when people curse at me. Your heart beats so fast when they insult me. I appreciate your sympathy, but don't need it."

Rise still said nothing and merely watched the town work. Many water troughs were built. The wives would boil the lake water and then strain it into the wood troughs. After it was cool it was suitable for drinking. One or two of the tree houses had a rope pulley that moved buckets from the ground to the top level. Such mean people had such ingenious methods.

Every time another passerby made fun of the old lady, Rise felt his heart beat faster. She must have heard him somehow.

Finally, the dark clouds began to follow the night. The community began to put out their fires and go to their tree houses or ground level homes to sleep. The old woman eventually moved and pulled herself under the hollowed-out hole with the board over it. She bedded down on a bundle of old blankets.

When Rise was sure every angry person in the village was asleep, he ventured out and grabbed the old lady's water bucket. He went over to a trough, stole some water, quickly walked back, and placed the bucket down.

"I thought you might do that."

The old lady startled him.

"No one else brings me water. I normally wait until they sleep to get some, and then find some scraps they didn't eat."

Rise asked, "Why do they hate you?"

"Because," she said mater-of-factly, "I am blind."

"That's no excuse. You should be respected all the more."

"I think so too." Rise could not see her smile under her cove.

Rise saw the silhouette of a water skin dangling from a post near the house of a sleeping family. He crept over to the house and looked around. He took it and freely used their water basin to fill it. He drank his fill and grabbed at some vegetables from a wood bin they forgot to seal up with a lid.

He walked over to the lady who had said nothing more. "Do you need anything else, before I go?" he whispered.

"No," she said. "But you do."

Rise was silent for a while, not sure whether to answer. Finally he whispered, "What do I need?"

"Information, my sweet. But first, you must answer one question, and do so honestly. Is your hair white?"

Rise felt his heart begin to pound slightly harder.

"My, my, don't get nervous over that question, just answer it. I can't harm you, I am very old," she chuckled.

The fact she felt his nervousness made him even more uncomfortable.

"How do you know..."

She cut him off, "Please, answer my question."

He sighed. "Yes."

She giggled delightfully. "Oh, so you are the one. My dear son, if I could move more freely I would kiss you."

"How do you know so much?"

"My eyes may be dead, but my ears are more alive than yours will ever be. A lifetime without eyes will do that for you. Your heart beats faster every time someone cursed me. It beat faster when you were nervous about my knowledge." Her voice was getting a little louder, "Your beat stayed rhythmic when you answered what color your hair was... in other words, my boy, you were telling the truth."

Rise gestured with his hands, forgetting she was blind for a moment, "Please, don't speak so loudly..."

"Oh hush. I can hear nearly everyone's deep breathing. Everyone close by is sound asleep. Thank you, for the water, by the way."

"I must go while I still have the color of night."

She chuckled again. "Oh no. I wouldn't if I were you. The sheriff and his friend had some interesting things to say today."

Rise looked over through the night at the spot he saw them talking. "You heard them, from here?"

"Yup." She was smiling in the dark. "Is it true, you killed a sheriff? And whatever an elite guard is? And that you wounded still another sheriff? Pushed him right down a well, I heard. Glorious."

Rise did not answer.

"No matter," the old one said, "they think you did, and they want you dead! Boy, do they ever want you dead.

"The sheriff's friend said the King did not think you were a terrible threat, just a man who happened to luck out. Fortunately for you, I don't believe in luck. I believe in fortune. For instance, it was fortunate for you that you threw me an apple instead of a rock. I was ready to squeal on you like a pig ever since you crept into those bushes. The sheriff has spread the word through the town to kill or capture a white haired man, and he would spare their family from ever being arrested. A nice prize to be sure."

Rise wanted to leave, however the old lady would not stop her rambling. He feared she would wake someone up if he walked away, and he dare not try to upset the delightfully crazy old bat.

She said, "I don't believe in luck, I do believe in fortune and chance. Chance would be if you did happen to kill two invincible monsters, but you turn out to be no better than the rest of the people here. Fortune, is that you actually turn out to be a nice man, and that is the key. You have fortune about you, which means you can shape the world."

Rise had no idea what she was talking about. "How do you know I didn't just act nice to gain your trust?"

"Hush up, I'm theorizing." She giggled again. It must have been a long time since she held a conversation with anyone. "Chance would have been if you were a nasty person and not run into me. Even with all your accomplishments, you would be dead, because I would only tell the nice, fortunate soul that the sheriff and his troupe of skelguards are guarding the plains of this forest tonight. They want to make sure his white haired prize is not hiding out here in the woods. In other words my boy, you are fortunate not to go to the plains tonight."

Rise shook his head, "Then it was a mistake to linger. I should have left sooner."

"My boy, go back to your hiding spot and get some sleep. You are fortunate. Things will be better tomorrow. His friend said you lucked out if you are indeed hiding in this sector, because his thermal vision had trouble seeing through trees and brush. Whatever that means. The sheriff and his friend are going to have another chat tomorrow about what to do against you. Since you are a fortunate man, just watch and see how things work out for the best."

She was strange, like the old man. Perhaps they had met on one of his previous journeys. He smiled to himself, realizing he now fully believed in everything the old man had ever told him.

"Tomorrow you will see how lucky you are," she said.

"I thought you didn't believe in luck."

There was silence followed by her amusing chortle. "I changed my mind. You're going to need it."

Chapter Two:

Reluctantly, Rise went back to his spot in the bushes. He heard the soft patter of rain above him. Fortunately, only a few sparse drops managed sneak through the canopy maze. It was cold, and his jacket was just barely enough to keep him from freezing. Just before he fell asleep he threw leaves over himself to keep warm.

Awaking with a start he lost all concept of time. He slowly pulled leaves off his head and looked around. It was morning, and he could see the sun leaking through the trees. He heard a few ramblings of the town life but felt comfortable knowing he was invisible in his hedge. He peeked through the leaves and saw the old woman, sitting as straight as ever. Her water bucket was half-empty.

He heard a father yelling at his son for losing a water skin.

Once again, Rise endured watching the arrogance of the town spit and throw things at the poor woman whenever they would pass by. He saw a few fights break out before noon.

Every now and again, when he was sure no one was close enough to hear, except the old lady, he would take a bite of one of the apples he still held in his pocket. His legs were getting stiff, yet he did not wish to move.

In his silence he thought mostly of Beline, but his mind would stroll over to other images as well. He wondered if he should just cut his hair off entirely, but that would require a small blade. He rubbed his chin and wondered if his stubble were white as well. Never before had he gone this long without shaving.

His daydreams threw him off guard, his mind

wandering to less important subjects. There was no way to know how long the sheriff had been standing there. He stood 300 feet down the lake. Rise counted two skelguards, but had a feeling there was a third somewhere. There usually was.

He looked to the sky for the elite, feeling uneasy.

He saw the third skelguard surprisingly close. It was circling the lake, walking very near to the huts and tree houses. It did not come in his vicinity, but he was feeling nervous about it.

"He's coming," the old woman whispered. The words left no mystery as to whom she was applying them to.

Rise saw the figure in the sky, coming from the west, flying just above the trees. The elite floated gracefully down, like a bird with invisible wings. The lights on its back turned off when he touched the ground in a small cloud of dust and leaves.

He could discern that he and the sheriff were talking, yet he found it impossible to believe that the old woman could hear it. It was an agonizing three minutes. Finally, the elite nodded and then took off into the sky again, leaving the sheriff to yell orders that echoed across the lake. Before he left, he ordered one of his dead followers to burn a home.

The skelguard pointed its staff and set the home ablaze. It then followed the sheriff out into the woods again. Rise saw a mother carrying two babies, one under each arm, run out of the home. The husband was grabbing pails and running to the lake to grab water while the neighbors watched in mockery.

"What did I tell you?" she said as soon as a mean young man had walked by. "You are fortunate."

"I don't believe fortunate people hide in bushes for two days," he whispered to confirm how good her hearing really was.

She giggled. "I do. Especially if it saves their life. You may leave this sector any time. I'm still not sure how you do it, but I will let my imagination handle that. I hear it's quite impossible. But, so is killing a sheriff."

"Please, what exactly did they say?"

"They said you were from 2128 and that you had two companions..."

"What did they say about them?!" Rise asked, almost too loud.

"Nothing." She heard his knuckles pop as he squeezed his fists. "They said you probably did not make it this far so quickly, and they believe you headed east to backtrack, but that he would tell another sheriff in the one west of here as well. They also said that

Sector... oh what did he say? Sector 2127 I believe, was not worth bothering with, because if you did go south from here, you would be as good as dead anyway... sounds like that is where you need to go. He said something about how the people of 2127 kill anyone who looked unfamiliar to the territory. Sounds like the safest place to me."

"Sounds like it."

"I would still wait for dark."

Rise nodded, half-thinking she could hear that subtle movement.

"Then I'll do as you say and wait for one more night. Is there anything you need before I leave?"

She giggled. "Just fill up my water bucket and give me an apple!"

Rise nodded and took a drink out of his new water skin.

Chapter Three:

Rise left the old lady at night. He was lost most of the night in the woods and slept during the day. In the evening he traced his position from the direction the clouds were coming from. They always came from the north. He then went on with his journey. He traveled half the night. Rise found another apple tree near the southern wall and stuffed his pockets full after eating four of them. Sleep was a necessity so he rested until morning. He sat under the tree feeling somewhat protected and opened the book. He turned to the pages about Sector 2127. Not much was written:

What a strange place. The prominent ones speak only in the old tongue. The people here are obsessed with riches. The smart ones hide their riches under dirty clothing. I saw three people killed for their shoes. A month is too long to stay here. I shall try to keep it down to a week. The yellow metal is very precious here.

"If they kill outsiders, it would be best to speak in the old tongue; try to fit in." He almost expected to have the old lady yell a reply across the sector at him.

Rise looked down at his boots. They were muddy, but still in good condition. His long black jacket was good too. Taiya had sewn up most of the cuts and holes. His sword was sharp and ready to defend.

His stiffness was all but gone. His toe still hurt when he walked on it, and his shoulder felt tight when he shrugged. Other than those petty things, he felt good enough to risk his life again.

Rise used some fat branches to pull himself up and down, regenerating his muscles. He remembered his younger days climbing trees with Bespin, and then his young adulthood sitting under them with Beline. He remembered the conversation they had one hot day, although he could hardly call it a conversation, she did most of the talking.

"Did you ever wonder what would happen if the walls fell?"

Rise was propped against the tree with his head low; back in those days he had a short sleeve shirt that was a plain gray color. Instead of a well marked, trusted sword, he had a shiny new weapon hardly used in combat. Instead of the pains and scars on his body, he had the flesh of youth. He remembered his pensive response, "Huh?"

She held her hands on the back of her head, looking up at the leaves. "Instead of looking up all the time, we could look straight ahead and find beauty. Instead of those dirty walls we could see... I wonder what we would see." She laughed.

Rise was silent, yet enjoyed listening to her talk.

She edged just a little closer to him. "Well, I think these walls will fall someday. I think you'll have a part in it."

Rise chuckled, "What about you?"

"Me? Oh, I don't know. I'll let you handle the wall, and then I'd plant a tree right in the middle of it. Water it, watch it grow in spite of what used to be there."

"A tree?"

"Yes a tree! Why not?"

Rise just shrugged as he stared at his feet.

"I think planting a tree would be a great thing to do. What better way to defy separation than by growing something. That way, the children of the different sectors can climb the tree and look all around without those horrible walls there."

Rise thought it was a perfect idea, but he knew the walls would never fall. As far as he knew, the walls had always ben there, and always would be.

"Your hair is starting to get white, just around the edges." She smiled. "Old man."

She pulled just a little closer to him, almost into his arm.

At that point in his young life, he was not afraid to

admit his love for her... to anyone except Beline. Most people in the living space knew about his love for her. His biggest decision at that time was whether to put his arm around her. It surprised him how the whole world seemed to stop and wait for the answer, just for him and Beline.

Rise awoke from his daydream and found his arm around the base of the apple tree. He quickly took it away. As much as he wanted to change the past, he did not put his arm around her. He had waited too long to make a decision.

Coming back to the present, Rise realized the most evil word in his vocabulary. Regret. He hated it. He was The Giver. He fixed things. Regrets were impossible to fix and therefore the bane of his life. Yet, he would get this one use out of them: he would learn from them. Never make the same regret twice. Not anymore.

He stayed next to the lone apple tree the whole day, reading again and again the book of the old man. He wanted to be ready for anything. If he had to flee from a sector, he wanted to be confident of what was in store. There would be no way to memorize the book, but it did not hurt to review it.

Finally, he could see his breath. The nights were getting cooler. The horrible clouds were coming again from the north. He shuddered and made his way to the southern wall.

The difficult and nerve scratching motions he once went through to scale the wall were gone. He used the grapnel as though he were simply pointing his finger. He barely feared the skelguards at the top. They had not seen or heard him before, and he was confident they would not hear him this time. He was already at the top looking down. The skelguards were 50 yards away from him. They had their backs to him, continuing on their patrol. Below him were many, many buildings. Most, like all the others he had seen, were destroyed. However, these were repaired better. They almost looked complete, even though the stitches of new masonry were apparent.

Rise descended into Sector 2127.

Part Six: 2127
Chapter One:

There were craters everywhere, a dirt and rubble mixture sinking its teeth into the land. It was a dirty, dusty sector, and he needed to fit in. Rise planned to find a spot to hide and remove his jacket, maybe rip a few holes in his clothes and cover himself with dirt. Yet, without the jacket he could not conceal his sword or grapnel, objects that would get him killed quicker than his nice coat.

He compromised by throwing dirt on his long jacket and boots.

Rise walked out of the small crater and continued through the night, hiding behind buildings. His eyes were trained after many years to see fairly well in the dark world, just like everyone else in the sectors. Not as well as a Writh, but decent enough to navigate. He went a few hundred feet in before he saw bouncing light between buildings and heard voices. He leaned against a concrete building and peered around it. He could make out shadows of people made giant against another wall, apparently a group around a fire. He could not discern what they were saying.

He pulled himself away from the building and was startled to see a man huddle against a rock not three feet from him. He was looking right at Rise. His face carried a young beard and very dark eyebrows. His eyes appeared as two devious lights from the reflection of the bouncing light.

"Nice shoes." The man's voice was shaky. He stood up slowly.

Rise made no move but started to pace his breathing.

"Nice jacket." The man wore a tattered cloak with a hood, which he kept around most of his head. The man wore no shoes, but dirt coated feet that were scarred many times over. He had a wood plank in his hand with nails driven through the end.

Rise opened his fist, his hand slowly reaching into his jacket for the sword, but the man made no move.

After a long while the man spoke, "I never had shoes, or a jacket." He smirked and chuckled nervously. "And here you are, a man with everything, who just dropped off the wall." He scratched at his wrist holding the club and in doing so pulled up on his cloak, revealing an amazingly thin wrist. "I have not had anything to eat for 10 days."

Rise took his hand away from the sword and placed it into the pocket of his jacket. He tossed the man an apple. It hit him in the chest softly, and he made no effort to grab it. He smirked again as it hit the dirt, his eyes following it. He looked as if he wanted to reach for it, yet he did not. He looked back at Rise. "That doesn't matter. I'm at the bottom here, and I'm doomed to starve sooner or later. Twenty three years is enough for me. Tell me, have you ever looked into the eyes of a dead man?"

The strange man began running and yelling towards the flickering light and voices. Rise saw the shadows stop gesturing and perk up to the new sound. Then in the old tongue he heard a yell from the shadows, "KILL HIM!"

The stranger ran to the left behind the building and Rise saw his shadow appear against the wall. It was quickly beaten to death by the other shadows surrounding the fire.

Rise bent down and picked up the apple. He put it back in his pocket. He doubted he would get a chance to ask someone here for food. Rise walked a different direction, circumventing the murderous group he never saw. Most of the sector was quiet. He passed many buildings, and every now and again a face would appear through a window watching him walk by. As soon as he was a respectful distance away, the face disappeared back into the shadows. "A community that never sleeps."

Rise found that staying in the darkest shadows was the best way to avoid unwanted contact. He wished he could just snake along the wall to the adjacent one, however, the watchtowers of the sector were too close. He would have to find the epicenter of the west wall to make his journey to 32 easiest.

Rise came across a strange sight. A part of the ancient city looked almost intact. The buildings still had their original roofs. The windows were broken and there was a sparse amount of debris. The concrete pavement was still solid despite a few cracks. The pavement rose eight inches when it got to be within four feet of the short buildings. Faded yellow lines were long ago painted down the middle of the hard black ground. He poked his head from the shadows. He did not want to enter the open space, merely observe it. He turned his wristlight on and shined it down the ancient street. It was starting to fade. Soon, he would need to find a replacement power source. Bespin had been the one to find them and he had no idea where to look for the small silver cylinders. Rise turned the light off to conserve any power that was left.

That was the first time he made the connection to magic. It was strange how they were so similar. He never viewed the wristlight as magical before.

There was a rumbling noise. It echoed off the buildings like laughter from a concrete throat. The noise was constant and growing louder.

He pulled back into the shadows and watched from his position behind the building. The empty paved street had visitors.

A quieter shadow appeared down the street. Rise had no idea what it was. Whatever it was, it was fleeing from the stronger noises that were about to come around the corner.

The first shadow drew closer. A woman's figure was on top of a strange device. It had a slender metal frame with two thin wheels. She peddled the small vehicle and had her fists gripped tightly on two handles that protruded from the center. She had black hair with a pale face, and a one-piece shirt and pants clothing made up of rags. She wore a pack strapped to her back, and her face showed the terror of fleeing for her life.

Louder shadows, the source of the first noise, came racing down the street at a much faster pace. They squealed as they came around the tight corner of the buildings. They were larger shadows.

Rise saw the girl coming closer on her strange device. The other two shadows were vehicles of some sort, like the ones he had seen the sheriff use to arrest people, only these were much smaller. They had four wheels and were boxier, four feet by four feet. Both of them had two blinding lights on the front. They had handles just like one the girl used. Her chasers were men, three of them, on two vehicles. The machine itself was only four feet high, yet the monstrous noise made up for it.

Rise felt uneasy, loud noises were against the law and could get you arrested or killed. He did not want the attention of the King in his area.

The vehicle with two riders was closer to the girl than the other. The man in the back of it pulled a bow and fired with tremendous accuracy. The arrow struck the girl just as she rode by. The arrow went deep into her left shoulder. It jerked her to the side. Rise heard the girl lose balance and fall. He wasted no time.

Rise pulled the grapnel from under his jacket and fired at the building across the street just before the followers approached. The grapnel sank into the building and hooked. Rise pulled the cable tightly around a fallen concrete slab and felt the vibrations in it as the followers were ripped off their vehicles. The force nearly pulled it out of his hands.

Rise stepped towards the street and retracted the grapnel. The two vehicles crashed on opposite sides of the streets. One was halfway through a large window that was previously boarded up. The man with the bow was unconscious, and the other two were groaning, not moving much.

The girl had fallen off her machine and was struggling

to get back to her feet. Rise ran over to her, glancing back at the fallen chasers. They would not be moving anytime soon.

The girl pulled herself away from him with her good arm. "Go away, thief!" she yelled in the old tongue. She made a desperate glance for her bag which had fallen a few feet away.

"I'm not going to rob you." Rise responded in the same language.

Rise grabbed her bag and set it next to her. "You need to get that arrow..."

Another noise. It was identical to the one the girl had been riding, a soft rolling noise. Then a man's voice from down the street echoed, "Touch her and die!"

Rise saw another shadow quickly grow into the shape of a man who looked to be the brother. He left his machine while it was still moving and let it fall on the ground. He approached Rise and drew his sword from a sheath on his back. It was a quickly made, thin sword that Rise knew would pose no threat.

"No!" the girl said, grimacing at the pain. "He... actually helped me."

The man pointed the tip of his makeshift sword at Rise, and moved between him and his sister. He backed up so he could watch both his sister and the man with white hair.

"Candra, I'm so sorry, I thought you were following me, and then they came..." He spoke quickly, but from his heart.

"Just get this out of me, Jacob!" She motioned at the arrow, a few tears of pain dropped down her cheeks.

Jacob's eyes were the same as the girl, though less confident. He nervously looked at Rise and his sister, not wanting to abandon his sword.

Rise spoke, "Have you ever removed an arrow before?"

Jacob did not answer.

"Let me do it, you make sure those guys don't get any closer." He moved his head at the fallen shadows.

"Jacob, let him. It hurts so bad!"

The brother backed away. He glanced to make sure the shadows were not moving, and then strictly held his gaze at Rise.

Rise knelt down and the end of his scabbard stuck out from his jacket. Jacob took a step closer after seeing it.

Rise examined the wound. The arrow had an equal length sticking out of both sides of her shoulder. The feathers were well picked, smooth and large. The tip was light and very sharp. An expert had fired this shot.

He grabbed the end and snapped it off. He did the same with the other end. Candra shook a little.

"Lay back."

She seemed to trust him with his gray hair, and she did as instructed.

"Close your eyes."

Rise quickly put his boot on her shoulder and both hands on the arrow and pulled as he pushed down with his foot. The arrow quickly slid out as she screamed.

He drew his sword and cut off the strap of the pack the sister had been carrying. He did his best to tie it around her shoulder to prevent too much blood from escaping. Rise helped the girl to her feet and saw she could not be more than 18. The same was true of the brother who was growing less suspicious, but grabbed the pack quickly.

Jacob walked to one of the vehicles of the pursuers. The machine was rumbling softly. He pulled it right side up with effort, and threw the pack under the seat. "Get on."

Rise helped Candra into the rear of the seat.

"Come with us," Candra said.

"No!" Jacob hissed. "He..."

"Quiet! He deserves at least a safe night to rest." She practically pulled Rise next to her with her good arm. "And don't forget the bicycles!"

He sat down awkwardly on the strange vehicle while Jacob placed the bicycles on the back.

The vehicle shook constantly, but the seats were very comfortable. Some sort of soft fabric he had never felt before.

Jacob assumed the front position behind the handle bars and pulled the trigger. The machine roared and with a kick of his foot the wheels pulled the vehicle forward with more ferocity than Rise was expecting.

The brother laughed, "It's like the old one father used to have, Candra!" He could just barely be heard over the noise. "Too bad we don't have any liquid coal to keep it running for long."

Rise felt uneasy. Jacob was driving it down the street and eventually took it between the buildings onto a dirt path. The noise it made was almost deafening by itself, but the bumpy tires added another level of noise.

Candra saw Rise's doubtful expression and yelled over the rumbling, "Don't worry. Jacob used to drive one of these for fun when he was little!"

Rise was certain that no one in their right mind would drive one of these things for fun. The brother was trying to scare him by the way he would drift off the path just to squeeze between close objects. Rise had to admit, as unsafe as he felt, it never seemed off balanced and he never hit anything.

The buildings were gone now and replaced by a dead forest. All the trees were rotted and short. A crumbling stone wall four feet high ran parallel to the trail Jacob was following.

Candra said, "This is much faster than the bicycles."

There was a small break in the wall, five feet across, and Jacob went off the trail between a group of dead trees and through the break. The dirt gradually turned to gravel, then back to pavement, and the buildings were once again shooting by at a speed faster than Rise felt possible. The pavement seemed to fly out from under them. He wanted off. He hated the thought of his life being in the hands of the youth.

A small house was at the corner where four old streets met. Rise saw a few faces peek through the windows of the adjacent houses, yet they quickly went back into the shadows. Each of the dwellings had smoke rising from them; a cozy look. They had taken him to the living space of the sector. Many dwellings stood along the different paved streets, each with a disparate color or style. None were taller than two floors, and they were well kept. None had old paint, and none looked as if the slightest breeze would crumble their hospitable walls. Much nicer buildings here than anywhere else he had been.

"We're home," Candra cringed, dismounting from the vehicle cradling her wounded arm. Jacob slowly pulled its rumbling body to a stop in front of the blue corner house. Many curious faces were peering against the windows.

"Wow, actual windows," Rise whispered to himself. He was amazed at all the treasures this sector held.

Chapter Two:

They pulled the bikes and the vehicle behind the house and hid them in a shed with a lock. They took Rise in through the back door, which was covered by a thin metal plate.

The two parents each held magic sticks similar to the one Morceff used to carry. The mom still held hers on the back strap, but the father had it ready by his side, staring at Rise.

The mother was almost as tall as Rise. Her round face stood on a skinny neck and long body. She wore a black shirt and pants with a belt around her waist and shoulder. The belt held bronze cylinders; ammunition for the weapon. The father was shorter by a couple inches. His arms and legs bulged against his matching clothing, just like his gut. Rise knew he could match the agility of this man easy, yet he would stay clear of the arms and legs, should a fight ensue.

"Don't worry!" Candra said, "This man saved my life."

The mother hissed at her daughter in the old tongue. Rise had not held a conversation in the old language for a long time, however, he could still keep up as she said, "Quiet! Speak in the old tongue, we're not some dirt peasants! And what happened to your arm? If that ration rat hurt you..."

She pulled her weapon from her back.

Rise spoke in the matching language, "If you don't want me here I shall leave..."

The parents seemed a little surprised the dirty stranger knew the language. The mother was slightly embarrassed.

"No!" Candra grabbed his arm and pulled him back as he was turning around. She squinted in pain as she accidentally used her injured arm. "Stay for one night. Our hospitality is the least we can do for you."

The father spoke, "Tell me your name, stranger." His deep voice was skeptical.

"Rise."

"What happened to your arm, Candra?"

"The smugglers shot me, this man saved my life, and look!" She pulled the bag away from Jacob and handed it excitedly to her mom. With her free hand she held the bag and did not shudder from the weight.

"Twenty pounds. Good job," the mom said, holstering her weapon.

"Go help her clean her wound," the father said. "Everyone inside." He pointed the weapon to the opposite end of the hallway. Jacob, his sister, and mom moved down the hall.

Rise heard the rain start to come down and it made him feel at ease inside a warm house, despite the barrel of the weapon still pointed at him. The house looked a lot like the one Beline used to have. He felt peaceful.

"Do not make me shoot you, stranger. Stay away from my children..."

"And the gold!" The mother's voice echoed from the other room.

The father said, "You best behave, or my gun will blast a skelguard-size hole in your back."

"Father!" Candra said, "He won't hurt us." They were still using the old tongue.

Rise did not like the feeling of a magic stick at his back. He walked through the hall and came to a massive carpeted room with fresh looking furniture. This furniture was not scrounged. It was created. Huge padded chairs, couches, and even some newly hand carved wooden chairs encircled a large table with a green top. The mother was eagerly weighing the gold on a scale, while Jacob was attending to his sister's wound in the adjacent room. A substantial barrel with water, towels, and a mirror occupied that space.

"How is she?" the father asked, still standing behind Rise.

"It's deep, but a clean exit thanks to that man," Jacob said.

The father nodded. "Have a seat, stranger."

The wife muttered something about how filthy he was, but did not protest as she counted her gold.

Rise sat down on a mountainous padded seat and only then noticed the stairwell close to the hallway. It was a fine crafted wood staircase, completely intact. Three small children had their heads poking out from the railing, watching him. They all had black hair. The eldest was probably ten, a girl. There was also a boy who was eight, and another daughter who was five. They had their tiny hands wrapped around the carved posts, staring at the new guest.

The father finally lowered his weapon while still maintaining a firm grip on it.

The mother squealed, "Twenty pounds exactly! The Mauz will love it!"

"Is that horrible man showing up again?"

"Of course he is! And don't call him that! He's our only way of joining."

The father shook his head. "I don't trust him..."

"Then you still have the mind of a peasant!"

Rise could feel the agitation of the father. It was awkward for him to argue with his wife in front of a guest. While the mother covetously put the yellow metal bricks back into the pack, the father took a seat next to the guest. As he did the three children came running down the stairs and jumped into their dad's open arms, the mom pushing her way past them towards the stairs. The father laid the weapon on the ground.

The eldest girl asked, "Who is he?"

"Where is he from?"

"How old is he?"

The father chuckled, "What is your name again, stranger?"

"Rise."

The father nodded. "A good name. Mine is Haset. My wife is Avidity. You have already met my two eldest children."

The young girl on her father's lap spoke in common speech, "My name is..."

"Hush!" The father whispered in the old tongue, "Your mom will not like you to talk in anything but the old tongue. Besides, the stranger probably does not care..."

Rise asked, "What is your name?"

"Abravail."

"What a pretty name." Rise smiled, "And what are your names?"

The boy said, "Hasten."

The youngest said, "Laurel."

"It's nice to meet you all."

The father shifted his weight to be more comfortable with the children on him, "You can excuse my suspicion. We get few guests who I... trust."

Rise watched as Candra and Jacob came and sat down. "You have much to protect, Haset. As a father it's what you must do."

"Why are you here? You speak the old tongue well enough, but I doubt you're from... this sector."

"Simply passing through."

"Where are you going?"

"Sector 32."

Haset glanced upstairs to make sure his wife was still out of audible perception. "Why?"

"Hopefully to find some friends."

The rain was pouring down in thick wet blankets. The drops were racing down the windows overlooking the dark street. A few reflections of candlelight from nearby houses made the street glitter. It was quite pretty. It was a rare treat to have rain make it through the swirling clouds of night.

Two red eyes appeared in the window. The nasty skull

with red eyes and strands of hair was walking by. Rise started as the beauty was instantly destroyed. His heart began to pound.

"No worries," Haset said. "It always comes by, making its rounds I suppose."

Rise was silent, watching it. It walked by and continued down the street, its spear ready. Each time a drop hit the monster, a glow of red echoed back from the protective magic. Rise wished he still retained the magic breaker. He wanted to destroy the beast.

"That is the reason my wife wants to impress the Mauz."

"I don't follow."

"The Mauz... the descendants of an ancient royal family. They still have ties with the Dark King himself. If our family can join with theirs, we will not have to fear skelguards or sheriffs."

Rise pulled an apple from his dirty coat and took a bite. "You don't seem that hopeful."

"The Mauz are an over-gloried gang. They want nothing but the control that comes with their territory. I even have my doubts whether they have influence over the skelguards and sheriffs. But my wife is confident."

Rise swallowed his bite, "I've had my fair share of dealings with gangs. I don't like them either."

"Everyone needs hope in this horrible world. Gangs have that allure to the young minded." Haset squeezed his children playfully tight, "But hopefully I have steered these precious young away from that. Hopefully, they will grow to hate the Mauz as well..." He spoke too loudly.

The mother came down dressed in the most beautiful garment Rise had ever settled his eyes on. For a brief superficial moment, he thought he saw someone more gorgeous than Beline. She had her long black hair draped down her shoulders. The long dress was blue and fitted perfectly. The candlelight of the house caught it and made little glimmers bounce off the dress. She looked almost more than human. Her anger quickly melted the beauty away. "Grow to hate the Mauz?!"

Rise was thankful she no longer carried the weapon. She must have put it away to put on the dress.

"Hate the Mauz? They're our only chance!" She stomped down the stairs, and the children fled from Haset's lap.

Her dress flapped viciously by Rise's legs and she stood standing over her husband. "Avidity, I was only..."

"Quiet!" she hissed. "They will be coming any minute

210

now, and this place is a mess!" She turned as if she had not noticed Rise until now and practically shrieked, "Ah! Look at him! He's filthy! How horrid! Get out of my chair!" She made an effort to seize him by the shoulders, but reconsidered for the sake of her dress.

"Mom, calm down!" Candra said.

Rise rose himself from the seat and asked, "Is there some way I can help?"

"Yes! Hide while the Mauz is here... and don't touch anything!" She pointed to the room with the water barrel.

Rise bent down and picked up a piece of apple that fell, and then walked towards the cleansing room.

Jacob said, "Mom, he did save Candra's life, at the very least you could let him sit in while the Mauz is here. You make all of us do it!"

Rise said, "It's all right, I don't want trouble, just a roof for the night. I've slept in worse places than a small room."

Avidity glared at the filthy trench coat. "I'm sure you have. Why can no one see what I am trying to do for this family? The Mauz can offer us protection for our entire lives, how can you turn that away? Just think! No more fears of skelguards or sheriffs in the night!"

Jacob looked down at his feet. "I don't like the Mauz." He mumbled it in the common tongue.

"What did you say?" She lowered her head and clenched her teeth.

Jacob looked up and said it a little louder, emphasizing each word, "I don't like him!"

Rise was standing in the doorway to the cleansing room, but could not bring himself to close the door just yet.

The mother was all out yelling, "You do not speak like a peasant! We're more than that! Look at this house! How much gold do we have? You don't speak like that! You sound just like your father!"

Jacob said it louder but sounded out each word in a slow controlled yell that told Rise just whom from the family he got his temper, "I - DO - NOT - LIKE - HIM!" Each word in the common tongue seemed to drive a nail into Avidity's ears.

She screamed and swiftly pulled the father's weapon from the floor and aimed it her son, "GET OUT OF MY HOUSE! AND DON'T COME BACK! EVER!"

"FINE!" Spit shot from Jacob's mouth as he yelled and turned to the door.

The mother continued, "YOU WILL NOT JEOPARDIZE THE REST OF THIS FAMILY!"

Candra was almost in tears while the father just gawked in surprise and anger. The young children seemed to have vanished.

Jacob tromped out of the house and slammed the back door. The mother seemed inanimately frozen by her rage, and like a fist she was keeping her entire body clenched. She finally screamed, "PEASANT!" She then stomped back upstairs carrying the weapon.

Haset turned his head and looked at Rise. He whispered, "It's all right. My gun was empty. Don't think ill of her..."

Candra said, "Dad, we need to go after him..."

The mother ran down the stairs pulling her dress up slightly so as not to trip. "The Mauz is coming!" She almost squealed in delight, but quickly wiped off a single tear from under her left eye. "You! Back in the room and close the door. Not a sound."

Rise closed the door and contented himself with looking through the keyhole. The Mauz was about to enter.

Chapter Three:

Avidity ran over to the door and eagerly threw it open. "Mauz! You are always welcome, please come in!" She stepped aside, and Rise got his first look at the Mauz.

The rain was pouring down a waterfall from the clouds. Behind the Mauz stood two giants. Their noses came to the top of the door frame. They all wore black shiny coats that were buttoned and tied across with new looking belts. The water cascaded easily off the coats to the ground. Rise was surprised by the Mauz to say the least. He was small. Very small. Child size. He wore a rather large black leather hat with a wide brim and shiny shoes that looked recently made. He was only four feet tall with broad shoulders and tiny feet. His body was almost a V shape as he stood with his legs together. He had the slightly darkened skin and slanted eyes that Chuce had, and a mustache comprised of parted whiskers, like a cat's. His eyes never looked up, he always looked straight ahead when he spoke.

"The Mauz is very busy," the small man said of himself.

Rise did not like the deep yet cracking voice, and he hated it more that the little man spoke about himself. Jacob was right, Rise did not trust him either.

"Hurry about the business," the small man spoke again, still only looking forward, never making eye contact.

"Certainly!" Avidity said, "Please come in and sit down."

The small man took six steps before the lumbering protection bent under the door. They too had similar suits and hats, yet their skin was as Rise's. He could not help widen his eyes as he saw them walk in. None of the monsters he faced before were this huge. They really were giants. The floor creaked in pain as they walked in, the wood boards bending slightly under them. They each consumed a chair, and the small man stood between them.

"I will be right back," the mother said, closing the door behind them. "I will retrieve the gold."

She hurried up the stairs.

Candra and Haset said nothing. A tense silence filled the room.

The Mauz yelled over his shoulder up the stairway, "You know, your family has almost paid off the entrance fee. Maybe soon you will be able to call yourself a Mauz." He still did not look up.

"Oh, that would be wonderful!" Avidity called back down the stairs.

"Although that other family, a few streets down, they are close too." He inspected his clipped nails with the arrogance that came along with speaking the old tongue.

The mother was making her way down the stairs. The father sat silent the entire time, as did Candra.

"What are you saying?" Avidity asked with a false smile.

"The Mauz wants only one family a year added. Our connections with the King only allow one. If the Mauz found out you were lying to him, he would count you out for this year and any others to come."

"We have been nothing but loyal to your family." The wife gently handed him the bag. The small man nearly fell over from the weight, but his larger counterparts quickly took hold of it. They were silent with their clean shaven faces and angry glares. The giant men sat like boulders, their eyes roving around. They just sat there, soaking the floor and chairs.

"Is that so?" The Mauz asked.

"That is the honest truth!" Avidity pleaded.

"Hmm." A horrible smile cracked across his face. "The family that is your biggest competition, the family that has paid as much as you, says that you have more than two children. Is this so?"

213

Rise saw Candra and Haset get uneasy.

Avidity said, "No! Absolutely not! We know that the Mauz will not even consider a family that has more than two children. We would not waste your time..."

"I certainly hope not. If you toy with the power of the King, you toy with your own death, but since you have nothing to hide, you will not mind a quick, but... thorough search?" His smile turned to a glare. "Boys, search this house."

The giants stood up and removed two small magic sticks from their coats.

"No!" The father said. "Yes, we have other children, please don't hurt them..."

"He lies!" The mother said, "You can search this house, feel free..."

"Children!" Haset said, "Please come out."

Rise was surprised to see them come out of assorted hiding places. One from a cupboard, one came down the stairs and ran by the giant to the father, and one even came out from under the chair of the father.

"What are you doing?!" Avidity screeched.

"Mauz, these are my children, please spare us any trouble, and we will not bother you again."

The Mauz clenched his tiny fists in anger, "The Mauz could bring a whole army of skelguards upon your house if the Mauz wished!"

Rise almost scoffed at that remark. This man had no power of any sort, just a false reputation. It angered him.

"We know that!" Avidity pleaded, "Please, take the gold. Please don't put us out of it. We are loyal to the Mauz. Please..."

"Enough!" The Mauz held up his small hand. "Very well. The Mauz will forgive you... conditionally. A few gold smugglers are seeking some... tiny bodies for their purposes. You give us those three small children, and you can still have a chance to join with us."

"You better not be serious," Haset said, pulling his children close.

"Boys, take the children!"

Rise watched in terror through the limited view of the keyhole, his breath fogging the chrome door handle.

Rise reached for his sword and suddenly remembered his oath. No more death. He became flustered. There was no way to

214

fell men so huge without running them through. He looked around the sparse room and found nothing he could use.

He looked through the hole. The two giants had put their guns away and were approaching Haset. He put his children down and stood up. He was half their size.

"Run!" Haset yelled to his kids. They took off for the front door before the two large men even made a step. Candra ran after the children through the door into the rain.

The giant men looked to the Mauz for their orders.

"I am sorry you did that. You are out of any chances to join us... permanently. Kill them."

Each giant grabbed a parent by their neck and easily lifted them, their leather jackets squeaking as they raised their massive arms. Haset punched and kicked making no real threat to the giant while Avidity pleaded with the Mauz until her face became red, "Please, please, we will give you anything you want! Please! We are a Mauz family, please!"

Rise was completely addled, no idea what he could do. His fist clenched a towel near the water bucket. The towel.

He pulled his grapnel from under his dirty coat. It was still holstered around his shoulder. He quickly wrapped the end of the grapnel hook with the towel until it was as thick as he could get it.

He threw open the door before they could even turn their heads in surprise and fired the grapnel. His shot was good enough. The padded spear end slammed into the giant's cheek. The force was hard but the towel kept it form piercing him. He collapsed instantly, releasing Haset.

Rise hit the recoil switch but the second giant saw the cable going back to the machine. Still holding Avidity he reached down and grabbed it like a stray piece of thread.

Haset jumped onto an end table and grabbed onto the side of the stair railing. He quickly threw his body over the railing and disappeared upstairs.

The Mauz reached into his jacket for something. Rise took two long quick steps to the midget and kicked him hard in the face before he could draw his would-be weapon. The small man fell on the table and slid from the wet coat he wore. At the same instant, the cable caught up to the giant's hand and wrenched Rise onto his back.

Rise saw a huge foot looming towards him. His muddled head admired the nice shoe as it came down for his face.

A loud bang echoed, and the giant's face strained. He stumbled and the foot missed most of Rise's head but still stepped on his ear. Another bang and the giant dropped Avidity. The third shot sent him reeling over Rise, and he broke through a chair as he fell, his enormous weight crushing the fine furniture. It looked like a tree snapping in a storm.

Rise saw Haset standing on the stairway with the smoking magic stick. His eyes were blazing with anger. He pointed it to the short unconscious man on the table.

"No!" Rise struggled to talk, the air was knocked out of his body. "Enough!" He coughed it out.

He pulled himself up, and the husband ran over to his wife. She was coughing as she kneeled on the ground. "They tried to kill us!" she said between sobs. "How could they? Why?"

Rise moved his shoulder around and realized with agony the giant had pulled something out of place. "Figures." It popped once as he rotated it, but the pain was still there.

The wife stood up and looked at Rise with confusion. She quickly figured out she was angry with him. "How could you? Now the skelguards will come and kill us all! YOU HAVE KILLED MY FAMILY!"

Rise just smiled as he rubbed his shoulder. "I've got an idea."

Chapter Four:

Candra eventually came back with the children. Now the entire family, less Jacob, sat with Rise watching out the window. It was still raining as hard as before in the dark street. The difference was one large dead body, and two unconscious ones were tied together in the middle of the street. They were tied next to the vehicle Jacob had been driving. It took the effort of everyone to pull the giants out. Haset had angrily grabbed the Mauz, flung his body over his shoulder, and carried him out there. They had quickly tied them together.

Rise asked, "How much longer until the skelguard makes its next round?"

"A few minutes," Haset said.

"Don't do this!" Avidity pleaded, "He'll tell the skelguard to kill us all!"

"I don't think that fool has any control. He's only a little thief," Rise said. "And I'll prove it to you. Rule number three of the sectors: no loud noises."

Rise instructed Candra to stifle all the candles in the house. He then walked outside to the conquered villains. The would-be child killer was waking up first. The Mauz tried to speak, but his mouth was stuffed with cloth.

Rise knelt down so that he was at eye level with the Mauz. He shined the light from his wristlight into the tiny man's eyes to get his attention. Shutting it off, he made him look directly at him. "I don't like thieves. I especially don't like small men who would murder a family. Normally, a beating would be enough for me, but you also blasphemed. You say you can control the skelguards? Let's see it."

He stood up and reached for the vehicle. Turning the key as Candra instructed him, the machine growled to life making the deep rumbling noises. He saw a few faces appear in the windows of the neighboring buildings surrounding the street. He had everyone's attention.

"Rule number three." Rise looked down at the Mauz who shook his head violently but could make no sound. His eyes were filled to the iris with hate.

Rise walked back to the house and slammed the door. He took his position with the rest of the family and waited in the dark. The father put the small ones to bed with the instructions of not looking out the windows tonight. He waited impatiently next to Rise. The mother was sulking in silence, convinced they should have run, that they would probably die.

"What is that?" Haset whispered, pointing to Rise's wristlight.

"It helps me see in the dark." Rise pulled his sleeve down and covered it. "It's almost out of magic."

He nodded. "I've seen that magic before. It takes those cylinders to power it. I know of a woman who could find some for you."

He did not say anything more, the red eyes and glow of the barrier could barely be seen walking down the street. The skelguard was coming. Two more quickly became apparent. They were coming to the noise.

It took them a minute to stalk their way up. The three of them looked down on their prey. Their blank horrible grins made no sympathetic gesture.

One raised its arm and brought it down on the vehicle.

The magic barrier flashed red as it made contact with the metal. The blow made a huge dent and pieces of the mechanism shot out from under the hood. It slammed again, and the machine began to sputter. Another hit pounded it deeply into the ground, and the machine became silent.

A second skelguard grabbed the unconscious giant and effortlessly pulled it. The Mauz was still shaking but was tied to the giant. One skelguard easily pulled the three of them through the street.

Rise whispered, "The Mauz has just been arrested."

The wife seemed more aghast at this than she had been at the Mauz for trying to kill them. "But... but he said..."

Haset said, "The word of a thief."

The mother began to sob and covered her face. She ran up the stairs and mumbled something about Jacob.

Rise said, "What about your son..."

"He will return. He always does. Don't worry."

Rise nodded with relief.

Haset suddenly remembered something, "Oh, by the way, those cylinders that power your light, a woman by the name of Kessi, she lives close to the middle of the west wall, lives in a completely tin shack, she might be able to help you find some."

"I appreciate the help."

"No problem. Rest here for the night and eat with us in the morning."

Haset patted him on the back and walked up the stairs. At the top step he spoke to Rise, who was still staring out at the rain, "And Rise... thank you. I cannot express how deep my thanks goes. If ever you need something... let's just say you have more than the word of a thief in your debt. You have the word of a father who owes you his children."

Chapter Five:

Avidity was the one who woke up Rise, not intentionally, but she was busy preparing breakfast. A complicated stove was used, and the food smelled delicious. That was what brought Rise up. His hand was clasped around the green necklace. He heard the wonderful noise of children playing upstairs, a noise that seemed out of place to him. He even heard Jacob and Candra talking. Haset was beyond his perception.

218

The windows let in a wonderful light. The rain was gone, and the street looked clean and purged, except for the battered vehicle that lay wounded in the middle of the road.

He heard Jacob say from the kitchen, "I didn't go far. I was close enough to see the Mauz taken away. Beautiful."

Candra giggled, "That Rise guy comes in handy."

Avidity said nothing, although she was not in a bad mood, more of a silent thoughtful mood. She had much to overcome in her own mind.

"Hey! Rise guy is up," Jacob said.

The older children walked over to him and sat down on the other chairs.

"I must have slept in." Rise ran his hand through his hair. It was getting long. He knew he needed to shave and bathe again.

"Yeah," Candra said. "We kettled and filled the bath, if you want one."

Rise silently chuckled at the hint.

"I left some shaving supplies next to it, with a mirror." Jacob reclined lazily in the seat.

Rise nodded, "Thank you. You read my mind. This family gets along a lot better when you're not pointing guns at each other." He never really focused on the word gun before, but Haset used it a few times last night. It made it seem so much less magical.

Rise stood up and heard his legs crack. He was stiff from the couch but well rested.

He closed the door to the washing room and saw the large bucket bath. Rise dipped his hand in the water. It was still hot. He smiled.

He stripped down and noticed forming scars received from the massacre at the tower. He had been hit more than he thought.

Lowering himself into the bucket relaxed his entire body from his feet to his white hair. He let out a long sigh of relief and let his arms hang out of the bucket so his body could enjoy the contrast of temperature.

After a long time he finished washing and shaving; a small razor device with a special soap lather gave him the finest shave of his life. He paused as he reached his hairline. Everyone was looking for a white haired man. He tugged at the edge of his temples. For years, his hair gave him the benefit in battle, the misconception that he was older than he was. A looming fear hung over him that more battles would be on their way. When he grabbed Beline in his arms, he wanted her to see him as he was. He decided to let his hair stay. After all, there were many people with white hair in the sectors, and it would still save him in battle.

The children were still playing upstairs, and he heard them running and screaming. They were playing skelguards and sheriffs. It was morbid and endearing at the same time. The water cooled down slightly, and he almost felt like falling asleep again. The noise of children playing was surprisingly soothing. He wanted kids. Children of his own.

He saw the necklace on top of his coat.

Children who had green eyes like Beline's. Blonde hair, like Beline's. Tapered cheek bones, like Beline's. Maybe his jaw. He liked square jaws for boys, but not for a girl. No, hopefully his girls would take all their appearance from Beline. The boys would have his determination, and their mother's compassion. Beline's compassion. He saw five of his children in his mind. All beautiful. One with lighter hair than the rest. Five wonderful, beautiful children, with the most gorgeous wife of the sectors.

Rise became angry. He quickly got out, dried himself, and dressed.

He opened the door and walked out into the living room.

"'Bout time, Rise guy," Jacob said. "Thought you drowned. Breakfast is cold."

"Thank you for your hospitality. I must leave." Rise said it in a curt, uncaring way.

"What?" Candra asked. "Why? Stay, eat with us." She pointed to the bandage on her arm. "It's the least we can do."

"Yeah, come on Rise guy. I... trust you more now." He chuckled, "I don't really trust anybody, but I trust you. Please, sit."

"No." Rise said, "I have wasted enough time. I have to continue my search." The food smelled flat and plain to him. No more appealing than the apples in his pockets.

As he walked to the hallway Haset came stepping in. He had on worn clothes. Rise had almost suspected the family owned nothing but new ones. He was covered with black grease and held a silver tool. "Couldn't get the vehicle running, it's far too damaged, but I managed to strip the parts. Left them in the basement. Oh, morning Rise. Did you have breakfast?"

"No, thank you. I must leave. Truly, thank you." He did not even convince himself of his sincerity. It shocked him at how

220

grumpy he currently was.

Haset eyed him and then finally said, "Well, you do what you must. Remember, west wall, Kessi. And remember, please, if you ever need anything, you can ask me. Thank you." He shook Rise's hand and walked by him to his family.

Rise pondered in his mind how hundreds of people in his old sector told him that. He believed none of them apart from the old man, Bespin, and Beline. And now Haset.

He walked outside into the beautiful bright morning, amid crowds of gold smugglers and skelguards making their way across the street.

Chapter Six:

Within a quarter mile of the west wall a marketplace was erected parallel to it. The buildings closest were all brick, older ones, that had been carefully and constantly repaired. The market was full of people trading gold for food, water, and fruits he never saw before; even a few small animals. Everyone murmured in the old tongue with an arrogant pride sifting through the air.

He chuckled to himself, "The nice part of town." It was a long journey, and he hated arrogance almost as much as stupidity. This sector had plenty of each. The crowd only silenced or parted when a skelguard journeyed the street. Once the skelguard was a respectable distance away the crowd slowly engulfed the empty space like a puddle of water filling up around a rock.

The market existed of small wooden stands with tarps or cloths hung over the tops of them. They lay single file for a half-mile in either direction.

Rise let the crowd carry him through their business. Hundreds of the rich dwelling in their false sense of security. He wanted them to be brought back to reality. He wanted to grab each one by their expensive shirt necks and shake them back with the new tongue. Sadly, it happened for one man.

Rise saw the sheriff and it startled him that he had not been watching for one. Rise started to second guess his decision about not shaving his head. Without his hat, his hair would be a giveaway. He buried himself in the crowd and watched from afar.

The sheriff was big. Rise felt cursed that every villain (aside from the Mauz) would be a giant in this place. He had much hair on his head and thick pointy sideburns that stuck out from his face a good five inches. He looked like a dog with the strange fur-like hair for his sideburns and pointy face. His hands were small for his size, almost paw-like. The man was probably six and a half feet tall with broad shoulders. He had a slender waist and long legs. He would be fast and strong. The man possessed two long barreled magic sticks strapped to his back and two swords on one side of his waist. To fight him would mean...

No! Rise would not let himself think like that. There would be no fight. Only safety. He felt that his luck was gone. He would just have to avoid him.

Rise tapped a passing woman on the shoulder, "Excuse me." He almost forgot to speak in the old tongue. "What's the sheriff's name?"

She looked at him with her round face. She lifted her chin upward when she spoke. Rise realized he wanted to slap the snob out of her. "His name, is Sheriff Wolf."

Rise nodded. "Figures."

The snob walked on.

The sheriff saw something that perked his instincts. He stalked over to a man buying fruit. The man wore a fur coat that was tailored to fit; appropriate for the temperature that was gradually declining in these days. The man did not see the sheriff coming. His only cue was that the shopkeeper and all those around him walked away quickly.

The snob turned to face the wolf, his chin higher than it should have been. The fear was obvious along with his pride.

Wolf plucked a few hairs off the fur coat and inspected them, as if the man had slain a relative of the sheriff's.

Rise felt sick as the sheriff killed the man with the swords. Arrogant or not, it was horrid. He shook his head in regret over his previous thoughts.

Morceff. Rise remembered his old sheriff. He grew up thinking how honor-less that monster was by using his magic weapon on people instead of fighting them with the sword. This sheriff used the swords knowing full well they could not defend themselves. He enjoyed it more, unlike Morceff who was bored with it. It was sicker. This sheriff thrived on the torture.

Wolf spit on the body and replaced the two swords. "How dare you, peasant? Buying vegetables? Is the Lord's food not good enough to keep you alive?"

The sheriff did not slay the shop owner. He left the shop owner knowing his presence would scare away any future customers.

Wolf stayed close to his kill, eyeing everybody. Except for one; Rise walked with his head down and coat collars up. By the time he finally found the building, it was just starting to get dark. Hopefully, he could hide in the darkness from Wolf and his underlings. His coat was dirty from his first entrance into the sector, and it was another sign that he did not belong here.

Rise finally found what he was looking for. A shop that actually had a sign, "Kessis." A red haired, pretty woman sat in front of a beige curtain, resting her back against it. The shop was very deep, but the curtain cut the view off a few feet in. The rest of the shop was a mystery sitting behind the curtain. The lady was smiling; she was probably ten years older than Rise. There were slight bags under her eyes. Wrinkles around the sides of her lips and eye corners were just barely visible. She was selling small metal spheres. Some as small as insects, some as giant as watermelons. They were perfect spheres made of iron, good for pummeling grain or herbs. A perfect sphere. That intrigued Rise. No one he knew could craft such a thing. He had to talk to her.

Sheriff Wolf was too far away to cause any danger, but he still felt that his white hair might as well have been a flaming beacon on top of his head. He approached Kessi who was sitting with her hand on her cheek against the table, still with a delicate smile. She perked up when she saw a customer.

"What are they good for, you ask?" She started her sales dramatics, "Well, I'll tell you. The larger ones are great for grinding wheat or herbs, the smaller ones can do anything from entertain children to deadly weapons in a sling..."

Rise interrupted, "Excuse me." He pulled back his coat sleeve and showed her his wristlight. He pointed to the cylinders that powered it. Her eyes and smile opened wide. "Do you have any of these? They're getting low on magic."

The stand to the left had an irritating fat woman selling fruits that were half-rotten. Despite her whining loud voice, Kessi's interest in the wristlight would not be disturbed. She finally looked at him. "Step around back, please." She quickly rolled straight back on her chair through the curtain.

Rise heard a deadbolt around the side of the hut unlock. He squeezed between the fruit stand and Kessi's and opened the door. He closed the door and turned to Kessi. The sight startled him. He did not know whether to pull his sword or vomit.

There were two of her. They were twins connected to each other by a lump of skin at their lower backs. The shirts they wore had holes cut out of the back to accommodate their position. Two rolling chairs with the backs cut off were fastened together, and they used each other as their backrest. The curtain at the front of the store perfectly hid the other one from view, even though they had been sitting back to back the entire time.

"Stop staring idiot," the twin said.

"Sorry. I've never seen... how?"

The first one he met said, "Just born like this."

Rise nodded. He looked around the back of the shop sealed off by the curtain. He had to look at something else. He was not used to such a sight. The room had many small tables. Piles of mechanical objects, many Rise never saw before. A table sat with colorful liquids in strange shaped glasses. Some were bubbling while others just sat there. The entire room seemed to be covered in colorful wires, like the ones on his wristlight.

The mean Kessi sat with a silver tray across her lap. She never looked at Rise. She was piecing together some strange metal invention with wires.

Rise suddenly felt uneasy. He was in a room full of inventions. If a sheriff saw this he would burn it and kill the owners. Although, an owner like Kessi might be put to death instantly just for being... different.

"You two run a dangerous business."

Someone outside was saying, "Hello? Anybody there?"

"Customer," the first Kessi said. On command they wheeled over to the curtain and she quickly, but carefully, pulled herself through the curtain and closed it behind her, blocking the view of her sister so she could take care of the customer. Rise was left with the mean one in the hidden portion of the shop.

She finally put the tray on a table, "I will have to finish it later."

She looked at Rise and said, "Just call me Kessi. What did you come here for? Who recommended you here?"

"Haset."

She nodded. "Good man. Hard to find one like him. Him recommending you here is a rare thing, a character judgment. What do you need?"

Rise showed her the wristlight. "I need more magic for it."

She shook her head. "Sorry, no magic here. I can give it energy though."

"Is there a difference?"

Mean Kessi pointed to a drawer on the far table. "Open it."

Rise slowly opened the drawer and found hundreds of the small cylinders, all various sizes and shapes.

His light always lasted about two years before the dual cylinders needed replacing. He took six and brought them over to Kessi.

"These are the same size as the ones I have..."

The chair wheeled away from the stand as the first Kessi was done dealing with the customer. As the chair turned so the first Kessi could talk to Rise, the mean one grabbed the tray and began working again. An entire life dependent on the movements of another person. Rise was astonished at their agility. They wheeled around so gracefully Rise wondered if they shared thoughts as well.

The nice Kessi took over business with Rise. "Okay, six of them. What do you have to trade with?"

Rise was silent. It seemed like forever since he bartered.

"I don't really have anything I can trade."

The mean one groaned without looking up from her work. Nice Kessi said, "That's all right. What do you have on you?"

"Nothing I can trade, aside from some apples..."

"Let me see what you possess."

As Rise pulled his coat away she instantly caught sight of the grapnel. "That! What is it?"

He removed it and showed it to her. She gawked, "This is amazing. If the sheriff caught you... I like it. It seems completely compressed by springs, retractable tip... bad cable, that needs to be replaced... what do you use it for?"

Rise did not really want to tell her, but quickly realized there was no choice, "That's how I came to this sector."

She lifted one eyebrow, "Those walls are 300 feet tall. Are you seriously saying this machine, without any form of chemical compression, can propel it fast and far enough to penetrate the wall?"

"Sure. A number of times now."

She smiled, "How did you make it? How can you compress the springs enough..."

"I didn't make it. An old friend did. But as I said, I can't trade it."

"So you're no inventor yourself?" She seemed disappointed. "Perhaps one day you will become one. Inventions are really the only weapon we have against the King." She paused as she collected her thoughts. "The King has absolute control. Through

225

magic, power, or corruption, whatever people want to call it, the point is, he has control. Do you ever wonder why the sheriffs act like they do?"

Rise was silent. He honestly never wondered about it. It was always an accepted fact. He knew they were monsters. But, she made a valid point. Even gangs were not as horrible as some of the sheriffs. What could cause a man to forget what he was and become a soulless slave beast?

"The King keeps his control by enforcing strict laws. No inventions, no loud noises... stupid things of that nature. Why do the sheriffs act with such voracity to these rules with complete devotion to their King? Control. They see an invention, they see a threat to all they know; the control has become security for them. That security has become a strange, demented, passionate love for their King."

His face showed how lost he was.

"What I'm saying is, by inventing we threaten the laws, the control, the sheriffs, and in turn the King. Our weapon. Technology."

That was another new word for Rise. "If what you say is true, breaking any of the laws should challenge the King."

She nodded. "That is true. So by you traveling sectors, in your own little way, you have challenged the Dark King. You broke one of the barriers he set."

"Killing a sheriff or two wouldn't hurt either." He realized his mistake.

She scoffed, "Yes, but that's impossible..." The color drained from her face as her eyes widened. "White hair. The man with the white hair." She scratched her head nervously. "Uh... I don't know whether to believe the rumors or not. I didn't think they were really true."

Rise regretted he said anything.

She finally just asked him, "Are you the one the rumors are about?"

He nodded.

"Did you really kill a sheriff?"

He nodded.

She smiled and her color returned. "Hope is always there. I believe you have challenged the King more than anyone else."

"I wouldn't say that. I hear there is a rebellion, what do you know of it?"

"Nothing. This is the first I've heard."

Rise nodded once more. "I see."

"What is your name?"

"Rise."

She said, "Well, Rise, I'll tell you what. Stay in the sector for one day, you may keep the power cells, but leave me the invention. I will make it better by this time tomorrow, at the very least let me replace the cable. It's wearing thin in some parts, it could snap at any time. I would love to examine it. My efforts at duplicating combustion are slow, having a compression system like this could help in other ways."

Rise hesitated.

The mean one spoke again without looking up from her work, "Listen, Sheriff Slayer. That's the best deal you'll get."

He knew he had no choice. He did not want to be in need of a power source for his wristlight later, especially should he be chased. "All right. This time tomorrow."

The mean one spoke again, "Shave your head. It'll hide your identifying mark."

Rise felt awkward about that. He relied on it for battle, and Beline always said it made him distinguished. He would find a hat instead, one made of anything but pig skin.

Chapter Seven:

Rise did his best to avoid any sightings of skelguards or the wolf sheriff. It took him a while, but he finally found a scrap heap. No one in this sector wanted to scrounge, and he soon found that he had the whole pile to himself. He pulled a few sheets of metal out and leaned them together until he created a half-decent shelter, just in case it should rain, which he hoped for. His water container was almost empty.

He did not find a hat, but he did find half of a pant leg from the cuff to the knee. It was in good condition other than being old and muddy. Rise tied the end up and it fit snugly on his head. From what he could feel with his hands, it covered his white hair. It also probably looked worse than the pig hat. It looked like a bad bandana.

The swirling clouds were coming again, covering a dark blue sky; no rain. He could not believe how much he wanted alcohol. He could see his breath which meant dew in the morning. With the little light remaining he searched until he found the cleanest cloth remnant he could. He laid it on top of a smaller metal slab to keep it from touching the dirt. It would collect some dew in the morning.

Before he fell asleep he listened to the ear piece again. To his great sadness, Bespin's voice still did not call to him. As he drifted to sleep in the cold night, he dreamed of Beline again. Another memory he could not let go. They were sitting on the roof of her house. Rise helped her patch a leak that day.

She brought up some wine which he eagerly drank. She just sipped it slowly.

"I aged this myself, it didn't turn out so great."

Rise looked at his empty glass. "Good enough for me."

"Glad you liked it."

They just sat there, watching the swirling clouds come over the sky, consuming it like dark blood in a puddle.

"Why do you fear the clouds?"

"I don't."

He was staring at his feet dangling off the roof.

"Maybe fear is not the right word. Of course, the great Rise doesn't fear anything." She teasingly mocked him and smiled.

He grinned for a few seconds.

"Why do they make you uneasy?"

He was silent for a while. "They don't."

"I see." She let out a long breath and finished her wine. "I wonder what the King is hiding."

She had caught his attention. "What?"

Even in the memory Rise felt stupid for his one word answers. Why could he not have talked to her more, while he still had her?

"Well," Beline said, "I have never seen the night sky. It's always covered by those clouds. The only one here who remembers is the old man, but he said he was very young when he last saw it. What is the King hiding from us?"

Rise was silent.

Finally Beline spoke again, "Oh well. Everything important is right here under the clouds."

Rise remembered the conversation went on about many other things. He knew she had done most of the talking, as always. He knew they talked about the house. He knew they talked about the last encounter with the Wriths. He knew they even talked about getting a pet bird. But, he let the memory pause with Beline's words. *Everything important is right here under the clouds.* It would help him sleep deeper. Just the thought that perhaps she could see through the thick silence he created. That she saw him, and perhaps even loved him. He enjoyed the best sleep he had since his journey started.

Chapter Eight:

It was noon by the time he finally awoke. He felt completely refreshed, his energy returning. He emptied the water container into his stomach and wrung out the damp cloth into it. It filled halfway. Good enough for a day.

He began to think of what Kessi said about the sheriffs. He never really believed they had motivation for their actions. They were monsters and behaved like monsters. However, what if they were not monsters? Did they have families? Even a so-called heart? The King controlled them, and they were devoted to him. What went on in their minds? Why would they arrest some and kill others? If he got arrested he might have a better chance of seeing Beline anyway, or they could just kill him. Or worse. They might just torture him for killing a member of the King's army. He began to wonder if all the skelguards he destroyed would count against him in his crimes. They were not really people, but they were also part of the King's army. No. They were not people. Neither were the sheriffs. No person could have an excuse for such gruesome behavior. They were monsters.

Rise spent the rest of the day finding a water source and filling his container. It was no easy task. Every snob he ran into would not let him have any without trading something. He finally found a well in the middle of four buildings. When no one was watching, he quickly filled his water holder and moved on. With any luck, he could avoid the wolf-like sheriff and skelguards.

He chuckled to himself. Now his days had only two fears, the sheriffs and skelguards. Not gangs, thugs, or muggers. Even the swirling clouds had taken a step back as a threat in his mind. After defeating numerous skelguards, the incident with Morceff, and the elite, he felt he overcame the common fears and only retained the true ones.

The tower massacre. He survived that. Hopefully, others made their way out, but he survived.

"My luck will run out if I push it." He was not sure why he said that out loud. He was making his way through a collection of buildings. No one was around. He could just barely see his breath. In the cold loneliness, Rise knew this was the way it was going to be. Him, alone, and cold. When his luck ran out, it was going to hurt.

He was closer to the stands now, just barely hearing the crowd of the marketplace through the spaces between buildings. As he came nearer to the crowd, a positive thought crawled up his mind. What if his luck held out? What if he found Beline? What if he told her he loved her and she loved him back? He almost laughed out loud from that. There was no doubt he would find Beline. He knew he would. But, to have everything work out perfectly was laughable. "Don't push my luck. Get the grapnel and get out. No distractions."

It was later in the evening when he finally made it back to Kessi's.

He stood in front of her shop, a lone figure in the dark street. "Get the grapnel and get out," he reminded himself.

Chapter Nine:

Rise went through the back door, anxious for his grapnel. Kessi was eating out of her ration bag. He was not sure which Kessi.

Her eyes lit up when she saw him. They both drifted their eyes from his face to his "hat" and laughed. "What is that?" The mean Kessi sneered at him.

"It covers my hair..."

"And I thought me and Kessi had a hard time putting on clothes, you got pants on your head."

"Did you get it finished?"

The nice one folded her arms with her beaming smile holding her head up, "Of course I did. You needed 315 feet of cable... to be on the safe side. Lucky for you, I had just a little more than that in one of the strands. Cable is not a very big seller here. No one has tools to really manipulate it. Speaking of tools, this machine is amazing. Ingenious. It also helped me with my research on compression. It's amazing how much insight this..."

"Can I have it back?"

She seemed disappointed he did not wish to listen about her life changing spring discoveries. "We have a customer at the moment. He'll be done shortly." The nice twin wheeled her side through the curtains while hiding her mean sister, who now was looking at Rise with a mouthful of ration.

"Can I have my device back, please?" Rise felt he was spending too much time in one sector. Images of that wolf of a sheriff plagued his mind.

"My sister has something to ask you," she said quietly while chewing her ration.

He heard the sale outside wrap up and nice Kessi rolled themselves back behind the curtains.

She reached over to a metal cabinet and opened it. She pulled out the grapnel. It glistened as if it had just been created. The cable did indeed look stronger, and she even took the time to polish it. "I took the whole thing apart..."

"Ahem..." Mean Kessi cleared her throat.

"*We* took the whole thing apart, cleaned the pieces, adjusted a few springs, a whole day of work..."

Rise stared at her. "You took it... apart?"

"Don't worry, it still works. We tested it." She pointed to a newly acquired stone slab on a table that had a long thin hole punctured through it. "If anything, it works better."

Rise reached out and slowly took the device. He could not really tell if it felt different. He knew there was more cable and just assumed it was a little heavier. Once he replaced it back over his shoulder, he realized his body had gotten used to the extra weight it added. He felt slightly more at peace with the old man's invention back in his possession.

"I have something to ask you," the nice Kessi said. "I need you to retrieve something for me, on the east side of the sector."

"Our deal is done, I have to continue on my journey, and unfortunately, that lies westward." Rise almost second guessed his answer. All his adult life he had been The Giver, one who gave of his time to make a living. Now he was saying no to an offer of someone. Someone who helped him. He feared he was growing selfish.

"You are a wanted man. A sheriff killer."

"Don't threaten me..."

"She's not threatening you, idiot." Mean Kessi interrupted, and the nice one quickly said, "You killed a sheriff, and I think I know how."

She reached down to a floorboard and pulled it up. Hidden underneath was a square box with a key latch. She unlocked it and pulled out a device Rise never expected to see again. It was a barrier breaker like the one he used to kill the sheriff. His eyes grew large at the sight.

231

Kessi smiled. "As I said, you're a wanted man. A sheriff killer. Someone in your position could truly appreciate this device."

Rise wanted the weapon, that was obvious. He hesitated.

"I will tell you, however, as a gesture of good faith, that it has low energy. Despite my efforts to charge it, no known device I have is compatible. So just assume it has only a few shots left at most. Still, I think you want it."

Finally Rise said, "Of course I want it. Anyone would want it. Why have you saved it? It's worth a profit far more than I can give. The rich ones of the sector would pay anything for a magic destroying weapon."

She laughed when he said the word magic. "Yes, *magic*, whatever you say. The issue here is that I have tried to barter it with news gatherers, even other... special individuals, but none seem to want to do the task I ask them."

"Which is?"

She smiled. Rise could tell she knew she would get her way. "Years ago, before our known history, when the rubble you see used to be a city that reached into the sky, taller than the walls of the sector, a *magic* being was made." She did not attempt to hide the sarcasm of the word she enjoyed so much. As she talked she put the barrier breaker back into the box under the floor. "The creature was built like a man, yet metal, with a square core of power. It was going to be a new warrior I suspect. For reasons only the past can tell, the being was never used and stayed in its place as the cities turned to rubble.

"A scavenger friend of mine found the beast and brought back the historic documentation of it; did you know people of the past had a much better way of documenting things? It was a book with tiny binding stitches I don't think hands could make, with small lettering, hundreds of pages in a tiny book. Anyway, he found the being, and the documentation. He did not touch the being for fear of its *magic* powers. He did, however, grab the book and bring it to me.

"I want that power of the metal being."

Rise did not hesitate this time, "Where is it?"

"I have exact coordinates, but my research of this being obliges me to warn you. It was built to be a warrior. If it awakens while you try to remove the power core, it will try to kill you if you do not have what the document referred to as an I.D. Badge."

Rise was almost surprised she could read, but then remembered he was using the old tongue, the language of the ancient people. Probably everyone here could read.

"That is why everyone rejected the offer of the EMP gun. Sorry, I mean *magic breaker*. The being has inhuman strength, skill, and cunning. Should you run, it will find you. If you do not awaken it, and successfully remove the power, no problem. Easiest barter of your life. Should it awaken, it will find you and it will kill you."

"Where is it?"

Chapter Ten:

He could not sleep.

As he pulled out the book of the old man he turned on his wristlight and began to read of Sector 2124. After he retrieved Kessi's treasure he would have little time to review his next sector. Sector 2124 would be the next place he explored. There were only three entries from the old man:

What evil place have I stumbled into now? Dark rumors of a beast that eats men alive? Though I do not believe it, the people seem scared enough. If it does exist perhaps the sheriff released it for his own sick pleasures.

I found a family to stay with. They are a cattle family. This whole sector works with a view to pelts, meats, and milk. Some of their beasts I have only seen in this sector. I have added a few more to the animal index, as well as a few new remedies for illness in the medicinal. They have a small boy who wants to be a hunter when he grows up. He's probably at least 1,500 nights old. Their other child is a baby not more than 120 nights old. The elder child leaves meat out at night to lure the beast of the sector. His little spear is almost comical. He asked me not to tell his parents because they would make him stop. The child explained to me that his family loved the baby more than him. The child told me his father would make him stop hunting the man-eating beast, not out of fear for him, but out of fear for their baby. I think the father beats his elder child. He continually tells the child he is useless and will never be a great hunter in his manhood. But, there is no beast, so there is no worry. This child intrigues me. He is missing a finger on his left hand and feels he must compensate for his loss by growing stronger, being a mighty hunter. It would not surprise me if the child lost his finger due to the discipline of his father. I go to sleep now on a full stomach of meat and milk. Best I've ever had.

I have made a horrible mistake in judgment. It has been a week since I have written; my heart can finally bare the pain. What a fool I've been! FOOL! The beast is real! It came in the night. I heard the screams. I grabbed my sword, but it was too late. The baby was gone. We followed the blood trail, but it quickly disappeared. If only I warned them of what their eldest child was doing. IDIOT! I write this from another sector, for I took the cowardly way. I helped them search for three days before I could not take it anymore and left. I must sleep now.

Night came, and Rise was even given a blanket and padding for him to sleep the night at Kessi's. Another gesture of good faith. She also gave him a map. It was poorly drawn, but discernible. It led to the location of the power she wanted. She also left him a tool to extract the power with. Wrenches were fairly common, but rarely used because of the lack of bolts. He trusted her, the nice one more so. She did not have to tell him about the danger of the being. If she were not worth trusting, she would have lied and told him it was an easy task. Or she might have warned him simply because he maintained a better chance of surviving if he were not caught unawares. She knew that he would take the job. That all, of course, was mere conjecture if his remote secondary suspicion were true. It could be a trap from the sheriff. How else would she have that device, that EMP gun as she called it? But, then again, he also had found one of the guns. She could not be a royal simply because she invented and that was illegal. Perhaps that was part of the trap.

His head hurt. Going over the different scenarios in his mind meant nothing in the end. He eventually went to sleep despite the noise the connected twins made with their inventions. It was as if they never slept. They rarely spoke, whether it was part of their adopted routine or if their minds were joined as one also.

It was another night with dreams of only Beline. This time a more recent memory centered in his dream. The two of them were collecting wood in the forest. Rise, the night before, received two bottles of a dark brown alcohol that Beline told him was too strong. He could not tell anymore. Alcohol was all the same. One was almost empty, and it had not yet phased him.

"Take a break, Rise, talk a little."

He removed his black leather coat and left it on a stump.

It was a hot day but he was only perspiring a little. The shade of the trees helped. He stuck the axe deep into the side of a large tree and sat down next to Beline, who spread a large tattered cloth on the ground. She had her collection of 30 small saplings in a wheeled cart. Each one was in a tiny clay container. It was common etiquette of all those who chopped down trees to replace them with a newly growing one. Of course, there were the occasional gang members who took more than a fair share without replanting any, and the sheriff who would burn down a few trees out of spite for the peasants, but for the most part, everyone respected the trees for the life they help sustain. Beline was one. She grew trees, and Rise chopped them down. She loved to grow things.

Rise relaxed in the shade with Beline. She carried a water bag and offered some to Rise, who took another taste of his alcohol.

"I had a dream about Forester Day," she said.

"What about?" He was feeling talkative today.

"I dreamed we came to chop down some wood for lumber, but when we got to the forest there was only one tree left. The entire forest was gone except for one tree. I could not cut it down. Then those horrible Wriths came with axes." She paused and smiled almost shyly, "Then the hero came. You stopped them and saved the tree."

Rise laughed out loud, almost spitting his precious alcohol to the dirt.

"Why are you laughing?" She pushed him playfully, but was still obviously a little hurt by his lack of concern.

"Because," he laughed a little more, "I'd probably be the one chopping down the tree." He nodded his head to the axe dug into the tree's body.

"If there was one tree left, you'd cut it down?"

He shrugged.

It was a sour memory for Rise. She was apparently hurt but did not want him to know. He thought it was foolish woman talk, but he knew he missed something. It was not until his present dream that he realized the connection between her love of life and that forest.

Rise awoke feeling tired, yet he knew it was time to move. The two Kessis were still at work playing with some sort of gadget. Morning light was glowing around the edges of the curtain blocking the view of the outside. The wall to the next sector was close, and now he had to go back to the east wall. It would take him a day and a night to reach the wall if he hurried and did not sleep.

"I'll be back in three days."

Chapter Eleven:

His progress was slowed by muggers, thugs, and bandits. Muggers would sneak upon men and women and take their possessions. Thugs would kill just for the sport. Bandits were like the first two, except they attacked in groups like a small gang. He heard the stories of the gold smugglers; gangs in their own rights, and was fortunate enough not to interfere with them. They were the greatest threat aside from royalty in this sector.

The two muggers were easily enough dispelled when they realized it would be a fight. Rise let them both go, he was in a hurry.

Thugs, however, wanted a fight, and felt shamed if they lost. The first one looked as if he never lost a fight in his life.

Rise jogged around a corner between two desolate buildings. He was almost 25 miles into the sector, halfway. He abandoned the "hat" idea because it brought more attention to him than when people just assumed he was old. A large pale man with a shaved head, beard, and deep voice stood in front of Rise. "You move quick for an old man." That was the only warning Rise received before a fist the size of his head came whistling through the air. The thug missed, but not by much. Rise would not let him get that close again. He was irritated by the delay.

The thug was alone and for a moment Rise felt that relieved him of his promise never to kill again, but quickly realized that had nothing to do with it. He knew that if he pulled the sword to scare the man away it would not work, thugs never ran. He was no mugger either, they came from the back. The next swing Rise easily sidestepped and pulled his sword. He spun around and left a deep gash along the man's left thigh. He would not run again but at least he would live.

As the large thug clasped his leg in surprise, Rise purposefully raised his left leg and kicked the man in the side of the face, knocking him to the ground. He continued on; the thug did not pursue, more than likely because he would never pursue again.

The next thug was the victim of bad timing. An open dirt field just out of the ruins held a host of undesirable people. They huddled for warmth around a large burning bin. Many held clubs, some carried swords. Rise knew they would see him. He walked quickly, keeping a good 30 meters distance. He only needed to go another ten miles.

An arrow struck the ground three feet ahead of him. Either a perfect warning shot or lack of skill. Rise turned to hear one yell, "Don't move or you'll die."

Rise gritted his teeth.

"Come here and you might live."

Rise knew he could make it if he ran. Only one had a bow which meant little chance of being hit. He did not know if it was the cold that aggravated him, or just the sense of wasting time on an errand. Or maybe it was the smell of the place. Or it could have been that Beline was out there somewhere, and he was stuck dealing with thugs and muggers who were below him. Yes, that was it. Beline was out there. That was the reason he was angry, and it was because he was angry that he approached the thugs.

The one with the bow was the leader, for he was the only one who spoke. "Friend, this is your lucky day. You have a chance to live. I have one gold bar riding on your survival." The leader was not tall, nor very big, but he had confidence alone that could win battles. He nodded his head to a rather short, wiry man, who wore only a pair of green tattered pants.

The short man had unbelievable muscles for his size. There was not much of him, but what was there was pure muscle. Not bulk muscle, well toned, used muscle.

Rise felt Green was a good name for this one. Green came running like a berserk fool, screaming and spitting.

Rise lost all control of his temper. He stabbed Green in each arm and once across the back of his calf. Then he beat him into the dirt with the handle of the sword. He was pushing his promise of not killing, even in self-defense. He regained himself at the last instant, letting the man live through his fury.

He arose, and the leader patted him on the back. "You just made me a little richer. Now get out of here before I change my mind..."

Rise grabbed his arm and snapped it at the elbow, then broke the leader's nose as he pulled the bow away from him.

He heard wild laughing from the rest of the thugs and decided he had to leave before he did break his promise. He cut the bow string with his sword and walked angrily through the field, leaving his two victims in the mud, their "friends" laughing at them.

Rise made only one other stop to refill his water

container out of a puddle that collected on the large leaf of a strange bush. Three miles to go before the map indicated a concrete rubble wall. There would be a trapdoor leading down into the earth under it.

Night was upon him, and Rise consumed the last of the fruits he carried in his pocket. He was tired and just wanted to get this whole thing over with. An ancient fence made from thick wires surrounded his destination. He saw a dilapidated building with a large object mounted on the roof. It looked like a big white bowl with a stick pointing out of the middle. Moss and other plant life were the only residents of the brown building. He went through the gaping whole in the fence and quickly spotted the concrete rubble.

He heard the wood under his feet as he approached. The well-hidden trapdoor was directly beneath him. Below lay a being that had been described as a warrior without mercy. That being was ultimately standing between him and Beline. One more obstacle. He reached down and opened the hatch without a moment of hesitancy.

Chapter Twelve:

The air was old. The top layer of dust from the stairs escaped as he opened the hatch. Rise took his first step down before turning on his newly powered wristlight. The beam seemed stronger than ever. It was enough to light the entire room. Thirteen stairs down revealed that most of the room suffered from a cave-in. The room was probably huge, but only 50 square feet remained. Tables were everywhere; each covered in a skin of dust. Square boxes with glassy dark fronts were aligned on each table. They were like the machines Bespin operated in the underground ruins.

He shined the light across the entire room. Rise jolted slightly when he saw the shape of a man pinned to the wall on his right.

The metal warrior was strung against the wall. A form had been fitted for the creature in the wall. A metal strap held the thing up by its waist. To Rise's relief, the being was all metal. It was not human. It made no movement. It was a metal man, almost like an elite hunter, except devoid of any flesh and any shred of humanity. Its head was bent forward, almost like it had fallen asleep in position. Tubes and chords ran into the man-machine from the wall, and one of the boxes with glass was hanging from the ceiling over its head.

Rise just stared at the being for a long time, making no

movement, not sure if it were alive. It was seven feet tall with long skinny metal limbs and fingers. He had a vision of the metal monster springing to life and choking him with its cold long fingers. They seemed like perfect hands for strangling. He forced himself to take a step closer.

It did not move.

Something created to defend and destroy. That was what Kessi said. Do not awaken it.

Rise pulled out the tool she gave him. It had a small hollow cylinder at the end. She said it was used to take the metal caps off. There was a small sharp inlet on the side of the handle she said was used to cut the wires.

Rise took another step and was now looking up at its lowered face.

It did not move.

On the chest of the being was a square metal plate with four octagonal knobs at each corner. He would have to remove them with the wrench, cut the six green wires, two red, and one blue, and then take the four caps off the magic.

He took another step closer.

It did not move.

Do not awaken it.

He was going to take the beast apart, and he could not wake it up. He nodded his head in smug disapproval.

Kessi told him the best possible scenario would be that the beast was too old to work, and the power source would easily come out. He wished she had not told him that. Hope for the best, but prepare for the worst.

He took another step closer.

It did not move.

Rise looked back with his light. Only one table was in the way of a quick retreat, should the beast awaken. He wished he had waited until morning, when a small amount of light could seep through the trapdoor.

He looked back at the being and swung his light across the face. As he moved the light across the face, the two eyes glowed red as quickly as they stopped. A shiver went up his spine.

He moved the light again and held it on the eyes. It was only the light reflecting that made them appear red. He moved the light off, and they returned to their normal dark, empty color. He let out an exhale, blowing dust particles in front of him.

He took his last step closer.

239

It did not move.

He stared at the beast, his head coming to its chest since it was held a foot from the ground. The creature was as tall as a skelguard. He peered up at the face. Should he fight it, the neck looked like the weakest point; a thin metal rod with a tube spiraling up to the back of the head. He had to know if it would wake up.

He cleared his throat. "Are you going to give me trouble?" It was almost a whisper. He forced himself to say it louder, "Are you going to give me trouble?" His voice echoed through the empty room. It did not move.

Rise took the tool and lightly poked the being. It made a sharp bang as he prodded it.

It did not move.

He took a deep breath and placed the cylinder over the first cap. He looked up at the face of the being. It was staring at him because of the tilt of the head. A cold, metal, lifeless gaze. It looked like it was watching Rise about to take him apart, yet it did not move.

The tool would not turn, the bolt was on tight. He pulled as hard as he could and felt it give slightly. Rise turned the tool and felt the cap turn with it, slowly loosening.

The creature moved.

Chapter Thirteen:

Rise jumped back leaving the tool stuck on the cap. The metal arm wrenched the chords from the wall as it swung at Rise, its head following his movement. Rise felt the cold metal just graze his throat.

The being's eyes were red with no emotion on its face. No mouth to yell or communicate, just red eyes and flailing limbs. The metal bar around its waist held it tight. It looked down at the tool stuck to the cap on its chest and yanked it off.

Rise ran and jumped over a table and pulled it down right behind him for a shield, knocking the square boxes to the ground and breaking their glass faces. He turned and saw Kessi's tool sticking halfway through the table next to his face. The metal man hurled it with deadly accuracy. The thick frame of the table saved the back of his skull from being bashed to pieces.

He peeked over his makeshift shield and saw the machine trying to pull the bar out of the wall. The wall bulged slightly but held.

Rise once again focused on the weak looking neck and decided it was time. He jumped over to the pinned beast and raised his sword.

The wall cracked right at the edge of the struggling creature.

Rise lowered his sword and ran for the exit. He heard the bar being ripped from the wall as he made it back to the stairs. He took four at a time, reached the outside, and threw down the trapdoor.

He quickly looked around for something heavy enough to cover it, but there was nothing around that he could move.

Rise ran for the hole in the fence. *Forget the prize, just escape the sector.* He stayed too long.

"I need a drink."

He ran towards the small forest that surrounded the abandoned compound. He saw a tree that miraculously still had most of its leaves this time of year and climbed it. He knew he probably could not outrun the creature if it were anything like an elite guard, but maybe he could hide.

The trapdoor burst open and the being came running up the stairs. It looked around and almost instantly focused on the tree Rise was hiding in.

Rise groaned. "So much for that." He jumped down as the beast began to run for him. Rise landed on the ground, rolled to distribute the fall, and ran.

He looked back, and thankfully the being was not terribly fast, it held a quick but awkward gate and could not jump rocks and stumps as Rise could.

At that moment he heard only two sounds in the world: his heart pumping blood to his lungs, and the loud thuds as the metal man ran for him.

There was no way to surprise this thing. It would probably guard its neck, and Rise was not strong enough to cut through the metal of its arms. He thought about shooting it with the grapnel, but if that did not work he would lose the grapnel and be stuck in the sector even if he managed to escape the hunter.

For now, Rise could tell he was making a little distance, as long as he did not fall or get cornered he would be fine. Unless the beast made him run all night.

He glanced back and knew the machine would not stop. He wished he had waited until morning.

Rise slowed down just a little, still enough to keep a distance, but not so fast as to wear him thin too quickly. He had only one hope. The thugs.

Backtracking always bothered him, but this time he found new interest in it as he ran for his life. He cursed himself for being so foolish and greedy and stupid. He could have left, but he didn't. He felt he needed that weapon from Kessi. His luck had run out, and it was going to hurt.

The dark swirling clouds had been churning for hours by the time Rise found what he was looking for. The thugs were huddled around the same fire, one was bandaged up, the other nursing a sore nose. He came running through the field. The being had been gaining ground slightly as Rise grew tired, and it was now a steady 50 feet behind him.

The thugs looked up and a few grabbed their weapons.

With a hoarse voice Rise yelled, "Six gold bars for whoever can kill the metal man!"

At that moment the being came around the hill corner into the field and began slipping on the wet ground, kicking mud into the air as its feet staggered slightly.

Twenty thugs grabbed their weapons and ran for the beast in the muddy field. He had to hand it to them, they were fearless. Stupid maybe, but fearless. Rise collapsed to his knees to catch his breath.

Swarming the metal man like flies, the thugs seemed to all jump for him at once. Rise saw three heavy men thrown twice their height into the air. He stood up and ran again.

He made it back to the ruins and began to weave through the alleys between the collapsed buildings. He had to lose that thing and escape to the next sector. He had been running for hours.

"Let's see you climb a sector wall!" Rise whispered.

It was completely dark, but morning could not have been more than two hours away. Rise felt lost in the ruins. He knew he was probably halfway through the sector but was not sure. His lungs were going to suck themselves dry, his throat was going to collapse, and his legs were warping like wet floor boards. His pants chafed his legs from the constant motion.

Despite how tired he felt, Rise thought he finally outran the beast. The thugs delayed it just enough, or so he hoped.

He came trudging around another corner.

A large flat board swung from the dark and caught him

in the face with a loud crack. His vision watered and blurred as he spun to his knees. He could not raise his neck higher than the waist of his assailant. His body was too tired to take it, and he collapsed. The last sensation was the tingling feeling in his neck.

Chapter Fourteen:

His thoughts were slowly returning. It felt like an axe blade stuck in his head was slowing the thinking process. His eyes were still dark, and he could not move or make a sound. The only presence was his headache. And a deep humming sound that was a constant nuisance.

Then he heard the voice. He could not tell what it was saying; it blended in too much with the humming. He could not tell if he were standing or lying, going forward in time or backwards. The voice slowly became more audible.

"... killed larger men than that. This one is strong."

Another voice, "Hey, white hair. You don't think this is the one..."

The first deep voice, "The Sheriff Slayer? That would explain him not being dead. Any other man would have died from how hard I hit him."

Rise groaned from his headache. His first auricular sound.

A third voice, "He's waking."

Rise tried to reach up to touch his sore face, but his hands were attached behind his back. He was sitting against a wall.

The second voice, "Why was he trying to steal our gold?"

"I don't know." The first deep voice said, "I was loading the last of it and I heard him come running around the corner. I grabbed a board and cracked him in the face. Hard. He should be dead."

Rise still could not open his eyes, the pain in his face pulled his lids shut.

The third voice, "He should know not to mess with us, everyone else does."

Second, "If he's the Sheriff Slayer he's from another sector and wouldn't know."

Third, "Why would a Sheriff Slayer need gold?"

First, "To bribe the royalty to let him live." He laughed

loud and deep. "He can't be from another sector. No one travels the sectors."

Second, "Yeah they do. The news gatherers do..."

First, "Bah! News gatherers. Bunch of liars. I killed me one of them last week. No one can travel sectors."

Third, "And no one can kill a sheriff, right? Apparently someone has. Never seen the royalty all riled up like this before. The sheriff and his skels are going mad. He'd pay up in gold for this one's return."

With all his effort Rise opened his eyes. He was in a wooden room with a stairway in the far left corner. He was surrounded by crates about half his height. Three men stood in the middle looking at him. He began to match faces to the voices.

The first deep voice was the one that hit him. He was as tall as Rise and twice as thick. He wore a green tattered shirt and black pants. His dark skin was moist with sweat. He had short curly hair and a large flat nose. "It would be better for you to have died." He pointed a large finger at Rise.

"You gonna pay. You don't take from us. You are gonna pay." The second voice was a very tall, pasty man. He was as thin as the board that hit him. His forearms were about the size of his head, making him seem more like a child's drawing than human. His hands were probably strong enough to crush a skull. His clothes were too short for his height. He wore a jacket of normal size, and the arms only came down to his elbows.

"I think we should hear his story. If it doesn't match, feel free to kill him." The third voice was a short man, well bundled for the cold. He had dark skin like the first, probably his younger brother. He had a warm coat wrapped around him that draped almost to the ground, and a wide brimmed hat to keep his head dry in the rain.

He walked over to Rise and bent down so they were eye level. "Are you the Sheriff Slayer?"

The pain in Rise's face made him close his eyes again.

"Why did you try to steal our gold?" The stranger tried a second question.

Rise remembered the metal man chasing him and forced himself to speak, "How long has it been since I was hit?"

The short man was very calm, "I asked you two questions..."

"How long?" Rise snapped.

The man made an irritated sigh in his throat. "Five, ten

minutes."

"You're going to regret not letting me just pass through."

"Why is that, Sheriff Slayer?"

The one that struck Rise said, "Just let me finish him. One more hit, that's all."

"I wanna snap his neck. I haven't done that for a while, need to see if I still remember how," the gangly man said, rubbing his giant hands together with a crooked smile.

The short leader said, "You better start answering some questions..."

Rise asked another, "Who are you?"

The short man scoffed, "Who are we? Heard of the Gold Titans?"

"No. I'm not from around here."

Rise just barely heard loud footsteps outside.

"The Gold Titans are *the* gold smugglers of the sector! You don't know the mess you're in. Did you kill a sheriff?"

The footsteps were closer and more familiar. Metal footsteps. They came to the door.

"One more question," Rise asked, "can you men fight?"

The deep-voiced one said, "Slumped you out cold, didn't I?"

"We'll see." Rise glared at him.

The door burst open in a splash of splinters as a metal arm wrecked through it.

The three men whipped around to their new assailant.

"What..." The tall lanky man spoke first but was not able to finish. A thin metal fist whipped across his jaw knocking him his own height backwards into a wooden wall.

The dark man who had hit Rise ran through the door into another room while the short one yelled, "Get the other magic sticks!" The short one drew his own weapons from under his coat, two small guns. He got one shot off into the creature's sturdy chest before he was picked up and thrown through the window over Rise's head. Rise heard the man fall into a puddle outside and grunt in pain.

Rise tried to stand up but the agony prevented him. He collapsed back down; it was like a bad dream. The creature bent down to reach for him, but a force knocked it over sideways.

The Gold Titan returned from the other room and stood in the doorway with the barrel of the magic stick smoking. It was resting against his shoulder.

The creature had a hole in its chest and left shoulder. Tiny flashes of light emitted from the holes and little arms the size of strings reached out of the holes and pulled the creature back together. It was healing itself.

Another shot to the creature's foot pushed the legs out from under it. The gangly creature cracked into the floor.

Rise finally made it to his feet. The dark man pointed the gun at Rise, "Your turn."

The metal creature sprang the 15 feet over to the gold smuggler, ripping the gun from his hands.

Rise made a run for the stairway with his hands tied behind his back, his head floating from the pain. He thought his hearing was fading because the humming seemed to get louder the higher up he made it. His shoulders hit the wall of the stair hallway more than once on his ascent.

More shots were fired below as the short man climbed back in through the window to help his companion.

Rise made it halfway up the stairs before realizing his weapons were stripped from him. His coat was gone as well. They replaced his belongings with the rope around his hands.

He made it to the top floor to find a large device venting the humming sound. A complex machine with a mechanical arm was stirring a large vat. The vat was ten feet across and stirred a very thick, yellow liquid. The vat was stirring liquid gold. The heat was amazing, more intense than any bonfire he ever constructed. More boxes with gold bars were scattered through the room.

He heard one less voice yelling downstairs as the fight continued with crashes and screams. No more shots were being fired. Rise looked frantically for something to cut his rope bonds. Nothing was sharp enough. He fell to the ground and pulled his hands under his buttocks. He slowly forced his feet through the loop his tied hands made. He had never been that flexible and his lower back burned from the procedure. Finally, his hands were in front of his body. They were still tied but at least in front.

Rise looked frantically for something, anything he could use as a weapon. Nothing. A silver box with controls for the vat was against the far corner. He ran over and began to look at the levers. No marks as to which control did what. Two buttons and three levers. He hit one button and the humming slowed. The arm stopped churning the molten gold.

A loud footstep echoed from the bottom of the stairs.

Rise jumped to the top of the control box and reached

up with his bonded hands to a rafter. He pulled himself up and rolled his leg over the top. With his hands untied it would have been effortless. He strained new muscles making his circumstance work. He finally lay on the rafter with a spinning headache just as the metal man came into the room.

It looked around and then up, instantly seeing Rise.

He forced himself up to a crouching stance. The five feet of room between the rafter and the roof was not enough.

The creature leaped and grabbed onto the nearest rafter. It quickly pulled itself up. It reached and pulled itself over to the same rafter Rise was on. The vat was directly below them. Either the concussion or the warm fumes were beginning to move the room around for Rise. He could not tell if the vat were ten inches or ten feet from him.

The being quickly scrambled across the rafter towards him like a hungry wolf.

He needed to knock the creature into the molten gold.

Rise took a step back and his foot slipped off the side. He caught himself with his hands, his feet dangling over the vat, and looked up as the creature raised a thin arm.

A loud explosion erupted from the left shoulder of the creature. It knocked it off the beam. To Rise's disappointment, it only grazed the side of the vat and landed on the ground. It sprang to its feet, and the tiny machine hands began to fix the shoulder.

Rise saw the black man who hit him earlier standing at the doorway. His shirt was ripped and his face bloody. He held the long barreled gun at his shoulder.

The creature jumped over the vat and landed on top of the man. He hit the ground before he could fire a second shot. His body smashed to the ground, the weight of the metal man keeping him from bouncing. The weapon went sliding across the floor.

The metal man placed its fingers around his neck.

Rise shimmied along the rafter with his feet dangling. Rise felt dizzy but forced himself to fall from the rafter. He just barely missed the vat on his way down and he felt the heat curl hairs on the back of his neck. The room spun twice before he was finally able to pick up the weapon with his bound hands.

He aimed for the weak neck and pulled the trigger. The butt of the gun flew back and hit him in the stomach. He instantly knew the feeling of his skin beginning to bruise. At the same moment, the creature's head blew away from its neck. Blue crackling light shot from the hole in the neck as the body went limp on top of the man. The metal head bounced off the wooden wall and landed face down on the floor.

Rise collapsed on his knees from the pain in his stomach, trying to catch his breath from the butt of the gun. The room was still revolving around him. He fell back and closed his eyes letting the weapon fall from his hands.

He could not move.

He heard the sound of the dead metal creature flopping over as the Gold Titan pushed it off with a heavy grunt. He even heard the footsteps, and the gun being picked up. He felt the poke in the ribs with the barrel, and yet he did not wish to speak or even open his eyes.

He heard the man swear to himself and say, "I really wanted to kill you. Makes it hard when you saved my life."

A giant hand; Rise was just grateful it was a warm human hand instead of a cold metal one. It lifted Rise up, and he felt himself draped over the man's shoulder. The last sensation was being carried down the stairs before he went unconscious again.

Chapter Fifteen:

He woke up startled. The three damaged Gold Titans were sitting at a table playing a gambling game with three small white cubes. He was lying down on a comfortable cot. Instinctively he reached for his sword and was surprised it was there. They replaced all his weapons. His head felt heavy, and he reached up to find his hands were unbound and a bandage on his head.

They looked up from their game and cheered. "Ten got up," the man who hit Rise said.

Light came in from the broken window where their leader had been thrown out. Outside it glittered like gold from the dew mixed with the morning sun.

Rise searched himself to make sure he had everything. The book, necklace, it was all there.

"Stop looking," the short man said. "All of it's there. We even made you a lunch, if you're hungry." He pointed to the ground next to the cot. Bread, meat, cheese, and his full water container were there. It was a long time since he had eaten cheese.

He picked up the plate and began eating.

"You didn't kill me, you gave me back my belongings... and you gave me dinner..."

"Breakfast," the lanky thug said as he rolled the cubes across the table.

"Breakfast," Rise finished.

"So?" The short leader seemed offended.

"So? It seems a little... noble for smugglers."

"Because you rolled a ten," Rise's assailant said.

"What?"

The leader said, "You brought that curse to us. However, you did save Twelve's life, so we rolled for ya. Had you been a nine or lower we would have thrown you into the vat and smuggled ya. You're pretty lucky, Ten."

Rise asked, "Where's the metal man's body?"

"Still upstairs. After the current vat, we're going to make him worth a little more. Titanium's the barter of a lifetime."

Rise saw a metal bar with a thin head laying against a crate of gold. He picked up the bar and went upstairs.

"Good thing you hit him when he wasn't expecting it, Twelve. Ten has anger issues. The metal man is dead and he still wants to beat on it," the lanky man said to the one who hit Rise.

"Shut your mouth, Fourteen."

Rise found the body on the ground. Without the head, it wasn't so menacing. Rise stabbed the chest with the bar and forced the thin head of his bar through the square line. He forced it open, ripping the bolts from the frame. He used the end of his sword to cut off the six green, two red, and blue wires from a metal box that was resting in the chest cavity. Rise pulled it out. It was about 20 pounds, enough to slow his progress for the day, yet he finally had the power source of the metal man.

On the side of the metal cube was a small rectangular glass window. It glowed a yellowish-green and hurt his eyes when he stared at it.

He took one last look at the machine before going back down the stairs. Just a scrap of metal.

The thugs were still playing their game.

"What you got there, Ten?" the leader asked.

Rise did not answer and began to walk to the door.

"Oh, mysterious I see. Well, I guess if I killed a sheriff I would be mysterious too. Anything else we can do for ya, Ten?" The leader asked the question with a smirk.

Rise wanted to say no, but he was in a hurry. "I need to make it to the other end of the sector by nighttime, without interruptions from any of your thug friends."

"Fourteen, you feel like stretching your legs?"

Twelve stared at Rise. "You really weren't after our gold, were you?"

Chapter Sixteen:

Rise stayed an extra ten minutes at their building to pack himself food for the trip and fill up the water. Mostly bread and meat because the cheese would go bad too quickly, although he loved the taste.

Fourteen carried the power source for Rise. It practically fit in his giant palms. Rise did not like being followed; he had always been the guardian. The Giver had always been the bodyguard. This man dwarfed him and kept the thugs at bay. They really did have a respect for his smuggler bodyguard. He knew it was simply because of how much gold they moved. Even the thugs were vain.

The only slowdown the whole day was a troupe of skelguards making a couple of arrests and executions. They loaded a few people into the large gray vehicles and drove off while Rise and Fourteen hid behind a building.

His injuries took their toll and cost him another day of rest. They finally continued on the next day, Rise feeling tense from all the lost time.

Rise only relaxed when he saw Kessi's booth and had not seen a trace of the wolf sheriff.

"Thank you."

He handed Rise the box. Fourteen said, "That's it? No long goodbye?" He chuckled. "Just like Ten. Anyways, the swirling clouds are not in sight yet. I might make it back by morning if I hurry."

His smuggler bodyguard took off at a jog.

Kessi looked up and gave a high pitched girlish giggle. "You made it! Quick, around back."

Rise went through the door and saw the mean Kessi working on some mechanical gadget on a tray. She was pushed aside by the nice Kessi and spoke as they rolled towards Rise on their communal chair. The mean one never really looked up at him. "At least the bandage covers your old man hair."

Rise handed the nice Kessi the box.

"So, you didn't wake it? I thought for sure you might...

unless that's what the bandage is for?"

"No, just made a new friend. Can I have the magic breaker?"

"Only if you call it an EMP gun from now on." She laughed as she began to take it out of the secret hiding place. "Rise, I wish you all the luck in the world."

"Might not be enough for what I have planned."

"Should be, unless you plan to siege the King's fortress at some point in your life."

Rise stayed silent. He always avoided conversations about the King's fortress. To him, the King was an invisible evil. The sheriffs and skelguards were tangible. He could see them. The King was invisible and speaking of a fortress for him would just make him too... real.

"Here." Kessi handed him the gun. "Please don't die."

"Thank you."

Rise went for the door when the mean Kessi said, "Where are you planning on going now?"

"Sector 2124. To the west."

"A news gatherer once told me about that place. He feared it because the people spoke of a flesh eating beast. He would not say if it were true or not."

"Thanks for the warning." He was a little surprised that she offered him counsel, despite it being a bit... bizarre. The old man's book already warned him of the flesh eating beast. Still he was touched.

Rise left and walked to the wall. The dark clouds were coming and people began to abandon the street. The booths went empty as the merchants locked them and left. He still heard the two Kessis at work in their place.

He waited a little longer than he felt he should have. It was uneasy for him to scale a wall when he felt so close to civilization. Finally, the skelguards passed each other on their watch and he ascended the wall.

The grapnel worked great. It was smoother and faster. He made it into the next sector in record time.

Part Seven: 2124
Chapter One:

He landed on the east side of 2124 and hit the grapnel

251

release. The cable quickly came back and locked into place. It was the smoothest descent so far.

This sector was more of the same. Ruins from the ancient cityscape. A large hill was located in the middle, although he could barely make it out in the dark. It looked as if it were cut straight across with a giant knife at 200 feet tall. The King did not even allow nature to grow taller than the walls.

Rise walked through the shadows away from the wall and sat down against the side of an old building made of brick. He heard arguing inside, something about food, between a man and a woman. It flustered him for a brief moment before realizing they were not speaking in the old tongue. He was back in a poor sector. Each of the houses had fences built around them where a few heads of sleeping livestock could be found. Hardly enough to consider them rich.

The people in the house he rested against had another argument about their last sheep being stolen. The door slammed, and he heard tiny footsteps run outside and around the house. A very scrawny boy with a bulging stomach came running out. The boy wore only tattered pants. He curled up against the shadows of another house and was crying. Inside his parents were still arguing.

The Giver stood up and startled the boy. The young one jumped up, and Rise quickly said, "Don't run. Here." He reached into his pocket and pulled out the food he packed.

The boy looked it over and decided it was fine. He walked over and began to eat it slowly but steadily. Rise handed him the entire wrap of food from his large pocket and said, "Give a little to your parents as well."

"Thank you," the boy said with a hoarse voice and ran inside.

Rise quickly left to find a place to sleep. A solitary place. He wanted a sip of alcohol so bad his stomach burned.

He instinctively began to head west, even though he knew he would have to rest sometime before the morning. His body was a bit stiff, and his head felt swollen. The only upside was the bandage on his head covered his hair. Hopefully, it would keep away the ones looking for him.

As if fate were reading his thoughts he heard the familiar sounds of the awkward walk of a skelguard. He quickly ducked down into the shadows under a low overhang from a nearby house.

He saw the figure walking, staff in hand. The glowing

red eyes, the skull face, and the strands of matted dead hair flowing down to its waist. The skelguard walked by without even looking at Rise huddled in the dark. It went to a house that held 20 or so sleeping sheep in the front fence. It stopped and looked at them for a little while. It lowered the staff, and the end opened up to release a fireball that engulfed most of the sheep.

The noise was horrible. The sheep were bleating in agony as the front door opened, and a man with a club came racing out. He held a half-empty bottle of alcohol in his hand. Rise found himself staring at the bottle. The man saw the skelguard and quickly dropped the bottle and the club. He turned and fled through the dark community. The skelguard went back to its patrol, leaving the sheep to die slowly. The man must have lived alone because no one else came out the door. All the neighbors were watching from their windows.

After the skelguard left and the sheep were long dead, Rise stood up and made his way eagerly to the bottle. He grabbed it almost lustfully and began to drink it. One gulp and it was done. Rise let out an exhale of blissfulness. It was not near enough to help him forget life's problems, but it was a start.

"So, you like whiskey?"

Rise drew his sword at the voice. He saw nobody. He did not like the fact that someone could so easily creep upon him.

The voice came again from a shadow created by an overhang on a house, "You are new here. I saw you come down from the wall. At first, I thought a skelguard had fallen from its patrol, which would have been funny in its own little way." The shadow moved and Rise was still irritated that someone followed him without his knowledge. That never happened. Ever.

Rise stayed silent as he observed the man. He was entirely in black with a knit hat that fit perfectly around the upper portion of his head. He held a bow across his back and a quiver full of arrows. He was equipped for a fight or a hunt, Rise could not tell which.

The man continued, "You are the first I have seen to climb a wall..."

"You stay awake too long."

"Probably," the man nodded. "You have to keep a watchful eye in this sector. There's monsters here that will eat the flesh off your bones."

"I'm only passing through."

"Ah, a visitor." He nodded some more. "Visitors are

always welcome, please, stay at my place for the night, you'll be safe there."

Rise shook his head, "Sorry. I've got to keep moving."

"Not tonight. A man who scaled the wall is a sure target for the sheriff in this sector. His eyes are keen as well. Besides, I have more whiskey."

Rise glanced at the empty bottle. "One night."

"Great!" The man grabbed Rise by the arm and said, "This way, I live on that cropped hill."

He recognized the cropped hill from his descent. Rise made out a house, one that looked like the one Beline used to live in. It seemed built out of the hill, as if a deeper part lay hidden in the ground. It was the only solitary house around. A couple gnarled trees grew around it like hands trying to choke it.

"What's your name, stranger?" He asked the question eagerly.

"It doesn't matter."

"Very well," the man sighed.

Rise hated the man's hand on his arm, it was not a tight grip, but the man had strength in it.

They made their way almost to the end of the housing area. Rise was grateful the man finally let go.

"Did you see that?"

Rise shook his head no.

"Stay here, I'll be right back!" The man placed an arrow in his bow and ran off into the darkness.

Rise leaned against the fence of a house that had three pigs outside. For a little while Rise could tell where the man was running by his footsteps, but that quickly died away and he was alone. The door to the house opened and startled Rise. Someone was staring at him. He began to reach for his sword but gave up the attempt after seeing it was a young woman, probably ten years younger than Rise. She wore a tattered brown dress, and her hair was scattered.

"Stranger!" she whispered.

"Yes?"

"Don't have anything to do with that man!"

The woman walked over until she was on the other side of the short fence. She leaned into Rise's face with wide eyes and spoke, "He is evil. Run before he comes back!"

"What?"

"You don't understand! He..." She made a quick glance

254

to the house on top of the dark hill and shuddered.

She lifted her head to one side. She grabbed his shoulders and shook him, "Run!" She gasped, "He's coming!" She ran back into the house.

Rise heard the footsteps again. The man was coming. Rise stayed where he was. He had fought too much evil to be scared, and the thought of an alcoholic beverage was extremely tempting.

The man came back with a small deer hung over his shoulders. Rise saw the arrow wound sticking through the head of the animal, "Got him on the move from a good hundred feet. Perfect shot. Looks like I can offer my stranger a drink and a meal tonight."

Rise looked at the house the woman came from. He could see two frightened eyes staring at him from a window, just barely visible in the dark. "What do you know about the people in that house?"

The man laughed. "They're crazy. Constantly trying to frighten others. Why, did she talk to you?" The man got defensive.

"Just curious."

"Good. I warned them once before. They lost a brother and a son not too many years ago, and they've never recovered."

They continued their walk to the hill. A path of small rocks was established to aid the climbing. Rise was glad to finally make it to the top and stood at the porch of the house. The wood creaked beneath his feet, and a stray limb from a nearby tree brushed against the side of his shoulder.

It was a view Rise was not used to. He could see the houses and a few scattered fire lights. Even a few shadows scurrying about the landscape.

"You have a great view."

Rise noticed even the spiders of the trees enjoyed the view. A few large webs were crafted between the fingers of the tree.

"Yes, yes, it's a great place for a person with my eyes. I can tell the color of a man's eyes at the bottom of this hill. Or his hair." The man cracked a small smile.

Rise said nothing and just followed the man into his house.

It was dark inside, lit only by a few candles placed in various corners. Very comfortable chairs surrounded a large wood table with only a few scratches on it. All the windows were boarded up, but left with one slit to peer through. Inside the floorboards did not creak like the porch.

The man disappeared into the dark hallway and was

gone for quite some time. He returned without the deer and without his weaponry.

A tall semicircle table with large stools was close to the left wall. The man made his way over to it. His black hat was off, and Rise saw his shaved head. It was hard to tell in the low light, but Rise guessed he was about 50.

"You promised me a drink," Rise said flatly.

"So I did. My name is Vor, by the way."

Rise said nothing as Vor pulled out bottles from a very well stocked drinking table. He poured Rise half a glass and brought it to him.

Rise swallowed it down. It was not the strongest he ever drank, but it was close. "More, please." Rise sat down on one of the couches.

"What is your name?"

"Rise."

Vor poured him another glass, this time full. Rise savored both swigs he took.

"I see you have white hair, Rise. That's interesting."

He reached up quickly to the bandage and felt a miniscule patch of hair that was sticking out. The man did have good eyes.

Vor continued, "Because there are a few rumors around that a man with white hair killed a sheriff."

"That's what I've been told." Rise motioned for a refill on his drink.

"Is it you?" Vor filled the cup back up.

Rise was not sure how he wanted to answer, so he took his time drinking.

There was a loud thud from upstairs. It startled Rise and he nearly spilled a few drops.

"Bah!" Vor grunted. "Be right back." He walked towards the black hallway and reached for a small knife in his boot just before the shadows of the hall consumed him.

Rise was left alone in the dark room with only the dancing candle flames to entertain his mind. The thuds came again. It was too difficult to tell if they were hitting the floor or the wall, but they came in almost a pattern.

Rise stood up and ventured over to the liquor table. It was a very nice table.

Thud.

The back slid open and must have held 50 assorted

256

drinks in it. The light was too poor to tell what they were.

Thud.

Rise reached into the dark for a bottle.

Thud.

Something caught his hand and seemed to wrap itself around it. Something bit him.

Thud.

Rise jerked his hand out, knocking a bottle loose. It cracked open when it hit the ground next to his boot. A spiderweb had entangled his hand, and a small red spot was visible just below his thumb knuckle. Inspecting his hand for swelling, he realized how unkempt and animal-like his fingernails had become on his journey. They were sharp and coated with dirt.

THUD.

Rise reached in for another bottle, quickly this time, and yanked it out. He took the cork out and drank it slowly as he walked back to the couch. The thuds stopped after that last loud one.

He put his feet up on the table and rested. The alcohol was finally having a minute effect on him. He was able to relax.

Something breathed down Rise's neck.

He jumped up and reached for his sword only to find Vor standing behind the couch. He had lurked up again.

"You would not believe the size of rats I get in this place, big as dogs." Vor had something dark on the side of his lips, but the light made it impossible to tell what it was. "Please sit down. Didn't mean to startle you."

Rise released his white-knuckled grip on the hilt and sat down on a chair facing Vor. He took another swig of his drink. "Rats? That was one loud rat."

"It was caught in one of my traps behind a dresser upstairs, kept knocking into it. What happened to your hand?"

Rise saw the barely noticeable bite mark from the spider. "A spider bit me..."

"A spider? Let me see that!" Vor jumped over the couch and grabbed Rise's hand, almost making him drop his bottle. "This is not good. This mark is from a small spider with black and white stripes, very poisonous."

Vor took his knife out again from his boot. It was clean and glistened in the low light. Rise started to pull his hand back a little, but Vor's grip tightened. He made two extremely fast flicks with his knife, leaving an X mark on his hand. He pushed down on it with the flat of the knife and forced the blood to come out. After a minute he said, "That should be enough. You should live."

"Thanks." Rise eyed his host.

"Don't mention it. How could I let a guest die in my house? Very shameful. Let me go get some wet rags, to clean your hand up."

"I've been bit by spiders before, I'm sure I would have been fine."

Vor just shook his head as he walked again to the lightless hallway. Just before he disappeared he made another sudden move. Rise was not sure what he did, but it looked as if he passed the blade of his knife by his mouth.

Rise dismissed it and went back for another bottle. This time he turned on his wristlight. He saw the spot where his hand was attacked. A nail was sticking through with a broken cobweb resting against it. It had not been a spider after all. That made the entire blood-letting ordeal useless, but better safe than sorry.

He swept the light back and forth across the selection. He saw a spider nest in one corner. Two more were just below it. He counted 16 white nests before he was done.

Rise grabbed another bottle and began to drink it. He was feeling more relaxed already. He plopped back down on the seat, checking the ceiling with his light and found more spiderwebs. He turned it off and enjoyed not being able to see the bugs. He saw Vor silently come into the light from the hallway with a wet rag. It was strange to see a person a few feet away before hearing him. He walked over to Rise and handed it to him.

Rise wrapped his hand in it.

"You must tell, did you kill a sheriff? I did just save your life."

Rise grunted, "Yes I killed a sheriff. And it was nothing special on my part. Just circumstance."

"You must be the greatest hunter alive."

Rise shook his head and took another sip of his drink. "You have a lot of spiders in this house."

"Of course. They keep the bugs out."

"I thought spiders were bugs."

Vor reached over to a candlestick on a small table next to the couch and pulled out a spiderweb. He collapsed it on the spider and trapped it in its own web. He let it dangle from his finger as it tried to break free.

"No. Spiders are hunters. Better than you and I put together. They're perfect hunters. Silent, deadly, proficient, and observant. They leave no waste. They can wait for days, for that perfect opportunity."

"Yeah, they're really something."

Rise finished the bottle and was at last feeling the blissful results he wanted.

"Let me show you something." Vor motioned with his hand for Rise to get up. It was the first time Rise noticed Vor was missing a finger.

Rise stood up a little shaky, but composed himself. He took one last drink and told himself that was it for tonight. It was hitting him faster than he expected.

He followed Vor to the dark hallway and Vor took a candle from a stand and led the way. The slope of the house changed, and Rise got the feeling that the house was buried deep in the hill. The hallway went on forever, lined with countless scratched doors. All of them were closed, and some boarded up.

They came to a stop somewhere in the hallway, probably towards the middle, but Rise had no way of guessing. He could see only a few doors down in each direction before the darkness enveloped them. Vor opened a door and walked through. Rise followed. His slight inebriation made the candle flicker twice as enchanting. The door opened up into another hallway with countless doors. Vor opened another and walked through it. Rise followed.

The endless maze of halls and doors went on for a good ten minutes. Rise had no idea how far into the hill he was. He felt like a fool for letting Vor lead him into this labyrinth.

Finally in front of them was a large door different from the others. It was completely metal with a fat lock. Vor pulled out a key with a spider head created on the end of it. He put the key in and turned it with great force. The giant lock snapped loose and Vor opened the door. Rise walked in after him.

Vor held the candle flame to a thin tray on the side of the wall that stretched all the way around the dark room. A trail of oil was in the tray, and it quickly ignited and spread across the tray lighting the room.

Horrible faces peered in the newfound light. Beasts Rise had never encountered before were huddled in the middle of the room ready to pounce. Rise stumbled back at the sight and Vor grabbed him. "They're dead."

Each of the beasts was propped up with metal rods, making them into ornaments. Many of them were large cat-like creatures with long fangs and golden coats. A few were larger and darker. One beast was nine feet tall with a furry coat with a round face and ears. It was propped up on two legs.

In the very back of the room, a wooden stairway led to another floor.

"What is this?" Rise asked.

"My collection." He said it slowly. "Did you keep a trophy from the sheriff you killed?"

"No, just some bad memories."

Rise could not believe they were dead. They looked alive in their poses and the flickering of the oil light added movement to their flesh.

"A very long time ago," Vor began, "when I was just a little boy, one of those monsters took and killed my brother." He pointed to the cat-like beast. "When I was 12, I killed my first one. Took me three shots with a bow. When I was 14, I killed another, using only one shot, straight through the head. The next I killed with a spear. The next two were cubs, which I used knives. That attracted the father and I used a sword to slay him." He pointed to the biggest. "This was the last one I killed."

A long grin spread hastily across his face like someone had poured water on dry cracking earth. His face soaked up the smile. "The big one, I killed with my hands."

Rise was feeling a little dizzy from the alcohol, and the last thing he wanted was this room of beasts to start spinning around him. "You have quite a collection."

Vor leaned close, "You have no idea."

He walked right into the middle of the beasts. Vor cleared his throat and rested against the big brown one, "You know the problem? After a while it gets too easy. Beasts make good food, and for the inexperienced they make good hunt. There's a problem though."

Rise shook off the dizziness but still had a dull headache. The faces of the savage animals seemed to get closer and farther. Perhaps the drink was a bad idea. "What's the problem?"

"I'll show you. Up the stairs please."

They left the beast room, and Rise followed Vor up a staircase that wound itself in circles. It spun extra fast in his vision. They reached another large metal door which he unlocked.

Rise never felt so dizzy from alcohol before. Usually he passed out before this amount of spinning.

It was another room and Vor grabbed Rise by the arm and closed the door behind them. Before Rise could look into the room, Vor blew out the candle.

Chapter Two:

He heard Vor whisper, "This way." Vor tugged at Rise and he followed. Rise was stepping on loose rocks which made crunching noises under his boots.

Rise hated being dizzy. "Light the candle, Vor."

"The problem with hunting beasts is they leave you wanting more."

More crunches under his feet.

"Light the candle, Vor."

"The problem is they soon are no longer a challenge. A great hunter needs... more challenging prey." The grip on his arm tightened.

Rise felt his heart slam into action.

Rise swung his fist at the invisible Vor. The grip released and Rise missed as he nearly fell over. Vor was too quick. He did not even hear crunches of the rocks as Vor took a few steps away, just barely escaping another punch.

Rise turned on his wristlight and shined it into Vor's face. Vor blocked the light with his hands, "You cheated."

Taking a step back to make a more comfortable distance between the two, Rise slipped on a large rock. He steadied himself and quickly glanced down at the rock.

A human skull was next to his foot.

Rise flinched and kicked his foot to get the thing away from him. He spun the light around and saw the white bones of men and women surrounding him. The whole floor was littered with them. He felt more dizzy than before. The bones seemed to be swimming around him, getting closer to his feet.

He forced himself to focus. He made himself stop shaking from the terror and anger. Vor was slowly walking around, holding up one hand to block the light from his eyes. "Do you understand yet? It's the only way to become a perfect hunter. Once you can hunt your own kind, then you become perfect. But you're different. You hunted a beast that can't be killed. You, Rise, killed a sheriff. You are a man-slayer, just like me. I know the taste of your blood. I want your power, and I will suck it from your bones."

Rise clenched his teeth together and began to reach for his sword.

Vor kept talking and walking in a circle around Rise who was fighting off another wave of dizziness. "I should have known I could not simply hunt you like the others, oh no." Vor slouched down until he was walking on the tips of his fingers and toes with his head tilted up to look at Rise. He was circling like a spider. "I could tell by your blood you would be difficult. You and a handful of others were not tricked by the dark. You have a special hunt waiting for you. All the others are on the ground before you."

Rise spoke through closed teeth, "Why?"

"My father was actually the first to kill one of the beasts that claimed my brother. By hunting him I gained his power. The more I hunted, the more powerful I became. You can't imagine the power, how it makes you feel, how much closer to perfection it leads you. So I continued my hunts until I became perfect. I was content with my lot for a long while, until the rumors of a young man with white hair who killed a sheriff began to circulate. A sheriff is a foe I felt was impossible to defeat. You. You murdered a sheriff, and by killing you I gain that power."

His eyes were reflecting the light, and his stance gave him the prowess of an animal. A predator.

Vor stood up slightly, still hunched over, "I was tormented for days that someone could kill a sheriff. But now, tonight, I saw you descend the wall. I followed you, spied your disguised hair, and now I will take the power from you. Feast on your blood and flesh."

As he circled, Rise kept the light right in his eyes. He caught the glimpse of a half-finished "meal" leaning against a wall behind him. Rise wanted to vomit. The dizziness was almost unbearable, but he forced himself to stay focussed. He felt beads of sweat dripping from the bandage.

Vor began to circle the other way, keeping a safe distance. He pulled out a vile from his coat and danced it around in his hand. "I thought this would have had more of an effect on you. Couple of drops should have paralyzed you. Can't quite seem to figure it out... oh, of course. I see. The alcohol. You were the first guest who wanted a drink. Foolishness on my part to mix it with alcohol."

Rise took a step forward trying to avoid smashing a rib bone. Vor took a step back, perfectly missing the bones behind him as if he memorized their exact scattered placements.

"You know how a spider hunts? It poisons its prey, immobilizing them. They are paralyzed when it begins to suck them

262

dry." He licked his lips. "The power of a perfect hunter. The power of perfection. I put a number of drops of my poison in your drink, and here you stand. I should have expected nothing less from you." He replaced his vile back in his pocket. "Prepare for the hunt, man-slayer."

Rise forced his foot down without looking, crushing an older skull, "You are wrong Vor. I am no man-slayer. I only kill monsters."

Chapter Three:

Vor stood up and ran once he saw the poison was having little effect. Rise kept his light on the fleeing man. Vor had just enough of a lead to swing open a door on the far end and fly through it.

Rise ran after him with his light and sword, just barely keeping the distance the same. The walls seemed to be moving, and the skulls on the floor danced around him. Vor reached out with his hand and snagged a doorknob on a passing door in another dark hallway and swung it open behind him, blocking the hall. Rise tried to stop but ran into it and nearly fell from the impact.

Something growled.

Rise turned the light in the newly opened room and saw four glowing eyes staring back. Two of the famished cat-monsters came running at Rise. The first jumped on Rise forcing him back into the wall, but running itself through on his sword in the process. Rise felt breathless for a moment from the sheer weight of the beast. The next one got a claw on his chest, and he felt the sharp nails rip through his jacket and flesh. He fell to the ground and pulled the sword out of the chest cavity of the first beast and rammed it through the second's head, pinning it to the open door as he screamed in pain and anger.

He gasped for air as he was forced low by 400 pounds of animal. He stuck his feet into the one on bottom and pushed out. He pulled the sword and rammed the door back into the animals until they were moved enough to get the door out of his way. Rise winced from the pain in his chest and saw the blood dripping down his front. It was not a deep wound, but it would bleed. He was glad he was not entirely sober. He felt less dizzy. The pain seemed to distract him.

Regaining the pursuit was easier than Rise thought. The hallway contained no more doors, just a massive span of hallway.

He ran until he found the one door at the end. It was merely a wood door that had been locked. Rise began to hack at it with his sword until enough was free to kick it in.

Rise opened it hoping Vor had no more dangerous pets.

The light was still going strong, but he was too late to catch himself. His foot caught on something and he fell. He felt his body bounce slightly. From what he could see, the whole room was covered in a rope net, knotted together every six inches or so. The room sank in from the doorway leaving a ten-foot gap of net and floor. The walls and roof even had this rope mesh all along them. It was a giant web.

Chapter Four:

He pulled his foot free and began to look around with the wristlight. Dangling from the ceiling were knots made of rope about five feet in diameter. There were at least 30 of them from what he could tell. A few were not hanging but wrapped to the floor. Rise clumsily made his way over to one tied against the wall, half-due to the unstable rope, half-due to the alcohol or poison. He was not quite sure which was having more effect. The dizziness was almost gone.

Rise was afraid of what he would find contained in the rope mesh, but he could not let it go. It took him a lot longer than he thought it would. Cutting through the rope was not easy. It was stronger than expected. And he was afraid of harming the content. He knew what to expect from a giant spider-like nest.

After a good 30 minutes he finally had enough to unravel it. Staring back at him was a young woman, pale and exhausted. Her eyes were wide until Rise shone the light on them. He quickly pulled it away. "Are you all right?"

She only winced her eyes shut from the light.

"The poison. That monster poisoned you. I'll have you out quickly."

Rise was finally able to free the young woman. She smelled terrible. She looked almost starved to death with long thin arms, black hair, and a tattered dress that showed her boney shins. He helped to get her comfortable against the wall, but she was completely limp and hard to place. He knelt down in front of her and said, "I don't know exactly what this poison is, can you understand me? Blink once for yes and twice for no." He made sure to keep the light out of her eyes.

She blinked once.

"Blink no."

She blinked twice.

"Good. I'm sorry I have no food for you. Can you open your mouth to drink?"

No.

"How many are stuck in here? Sorry. Do you think all of them are still alive?"

No.

"Do you think some of them are?"

Yes.

Rise nodded. "Will the poison ever wear off?"

Yes.

"I know you can't answer, I'm just curious how you know that."

She kept pointing her eyes to her thigh.

"Your leg?"

Yes.

Rise awkwardly touched the end of her dress, then looked up at her eyes to make sure it was still okay to proceed. He slowly lifted it up just enough to see the puncture wounds six inches above her knee. He pulled the dress back down.

"He has to re-infect you with it. Does he come every day?"

Yes.

"Every half a day?"

No.

Rise took a deep breath, "Do you know what he does to those he captures?"

Tears welled up in her yes. *Yes.*

Rise swallowed hard. "I'm sorry. I'll free you all. Last question, does he stay nearby?"

Her eyes grew wide, and she began to blink frantically. Rise felt warm air on his neck.

Chapter Five:

Rise turned and saw a shadow hanging from the ceiling, something metal glistening in its hand. Before he could put the light on the shadow, it seemed to swing into the dark away from the light. All he could see was the rope web shaking as it went. He took off after it.

Before he had gone even a few steps a large door in the dark slammed shut and locked. "I'll see you soon enough, Vor."

Rise made his way unsteadily back across the web, "I'm going to help the others now," he told the motionless girl.

As he went it got faster to free people. For those on the ceiling he would climb the sides and then have to cut them off the 12 foot drop to the man-made web. He found many still alive before he came to the first starved one. It was practically a skeleton. A man with a horrible look on his face, probably 50 years old. Rise placed him in a corner. After a few hours the corner became filled with casualties.

The only way he could keep going once he found a dead body was the thought of Beline. He was helping victims, he wanted her to see him. He wanted to leave this sector and continue his search for her, but she would not want him if he abandoned these poor people. He would slay this sector's monster and then continue on. No. He couldn't do that. He had sworn not to kill another man. Despite how much of a monster this man became, Rise could not kill him.

Many hours passed, and he freed 32 people who were still alive, 12 who were dead, and 2 who were questionable. Rise was sweating from the work and felt his muscles stiffen. The entire time he kept glancing around for any sign of Vor. It was not an easy thing to leave his back to the shadows as he helped free a person. He felt exposed. He unsteadily walked the web back to the first woman he saved.

Her mouth was open. It looked like she could barely move her tongue, but a muffled, numb word came out, "Thank... ooh."

"You're welcome. Can you drink now?"

She could not nod yet, so she blinked once. Rise took his water bottle and gave her a mouthful, which she choked on but got it down. "You seem to be recovering the quickest." Rise took a swig of his water. "I'm going to leave this bottle with you, once people are recovering, please give them some. There isn't a lot, so be sparing. I have to go after that monster."

He stood up and walked towards the door he heard lock when Vor retreated. He had seen it when clearing the far side of victims. It was another large wood door. During the whole ordeal he had listened for the sound of the door opening, just to make sure Vor would not sneak up on him again.

Rise came to the door and tried to open it. Locked.

He weakly began to swing his sword until enough was broken through. Rise did not notice his wristlight beginning to fade.

Chapter Six:

Rise was sure the poison had been sweated out of him. Now all he needed to deal with was the slight inebriation. His judgment would probably be slowed, as well as his reaction time. He would have to concentrate.

Another hallway led him by more walls with deep scratches in them, as if a beast had jammed both claws to the walls and drug them as it walked down the hallway. The light only let him see 20 or so feet in front of him, and this tunnel of a hallway seemed to be the longest one yet. He had a slight dread of Vor back tracking him and going after his prey once more.

Rise turned around startled. Nothing but dark hallway. He quickly turned back around and walked faster. He could have sworn he felt breathing on his neck.

The hall creaked and moaned under his steps. He finally came to a door. A door that was ajar. He took a deep breath and kicked the door open. Rise ran in and quickly pointed the light around him looking for the monster in the shadows. Nothing.

The room was the largest one of the house. It stretched out for a couple hundred feet where a crack was letting the morning light seep through. The light draped itself over a door at the other end of the long room. He was sure it was the exit door. Enough light filtered in so that he could just barely make out a line of large concrete columns on his right and left. He could only see the light reflecting off the faces of the pillars, and darkness covered the rest. Vor could very well be hiding behind any concrete column in the darkness. Rise took a few steps forward. An overhang by the crack in the roof blocked any of the light from revealing the ceiling, which was a good 20 feet high. Rise went to shine his light upward when it flickered and died.

His heart began to pound.

Rise grunted and reached into his pockets for the additional sources of power Kessi had given him. He never used his wristlight for a whole night before. The hours it took him to free everyone from the traps had drained his light. It was difficult to find the power sources, the only light that came through the crack showed

267

the exit door a couple hundred feet away, and the faces of the trail of pillars that led to the door. A perfectly placed light source that blocked just enough to make him uneasy. It was a room designed to instill fear. The door was false hope. He would be attacked before he ever made it.

Rise finally found the power sources in his pocket.

There was a slam behind him. Rise turned and dropped the cylinders on the ground. He heard them roll but was watching the shadow that closed the door and bolted it. The shadow seemed to float up into the darkness of the ceiling and disappeared.

The hair on his neck raised up.

Rise quickly found one battery by groping around the floor, but he could not find the second. He searched faster, more frantically.

He heard a strange noise. Looking up, but still searching for the cylinder, he saw movement crawl through the shadows of the ceiling. The shadow quickly descended to the ground. A long thin shadow traced from the ceiling down to the body of the monster. As it lowered, a noise like someone rubbing their hands together followed it. Rise saw the silhouette of this new monster. It stood like a man with long glistening six-inch claws at its sides. It reached up and quickly went back to the darkness of the ceiling with that strange noise. It seemed to float up and down at will. Like a spider crawling up its web, it vanished into the shadows.

Rise found the other cylinder on the ground and stood up. He practically ripped the dead ones out of his wristlight and heard the noise again. It was between him and the exit.

He whirled around and saw the shadow swing in at him from the ceiling, the claws reflecting the light. Rise fell backwards on the ground and saw the claws swing just over his face before the shadow returned to the darkness of the ceiling. Rise dropped one of the new cylinders and it rolled into the shadows. This time he heard a hissing noise scurrying around the roof. It was right above him.

Rise ran forward and heard the whoosh as it pounced. It missed and bounced back up to the darkness of the tall ceiling. He closed his eyes to listen for it. Nothing.

The heartbeat from his chest was the only thing he could hear. Behind the darkness of the pillars, something touched down. It was on the ground now. He heard steps as it scurried. Rise saw the beast running at him from the shadows with the speed of the giant cats he fought earlier. It rose its claws in the air and jumped for Rise out of the darkness. He pulled his sword and swung. The sword seemed to go through it without touching it. He had to duck and spin to avoid the claws. Once again the shadow returned to the darkness, this time on the other side of the trail of pillars.

Rise hit the ground in frustration. He had to get to the light.

A sound of something on the ceiling. The beast made it back to the roof. Rise pushed up and ran for the light above the exit. He heard the same strange noise behind him.

He glanced and saw it drop behind him and then back up into the darkness. It dropped again, closer this time. He was expecting it one more time from behind, but something from in front of him ripped his chest in the same spot as the animals had done earlier. It knocked the wind out of him as he toppled on his back, just in time to see the shadow slide back up to the roof. The cut had opened up the scabs that were forming from his earlier attack. It was beginning to burn.

Rise ran again for the light, he was not even halfway there. The shadow swung from his right side from behind the pillars, and he could not draw his sword up in time to block the needle-like claws from digging into his shoulder and pulling him. For a second he was floating with the creature as it swung through the air, only held up by his skin. The skin ripped with a horrible tearing noise, and he hit the ground again.

"Can't stop!" Rise forced himself to say it, to ignore the pain, to ignore the monster.

Rise switched the sword to his left hand because his right was predominantly useless from the last attack.

He had made it halfway when the shadow swung in from behind and scrapped along both of his calves. He tripped and fell to his face. His sword hit the ground and slid into the darkness behind one of the pillars on the left.

He rolled over and frantically searched for the monster. It was gone, in the shadows again. He sat up and waited. He closed his eyes again, listening. The silence was more frightening than if he heard it coming. How could a creature move without noise? He sat there in the dark for a good minute, just listening. No noise from anything except his own body.

Then he felt it. His hair stood on end, his breathing stopped. Warm breath on his neck. Something just bit him.

Chapter Seven:

Rise swung with his free hand to grab hold of the beast but he was too late. He saw the creature let go and begin the arc of another swing, this time towards the first door he came through, away from the exit. Rise felt blood drip from his neck.

With his left hand, he pulled out the grapnel. He aimed just above the creature and pulled the trigger. It shot and locked into the ceiling. The creature had just hit its lowest arc of swing when Rise hit the retract button. It snapped his body off the ground and he flew towards the creature, the leather strap around his torso pulling his aching body by his shoulder. He saw the head turn in surprise.

Just as it was making the ascending part of its swing back to the shadows was when Rise forced his body into its. The creature was knocked for a spin and it slammed into a pillar. Rise heard Vor grunt in pain and surprise.

Rise hit the release button and landed on the ground harder than he expected and quickly collapsed, his calves burning.

The creature stood up weakly and Rise reached into his pocket for another cylinder. He quickly placed it in allowing just enough time for the creature to climb its web-like rope back up to the darkness. Rise hit the release button and allowed the cable to pull back into the machine.

Rise turned on the light and looked up. A massive rig of pulleys and ropes was assembled with hooks for locking the rope into place after a swing. With this setup, Vor was able to swing like a spider all around the room and quickly retract himself to the ceiling.

He searched the ceiling for Vor's shadow but could not find it. The silent creature made his way to some distant shadow. Rise walked back to the pillar where he lost his sword and found it against the wall. The room was less menacing with the proper lighting. He saw a rope winch attached to the wall. Rise clumsily used his left hand and chopped the stiff rope.

Bundles of rope dropped instantly from the ceiling. Rise went in search of another winch to chop.

Not even a noise was made as something wrapped around his neck and jerked him back. His neck instantly stiffened. His feet flew into the air, and something else wrapped around them. He was stuck, swinging just above the ground. The dark shadow ran by and cast another rope web around his arms and pulled them tightly to his sides. He tried to swing his sword with his left arm but the rope caught his wrist and twisted it backwards, forcing him to drop his sword to the shadows again. The wristlight was stuck against his thigh from the rope, pointing uselessly to the ground beneath his dangling body.

The creature stood over him. The voracious monster was enjoying it. The claws were close enough to tell they were metal gauntlets with elongated fingers. Vor held a black vile, no doubt the poison it used. It slowly unscrewed the lid and dipped a claw into it. Rise struggled against the rope, but the pain in his shoulder and neck was too much.

He reached into his pocket for something. Anything. He found the magic breaker. He recalled its effect knocked the sheriff over with a strong burst of energy.

Just as the claw was coming for his neck Rise found the weapon and pointed it through his pocket. The force tore a whole in his pocket but also sent Vor flying a good ten feet back. It knocked him into a pillar, and he released the rope holding Rise. The ropes around him went loose, and Rise landed on the ground and instantly found his sword. He forced his wounded body to run at Vor, who was slumped against the pillar.

Rise knelt down and quickly ripped the gauntlets from his hands. Vor was dazed, the back of his head was bleeding from the impact. "How..." He struggled to speak. "No! Perfect... hunter..." Vor shook his head.

Rise pulled him close to his face, noticing the blood around his lips, and said, "Was that challenging enough?"

Vor spat in his face and Rise knew he could not hit him hard enough with his left hand so he dropped Vor and kicked him in the face. Vor slumped unconscious.

"Only one punishment for you. I can't kill you, but I'll bet some other people want you dead."

Rise picked up the gauntlet that still had the vile clasped in its hand. The paralyzing venom. He dipped the claw back into it and then rammed it a little harder than he should have into Vor's neck.

He screwed the vile cap back on and placed it into his hole-free pocket. He did the same for his other small items. Startled by the touch of the EMP gun, he took it out to check the power. It still had a light. He had at least one more shot. He let out a breath. He had not wasted all of it.

Taking the ropes that still draped his body, he tied Vor as tightly as he could and slung him over his good shoulder. He carried him back to the locked door. Rise searched Vor until he found the key and unlocked it.

He took Vor all the way back down the darkness to his horrible man-made web. Rise was pleased to see the first woman he helped standing up and assisting others who were recovering more slowly. It would have been a challenge without a light. She and two others were fully functional.

He dropped Vor violently to the web. "Don't worry. It's me."

The woman shielded her eyes from the light and breathed a sigh of relief. She came over and hugged Rise, who groaned from the pain of the cuts.

"Sorry," she said. "Thank you so much! You have no idea how long that monster has been murdering in our village."

A man who was walking came over and patted him on his good shoulder. "Nothing I can say can show my gratitude, friend. Is he dead?" He pointed to the unconscious Vor.

"No. He's all yours."

They smiled. "For too long this horrible man has haunted our sector, kidnapping our children, and killing any who pursued him. How can I thank you?"

"Bring him to the people of the sector and give him justice."

The man nodded.

Chapter Eight:

Rise gave them directions as best he could on how to find the exit in the large room, and then quickly left them. They would have no problem following the one remaining hallway in the dark. He was in too much pain for talking. He was sleep deprived and needed to find somewhere to lay down. As he suspected, the door at the end of the trail of pillars was the exit. He pushed it open and his eyes burned from the daylight. How long had he been in that terrible house?

He emerged on the other side of the hill, closer to the west wall. It looked to be half a day's journey there. Vor's fortress dungeon must have been built straight through the hill.

The mound of earth led back down to more communities. They were mostly tents, a few houses and buildings used for dwelling, but mostly cloth racks to keep the rain and cold out.

He stumbled all the way down the hill, his legs burning, his neck sore from Vor's bite, and his shoulder was ripped badly. The pain in his chest only hurt when he breathed. His coat was battered as well, new holes and gashes. He even needed to switch to the left pocket because of the new hole in the right one. The necklace was still intact. His sword was stilled, and the grapnel and book were still in good order.

Reaching up to touch his head he realized the bandage had fallen off. His hair was now exposed. He did not really care. He was in too much pain to care. The sector was a whirlwind around him.

The morning was warmer than it had been for the whole month. Rise found a large rock and wedged himself under to avoid the sun. He needed to sleep. He needed to heal.

He could do neither. If he were awake he was thinking about Beline, if he were about to fall asleep, a new pain would shock him awake.

Then he realized he had left his water container with the woman. Another stupid misfortune. He could not sleep so he stumbled around like a man who was sleeping. He made his way through the community getting mostly blank stares. He ignored them all, he did not care. Let the sheriff see him, let that horrible elite come. The pain was too much.

Rise journeyed for another few hours before sheer exhaustion pulled him to the ground. He forced himself up and kept walking. He was almost through the community of onlookers. Most were cooking meat over a fire, some were stitching and sewing their tents, others would only stare. He hated those ones.

He was probably a mile away from the wall when he could not take it and fell to the ground, thirsty, hurt, and tired.

Chapter Nine:

Rise dreamed of Beline. Another memory.

He had been sick, felt almost as if he was going to die. Beline had spent the entire week at his bedside, just like when she stayed with the old man before his death. Bespin would go and gather supplies and herbs for the fever.

Beline looked down on him with the most beautiful green eyes he ever saw. He loved those eyes. The pain was horrible in his body. His stomach felt like it was going to burst apart. His head was being dug from the inside out, and his mouth was dry. That all dissipated when he looked into her eyes. That wonderful smile sent medicine all up and down his body.

She would speak to him a lot, even though he could not reply. Talking mostly about other memories they shared. Rise remembered her stroking his hair from the front to the back. That was probably the most soothing touch he ever received. She would stroke his hair for hours with her small hand.

He could almost feel that now...

Rise sat up and startled a young woman who had been stroking his hair. She was a red haired girl, probably 20, and had freckles on both cheeks and arms. She wore a purple dress with a white hair bonnet.

He was sitting in a wonderfully soft bed. The warm towel fell from his forehead down to his lap.

"Sorry I startled you," she said with a soft voice.

"It's fine." Rise shook his head. Most of the pain in his body was still there, but duller. His shoulder and chest were bandaged, and it felt like his legs were also.

"You have endured a lot," the girl said.

Rise said nothing. He looked around the sparse tent shelter.

"My father told me to look after you. He said the Sheriff Slayer saved him from Vor and that I was to look after you. He found you collapsed just at the city limits, before the wall. My name is Katie Harn."

"It's not everyday you meet someone who still knows their family name."

She smiled, and most of her teeth were missing. She was actually considered quite beautiful, but not to Rise. Beline had perfect teeth, a step above beauty in the sectors.

Rise saw his coat on a chair with new patches on it. Even the hole in the pocket was mended.

He gasped and reached for his neck. "The necklace! Where is it?"

He shocked her again, and she nervously found it among his belongings she placed on the chair. She handed it to him, and he clutched it to his bandaged chest. "Thank you."

Placing it around his neck he said, "Where's your father?"

"He's being a witness for Vor's trial, out in the public square."

274

"A gathering like that will attract a sheriff and skelguards."

Katie said, "He promised to make it quick. More of a formality."

"I have to go Katie. I must leave for the next sector. Do you have a water skin I can have?"

She reached under the bed and handed him one. "Just filled it. I had a feeling you would be leaving." She sighed.

He gently touched the side of her face and said, "Thank you. I feel healed."

Rise readied himself and quickly left the house with Katie watching from the porch. He wanted to escape this sector while everyone was heading to the trial, before it attracted any royalty. As he walked through the sheep fence he said, "Tell your father I'm in his debt."

"Trust me, Sheriff Slayer, we're both in yours."

Chapter Ten:

That sweet girl had even cleaned his boots. He had the taste of medicine in his mouth, some sort of root extract. The wall was a quarter mile away, and he found a nice little pond with grass growing around it. The dark clouds were just about ready to make their nightly appearance, which meant in just a little more time he could scale into the next sector.

He realized he never asked the girl how long he was out. Could have been a couple days or the end of the same day. He did not know or care. He lingered too long here. It was time to leave.

The pain was not too bad. The tower had been much worse.

He pulled open his book and looked at the map. He was in 2124, so close to his destination. West one sector to 2123, west again to 2120, and then north to 34. North once more would get him to his rebellion sector. It sat along the north border of the map, the northern end to the sectors. There was no telling what was beyond the border. The idea of land and horizon without sectors was foreign to him. How far could a person see without a wall in the way. No ground was high enough to peer into another sector, the King made sure of it.

Rise began to skim the chapters of those sectors just as the dark swirling clouds came in from the north. They brought something else with them.

He heard something and put the book away in the inside pocket of his coat.

A sound from the side of the pond. He blinked twice at the sight. Footprints with no owner were walking towards him through the muddy grass. Something invisible...

Rise had no time to react.

The steps ran for him and he felt a metal post drive into his chin, knocking his already sore neck back. Rise stumbled and reached for his sword. His shoulder burned in pain and his eyes watered. He knew the sector wanted him dead.

The blur of movement from the elite guard dissipated as it came into view, revealing itself to its prey. Rise saw another horrible man with wires in the back of his head with a silver metal suit. It was tall, and the helmet only revealed its lower jaw and a little of its neck. Rise could tell from its movements that this one was not as arrogant as the first. This one was angry.

One hit and Rise felt all the pain in his body return.

The elite hissed, "For the murder of a sheriff, skelguards, assaulting a sheriff, the murder of an elite guard, trespassing sectors, and possession of invention, you will be punished by the King's holy laws!" He drilled a fist into Rise between each offense.

"Good! Arrest me and take me to your King!" Rise snapped back, rubbing his jaw. He thought about reaching for his EMP gun, but remembered the zero effect it cast on the first one.

"Arrest?" It took another step forward and hit Rise again with his metal hand.

Rise spat blood on the ground from his busted lip.

The elite grabbed him by his shirt and lifted him up with skelguard strength, "Arrest? No. My dignity lies in that I get to punish for the King, so he does not have to look at you filthy peasants."

The skin showing on this elite was his lower face and neck. The rest was covered in silver metal armor. Rise went to strike the face. With its free hand the elite caught him by the wrist and squeezed until Rise gasped in pain. His wrist popped and dislocated.

Bright lights were appearing before his eyes; the pain was intense. His breath left his body. He was going to pass out. He almost wished Vor had killed him... Vor...

While both hands of the elite were busy, one holding him, the other breaking his wrist, Rise reached into his pocket. He grabbed the vile with his left hand and snapped it in half with the weight of his hip, spilling the venom onto his long finger nails.

He squirmed from the pain and gasped, "You forgot something."

"What?" The elite asked out of spite and squeezed harder.

"One more crime. I threatened to kill your King." He gasped it out as clearly as possible.

The elite's eyes grew in fury and he barred his teeth. "You insolent PEASANT..."

Rise pulled his left hand from his pocket and scratched the neck of the elite with his finger nails. The elite let go surprised and dropped Rise before realizing what happened. It reached out again, desperately trying to grab Rise and ripped the necklace from him as Rise turned and ran. Rise carefully cradled his wrist and ran for his life.

The elite blurred its movements once again and moved at impossible speeds. Rise heard him coming. The elite never reached him. A few inches from grabbing Rise, the elite's legs failed to work and he landed on the ground face first. The elite was paralyzed from the poison, clutching the green necklace.

Rise ran for all he was worth. He made it the quarter mile to the wall and used his free hand to aim the grapnel. He needed to steady it on his elbow because his wrist felt about ready to fall off. He made it just in time; the two skelguards just passed each other on their patrol. Finally, a break from this horrible sector. Hopefully, the elite had been paralyzed before it could call for help. Rise made his most painful ascent yet, and very nearly fell when trying to pull himself over the wall as he yelled in pain. Soon, he was running for his life through Sector 2123.

Part Eight: Sector 2123
Chapter One:

He made it all the way using only his left hand. His right was in excruciating pain. It was not as bad as he originally thought, he could move it slightly. It was not broken, yet dark bruises marked a trail across his wrist. It was his sword hand however, so he was effectively defenseless.

Running was also slightly more difficult while cradling a fouled wrist. He took no time to notice the layout and he just ran west. He did notice that this sector was devoid of buildings. Thousands of tents were scattered through the valley. The ground seemed to dip slightly, like he was running through a giant bowl.

Rise remembered the first elite, and how it followed his invisible trail to that underground building. He hoped if he ran through a populated enough area, whatever trail he left would be confused with others. Everyone seemed to be asleep except for a few drunks. Rise envied them.

Whenever he saw anything that resembled the glowing eyes of a skelguard in the distance, he would alter his course slightly. He would not be caught. Not now. Not ever.

He smelled coal fire and leftover remains of activities of the day.

Three miles later he was coated in sweat. He had to stop. Rise collapsed to his knees and breathed deeply. He was far enough away from the first community of tents that he did not have to worry about waking anyone from their slumber.

Making a plan was more difficult. He needed sleep. He needed to bathe. Every time he formulated a process in his head his thoughts would jump back to wondering how long the poison would last in that elite.

His breathing was staggered from the pain in his wrist. It was hard to get enough air to compensate for the pain.

Rise forced himself to think. His breath came out as wisps of clouds in the cold air, and his brain seemed frozen also. Running aimlessly would not help him. Neither would just running west. The elite now knew he was in this sector. If he called the sheriffs of all the surrounding sectors to his aid... Rise would not let himself think of that. If he had to he would deal with it when it arrived. The simple fact was he needed a place to stay to mend his wrist. He awkwardly pulled the book from his jacket pocket.

Sector 2123 was no more than a short paragraph, but it offered much promise:

This is the only sector I would dare call "normal." It has skelguards, a sheriff, people, and not much else. No unique characteristics to speak of, just people trying to survive. It's oddly strange. Normally, an attitude is evident just by breathing the air. This one seems devoid of any human feelings. I found one man however, who is different. He is probably the smartest man I have ever met. Uzzah is his name, just a young man, but so smart. His father trained him before being captured by a skelguard and sheriff for inventing. I stayed with him for a full month, learning of inventions, chemicals, and application of the two. We have much to offer each other.

Rise realized that was how the old man learned so much. He experienced more than anyone else. It was his insight and experiences that caused others to think he was crazy. In retrospect, it was everyone else who was naïve. The people only knew of their little world in the sector walls. The old man brought knowledge from many sectors, not just one.

Rise saw a small map drawn with a black circle. After discerning the direction, Rise realized he held no choice but to make his way to the mark. It led him northwest through the sector, just on the outskirts of a valley forest.

He journeyed a long while until he came to the forest. It contained huge lumbering trees that had never seen an axe. It was beautiful. Draping limbs covered the forest floor like a protective skirt. He heard a chorus of birds through the main channel path that wound twisted like an old man's finger. It was a strange chorus; he never knew birds to be loud during the night. It was a unique call, one he was unfamiliar with, almost like a high pitched rumble from the back of the throat. The beauty was not tampered by the dark. It highlighted it. Rise felt drawn to this forest. He forgot the pain in his wrist. Small bugs that lit up the night with their bodies floated lazily through the air.

For the first time in a long while, Rise took a leisurely stroll through a forest. It even smelled better than the open air. Better than six dwellings each baking bread.

Beline would have loved it. Rise reached out and ran his good hand over the bark of a tall tree. Perhaps planting a tree right where the sector walls once stood would be a great idea.

Slow down, he thought. *You haven't made it to the rebellion yet.* He wanted to keep the thoughts of tumbling walls out of his head. As far as he knew, the walls were there, will always be there, and were always there to begin with. The walls were life.

He had to admit though, he changed his life by climbing them. He broke through. Beline would never believe it.

Rise saw a slight shimmer in the underbrush to his left, just off the barely maintained trail. Something reflected the meager light of the floating bugs. He reached down and pulled out a glass bottle with a dark liquid inside. Dirt and leaves fell off the bottom. His heart began to beat slightly faster in anticipation. He tried with startling pain to uncork it before using the other hand and the crook of his elbow.

He smelled it. The unmistakable smell of wine. A large smile went across his face. He almost raised it to his lips as he continued walking. The trees were looking down on him. It did not feel right.

"Come on, drink it!" Rise said out loud, his body trembling from his addiction.

His mind argued back, tricking him by using Beline's voice. *But it was that lure that put you in danger to begin with.*

"Yes, but it led me to those trapped people. No telling what terrors they would have faced before they died!"

His mind quoted Beline with a phrase she spoke before he started on his journey. *I found you drunk on the ground. I figured you'd be happier with the bottle, so I took my leave.*

Rise had nothing to say back to his taunting mind.

His mind did not stop. *Goodness! I can still smell it on you!* His heart sank and throat collapsed. Tears began to push their way to his eyes. That horrible memory. It made Rise feel dirty, pathetic, and naked.

He broke the bottle against the tree without further hesitation. The glass pieces fell to the ground and the wine trickled a descent on the tree bark. "For you Beline."

His mind allowed him peace as he continued walking through the beautiful land.

"No more killing and no more drinking. I'll be no fun when I find her."

Chapter Two:

Rise saw a house buried deep in the forest. It was old; probably many generations of a family lived there. The house was a single story with red paint that long ago grew patchy. The roof came to a point in the front but collapsed in the back and was supported by new boards. A heavy layer of moss coated the roof. Despite the dilapidation, it looked cozy with its warm smoke rising from the chimney. The map lead him exactly to the house.

Knocking on the door was awkward for him. He was not quite sure what he would say. The door was solid wood with a crafted handle of a bird spreading its wings over an egg. The egg turned as the door opened. An old man with a candle and knife opened the door.

An old man's voice said, "What do you want? Be quick or I might slice at you!" The knife was dull, a butter knife.

"Are you Uzzah?"

The old man was bald except for long strands along the sides of his head. He had a bushy set of white eyebrows and stubble. He wore a long white robe that was paper-thin and Rise did not like the silhouette that greeted him. He probably only weighed 110 pounds.

"Of course I am Uzzah. Who else would live here? Who else deserves to live here?"

Rise nodded and continued, "A long time ago, I have no idea when, an old friend of mine visited you. His name was Trek, in the old tongue it was pronounced Terk... do you remember him?"

"Trek? If someone by that strange name visited me, I would remember."

The old man began to shut the door.

Without thinking Rise shoved his right arm out to stop the door and the gangly old man took a swipe at it. The knife cut only the air but smacked against his swollen wrist which he retracted quickly. As he did, Uzzah caught a glimpse of the grapnel.

"What happened to your wrist?" Uzzah surprisingly showed some concern.

"A fight. Are you sure you don't remember Trek?"

"A fight? What's wrong with it?"

Rise decided to answer his questions, his body shivering minutely, "I don't think it's broken, but it looks horrible..."

"May I?" Uzzah asked the question but did not wait for an answer. He reached out with both of his small hands and gently, with the touch of an archer, felt along the wounded wrist. The old man never let go of the butter knife. "Oh, it looks worse than it really is. Mostly swelling. It will leave a nasty bruise. It does, however, need to be set."

The old man threw his weapon back to the eating table. "Get in here. You trying to kill me from a draft? I am an old man!"

Uzzah pulled Rise into his warm house and shut the door. The house was small, but as Rise previously guessed, cozy. One table, one chair, next to the only window. A large brick fireplace had a wonderful flame fighting off the cold. Many candles were lit around the room.

The old man went to a closet and pulled out a very thick blanket, woven from about six other smaller ones. He tossed it to the ground next to the chair. "Sit on that."

Rise did as he was told and Uzzah went into the kitchen and disappeared through a door. He returned with a strange looking hollow cylinder with screw-ends sticking out. There was a thin layer of tan leather around it. In his other hand he held a scroll.

Uzzah handed Rise the contraption and opened the scroll, placing an ancient book on one end and the butter knife on the other, to keep it from rolling up. Rise saw a remarkable outline of a human body filled in with detailed sketches of bones. After examining the wrist with squinting eyes, Uzzah turned and snatched the equipment from Rise. "You do know you are in the best of care, right? Better than you deserve, I'm sure."

He quickly and preciously slid the cylinder over Rise's wrist. "It's been a long time since I've used this, so I'll probably hurt you a lot." Without waiting for an objection, Uzzah tightened the first screw and the cylinder contracted around his wrist. Rise grimaced as the pressure built and Uzzah turned more of the screws. The pain was horrible, but only instantly. One loud and uncomfortable pop in his wrist ended the pain.

"Leave the setter on your wrist for at least a week, drink lots of water, and eat meat. And don't think even for a moment that you can just leave with my setter."

"Thank you." Rise could not move his wrist because of the tightened cylinder, but the pain was gone.

"Now," Uzzah continued, "about your friend Terk..."

"I thought you didn't remember him?"

Uzzah snorted, "Of course I remember him! It just took a while, I'm old remember? Besides, he went by another name at that time."

"What name?" Rise asked.

"If he didn't tell you, then you weren't meant to know."

The old man sat in silence with his eyes closed until he was ready to speak, "That was probably the only man who was worth the things he bartered for. He cared for people. He was very knowledgeable. The only man who easily traveled sectors, aside from the news gatherers. Wonderful inventor, we exchanged many theories. Actually, that setter is from his original design. What is my friend doing these days?"

"He died. Recently."

"Oh no." He sighed, "I'm truly sorry to hear that."

Rise pulled out the grapnel from under his jacket. "This was his. He passed it on to me after his leaving."

The old man had been waiting for Rise to show it to him

and nearly ripped Rise's shoulder out of place from the strap still attached. Uzzah said, "He showed me this contraption years ago. It was how he traveled so easily. But, it looks just recently constructed."

"It has had some touching up along the way."

Uzzah let go of the device and sat back in his chair. "Such a wonderful device. Man is a great creature to be able to discover such things. That fool of a King has made it illegal for man to do what he was meant to do. Invent. Such a disgrace to the very nature of humans.

"The only thing Terk loved more than that machine was a sword we crafted together. Black steel with perfect balance."

Rise did not bother to show him the sword.

Uzzah continued, "Do you know why the King made inventions illegal?"

Rise had no answer and Uzzah wanted none.

"I will tell you why. They threaten him. An invention strong enough to defeat him is the only fear he has. The law is poorly written to cover up that fact! The law only says inventions are illegal, punishable by whatever the King wishes. It's never stated if the inventions are what you made or found, either way, illegal. What's the difference between inventions, and items for bartering? Nothing! They both came from the same ancient civilization! And so what if we make a new invention? You know, to better us humans? He won't allow it! He's threatened. He can handle anything from the ancient civilization and that's why he conquered it. New things, new powers he has not yet confronted... those must terrify him. Think of it, that terrible King has a terror. All his power, all his followers, and he's terrified of inventions. Why else would he make them illegal?"

Rise wanted to change the subject, and he did have an obligation to warn the old man. "I am a wanted man."

Uzzah laughed. "So was Terk. And they never caught him. Don't worry, you're safe here."

Rise could not believe his old friend had been a wanted man. He loved him all the more for it. It meant there was a sliver of hope. The old man died, unnoticed by the King, with his adopted family close by. There was hope. He wished for his friend's advice now more than ever. His original idea of fleeing the sector did not seem so crazy right now.

"Thank you," Rise nodded his weary head.

"What did you do anyway?"

It was the first time Rise did not hesitate to say it.

"Killed a sheriff."

Uzzah laughed, "You just earned a pillow."

Chapter Three:

Rise awoke to the smell of meat stew. Uzzah was cooking it in a pot in the fireplace. He meticulously stirred it with smooth hands. Rise had slept on the floor, and despite his constant dreams of Beline, felt refreshed.

"Take a bath, you smell like scat." Uzzah did not look up from his cooking. "Through the kitchen door, first one on your right."

Rise walked through the kitchen and saw the bottles of liquor sitting on a boarded window sill. He used to love to take a bath with a glass of alcohol. He forced himself to look away from it. Not even a day and the temptation was itching his throat.

He found the room and was surprised at how small it was. Just big enough for the door and the tub.

The water was cold, and Rise missed his heated pipe water. He had taken it for granted. He never even really cared where it came from and where it went. It had just always been, but now he wanted to know everything about it.

After bathing Rise noticed a small broken mirror on the wall with a peg holding scissors. They were recently sharpened, and Rise used them to cut his growing hair back to the hassle-free trim. He loved running his hands through his hair now that it was short again, it reminded him of Beline stroking his hair.

Rise readied himself and nearly passed out. It was gone! The necklace! Then he remembered. The cold clutches of that elite ripped it from him. It had stolen it from him. "I'll find you." Rise growled it through his throat and nearly shattered the mirror in anger, yet refrained himself.

He walked back out and ate the stew. Uzzah was just as pointed and self-righteous as before. Rise loved listening to him. He was kind, but just a little selfish. It was strange to him how one man could be both those traits. Uzzah became one of the few people Rise felt good conversing with. They talked for an hour, Rise telling him his story of how he came to travel sectors like his old friend, and even about the death of the sheriff, and the horrible encounters with the elite guards.

"Tell me about your friend Terk, as you knew him. I'm

curious about what he did after he left this sector."

"The book he left me contains his journeys. It's also very sparse on details. I think he kept most of his real knowledge in his head."

Uzzah nodded quickly, "And he had a lot to store. We developed a theory together, well, it was mostly mine, about magic."

Rise laughed. "He hated magic. He always disliked using the word. I never knew exactly why."

"I'll tell you. Because it's a farce! It's a fake tool used by the cursed King."

"The effects seem real enough."

Uzzah grabbed Rise's arm. "Only to the idiot's mind. For example, your arm. It was wounded. What if I could fix your arm? Would that be magic? No! Because I used an invention to do it. Only human ingenuity. That's why the King hates inventions. It threatens his farce of magic. That was the conclusion me and Terk came to. We spent hours discussing the pros and cons of magic, and possibilities should it be exposed. People in this world are born to fear magic. That's all we ever knew. When we question it, use inventive logic against it, we start to see weaknesses in the system."

Rise was not completely convinced.

"Bad example, but think of the principle behind it. If I told you I could fix your arm with a magical hollow cylinder, it would seem amazing to you. Do you get it?"

"No." Rise looked at the cylinder on his healing wrist.

Uzzah mumbled. "Fine. Hmm. Oh, okay, how about this approach... go outside for a second." Uzzah ran back into the kitchen through the door.

Rise did as he was told and walked outside through the wood door with the carved handles. It was a cold, damp morning. Fog surrounded the forest. It seemed detached this way, no sector walls, no sheriffs, or skelguards. Just nature. He could not have picked out a sector wall if he wanted to. He could imagine the forest sprawled forever, uninterrupted by the horrible barriers. The birds were chirping in no discernible pattern and Rise was almost glad to be alive. Almost. He stayed in his "happy" state for about a minute, before the chill ran down his spine.

Thick gray smoke came from behind the house. Unnatural smoke. The wind carried it towards Rise, and he heard a deep rumbling voice that rang so loud his ears hurt, "You thought you could escape me? Now you die."

Rise drew his sword as his heart clung to the insides of

285

his chest. A dark figure was walking through the smoke. The elite had found him.

Yet, it stopped moving towards him. The wind finally began to take the smoke away from his presence and Rise was facing Uzzah, who had a large grin on his face. "Did you learn the lesson?"

They walked back into the warm house and Uzzah explained it, "How did I magically appear in a cloud? How did my voice magically become louder and deeper? Not as magically as you think. I want you to have these."

Uzzah dropped two small spheres in Rise's hand. They were the size of his thumb.

"Keep them in a place where they will not be crushed. The chemicals in those orbs react to changes in temperature and air content, producing a massive cloud. They might come in handy as I will explain later. Next, the voice."

Uzzah pulled out a pointed cone attached to a handle with a trigger. He spoke into it, and his voice seemed inhumanly loud. "This device magnifies sound. You cannot have this. I like it too much. This I have not yet figured out the principles behind it. I scavenged it years ago.

"And now the point you have been patiently waiting for. Now that you know how they work, they are less "magical." The King uses inventions of his own, ones that most don't understand, to frighten them, just as you were frightened by my appearance in the cloud, and strange voice. We mistakenly view this as magic. Some day, the invisible shields around the King's men will not seem so magical. Same with the fire from the skelguard staffs."

"Where did he get the inventions?"

"Me and Terk believed it was from the ancient cities, before they fell. An advanced race of men until they met their match and crumbled. Me and Terk believe the King uses inventions we don't understand. Why? To control us with fear that he is all powerful! That's why we have never seen the King. That's why inventions are illegal, because the more we invent the more we learn. The more we learn, the more we figure out how his "magic" works, and the less afraid we are. Because inventions lead to rebellion."

Rise had to absorb the information. He breathed in the word rebellion.

Rise retorted, "How do you explain the skelguards? What invention brought them back from the dead? Explain that to me."

Uzzah grew irritated. "Why do I bother with you?

Truthfully, I don't know, but I have found a way, on a small scale, to replicate their fire staffs. It's all in the chemicals. No magic required. Of course, they have the supplies for massively making it."

"That does not explain bringing back dead warriors."

"No. No it does not. It has bewildered myself and Terk. But, one thing is for sure. The staffs were magical until I figured out how they worked and made something similar. It's only a matter of time before we figure out the trickery he uses on the skelguards."

Rise felt something new. Curiosity of a new world. If Uzzah was right, everything would make sense. The old man's inhibition to use the word magic left a strong imprint on him. True, he used the word like any other, but each time he felt strange about it. It was too easy an explanation. If knowledge were the key to bringing down the King, he would learn it, because it would take him to Beline.

Chapter Four:

Rise spent two weeks with Uzzah, each day learning something new. It proved to be a haven from the sheriffs and elite guards that he knew were watching for him. Uzzah was a genius obsessed with his genius. He taught Rise the chemical reactions that made the small silver cylinders power certain devices like his wristlight. How batteries must have been everywhere in the ancient world. He taught him how to splice wires to accept most forms of power. He even showed Rise how to create a small column of fire that danced. After the first week, Rise stopped using the word magic. He did not even notice the natural transition of words. Words such as magic sticks slowly turned to guns. Uzzah was right, the more knowledge he took in, the less magical it seemed.

The beginning of the second week Uzzah showed him the principles behind guns, how they worked, why they were scarce, and how to replicate the effect in similar inventions. Hours of lectures of how the combustible powder worked, how much each bullet received and why. In return Rise shared the book with him, the knowledge of his long lost friend and of new sectors. Uzzah helped Rise to add new content to it, stories of his own adventures. Uzzah helped Rise to bind the new pages into the book. He warned him to always keep updated maps. If the ancient world had done that, many of the secrets would be unearthed. The tower of Sector 45 was crossed out. The depression lands of the mull were added. And

287

Sector 2128 was crossed out completely. It was King dominion explicitly.

Uzzah showed him syringes and how they worked, also some other medical tools. The last day was spent on combustion, and Uzzah revealed how the vehicles of the King worked. Rise had never viewed them before as magical, but they worked on the same principles of the other things he thought were magical.

Uzzah became one of the few people to know why Rise was willing to risk his life for his journey. Uzzah was surprisingly unselfish in his speech.

"Rise, you have found love, and the worst possible thing has happened. You not only have lost that love, but you're unsure of whether there is even hope of finding her."

"I will find her."

"That's right. I know you will. Fight for her. Let nothing become a wall. I have given you knowledge to make your own doors. The greatest gift to you I can give is my knowledge. With it you will not fear the King and his horrible actions. That monster has stolen your love from you. Fight for her, battle armies for her, swim rivers, and climb walls, all for her. Let nothing stop you." Tears filled his eyes. "I lost my love a long, long time ago. I did not fight for her. I let her be taken and I have been slowly eaten alive by the memories. I wish with all my heart," Uzzah clenched his chest, "with all my being, that I had fought for her. The most pure love I have ever seen is in you. Perhaps if I had fought for her, I would have died, and then I could not have been a tower for you in your time of distress. Your love is pure, untainted by the evil this world has created. You will crumble walls and boundaries, disintegrate kingdoms, all for love. Rise, you will find her, and when you do, hug her and kiss her and tell her you love her and never, never let go. Squeeze her for all that life is worth, because in the end, I know it's the selfless love you have that will recreate this barren world."

Rise was silent. It was the nicest thing anyone aside from Beline ever said to him. Yet, he could not enjoy it for himself.

"You say my love is pure and selfless? No. It is entirely selfish. I would die for her, yes. But only out of the chance that I could live for her. My life is nothing without her! I call that selfishness."

"I don't believe that for one moment. One day... no, not one day. *That* day, when you hold her in your arms, you will realize it. You did this for her. Not for you."

Rise was not allowed to speak, Uzzah interrupted him.

"Your arm is healed. Leave this place and find her. Watch the world crumble because of your love, watch your fears die in terror of your passion. The one thing you are lacking is in this sector. Don't leave without it."

"What is that?"

"More knowledge."

Rise was suspicious. "Where?"

"This sector holds the biggest vault of knowledge other than myself. Canyon is here. The leader of the news gatherers resides in this sector. Find him, and complete your mind. Then this horrible world will crack itself open for your cause."

Chapter Five:

Rise had been staring at it for hours. He rested in the crook of a tree that was half-bald of leaves. Not exactly a discreet place to hide, but the distance was right, and he was mostly covered. It was the best location he could find. The hours had been long and dull, not so much as a bird came close to it.

A fog was settling, which Rise was grateful for, less chance of being seen. He could only imagine what it used to be. A magnificent fortification at some ancient time. Large concrete columns rising to the sky with guards patrolling every inch. Now it lay desolate, a blended mesh of earth and concrete. No stone stood higher than ten feet. A few dilapidated pillars were scattered about. The complex was completely destroyed. Vines and weeds grew out of collected dirt from the sides of shattered concrete blocks and walkways. He was in there. Canyon was in there. The mysterious leader of the news gatherers.

Rise followed the directions westward precisely, and Uzzah was correct down to the foot. Uzzah himself never met Canyon, hardly anyone aside from his personal assistants had. At least those were the rumors. Uzzah said, shortly before he sent him on his way with his blessings, "Rumors are great. Only lies spread hope more quckly."

The ground was a cracked foundation of concrete covered with dirt and leaves. It spanned for hundreds of feet. The tree overlooked this sight and was the biggest piece of nature next to it. The cracked walkways teemed with grass. Rise liked the sight of the grass creeping up through the cracks. Given enough time, anything will crumble. Anything can be defeated.

He had not realized it, but he was moving the gas pellets around in his hand. Uzzah's gift. "Be creative," Uzzah had said, "But don't waste them."

Rise marveled at his change. The moment Uzzah made his point about taking in knowledge, Rise had changed. The more he learned of inventions from Uzzah, the more the veil of confusion lifted. It now made sense. The mysticism was gone, and the King and his minions were brought down to a new plane. His plane. They were human. And they were in his way. Rise had conquered his fear. He waited in the tree not as Rise The Giver. He was a new creation. He had the sympathy and care of The Giver, but without his old fears. He still feared losing Beline completely, but his experiences and knowledge morphed his thinking. He always feared gangs when he was simply The Giver. Then he killed a sheriff and faced an elite. He fought in a battle with an entire army of skelguards. He no longer feared gangs or thugs. He no longer feared the skelguards, the sheriffs, or the elites. Not even the invisible presence of the King stung him. And not even the swirling clouds and all the evil they represented could drag the fear back into him.

He liked the new person he was becoming. The slight anger he felt was driving him. He felt capable of ripping the ruins to pieces, finding Canyon, and taking the knowledge he needed. He did no such thing. He simply waited.

Then he heard it. Footsteps.

He looked towards the sound which was difficult to find. They were just faint enough to be above a whisper. He could not see anyone walking, yet he heard the steps. The steps grew quieter and seemed to disappear in the ruins of the complex.

The old Rise would have blamed it reluctantly on some unseen magic. Rise knew that it was a chemical reaction that made the person walking, probably a news gatherer, invisible to the human eye. Rise jumped down from his perch and trudged up to what appeared to be the old entrance. He was tired of waiting.

"CANYON!"

His yell echoed through the fog and empty broken landscape.

"SHOW YOURSELF!"

Rise heard them walking up behind him. He heard many steps in the fog. Many from different angles, and he could even feel the peering eyes of some staring at him from a few feet away on top of some of the taller columns. Some were perched like invisible vultures. He made no sudden moves. He did not need to. He did not fear men.

"Take me to Canyon, and none of you will be hurt."

He heard one of them laugh quietly, directly behind him.

Rise turned and reached out for the sound. He was lucky and grabbed what felt like a neck. There was no stubble, no roughness. He had grabbed a women's neck. He quickly let go, embarrassed. "I'm sorry..."

He felt a tiny fist jab into his stomach from the invisible source. His new ego just took a small beating.

"Wait!" A news gatherer slowly appeared out of the air. "I know him! The white haired Sheriff Slayer!"

Rise laughed out loud. It was that first news gatherer he met so long ago. "Hello, friend." He was clutching his stomach.

Chapter Six:

"After the tower fell, a warning for the news gatherers was sounded. We each had to hide. The sheriff was looking for us. He wanted information on the Sheriff Slayer, but of course they refused to say that. They wanted to apprehend "A criminal of the foulest nature." In other words, they really like you, Rise."

Rise was drinking tea in a dark room with colorful blankets hanging from the walls at all angles. The room had pillows for chairs, and large thick carpets. It was luxurious inside the complex. He was taken through a secret tunnel hidden by a giant wall of ivy, and seated in a lounge. One large wooden chair, almost a throne, sat uninhabited. Rise assumed it was for Canyon.

His nameless friend the news gatherer brought him in, seated him, and sent the word for Canyon. They now talked as old friends with the news gatherer guards looking both fierce, and ridiculously clothed. The bright colors and tight clothing were wrapped around large muscles and angry features.

"After that horrible massacre of the tower, I came back here to report of what happened to your sector, which was on my route. Canyon advised me to stay here for a while, to keep safe while he reworked the schedule."

Rise said, "You guys are organized. So much is changing though, how do you keep up?"

"We don't always. And we have been known to make mistakes at times..."

A blanket curtain was pulled aside by a guard on the other end. Canyon slowly walked into the plush room, a cane in each hand. The man was quite pale, almost painted that way. His head had no hair to speak of, except a few strands that made his white eyebrows. His garments were different from his followers, more toned down in colors. He wore a brown robe tied with a light red waist band, and a blue knitted scarf. His two guards slowly helped him to his chair which he graciously fell into. He leaned to one side, and then the other, staring at Rise.

Rise finally spoke, "What do you know of the rebellion?"

Canyon had a deep voice, like a falling boulder's echo through a cave, "What are the odds?" He spoke slowly, not one ounce of hurry came from his body. "Ever since the word was out that you killed a sheriff, my men have been following you. I instructed them not to help you in any way. You're quite the hearty cockroach. I need to bottle your luck and keep it with me. I'll need it if the King were to find my whereabouts."

Rise would wait for his first question to be answered, "Why would the King want you?"

Canyon chuckled, "Because I know his dirty little secrets."

The leader of the news gatherers leaned forward with effort and stared at Rise. "All of you leave us, and send for my supply."

Rise's news gatherer friend stood up and patted him on his shoulder, "I hope to see you again."

Rise nodded and watched them leave.

Canyon leaned close enough that Rise could trace each wrinkle with his eyes. "You are fighting against the magic of the King. You will die. His magic is too strong."

"I don't believe in magic." Rise did not move his eyes.

Canyon seemed to light up and pulled away, "Oh good! An educated man. Perhaps it was wise of me to let you in after all. You know of course, had you been any other wandering fool you would have been left outside to rot? A sheriff and an elite? You broke the arm of that one you shoved down the well, and then to escape the grasp of another elite? Not even Lars did all that. You must be the best combatant in all the sectors. Well, I shouldn't say that, there is RedLink of Sector 32, he's extremely proficient, yet he has not killed a sheriff."

"Sector 32? I have to get there..."

"I know, why do you think I brought it up? Why do you need information from me? You know where to go, Barb and Tad already told you."

Rise would not be denied. "You have information. About what, I don't know. But, something nags at me, and I need what you have."

"I could use a good man like you. Don't waste your efforts on the rebellion. I know them as they know me. We don't get along so great. They want to assault the King while I want to wait him out. Wait for the opportunity. The rebellion will only lose lives."

"No! I can't wait any longer! I have to join the rebellion. Beline is still out there; I can feel her!" It was at that moment Rise noticed a void. All this time he had been searching for Beline, felt her, somewhere, close by. Bespin. It was the first moment he realized he knew Bespin was dead. He shook from the thought. He could feel Beline, knew she was alive, but Bespin... there was nothing. The few nights he waited for Bespin's voice to come through the ear piece had been in vain. He was sure his friend was gone. Bespin would have tried to protect her and Rise was sure the skelguards had killed him for it. When he found Beline, he knew Bespin would not be with her.

Canyon saw the sudden weakness and used it, "The rebellion will not help you in the way you think. They're more selfish than you know. They'll use you, and in the end you will not even make it to the great fight they promise is coming. They have been waiting like me to some extent, yet they think their great war is drawing close. They've been thinking that for years."

Canyon put his fingers together under his chin and smiled. "I have seen many of their leaders come and go..."

Rise stomped his foot, tears in his eyes for Bespin's loss. "I will join the rebellion."

Canyon sighed. "Very well. Such wasted talent."

Another old man came in through the curtains with a tray. A syringe with a yellowish-green liquid lay on it. "Your supply, sir."

Rise stood up. It was the podium master from the tower. "You!"

The podium master jumped a little when he saw Rise. "I thought you would be dead by now."

"You'd like that, wouldn't you?"

He shook his head, "Not like that... you're the only one who... the tower..."

293

"Aside from you, you coward!"

The podium master was angry now, "You fled just as I did! You dare call me a coward?"

"You condemned those people to death! You trapped them there and made them stay! And then you fled!" He quieted down some, and regained his composure, "You have some luck though. I have sworn not to kill after that horrible massacre. But, I can still beat an apology and confession from you."

Canyon spoke with great authority, "Sit down, Rise!" He poked him with the cane in his right hand. Canyon took the syringe and said, "Leave."

The podium master retreated back through the curtain.

Rise sat back down.

"Rise," Canyon was twirling the syringe in his fingers. "The rebellion is a wasted effort. It has been going on far too long, but I will hand it to them. They have not been caught. Yet."

"Please," Rise pulled closer. "Tell me what you know, Canyon."

"I know what is happening in every available sector at this moment. I can tell you the King has taken a total of 103 sectors over the years. I can tell you time is running out for us. I can even tell you how many sheriffs and elite guards he has, how many skelguards are roaming at one specific time, and even their patrol pattern. But I won't. I have something more valuable. I have the history of how the King came into power."

"I'm listening."

Canyon smiled and began his story.

Chapter Seven:

"The world you don't know was quite different from this one. It was over 800 years ago. Huge nations, all divided against one another, yet amazingly dependent on each other. Over 500 of them, and yet ultimately two alliances. A great war was brewing, and everyone knew it. No one knew how long it would be before the final chords broke. Barriers, containments, and threats all added to the anguish of that time. The kingdom I was a part of was run by a royal family. A king with his queen, and their three children, two princes, one princess. They were a noble family, and the king was a good man, for a time.

"Small battles for the reserves took place; each nation

wanted energy and land to expand their exploding populations. The rival government was across a great sea, and governed by one man with his hundreds of advisors. The world united against itself, some coming to my nation, others to the one across the sea.

"Our king was Arthur Tetriach. Many called him King Arthur, a joke about an old story of a king with high ideals for his people. He felt obligated to live up to that role. His Queen was Martha Tetriach, a beautiful woman whose heart was only for her children. The oldest son, Prince Jacob Tetriach was a smart fellow, if somewhat arrogant. Many times his father would come to him for suggestions, and often enough they worked. The Princess was Meagan Tetriach; she looked just like her mother. She was not so bright, but I loved her as my own daughter. Her heart was pure towards good and peace and would sacrifice all she had if she knew it would provide one meal for a starving human. But it was the youngest son who would ultimately impact the world the greatest. Unfortunately, not for good.

"Everyone loved the youngest. He was so kind and focused his attentions at peace. His father and mother never knew he was contacting the "enemy" nations and speaking to their leaders. He would befriend them and plead for peace. I overheard a few of his conversations. He had them regretting the actions they took for war, and they spoke of how fond they were of him, and how they wished they did not have to fight his father's kingdom. He would laugh and... I'll never forget the closing words he used to every one of them, "Friend, we're all in this together. If all our troops put down their weapons at the same time, we could achieve a peace greater than anything we could imagine." It was amazing to see him befriend the so-called enemies. He was so charismatic.

"He would contact around ten nations every day and speak peace. In about two months time he would have completed talking to every nation. Every two months they would hear from him again. It went on this way for three years. They almost expected to hear from him on certain days, and they looked forward to it. He could actually get the most hardened leaders to regret fighting. But, they couldn't stop. Too much was at stake and the world was falling out from under everyone. If you took the nations all into consideration, then the whole world loved the youngest son.

"Arthur was growing impatient and after an attack had almost killed his wife he grew wrathful. Vengeance was next, and an all out attack on the opposing side was launched. As advisor to the king I had much to say, but he did not listen as he did at first. His mind was set on revenge and certain other advisors supported him. For a long time, it looked as if our nation would come out victorious. I lost many friends in those years. This tore the family apart, and they hardly spoke with Arthur... except the youngest one who was fighting to keep the family together. His family spoke ill of everyone in it, except for the youngest. They all loved him deeply. He was the son everyone wanted to have. A golden heart and the words to do all his heart instructed him.

"Then came the day when the world eventually spun out of control. A great migration took place, and the whole family of humans bonded together for their joint survival. Once safety was assured, there was talk of peace and forgiveness. The talk did not last one week before the battles started again. Sides were soon taken. The worst part, we were losing. The other half of the world was conquering us, slowly but surely. All hope seemed to be lost for us.

"It came from the sky. Our deliverance came from the sky. A great weapon fell from the sky right into our lap. It took many scientists to unlock its power. Before it could be used though, a surprise attack ended the lives of the king and queen, and wounded the youngest son terribly. The two remaining children were suddenly thrown into the position of running the huge nation and all the allies. My position became difficult.

"Instead of fighting, they used the weapon to save the life of the youngest. Yet the worst happened. Our dear, precious, young son, was corrupted by the power of the weapon, and he became the conquering ruler. At that moment, he became the King we know today. It is that King that runs the world today. It was that King who instituted the sectors to control the human family. It is that King that conjured the skelguards and sheriffs.

"That is my story Rise. It is my gift to you."

Rise was looking a little nervously at the syringe. "How is it possible... over 800 years ago... how do you know all this?"

"I saw it happen." Canyon jabbed the yellowish-green syringe deep into his own arm. "I was there."

Chapter Eight:

After the syringe was empty, Canyon let out a long sigh and relaxed in his seat. "That's the information the rebellion knows. I could fill in the details, but you would have to join my side of things. If the rebellion rejects you, please come back to see me and I'll tell you what you missed.

"It's funny in a way. They have bits and pieces of the past, but can't for the life of them figure out how some of it ties together. Once they inform you of what they know, I promise you will not fear the King nearly as much."

"I don't fear the King."

"Good."

Rise sighed. "And I don't fear you. But I am... puzzled. How old are you?"

"That's not the question you care about. You ultimately want to know how the King and I both lived so long? Well, I won't tell you. All you need to know is that experience wins the battles. The rebellion has long been in place and I remember it in its infancy... yet the leaders have all died over time. Therefore, you have 70 years max of experience with the rebellion. The King has much more. Yet I have more than the King."

"And still you do nothing with all your wisdom. That's why the King rules. He did something while you failed to act!"

Canyon shakily stood up, "The King rules because of that infernal... I never failed to act, don't think for one second I idly stood by and watched that monster torch the world! I did everything I could, and I'm still doing so to this day! But, if you're that ignorant you might as well join The Control."

"The what?"

"The rebellion."

Rise nodded and Canyon sat back down.

Rise said, "I will join the rebellion. No amount of skelguards, sheriffs, or elites will stop me."

Canyon laughed, "You don't need to worry about the skelguards. They were present in my time, though in different forms. Mindless drones. The sheriffs... I won't lie. They are trained well, and most know how to use their training. If you get lucky, you'll meet a cocky one you can outsmart. But, I suggest you avoid them.

"And then of course there are the elites. You should fear them completely. Unfortunately, you can't simply avoid them. They'll find you. You will have to engage in battle. May I ask how you killed the elite?"

Rise looked around hesitantly. "I... didn't. A friend did. She shot him through the head."

Canyon nodded. "I see. The cocky fellow took his helmet off. Don't count on that again. On his lower back is a small silver box that protrudes just slightly. Smash it. If you do engage, do not miss, you will have one chance. Destroy that and the magic..."

"I don't believe in magic."

Canyon smiled. "Of course. I knew there was a reason I liked you. Magic is for the ignorant peasants. What I mean, is if you destroy that, his fuse connectors will be damaged, and his power source fails, which means without the artificial strength the suit provides, that elite will be forced to carry 200 pounds of metal on his body."

"How do you know this?"

The smile on his face grew. "I helped design it. Years ago when our technology was cutting edge. Now technology is banned for fear we could conquer it."

"Why do the sheriffs have that barrier and not the elites?"

"Theoretically, the elites don't need it. They have other powers given to them. Those shields are difficult to produce. Sheriffs all have them because that is their gift, except one. But, if you indeed are going to Sector 32, you will learn of Sheridan later. He is the only sheriff without an invisible barrier. I promise you, he does not need one. More than anything else that will cross your path, you must avoid him at all costs. There is no running from him. There is no fighting him. There is only death. The only way to conquer a normal sheriff in your condition is with forceful trauma. Drop him off a building and his body will still impact with the shield creating... SPLAT!" He clapped his hands together. "Don't try that with Sheridan, though. Any other sheriff you have a possibility against, but not him."

"Or I could use this." Rise flashed the specialized weapon.

Canyon laughed hard. "You are a tricky one. I haven't seen an EMP gun in centuries. Rise... good luck to you."

"Thanks. I'll need it. But, I have one other question before I go."

"Which is?"

"Is it true that no one can defeat the King?"

He sighed. "Is it true? Who knows? I have not met everyone. Perhaps, there is someone who under the right circumstances and training could beat him... if the King has not already arrested him or her."

"That's not what I meant."

"Ah. Let me put it this way. The reason he now rules is because he fought an army of well trained soldiers and won. *By*

298

himself. He fought an *army*, and won. You thought the tower was a massacre? You should have seen that battle."

Part Nine: Sector 2120
Chapter One:

His quest for knowledge complete, Rise quickly moved under the shadows and scaled the west wall into the east side of Sector 2120. His heart was pounding. One more sector lay between him and 32. It was exciting. His journey was about to end.

The sector he now found himself in presented a new sight. He could see no buildings, just rocky, hilly terrain. Boulders were strewn everywhere like bugs caught in a nest of grass. He saw many boulders leaning against one another with drapes of cloth over the openings. These people dwelt in man-made caves. It was actually a refreshment. He never realized how much of an eyesore the worn and torn buildings really were. The grass and rocks were much more peaceful.

A skelguard appeared in the distance from behind a boulder. Without thinking it lit a nearby entrance cover with its staff and walked away.

"Just can't get away from them."

It did not notice him, and it continued on its patrol. It continued its stalk through the night and Rise made sure he kept himself a good distance away.

He walked uphill in a northwestern direction, moving quietly through the darkness. He had always been impressed with his vision at night. The swirling clouds did little to add to the ambiance, but over the years his eyes adapted on their own.

Rise made it to the crest of the land and was disappointed to see a building. It was a structure of some sort, a good mile away. It stood 150 feet tall at the point. A concrete shelf rested on a square column with a metal pole sticking up, dangling large coils of cable. A column of wood planks was set up as a ladder to ascend to the top. It of course, was the mere remains of something grander. The land weaved in a large trail underneath, like it used to be a river bed. Rise was convinced the structure was the remains of a giant bridge that held itself up by massive cables. Now, only half of it still stood. A small village was built under it. Little tents and scrap metal dwellings were spaced out under it.

It was between him and the north sector wall.

"Sleep," he told himself out loud.

He quickly argued, "No time. Just one more sector. I can make it before day if I hurry."

No you can't. His mind was urging him to be more cautious of his limits.

Rise began to jog. He would make his way to the village under the giant structure and camp there for the night. Sleep was sounding too good to pass up. He was so close he could almost taste the exhilarating coldness of his breath being taken away by the jump off the top of the sector wall. The amazing freeness it gave him. His days of that, he felt, were almost over.

It took him a few hours to make it. The hills were steep and he avoided many guards. They were on full patrol it seemed like. Or he just had bad timing. He could not remember how many skelguards he would normally see in his old sector. It seemed so long ago. His ignorant bliss in Sector 2128 was lost forever.

His first steps into the village under the silhouette of the structure were awkward. Masses of huddled people surrounded metal bins that they had built fires in to keep warm. They were all awake. A whole village of nocturnal people. Their clothing was even more patched together than most. Clothes normal peasants would abandon were preserved by these people. Alcohol bottles were strewn everywhere, and the occasional man or women of the village would pick up a discarded one and check for any remaining fluids.

"Bunch of drunks," he muttered under his breath, jealous of their inebriation.

The eyes were glaring at him. He was the newcomer. No one got up, nor did he expect anyone too. He darted his face towards the earth, hoping in the low light of the dancing flames they could not tell he was young with his white hair. He needed a hat.

"Move!" A huddled old woman pushed him away at his knees. His boot had been on top of a bottleneck. The woman checked it for liquor. After finding none she glared up at Rise. He heard her threaten, "You drank it! I will cut you in your sleep." She muttered some other words and hobbled off for her next victim.

He heard boisterous laughing of two men fumbling towards him. For whatever reason, the fear of being identified now was too great and wrapped around his neck like a noose.

The loud men were drunk and singing some song they just made up. They grabbed onto Rise's arms and began to pull him into their dance. The smell was horrid, alcohol and dung mixed with Rise's air and he pushed them away in disgust. He tried not to make eye contact.

"Hey!" The drunk man yelled slurring, "Nobody..." He tossed the empty bottle in his hand and struck Rise on the top of his head. The pain hit him just right, sending a small but irritating jolt to his feet. The dull pain angered him.

The two drunk men began laughing and just as quickly turned it into rage, "This guy! This guy? Yeah! This guy! You can't push me! You think you're better than me?"

His friend agreed in drunken stupidity, "He thinks he's better than you?" He tried to point at his friend but got fascinated by his large nose instead.

One of the less drunk women stood up from her circle and said, "He's probably from the north of the sector! How dare he! This is our home! Walk back to your own land, north rat!"

"Yeah!" Another voice yelled.

Rise looked up briefly as 20 men and women, most of them drunk, begin to encircle him. An entire mass of dirty, dingy, and smelly people came to trap him. The circle tightened as more joined the group, their faces ugly and twisted from the bouncing fire in the bins.

Someone was standing directly in front of him. The man reeked of mold and sweat. The nasty person leaned forward, forcing his dingy face into Rise's and pushed his head upward, "Look at me, stranger!"

Someone hit Rise across his shoulders with a wood board. Rise fell forward and knocked heads with the man in front of him who stumbled back, recoiled, and struck Rise across the face.

An empty bottle struck the ground next to him. Rise did not even have time to reach for his sword.

Chapter Two:

Rise felt utter hopelessness as the grubby, dirty hands grabbed, pulled, and scratched him. He feared that all his work, luck, and hope were ending in the mass of dingy people. Was this how it would end? Not by some skelguard, not by a sheriff, or the elite, and not by the King's own hands. Worst of all, he was not even in Beline's arms and it was going to end.

"WAIT!" A voice echoed under the huge structure and instantly the hands released him.

Rise saw the mass of dirty people jumble away. Another

301

filthy man with a thick brown beard was coming through the crowd. He wore tattered everything and a scarf wrapped around his shoulders making an extremely curtailed cape.

The man spoke, "Save your energy, delivery comes tonight!"

The drunken crowd lifted their arms and yelled in excitement.

Everyone seemed to have been disarmed, and they walked back to their stations of drunkenness. Even the two that started the attempted murder forgot their cares and continued walking arm in arm and singing.

Rise had to thank the man properly. His heart was racing, and getting words out was difficult between the heart beats. "Thank you."

"Name is Lowell." A deep husky voice stained with beer came out of a strong body covered by thick tattered rags. A whole society of bottom scrappers. Poorest of the poor. Sheriffs would often use them for target practice. Or worse.

"They always get a little feisty just before the delivery."

"I can see that."

Lowell put a smelly arm around Rise's shoulders. "Yup, friend, they see someone with a little riches in their clothes, and they get angry. But, don't fret so much. After the supply of alcohol arrives we'll have enough to get us through another year."

"How do you get a year worth of alcohol?"

He opened his mouth and revealed a shattered smile, "We know people."

"Right."

"Come on, I'll find you something to eat."

Rise tried to pull away, but the man was strong to a scary degree. "I don't want food. If anything, I need a place to sleep."

The man laughed. "Sleep? Maybe for a few hours, but after the fights start it'll be too loud to sleep."

"A couple hours is all I need."

"Very well," Lowell consented. "Follow me."

He led him through more of the same huddled masses surrounding a fire. A quiet anticipation awaiting them.

He took him to an empty cot beside one of the massive concrete supports of the structure. "This is my home, feel free to sleep in it."

Rise stared at the disgusting bed.

Lowell said, "I have to prepare for the fights." He removed his top shirt and was left with an even more tattered one revealing his arms. They were enormous. "I have won the last three years, going for a record tonight of four. Come watch if you want. Come watch me win the beer! I might even share some with ya!" He laughed and slapped Rise on the back before walking away, mock boxing the air.

Rise made sure Lowell was far enough away before flipping the mildew stained mattress of cloths off the cot. It still stank, but was more tolerable. Rise eased himself onto the moist bed and covered himself with the disgusting rags.

Chapter Three:

Rise heard thumping in his sleep. He heard shouting echoes. He heard people screaming. He heard dust being rattled off the huge structure as it creaked and moaned with deep booming noises. But that was not what woke him. Something was walking close to him. Rise opened his eyes was staring up at a skelguard. He was on his back, looking up to the tall monster. The glowing red eyes were not pointed at him, they were pointed ahead and it walked slowly by, staff in hand.

Rise felt every muscle in his body tense. He looked around with only his eyes, not daring to move. The entire area around him was deserted of any people. The crowd must have moved onto the large wooden ladders to the top of the structure. Now a patrol of skelguards was wandering the area. He saw the vehicles with their two round lights in the front parked just before the village under the bridge. The gray boxes with wheels had skelguards removing giant crates out of them and setting them on the ground. It reminded him of the food ration procedures.

The shouting and screams continued above with a monstrous echo. The deep rumble of a crowd gone insane. It was safer than being where he was.

Rise slowly lifted his head and saw that he probably blended in with the rest of the garbage left behind. The rags he was covered by prevented the skelguard from seeing him. He rolled himself slowly off the cot and quietly stood by the huge pillar. He hid behind it, his back to it. He heard steps getting closer from the other side. Another skelguard was making its way through the darkness.

A loud echoing voice came from the top. Rise could see

303

the boards shaking from the people stomping above it, shaking the dust loose. The voice yelled, "62!" Something fell from the top. A limp body was thrown onto a pile of other limp bodies that Rise did not notice until now. The body landed awkwardly with a slapping sound. The fights had already begun.

He could not sneak up to the top that way. That was the end where they were pitching the dead bodies.

The skels were on the other side of the giant support pillar and they were making their way around. Rise circled quietly to the other side, but had to stop from going to the next because of the glowing eyes of another skelguard in the distance, probably 50 feet away. Until that one moved away he needed to stand his ground. The steps of the one circling his pillar were getting closer.

Please, don't come this far, he thought to himself. *Please*. His heart was pounding. It was almost to his corner.

The far off skelguard slowly walked away and Rise quickly sidestepped to the other side and made his way to one of the tin barrels containing an almost dead fire. He ducked behind it and spotted the rest of the patrol. The heat of the bin was uncomfortable against his face, but he dare not move.

Rise heard another skelguard walking behind him and he rolled himself to hide under a large cot. He was afraid he made too much noise but the steps continued walking.

He was 60 feet from the closest ladder, a giant wood grid that sprawled to the top of the old bridge.

Rise pulled out from under the cot and brought himself to his knees and slowly crept for a large, thin, metal slab. The ancient sign was about 12 twelve feet square. It was green with white writing. Most of it was torn off, but in the old tongue read, "...mont Bridge." It was stabbed into the ground like it had fallen from the top at some point in time.

He hid behind it as the steps he heard were sneaking up from the other side. The next closest object was another pillar that was almost right next to the ladder he needed. He would have to run. He peeked and watched the skelguards walking. Two were far enough away that they did not matter. Three were too close and would hear him run.

"63!" The shouting continued and Rise heard something drop in the distance on the other side. He did not look.

The three that were too close were walking between the cots and garbage and finally made their way to the other end. Rise ran before the far ones turned around. He held his grapnel close to him so it would not jingle as he ran. He made it to the pillar and quickly ran to the other side. He took a moment to breathe. He would need to climb the ladder slowly, and quietly, if he were out of breath he could not do it.

Checking one last time for skelguards, he took three long steps to the outer edge of the ladder and began his ascent. The fights would be safer than dealing with the wandering dead.

Chapter Four:

He climbed the ladder all hundred feet to the top. The overhang blocked any chance of the skelguards seeing him. The support pillar continued into the air another 50 feet, but all the commotion was taking place on the walkway of the bridge. He poked his head over and saw the mob of bottom scrappers huddled. Most were standing cheering. He could not see through them, but he heard a fight in the middle.

There was a terrible crunching noise and the crowd screamed with excitement. The deep voice echoed, "64!"

A large woman pushed her way through the crowd and sat in what Rise guessed was the winner circle. He saw Lowell sitting prominently in it and yelling every time a good hit was thrown.

Next to the winner circle sat a small crate of alcohol. Each of the winners got one; their prize for blood.

Sixty five was called and Rise still did not see the face of the voice because the crowd was too big, 200 strong. The horrible death matches lasted five more lives. Most of the people apparently just came to watch.

The crowd separated for just a brief moment and Rise saw to his horror a sheriff walk through and stand in front of the winner circle. The same voice that was calling out the death count said with a horrible smile, "You ration rats have earned the privilege to live tonight. Who here is the best?"

The entire circle of winners shouted.

The sheriff wore the same well-fitted clothes as the other royals, brown tailored uniform with matching boots. The logo of an iron fist was patched on his chest. His face was clean shaven, and his skin was very dark. His hair was long and black, and it curled in the wind. His nose was almost square, and his chin was small. His build was more muscular than most. He held no sword, only two long barreled guns strapped to his back. "I thought as much. The winner of the final fight gets control of the large cases of alcohol! Take a few minutes to breathe before we start."

The bridge was a dangerous enough place. The ancient river it crossed dried up long ago. In place of the life giving water these bottom feeders had set up vacancy. The bridge still had its support structures on the side with the ladders; two towers that ascended up for 50 feet before they fell to pieces of cracked concrete and rebar. The bridge itself sprawled fifty feet wide, and went out 150 in length. The end of the bridge had long ago been torn away, and large support cables stuck out like veins of an ancient decapitation. The matching side of the bridge was nowhere to be found, as if it simply disappeared.

The sheriff began to turn his body towards Rise's direction. He let go of the ladder and fell a foot, just below the surface of the asphalt. He looked around for anywhere to hide. He could not descend, the skeleton guards were below, and going up was out of the question. He found a ripped open alcove of metal, and he shoved his body tightly into it. It looked like it used to house a smaller pillar that was ripped out long ago.

He heard the sheriff's boots walking slowly over.

Rise hastily glanced and saw the back of his boot a few feet from his face. His hiding place cut off the sheriff at the ankles. He was looking the other way and missed Rise. He removed a thin box from his belt and pressed a button before speaking into it. "E8, you gotta come see this one."

A scratchy voice talked back from the box, "Good, I could use a break. That murderer is still out there. When I find him I'll cut his throat out."

The sheriff laughed. "Save your blood lust for the fight, there are actually a few dirt peasants worth watching this time. Real killers. Dirty wastes don't even understand they're keeping their own population under control. All for beer."

"I'll be there shortly, Gerik."

Gerik placed the box back on his belt and stood watching the crowd get excited for the upcoming fight. "Horrible creatures." Gerik sighed under his breath.

Rise was ready to faint. The sheriff was standing right over him. It was a miracle he did not see him hiding in the alcove just below him on the edge of the ancient bridge. The skelguards were still below him. If he moved his body, he risked falling to his death.

Can't get worse, he thought to himself.

A few minutes went by, and then he heard it. The familiar rumbling sound from the sky. It was the elite.

Chapter Five:

His heart was ready to rip itself out of the alcove and drop the hundred feet below. Rise felt trapped and his sweat was beginning to drip. His only hope was that they did not look straight down.

Before the elite made his landing he turned invisible to avoid detection. A barely visible, blurry image, quietly landed next to the sheriff. His suit stopped making the humming noise and Rise could only guess at his location. While moving he could almost see the figure, like a heat wave blur. But, when the elite would stand still all vision of him was gone.

Gerik knew the elite was near and said, "I heard he escaped from you." There was a smile on his lips. "How did Sheridan take it?"

"He won't escape again," the invisible hunter said.

Rise recognized the voice of the elite that had attacked him earlier.

"I envy you. You get to find and slaughter him. He thinks he can just kill one of us? Morceff was loyal beyond compare to our beloved King. He was a good man."

The elite came into vision at that remark. He still retained the marks on his neck just above a green emerald necklace. He almost had tears in his eyes, "He'll pay for what he's done. This treachery will be punished. After all our Lord has done for these peasants, the forgiveness he has shown... How can supposed men behave like that?"

"These are not men. Filthy peasants. They've no idea what mercy is."

The two watched the fight continue.

"Nice necklace," the sheriff stated.

The elite clutched it, "A piece of scrap that murderer owned. The only tangible clue of his existence. One day, it will be my trophy."

Rise felt his hands shake in rage.

The elite disappeared again and Gerik said, "Good. For now, take your mind off your work. Enjoy the entertainment." He

307

turned to the crowd. "Move aside, peasants!"

The crowd split apart instantly. Rise slowly poked his head up to see what was happening. Bats, clubs, boards, nails, ropes with wood tied to them, assorted hand-made weapons were thrown all across the ancient bridge.

The elite whispered to the sheriff, "Make an announcement before the fight."

"Almost forgot." Gerik put his arms up. "Before the fight I need information. Anyone who has seen a younger man with white hair, last seen wearing a black coat must report him immediately to me."

Lowell stood up.

No! Rise felt sick.

"I've seen him! He's probably about 30 or so, but he had white hair!"

"What?!" The sheriff seemed surprised. He trudged over to Lowell and grabbed him by the beard and pulled him to his knees. The sheriff bent down to yell at him, "Where? When? Answer, peasant!"

"Tonight! He's sleeping under the bridge!"

No! Rise bit down hard.

Rise heard the elite start the humming noise again and shot quickly down to the bottom leaving a gust of wind like a giant hawk. Gerik grabbed his box and said, "Skel troop four: Command: Search area for Fugitive one."

Rise pulled himself back into his alcove, not daring to watch. He heard Gerik's voice, "The rest of you! Bring him to me!"

Rise heard the mob quickly stand up and he felt the bridge shake as they hobbled for the huge ladders. He heard people rushing past, yet none stuck their head down the alcove.

"What are you doing?" Rise heard the voices of the two drunks from earlier start to argue with Gerik. "You don't tell me what to do! You think you're better than us..."

A loud bang of the gun ended the conversation. Rise heard the sheriff push their bodies over the side and say, "I am better than you, traitors."

As long as no one looked in the alcove he would be safe. He would just wait them out. It was five minutes before every last person made their way down the bridge.

The elite's voice came back over the box, "He's gone. He must have fled. Too much foot traffic to track his steps... the trail is either gone or cold."

Something grabbed Rise by the hair. "Found ya!" He smelled beer as he looked up into the eyes of Lowell. He thrust his other hand down and easily pulled Rise out of his spot, his massive arms hardly working. He tossed Rise to the floor at the feet of the sheriff. They were the only three on the top of the bridge. Everyone else was down searching for Rise.

Rise was looking up into the eyes of Gerik. Hatred and disbelief flowed from the sheriff. Smoke from the end of the gun danced through the air. The sheriff was actually quivering with anger. He hissed, "You!" Gerik seemed more surprised than Rise.

"Let me kill him for you, sir!" Lowell said, standing at the edge of the alcove.

"How dare you!" Gerik yelled. "That's not your privilege!" Gerik shot Lowell and watched with disgust as his body stumbled backward over the edge. A sickening thump ended Lowell's reign as fight champion.

Rise did not know whether he should move. Fear was gripping him. All he learned from Uzzah he was forgetting for the temporary weakness of fear. The sheriff did not move. He just looked at Rise, up and down with so much disgust Rise felt he might actually deserve the death the sheriff threatened.

Finally, Gerik spoke into the box. "He's up here."

Chapter Six:

Rise saw the boot as it pinned his neck to the floor. "What is your name?" The sheriff popped Rise's neck as he twisted it.

Rise did not speak. He heard the horrible humming of the elite's flying armor bring him back to the top. The elite landed, turned visible, and marched over to him. "That's him alright."

The elite reached under and pulled Rise upward, dangling him by the throat. "This time, you die."

"This is it?"

The elite looked at Gerik. "What do you mean?"

"This thing is it? I was expecting a monster of a man, one almost worthy of our powers! And this is it? He's not better than a common peasant. I expected more." Gerik stared at Rise with all the hatred in his body. "You killed a friend of mine, peasant. A man with faith you could never understand. A good, loyal man until you murdered him. After that, you betray our King? A man dreams of the day he can execute perfect justice for his Lord. I never thought I would be the one to do it. And here you are, in my very own sector. What you did was all luck! You're nothing! Nothing but a peasant who got lucky."

Rise glanced and saw the scratch marks he left on the elite. His memories of the knowledge Uzzah taught him came back. The skills of the old man came back. His friendship of Bespin flooded his mind, and his love for Beline flooded his heart. All of his training, knowledge, skills, instinct, and luck had brought him to this point in his life. Triumph or failure. The scratches on the elite. They were only humans.

Rise dangled by his throat like a dirty shirt with his hands wrapped around the wrist of the elite. "A lot of people have been talking about my luck lately."

The elite pulled him close. "What's your name, villain?"

He stared into the eyes of the elite. "Rise. I used to be Rise The Giver. Now I'm Rise The Sheriff Slayer. And I'm giving you one chance, and one chance only. Where is she?"

They stared at him in incredulity.

"And I want that necklace."

The elite tossed Rise like a pebble. Rise went sailing and landed in the middle of the bridge. He felt his coat rip as it hit the pavement. The grapnel bruised his chest as he rolled to his knees amid the weapons the brawlers had been using.

Rise stood up and drew his sword, "Don't say I didn't warn you."

Chapter Seven:

The elite said, "Do what you want to him, but the death blow is mine."

"Fair," the sheriff said, pulling out his other gun.

The elite became a blur as he moved at unhuman speeds. Rise felt the punch send him upward and the blur of the elite followed his body into the air and sent a foot crashing down into his chest, sending him back to the ground. Rise slid on his back, rolled his feet over his head, and stood upright.

Rise put the blur between him and the sheriff with the guns, blocking any possible shot. Gerik was running after them now, trying to pick out a good shot. He could just barely make out the movement now, he saw the almost invisible feet running for him.

Just before the elite reached him, Rise jammed his sword into a crack and put all his weight on the hilt. The elite's feet hit the blade and tripped. He crashed forward with tremendous speed and tore up some ancient asphalt behind him.

Rise spun up to his feet again. He had to keep moving. Gerik was a few feet away and pointing one of the guns. Rise threw his sword and knocked the gun from his hand. He dove at Gerik as he tried to aim the second gun. He collided and saw the red spots of contact against the shield. It was like he tackled a boulder to the ground. He pulled the gun out of his hand and felt himself being lifted up from behind.

The elite grabbed him by his back and right arm and began to pull. He wanted to rip Rise's arm off. Rise pointed the gun at the exposed flesh of the elite's lower neck, just below the helmet. The elite quickly dropped Rise back onto the sheriff. Gerik kicked up with both his feet, knocking the wind out of him. Rise dropped the gun and it slid a few feet away.

Rise saw a board next to him. He picked it up and swung across what would have been Gerik's face. The shield knocked it away, but also knocked Gerik back over. He quickly rolled up as the blur came back and kicked Rise in the stomach. Rise wanted to vomit from the pain.

Rise made a desperate dive for one of the guns, but felt his feet being grabbed. For a brief moment, he was hanging in midair. He was being swung by the elite. Rise used all his strength to pull himself forward to grab the arm of the elite as he let go. He had just enough time to grab onto its arm before he was thrown. His feet were now free.

He felt exposed. He ducked in time to avoid a blurred punch to his face. The kick came from the sheriff who hit him in the lower back. Rise spun away and picked up the gun from the ground.

With his other hand, he pulled out his grapnel and shot at a large cable pillar. He strafed around the oncoming blur and pulled the retract button. The grapnel flew him across the width of the bridge. Gerik ran for the other gun and the elite blur was coming at Rise. Rise hit the ground and pulled the latch releasing the grapnel from the torso belt. He left the grapnel on the ground and ran straight for the blur. A moment before impact he forced himself to fall to the ground rolling. He rolled himself up and felt the sharp metal foot armor dig into him as the elite tripped over his fallen body. The elite landed on its hands. Rise quickly turned before the blur vanished and made out the small box Canyon described to him. Rise aimed and pulled the trigger. The gun knocked his hand back from the force and Rise watched as the box sparked and the elite came into visibility again.

A great force skimmed Rise's right arm, forcing him to drop the gun to his right as he fell forward. Gerik had grazed his arm with his second weapon.

The elite could hardly move, the power of the suit draining out of the box, making the suit extremely heavy. The elite pulled a hidden switch on the inside of his metal frame and the chest plate came off, relieving some of the weight. "KILL HIM, GERIK! KILL HIM NOW!"

Rise pulled the gun up and fired at Gerik. The bullet struck the gun from his hand, breaking the barrel in a burst of red barrier and gun pieces. The sheriff ran at him yelling into his box, "Skel troop four:...."

Rise fired again and shattered the box, knocking Gerik to his back.

The elite managed to remove the heavy armor and now stood bare before Rise. A scrawny, pasty man stood before him. To Rise's disgust, the man had wires coming out of almost every part of his body. His left arm was completely metal. He was left in a gray uniform that made him look weak. Anger was written all over his face and Rise knocked it out of him with the butt of the gun. He fell to the ground unconscious. Rise took the necklace off the scrawny man.

"This belongs to a friend of mine." Rise put the necklace on. He would not be stopped.

Rise turned to face the sheriff who was beginning to stand up. Rise had no fear left. "Only men." He pulled the trigger but the gun only clicked. It was empty. He discarded it.

He reached into his coat pocket and pulled out the shield breaker. He fired and watched the air distort as the shot struck the sheriff and sent him rolling backwards. The barrier distorted and then disappeared. Rise was now facing a man not a monster. The light on the bottom of the EMP gun was gone. He placed it back in his pocket, knowing it was out of power.

Rise reached down to the unconscious elite. He pulled the elite over to the ledge and tossed him towards the pile of bodies beneath. Hopefully, it would break his fall. Rise would not break his vow. Not to these worthless men.

Rise felt his blood dripping down his arm and torn jacket from the grazed shot.

Gerik stood up and grabbed a club that was on the ground. He ran for Rise. Rise found a metal bar with a point. "This ends."

Gerik swung the bat and Rise ducked to avoid it. Gerik kicked Rise in the face as he turned to recover his balance and then struck him with his other hand across the face. Rise stumbled back and then ran at Gerik.

The sheriff dodged the point of the metal pole and came down hard with the bat on Rise's bleeding arm. Rise screamed in pain and head butted the sheriff across the cheek.

The sheriff swung the bat as he stumbled. It was the first time he had probably felt pain. It angered him.

Rise saw a few heads of the bottom scrappers poking up from the ladders. They must have seen the body of the elite fall. Rise was glad the last order from Gerik to the skelguards was to search for him down below. Hopefully that order would hold.

Gerik was running for a discarded axe that was now a foot from the ledge. Rise quickly followed just behind him. Gerik dived for it. He grabbed it and spun so that he landed on his back pointing the weapon at Rise. Rise dove as well. With his free hand he grabbed the axe and forced it sideways as he fell. He did not let go. He rolled his body forward. Rise did not finish his turn and landed hard on the ground just above Gerik's head. They both maintained a grip on the axe. Rise struck him across the face with the bar and ripped the axe from his hand. His zeal for the weapon betrayed him as it slipped from his sweaty grasp and fell off the ledge.

He swung the metal pole and Gerik easily blocked it with the bat. The shock hurt both their hands. "How can you hate our Lord? After all he's done for you! I'll bring your head to the King myself, you worthless waste!"

Rise pulled back and swung again, hoping just to graze Gerik's ear, give him a stinging pain. He missed and Gerik uppercutted him with the bat. Rise saw lights before his eyes and the wind nearly finished tipping him over.

They battled across the bridge, Gerik just barely keeping the upper hand. Rise could not get a decent hit on him. Gerik was a skilled fighter. Rise saw his sword and forced the fight over to it. He pushed against Gerik and ran towards it.

Rise rushed passed him and Gerik reached down to a whipping rope that had been left behind from the fights. He pulled it up and whipped it around Rise's neck and pulled him backwards. Rise's feet left the ground, and he dropped the metal pole. His back slammed to the ground and his head followed. More colors before his eyes as the wind left his body.

Gerik jumped on top of Rise and forced his knee on his wounded arm. Rise was in too much pain from other things to realize it. Gerik reached over and pulled up Rise's sword. "I'm gonna take you to the King in the smallest possible pieces!" Spit flew from his mouth as he yelled in absolute rage. He pulled the sword up, and Rise kicked him between the legs. The intense shock went up and out of Gerik's body, and he dropped the sword in surprise. It landed across Rise's chest. Rise pulled his legs out from under the sheriff and pushed both his boots into his chest, knocking him over. Rise grabbed the sword and ran to the sheriff.

He grabbed Gerik's hair and pulled his head back and touched the cold metal of his blade to his neck. Rise was breathing hard through clenched teeth, "WHERE IS SHE?!"

The sheriff spat on him and Rise pulled the sword back and struck him across the face with the hilt. A crowd now gathered on the ladders, no one daring to climb to the top.

Gerik pulled a dagger from his boot and slapped it across Rise's chest, ripping his shirt open and exposing more blood to the air.

Rise cringed back and swung his sword. Gerik ducked his head and dived into Rise knocking them both to the ground, sending the sword sliding across the pavement. They were both sweating as the wind pulled against them. Two men struggling for life. Rise was blocking the dagger just above his neck as Gerik was pushing down. Gerik was stronger and the blade came down and began to press against his skin.

Rise did not want to think about the cold blade entering his body again. He closed his eyes and forced his body to react. He saw Beline's face for the thousandth time. She was smiling. She had green eyes. Beautiful eyes.

He felt the knife slightly graze the necklace she gave him. He opened his eyes as it just barely broke his skin. "Where is she?"

The knife came out of his skin as Rise's strength grew. The knife was being pushed away from him. "Where is she?!"

The knife was a foot away from his face, and he forced himself up to his feet and began to push the sheriff towards the ledge. Gerik stared in disbelief at the sudden show of strength. "WHERE IS SHE?!" He was practically running the sheriff to the ledge.

For the first time, Rise saw fear in a sheriff's eyes.

"Where's who?" he gasped.

"BELINE!"

"I... don't know."

Rise shook with anger and threw Gerik to the ground. He sat on top of him and ripped the knife from his hand and threw it over the side. He began to beat Gerik senseless with his hands. "WHERE IS SHE?!" He kept sobbing over and over. "BRING HER TO ME!" Long after Gerik had gone unconscious Rise finally stopped when he felt a hand on his shoulder. He looked up and saw the crowd had gathered from the ladder. One man held out Rise's sword to him. They were all scared with awe. He heard murmurs. "He defeated a sheriff..." Over and over they kept saying it.

Rise stood up from Gerik's body, tears streaming down his face. He took his sword from the man and asked them, "Where is she?" They stared at him.

Rise slowly walked across the battlefield of the bridge and screamed the name of his love into the cold wind, to each direction of the sector. He wanted the echo to be heard. He wanted all to know that he would not stop until he found her. He wanted his voice to reach the King himself. He made his way to the pillar and took a deep breath as he took the grapnel back into his possession.

Rise walked towards the ladder and the crowd split for him with the same respect they gave the sheriff. A silent respect. Rise hated it.

The skelguards had scattered out more in their search for him leaving wider spaces below, yet Rise did not notice. He just descended the ladder in a daze. He wanted Beline. He wanted her beside him. He fought great evils for her and she may never know it. It was worth it, just the thought of fighting for her was worth it.

Rise ran. He ran as hard as he could for the north wall, he wanted to leave this sector. The skelguards journeyed south in their search for him, leaving him free from their threat.

The rest of the night was a blur in his mind. A painful blur that hurt with every step and breath. Rise vaguely remembered finding a large growth of shrubs away from any man-made shelter. He buried himself under their leaves to hide as morning approached. He slept the day away and did not move until the clouds came back and the cover of night reappeared.

He ran hard and finally approached the wall. He was dehydrated and exhausted. He was injured and wanted to just sit down and cry for Beline.

He did no such thing. He pulled his grapnel and began

his ascent into Sector 34, just before dawn struck away the swirling clouds.

Part Ten: Sector 34
Chapter One:

Rise found a ditch a few hundred feet from the wall. He did not even notice the surroundings. He just saw the ditch and headed for it. He fell the five feet to the bottom and was thankful it was muddy and not hard. He lay in the ditch and finally fell asleep as he felt the sun's rays on him.

He was not asleep long. His mind pushed him up. He grabbed the mud wall with his face still in the mushy ground. Rise pulled himself up. His mind begged him on. *Keep going. Stop and you die.*

There was no telling how much of lead on his opponents he had. He smiled to himself as he climbed out of the mud hole. He had called them opponents. Equals. He did not fear them.

He was too exhausted to jog, which would mean it would take him about two days to reach the north wall to the final sector he would visit. If he made it that far. Where could he go? His victory won the battle, yet now the King was sure to unleash every bit of power he had left.

Rise pulled himself fully out of the pit and sat looking down at it. His arm was burning fiercely, his head was sore, his back was aching, and he felt something in his chest like shrapnel of some sort.

He glanced up at the sector. Another uphill journey. Another sector made up of ruins of the ancient cities. Another sector with thugs, gangs, and other murderers.

He wanted to go back into the pit, sit, and wait for his death.

Get moving.

How long did he have? An hour at most, before Gerik called in reinforcements? He could not run. He would not make it far. They must have known he went north. They would force the information out of one of the bottom scrappers.

Do it for Beline.

Rise bent his head down and began to sob. "I'm sorry. Beline... I'm so sorry. I can't do it. I came so close... my love, I failed completely."

Another voice, "Get up."

Rise looked around. No one was in sight. The villages were farther uphill and no one had seen him enter the sector. He was too far away to be bothered by the skelguards on patrol.

The voice came again. "Get up." A man's voice. Rise knew that voice.

He focused on the voice and heard footsteps. He could just barely make out the blurry vision of a man walking. A news gatherer appeared by twisting his ring. Something that would have seemed more magical just a few days ago. Now it was just an invention of a world Rise would never know, and he was forced to accept it as fact.

"I know you." Rise's voice was hoarse. He had no energy left in any recess of his body. Even the necklace that Rise would have carried through fire and thorns was getting heavy for his neck.

Rise was looking at his friend the news gatherer that he ran into so many times before. What was his name? Did he ever learn it? Rise could not remember. But it was the same one. The black hair, the boyish face, it was the same news gatherer that helped him before.

"My friend, Rise. Please get up. You have no time."

"Why did you follow me?" He just barely rasped out a voice.

"To be honest, there are three of us following you, and we made a wager of whether you would actually make it to Sector 32 or not. I got a very nice pair of boots riding on your victory."

Rise stared at him, and then cracked a smile as his friend laughed.

"Seriously, you have zero time. My companions informed me that the sheriff is awake and on the move. He massed 300 skels. My friends are trying to lead him west, bribing the bottom scrappers to give him bad information. Well, actually threatening them of lighting their beer crates on fire. You have to get up *now*."

His news gathering friend was tugging on him. Rise just sat there.

"I can't..."

The scrawny man pulled him up with amazing strength. "Liar! I've seen you do too many amazing things, and now you tell me you can't go one more sector?"

He began to pull Rise northward. Rise could only allow himself to be dragged, a bloody and muddy mesh of black coat and

317

brown boots.

"What's the point? If I make it one more sector, he'll just hunt me there."

"Canyon doesn't believe in the rebellion's effectiveness. That doesn't mean it's powerless. They have managed to hide their existence for hundreds of years from the King. You'll be safe and have all the rest and time you need to accomplish your quest. Now MOVE!"

Rise steadied himself a little and began to walk with his friend's help. "Why?" His voice was coarse.

"One sheriff has been done before. Wounding another, that has some skill. Defeat another sheriff, luck. Defeat two elites, you have power. Our Master Canyon was fond of you. He was quite impressed. He had three of us follow you to see if you'd make it. Even though I like you too, I was not going to interfere so much, but then you battled them on the broken bridge... and WON! You can make it one more sector."

They were coming close to the outskirts of a town of rubble. "We have a hiding place in this sector. Well, hiding places in all of them actually. You need to sleep until night. Me and my companions will try to slow down the sheriff's efforts. A couple false stories about which way you went should do the trick. People love a good rumor." He smiled.

Rise was pulled by his friend for a mile until they made it to a small shack. His friend unlocked the door, revealing that it was a thick metal frame with a complicated locking mechanism. A safe hold. Rise was relieved to see a very comfortable looking cot.

"Sleep until night, friend. I've tried to help you as much as I can, please... don't get caught," he smiled. "I might lose the bet if you do. Whatever started you on your quest, remember it, and cherish it. Don't let time fade it."

His friend tossed him a water bottle he kept at his side. "I don't think we'll see each other again. Good luck in your rebellion. Oh, and don't open the door to any strangers, especially skeletons."

His friend shut the door and Rise heard a loud click from the lock.

Rise drank the bottle greedily.

The room was completely dark, and Rise found himself falling asleep on the cot. He was so close.

Chapter Two:

She was in his dreams again. Her green eyes. Her smile that would disarm rival gangs. She was reaching out to him. His dream was replaying something that happened a few years ago.

She was crying. "Rise..." She sobbed, "My brother was arrested."

Before he knew what had happened she wrapped her arms around him and cried on his chest, her bottom lip curled in agony. He felt her heart beating.

"I'm... so sorry." He said. "I..." He began to cry as well. Their tears fell to the ground that day long ago.

He sobbed as much as she did, her pain was eating him alive starting at his heart. "I wish I was there! I'm so sorry I let it happen!"

"No!" She said, "I could have lost you too if you had been there! Don't ever say that!"

They hugged tighter. "They beat him, Rise." She took a deep breath. "They beat him and threw him into that horrible vehicle! They drove away with him! I ran... so hard, Rise. I ran after it. As hard as I could, and he was gone... my awful brother! He made me promise... when he saw them coming for him, he made me promise not to interfere, to hide and stay quiet! How could he?!" She hit Rise's chest.

She was no longer standing with her own strength. Rise was holding her up. "Beline... your brother did me a favor. If you had interfered, they would have robbed me of you. Your brother is not awful for that. It makes him a great man. I'll miss him dearly."

She hit Rise again, a little harder, "Don't ever leave me! EVER! You're all I have left."

Rise tried to force himself to stop crying. He wanted to be strong for her. He wanted to be a tower she could climb to be safe from all the troubles of the world. Yet, here he was, crying like a woman right next to her.

He gently pushed her back and looked down at her green glazed eyes, "Beline. I will never leave you. I will always protect you. If you're ever lost... I will find you."

She bit her lip and muttered, "Why?" She looked back as if she wanted to hear a specific answer, an answer Rise did not give.

"Because you are my dearest friend."

Rise shot out of bed in anger, snapping the dream away

319

from his mind. "Beline! I love you!" He was alone in the dark.

He remembered. His quest, his journey, what it was all for. All his pain, suffering, fighting, bruises, cuts, sweat, and tears were for one purpose. He was going to find Beline and tell her he loved her with his whole heart, life, and spirit. He loved her, and no sheriff, no army, and no King were going to stand in his way.

He opened the door and saw it was night. He had a sector to cross.

Chapter Three:

He ran north, the mud caked to his clothes and face and he was happy to see a small lake. He forced himself to take his clothes off and wade through it in the freezing weather to get clean and refill his water. He washed the mud from his clothes as well, trying to keep them as dry as possible. He held a strict course north and did not run into any skelguards. This sector was completely asleep in the dark night of the swirling clouds.

His slightly wet clothes impeded his running, yet it refreshed him even more. His energy was fully restored, and he would not allow himself to feel the pain in his body. He needed to ignore it.

He journeyed north through broken buildings, through sleeping communities of bottom scrappers, and also passed the tents of the wealthy. He still had not seen any skelguards all night. Perhaps his friend really had distracted the sheriff with false rumors. He could only hope.

Rise found a forested area he could take cover in and sleep before daybreak. He awoke in six hours and continued his long journey. Night was approaching again.

Rise saw the wall finally in the distance over the last stretch of uphill territory.

Rise rested against a tree and watched the wall. To his anger, he saw small camp fires directly in front of his destination at the center of the wall. Gangs. The area was completely surrounded by scrap metal shards; giant ones. No telling what invention they once belonged too. They looked like a metallic streak of evil grass ripping open the landscape. They must have been 200 feet tall.

So, you just gonna march up to them? His mind was beginning to talk to him. He was unsure if this was a good or bad development. Whatever helped him survive his burden should be a good thing.

"Yes."

Demand that they let you through?

"Yes."

And why are they going to listen to you?

"Because I'm the Sheriff Slayer."

Rise began walking north. He might need some energy by the time he got there. He drank some more water and wished he had something to eat. His stomach was a little scratchy, but he could wait.

Rise finally made it to the columns of the forsaken shards. He had no idea what they were or how they got there. They were 200 feet up, like a giant stuck them straight into the earth. Perhaps a great fortress once lay here, but was now blown apart from the inside.

Two pointed columns marked the entrance of the gang territory, which was covered with red paint and different markings that Rise did not recognize.

Rise invited himself in.

Hundreds of them were found doing their assorted duties. None seemed to even look up. They took his presence for granted. Many were constructing weapons, some were sharpening swords. They had their own town of evil.

You only made it this far because no one else is dumb enough to just walk into their territory.

He ignored his mind.

Rise was within 100 feet of his goal. The center of the wall. He was almost there.

Keep walking, don't push your luck.

"Hey! Is that the Sheriff Slayer?"

Crap.

Rise kept walking. He would not look back. He was too far beyond these foes. He held no fear of them.

The whispers were becoming murmurs. He heard some describing what happened on the bridge. Rise hated how quickly rumors spread. It was only recently he defeated the two in the bridge battle, and now an entire sector away heard of his feat.

More whispers and he heard them dropping their chores. A crowd was following him. He did not look back. He was walking through a horrible trail of blood-lustful men and women.

He started seeing the people in front of him looking up. They had noticed the crowd.

Fifty feet! Keep walking!

He heard the whisper he did not want to hear. "Look at him, I can take him!"

He was alleviated to hear a whisper in response, "You kidding? That guy killed six sheriffs!"

Rise smiled for a just a quick moment. He hated rumors. They grew as quick as they spread.

Rise was watching the wall. The skelguard patrol had not crossed each other yet. He would have to stall for time. Not long, just a minute.

Rise stopped and the crowd stopped as well. They were watching him.

Rise turned around and stared at them. The crowd followed him all the way to a safe distance from the wall. There were more than he thought and they had not dropped their weapons along the way.

He enjoyed the fact that his heart stayed calm. He truly did not fear them.

"You the Sheriff Slayer?" Rise could not see who asked the question.

"Yes."

Another voice, "What's your name? We need to put something on your grave!"

"I might just inscribe Rise on your own grave if you take one step towards me. You fools don't know what you're dealing with. I'm more powerful than you can imagine."

Great. Just keep pushing it.

Rise remembered the gas pellets Uzzah gave to him. "Be creative," Uzzah had told him.

Come on, just one more lie, let them sweat it out. Then you know what to do.

"An army of skelguards couldn't kill me! Sheriffs couldn't kill me! Even the elite guards of the King himself could not kill me!"

You could use his name. That's it! Use it. Why not? No one else does for fear of the power it holds. Use it.

One of the men of the mob yelled back, "KILL THE SLAYER!"

The mob was moving towards him.

Rise yelled with all his might, "YOU WILL KNOW A NEW TERROR! THE KING IS NOTHING AND AFTER I KILL HIM, I WILL COME BACK FOR ALL OF YOU! DO YOU HEAR

ME? RASS WILL DIE!"

The mob stopped at the mention of the King's name. No one spoke it aloud after being taught it once. The superstition was too strong. Rise shattered it like glass. That one word stopped the mob.

Rise threw down the pellets and in an instant he saw the smoke rising between him and the mob. Rise aimed the grapnel and fired just as the two skelguards passed each other on the wall.

He was at the top way before the smoke cleared, leaving the thugs to worry about how he disappeared, and whether or not he would indeed return for them.

Rise retracted the grapnel and slowly walked over to the ledge, slightly amused by his performance, and a little disappointed. Beline hated it when people lied. Yet, he was sure he would have had her blessing.

Another day was about to begin. His journey was almost over. He saw a varied sector before him with tall buildings, forests, scrap piles, a lake, and tents. It was like five different sectors rolled into one. And in that sector was his future. The rebellion was his only hope. He would break the King's laws one by one to find her. He would defeat every sheriff, elite, and skel that crossed his path if he had to.

He breathed in the cold air, taking his time, not fearing anything atop the world.

"Beline, I will find you. I swear on every shadow of strength I have in my body and mind, I will find you."

Rise descended and his first journey ended.

Made in the USA
Charleston, SC
23 January 2011